Printed in the United States of America

First Printing, 2018

www.stephaniekeyes.com

ISBN 978-0-9998467-2-8

Cover Design by

Najla Qamber, Najla Qamber Designs

Editorial Services by

Michele Coppola Ames

Laura Whitaker

Ashley Turcotte, Brown Owl Editing

THE SPELLBINDER'S SONATA

STEPHANIE KEYES

DEDICATION

To my readers who are grieving, you are not alone. I see you, and I am right there beside you.

PROLOGUE
GRIFFIN

Wednesday, December 17th, 1902— Pittsburg, Pennsylvania, US—Byrons Estate

THE CIGAR SMOKE FORMED A THICK, UNFORGIVING VICE around my neck. It drew the air out of the room, leaving a haze hanging above head level. I detested everything about cigars. Their unpleasant aftertaste, their weight in my hand, the way the ash burned when it landed on my fingers.

My hosts, the self-proclaimed Lord and Lady Byrons, had left a box of the finest Cubans (or so I'd been told) in my room as a welcome present. I did not feel welcome in the least.

The entire estate oozed moodiness, as though covered by a cloak of despair. It reminded me of my childhood residence in Warwickshire, England; more than a few spirits roamed that home. I'd had too many run-ins with impossible shadows and unexplained cold spots to assume otherwise.

Clasping the red brocade curtain, I drew it back, surveying the road and other homes beyond the estate's walls. They called the thoroughfare "Millionaire's Row." True to its name, only the richest of the rich resided at its edges. The row bustled with those hoping to be seen and those *needing* to be seen.

The garden, in comparison to the public street, had a stagnant look about it. I could almost envision it in the spring, partially alive with carefully controlled color.

"Griffin, come away from the window. There's a good lad." Jiggory Underhill, my manager and constant companion, walked into the room. "You'll catch your death."

It seemed Jiggory's mission to control my welfare during my every waking moment. I permitted it only because it had been Jiggory who'd found me. Jig who'd rescued me from the tertiary country estate my father, a titled lord, had reserved for his only bastard son: me. It had been Jig who'd propelled me into the midst of celebrity.

He had helped make me successful. Years later, few hadn't heard of the young piano virtuoso, Griffin Dunn. Jig was the closest thing I'd ever had to a friend.

"Are you nervous about tonight's performance?" Jig rolled his cigar between his fingers.

I dropped the curtain, moving away from the December chill that stealthily snaked through the panes. "I am *never* nervous." I straightened my collar and smoothed my jacket. "What sort of place is this anyway, this so-called Byrons *estate?* I've not even been assigned a valet."

"It's America, Griff. They do things differently here." He shook his head, his smile turning smug. "Besides, you're a child, not quite a man."

I locked eyes with Jig. "They pay me as they'd pay a man." How many chaps of sixteen could claim wages equaling mine? Five hundred and fifteen pounds per annum was practically unheard of in the circles we traveled.

Only last month, I'd performed to a packed house in London. That night's pieces had included an orchestral arrangement of Beethoven's *Moonlight Sonata*, featuring me as the star. I could still smell the tension that had built within the auditorium—a palpable thing that did not dissipate until the final chord resolution. I'd brought them to their feet.

"Drop the surly bit. You need a benefactor, and you'll only get one if you invite 'Charming Griff' to the party," Jig said. "Caring for your mother has taken what little earnings you've assembled. You won't be able to pay my salary. I'll be forced to leave."

It was the same story he'd been touting for months, but I wasn't living on my salary alone. My inheritance had allotted me an extra 5,000 a year. I didn't need my income to survive.

"Pity."

"You might think differently when you're on your own. You've never had to do that before. What better place to achieve that than in the Americas? They're throwing money at everything here." Jig's jaw set, his eyes glinting with the steeliness that made him a good manager.

"Byrons is an insufferable fool." The evening would be torture. If I'd been at my home, Fulton House, I would have played a piece of my choosing, composed another work for my journal, or perhaps even spent the night with Clarissa. She did profess to love me, after all.

Jig shrugged, the tension from the previous moment trailing out of the room like long, smoky fingers. "No matter.

You'll win over someone else. Carnegie is supposed to attend your concert, and maybe one of the Vanderbilts. There are plenty of robber barons to choose from. Only you can determine your own success."

My anger rose, a viper poised to strike. "I think not, Jiggory. *You* will find a way to ensure my success, or you'll never manage another performer."

Jig's entire expression shifted, his eyes narrowing, his mouth reshaping into a hard line. "You overestimate your influence."

"Do I?" The silence between us stretched, only to be broken by a knock on my door.

A voice rose from the other side. "Mr. Dunn?"

"Finally, a valet. It's about time. Aren't you going to get that?" I cocked an eyebrow. "You *do* still work for me, as I recall."

Jig held my gaze for several beats longer, before sighing and moving to the door. With a twist of the knob, he revealed not the valet I'd been expecting, but a small boy, dressed in fine knickerbockers, a white shirt, and a jacket that rivaled my own in quality. The boy didn't enter the room, but stayed at its fringes, resting his face against the doorframe.

"What is it, lad?" Jig asked, his voice more patient than I'd ever heard it.

The boy jumped but remained in the opening with his face pressed against the doorframe, as though something barred him from entry. He couldn't have been more than ten years along. "Mr. Dunn, sir, I'm Jonah Byrons. I was hoping you could teach me to play, sir. See, I've always wanted to learn and I've heard you rehearsing. You are the very best."

What a delightful child! Still, I had little experience with children. My own childhood was isolated, restricted to our few servants and Mother. Children were better left to their wet nurses and nannies.

Jig obviously didn't feel the same. He got to his knee and gave the boy his best, most welcoming smile, catering to the child as though he were royalty. "Come in. Speak with us a moment."

The boy quivered as though he might wet himself. In truth, I half expected him to run away. To his credit, he did not. He stepped over the threshold, finally allowing us to see his face. His green eyes widened as though he'd never seen an Englishman before.

Instant horror filled my person. I drew back, only realizing I'd crossed the room when I'd bumped into a chair.

The child was grotesque. One side of his face had been horribly disfigured, as though he'd been caught in a fire. I dimly recalled hearing about a gaslight fire on the estate the previous year. One of the boy's eyes appeared half shut, while his cheekbone had been distorted into a series of fleshy ridges. *What a horrid child!*

"I—I—uh, what did you, er, say your name was?" Jig seemed surprised, but not horrified. How could he speak to *it*? Surely, forcing a smile for that mongrel stole all his energy.

Footsteps sounded in the hall. A moment later, a thin, blond woman of average height strode into the room. Her manner of dress was a plain, gray wool creation—the uniform of a Byrons servant. She placed a hand on the boy's shoulder. "Jonah. Why aren't you in bed? Come with me at once." She spoke with a thick German accent, diverting her eyes to the floor.

"Wait, Nanny Minna." The small boy broke free and rushed forward to tug on the hem of my jacket. "May I come to the performance tonight, Mr. Dunn? May I sit beside you?"

Pulling my jacket from his grasp, I focused on the boy's slim fingers—anywhere but his face. "Absolutely not. The cream of society will be there. There will be no room for the likes of *you*."

The boy's face fell, but I could muster no sympathy. Far better he learned the true cruelty of life at a young age.

Nanny Minna drew herself up. "Jonah, do not let Mr. Dunn offend you. You're better off not being in the company of one such as this."

One such as this? How dare she! A servant calling *me* into question? "I beg your pardon, madam, but it is this child who is the monster."

Narrowing her eyes, the nanny's firm lips curled into a cunning smile. "Perhaps you do not see who the true beast is, Mr. Dunn. I, however, am not so blind as that." She turned and exited the room with the same determined gait as when she'd entered, Jonah trailing in her wake, head hung to his chest.

Relief swamped me the moment they'd gone. "Thank goodness. Better she take the little monster away now than leave us to suffer him another moment."

Jig shook his head. "Given your own birthright, I suppose I expected better behavior from you. Your mother would be most disappointed, had she lived."

My throat thickened, pressing and halting the flow of my breath for a moment. A memory of her taking my hands in her own and spinning us around filled my head. Her spun-gold hair had flown behind her. We'd fallen to the ground giggling and laughing, her smile infectious. But the moment faded as quickly as it had appeared.

Mother was gone.

The clock in the hall chimed eleven. All thoughts of the boy faded away. It was time for my performance.

Jig flipped open his pocket watch. "We must go. After you."

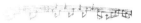

TALL WINDOWS LET IN THE MOON'S GLOW AS I LED THE way down the polished hall. Alternating shafts of light formed a pattern across the floor. With only 8 days until Christmas, the requisite pine boughs adorned the banisters leading to the parlor, but otherwise, there seemed to be little to mark the season. Very different from how Mother once—

"Ladies and gentlemen, I give you *the* Griffin Dunn!" Jig had somehow moved ahead of me and had made my introductions. A sea of society awaited me. No time for childish reminiscences.

Forcing my grin to its widest possible reaches, I nodded to the patrons. Applause rang out. The crowd parted for me and a hush fell over the room. Moonlight from the tall windows bathed me in a glow as I took my seat at the piano.

"Mr. Dunn. Some water for you sir?" A servant stood to the side, a pitcher and an empty goblet in hand.

"Take it away, you fool. Don't you see I'm about to begin a performance?" I muttered.

The servant nodded, drawing himself back into the shadows and taking the water away. Finally, the moment was perfect, and the spotlight was mine.

The stark white keys of the Byrons' prize Steinway glinted beneath a row of gaslights. I laid my fingers upon the keys and it was as if I'd come home. No music sat on the stand before me. The notes simply appeared in my brain as though they'd been *burned* there—mine to remember for all time.

The Byrons had chosen the program for that evening, but it was *my* performance. Instead, I launched into an impromptu selection on my part—one of my own compositions—*Redemption*.

Tipping my head back, I let the music take me over. The complex chord changes pulled me in. The notes reverberated throughout the parlor. They'd never heard anything like my music before. It broke all the rules of theory, with chord changes a beat away from tripping over one another in their ferocity to resolve themselves. I could almost smell the applause as I struck my final chord.

Yet, my standing ovation never came. The sound of shattering glass obliterated the moment. A swift, hard thud followed, sending tiny vibrations across the floor, replacing any accolades I'd hoped to receive. Instead of cheers, there were screams—shouts that grated my nerves and rang in my eardrums.

I pivoted on the piano bench and wished I hadn't. In the middle of the parlor floor, on a blanket of shattered glass, lay the deformed little boy I'd met a short time ago. The one who'd begged me to teach him.

He should have seemed even more monstrous then, with a trail of blood seeping from between his lips. Instead, there was only innocence in his pale, sleeping face, hideous even in death.

"Jonah." Lord Byrons fell to his knees. He stretched a meaty hand forward, brushing his fingers along the boy's cheek. Mrs. Byrons stood apart from him, one fine, shaped eyebrow frozen aloft.

A banshee-like howl shattered the moment's hold as Nanny Minna rushed into the room. An audible gasp broke the silence as she pushed Lord Byrons away to reach the boy. She collected Jonah in her arms, clutching him against her. A sob ripped from her throat. Each of us bore witness— a helpless audience to the tidal wave of the woman's personal despair.

After a time, Nanny Minna lowered Jonah slowly to the ground and rose to her feet. Gone were her light, critical eyes. Soulless, black pits had sunken themselves into her pale face.

She thrust a finger in my direction. "Murderer!"

Her accusation slammed into me, along with the realization of what Jonah had done. He must've crawled onto one of the interior skylights in an effort to see my performance. But still, that did not earn me the title of murderer.

"Madam, I did nothing." It was true. I'd been performing. I hadn't forced the child to watch my concert from above.

Minna shook her head, her jaw rigid, her eyes surely as cold as the ice crystallizing within her heart. "You would not help him when he asked. Your own selfishness cost this child his life, and you've taken my heart from me. You will pay for what you have wrought."

Raising her hands into the air, she closed her eyes as she said: *"May he be bound to this house until true love finds him ..."*

But any hope I had of understanding her was lost as she switched to German, chanting a string of dark-sounding, guttural words in a language I didn't understand. Before my eyes, the shards of glass from the broken skylight rose above the ground to hover in mid-air. Nanny Minna waved a hand and the pieces began to spin, faster and faster, moving closer and closer, until they'd formed a tight funnel.

Before I could take cover, she pointed at me and the shards of broken glass, still covered in Jonah's blood, pummeled my chest and drove the very life from my body.

CHAPTER 1
KATE

Monday, November 21st—114 years later Pittsburgh, PA

THE BUS DRIVER GUNNED THE MOTOR AS WE TORE across the Sixth Street Bridge, the bright yellow metal of the dramatic structure rising toward the pre-dawn sky as it closed the gap between downtown Pittsburgh and the North Side. Technically, it was referred to as the Roberto Clemente Bridge, but only out-of-towners used that name. To those born and bred, it was just Sixth Street.

The only thing I wanted to do was sleep, but my clarinet jury at the Byrons School of Music was four weeks away. Jury week was the once-a-term intimidation party when I had to perform in front of an audience of five teachers.

I'd only been a student at the Byrons School for about four months, but competition was intense. The school accepted twenty-five students in grades eleven and twelve, which meant each of the fifty spots was highly coveted by the wannabe students on the extensive waiting list.

Somehow, I'd not only gotten in, but earned a full scholarship, so Mom and I had made a deal: I could go to Byrons, Dad's alma mater, if I paid for any incidentals and kept my scholarship. Apparently, taking responsibility for my own education would give me "valuable workforce skills."

So, I got up at four a.m. Monday through Friday and rode the bus. It took fifty-five minutes and two busses to get to the creepy Byrons School of Music, in the converted Byrons mansion in Pittsburgh's North Side. Then, when classes ended at three p.m., I did the same commute again.

Frigid air seeped through the window, promising me the cold would be waiting when I got to school. It was two degrees, with a windchill factor of minus twelve. I'd lived in Pittsburgh all my life; you'd think I would have gotten used to cold winters. Instead, the sudden drop in temperature from cold to downright polar ice caps every November still caught me off guard year after year. I yanked the drawstrings on my fleece hoodie tighter, snuggling deeper into the down parka I'd layered overtop.

If only we could get to Byrons sooner. The school would be creepy, but a *warm* creepy. *I wish* . . .

Oh shit, I couldn't believe I'd almost made a wish *in public*. I'd promised Dad. What a stupid thing to almost ruin everything over.

The familiar hurt sprung up on me, the way it always did when I thought of Dad. Not only had I lost a father, but a teacher. Maybe one day, I wouldn't miss him so much. Or maybe it would get worse.

The Funeral March by Frédéric Chopin began to chorus inside my backpack. Mom's smiling face filled the display as I seized my phone. Of course, Mom wouldn't know Chopin if he rose from the dead and smacked her on the butt. Ignoring the call, I shoved the phone back in my bag.

She probably wanted to give me more info about her ever-changing work schedule. Mom had spent more time in airports since Dad's car accident than she had with me. If she went anywhere for more than a night, I got to crash with my boss at Coffee á Rena, Rena Lane, who I'd gotten tight with after Dad. That was the only good thing about Mom going MIA all the time.

The bus sped through the slowly changing landscape of the North Side. Past renovated warehouses, brownstones that had been transformed into trendy yoga studios, and restaurants that would bring any foodie to her knees. My grandma told me that the entire city used to be filled with steel mills, and a thick cloud of smog had made it look dark all the time.

I couldn't reconcile that image with the Pittsburgh I knew. The one with top-notch universities and a series of vibrant neighborhoods that had gotten it touted as "The Next Brooklyn."

The bus turned onto Ridge Avenue, swinging past the Allegheny Commons section. A college campus neighbored Byrons, making the area normally a pretty busy place—but not that early in the morning. Few cars were on the streets, and even fewer students.

When the school loomed ahead, I stood and wrapped my fingers around the worn canvas of my bag's shoulder strap. My ride jerked to an uncomfortable halt outside the school gates, its large tires squealing across the pavement from the effort as the back door opened.

Waving to the driver, I climbed down the bus steps and

walked into the darkened courtyard. The brick building loomed over me. No interior lights were on, except for the low glow of some security lighting on the first floor.

Chills swept up my arms and not from the cold, either. There was something about the house. The shadowy corners and unexplained cold spots, combined with the heaviness that rested on my chest whenever I pass through the gates said it all. Something bad had happened there.

A blast of wind stole my breath, and, before I could catch it again, the iron gates slammed shut behind me.

Charlie, the school's night security guard, rushed out from the guard shack and opened the gates once more. He fastened them to metal hooks protruding from the brick walls. "Sorry about that, Kate."

"Hey, Charlie. S'okay."

"Morning." Standing straighter, he smiled and tipped his hat like gentlemen did in those old black-and-white movies Grandma Covington watched. Something was off about him, though. His smile didn't reach his eyes. Only one thing had ever kept Charlie from smiling.

"The piano again?"

He nodded. "I've heard it before, but lately it's been all the time."

"I've heard it, too, you know." I'd only been attending school there a day when I'd first heard the ghostly music. A haunting melody—pun *totally* intended.

I forced myself to glance up at the imposing four stories of Byrons School. One long building, it sat trapped behind iron gates that reached above my head. The mansion formed an L-shape, with a porch running the length of both sides of the house. A brick courtyard led up to the grounds. A forgotten garden dominated the back.

The place probably looked the same as it had back in

the day, Charlie's guard shack on the far side of the court-yard being the exception.

"Are you sure you want to go in there?" Charlie asked.

Nope. "Juries. I have to practice. You know how it is."

Charlie nodded. He did know. He'd been a guard at the school for five years. Long enough to know the M.O. of a music student.

"Hey, wait a minute." Turning, I reached into my bag and dug out the leftover cinnamon bun I'd taken from home, handing it to him. It was partially stale, but Charlie never cared. He lived alone, and I didn't think he ate very well, judging by his chicken legs.

"Thanks, Kate." He unwrapped the pastry I'd covered in a layer of aluminum foil and then bit into the roll. "This is great. You don't have to bring me breakfast every day, though."

"I know. See you later."

Charlie shook his head as he moved toward the shack. "See ya, Kate."

Leaving him behind, I climbed the few remaining steps, then pushed open the bulky front door before moving into the hush of the dim lobby. During our new student orientation tour, the guide had raved about the décor, how one side was done in classic Victorian and the other clearly Edwardian. Most of my classrooms were on the Victorian side. Thick mahogany furniture, paneling, and flooring absorbed any illumination like a sponge, leaving only shadow behind. There were ninety rooms in the place, though students only had access to some of them.

The dark hardwood creaked under my feet as I crossed the space. At least there was no piano playing going on. Warmth crept up the side of my neck as the sensation of being watched took me over. The air grew heavy, as though someone stood beside me, about to speak into my ear.

I'm okay. I'm okay. Keep moving.

I let that mantra play in my head as I flicked on the lights, careful not to look down either of the hallways flanking the entranceway in case something really was there. I headed to the practice rooms downstairs.

The basement level had been remodeled the previous year, with thin, blue carpeting and freshly painted walls. It still managed to be just as creeptastic as the second floor where some classrooms and most of the administrative offices were located. Fortunately, most of my classes were on the first floor, which meant I only had to be a nervous wreck in the early morning.

My practice room was the first one on the left inside a larger orchestra rehearsal space. Passing dozens of abandoned music stands on the way to my room, I glanced at the three name plates affixed to the wall beside the door. *Igor Bramanhov, Kate Covington, Antony Deets.* I touched a finger to my name—my daily ritual since day one.

You'll do great, Kate. You deserve to be here.

Flicking on more lights, I dropped everything onto the only chair. I had little space for much else besides a music stand. The area was so tiny, I could stand in the center of the room with my arms extended and touch the walls in either direction. The only other area in the room was a small set of lockers, where we were supposed to keep our books. Locker space was at a premium, so only seniors had lockers on the upper floor. Juniors, like me, had to use the ones in our practice rooms.

Unzipping my ratty messenger bag, I peered inside. My B-flat clarinet, Benny—named by my dad after Benny Goodman, a clarinetist from the swing era—rested in his padded sleeve. From my bag, I snagged a pencil, a shot glass, and a long, thin, velvet-lined box that held my clarinet reeds. The reed box made a soft clinking sound when I set it on the ledge of the music stand.

I shoved the pencil behind my ear—part of my regular fashion regimen—and then walked through the large rehearsal space and down the hall to the ladies' bathroom. Turning on the tap, I filled the shot glass partway with luke-warm water so I could soak my reeds.

When I returned to the room, however, my reed box lay open on the floor. Reeds had scattered everywhere.

"Aw, come on!" I dropped to my knees. The reeds had to be saved. Otherwise, it would take days and a lot of sand-ing, plus trial and error, to get a new set to play the way I wanted.

With care, I picked up the reeds, checking the numbers I'd marked on the back of each for preference. I wiped numbers two and three on my jean-clad thigh and popped them both into the shot glass to soak. Hopefully, the five-second rule applied. I didn't have time to prep more reeds before classes. Naturally, my favorite that week, number one, had disappeared.

I crawled all over the floor. Number one wasn't anywhere . . . until it was suddenly *somewhere.*

The slim piece of bamboo had been jammed into the air vent next to the chair. The reed had actually split down the middle where the white slat pierced it. There was no way it could have gotten there on its own.

Strains of the phantom pianist's music started up. The skin on the back of my neck prickled with a wash of goose bumps.

Shit.

CHAPTER 2
GRIFFIN

THE SUN HADN'T YET RISEN, AND DARKNESS STILL HELD the house in its grip. That morning, I'd sought out my sole refuge from my torturous half-life: the piano. I understood the fear my music embedded in the souls of the building's security team. Yet, if I was to be forever bound to the former Byrons estate, surrounded by music students, I should be permitted some respite.

Though everything around me had changed and grown, I myself remained forever frozen at sixteen.

May he be bound to this house until true love finds him . . .

They were the words of my curse—one uttered by a distraught German nanny. They'd haunted me ever since. Of course, I hadn't realized I'd been cursed when Nanny Minna had sent broken glass thundering into my body.

But those words had plagued me from the moment I'd

opened my eyes to find myself looking down at my own broken body on the floor. I'd heard them when I'd watched Jonah's soul leave Earth, bathed in white light. When Jig had taken my body to be buried far away from my beloved English soil.

I'd only learned they were part of a curse, when Minna summoned my spirit weeks later. Grief-stricken though Minna was, there'd been no shortage of anger in her eyes. "Ah, the ghost of Griffin Dunn. Now you'll know pain, for you will rot here, waiting for your true love. Only then, will you have the chance to be free."

And so, I stayed at Byrons house, a spirit. Any attempts I made at leaving resulted in me being pulled back over the property line and forced to relive Jonah Byrons death, as well as my own.

And I'd waited.

But the words of the curse continued to haunt me, even when the Byrons family had quit the house, unable to bear the reminders of their son's death any longer. In truth, I'd heard them long after I'd found myself left to roam the hallways of the abandoned manse.

The house had eventually fallen into disrepair, only to be fixed up again and refitted to serve as a branch of the Red Cross in the forties, and later as a women's shelter in the fifties.

The interior skylight Jonah had fallen through had been boarded over. By the late sixties, the house had been converted once more, into its current incarnation: the Byrons School of Music.

I'd been left behind to witness it all, unseen, only heard. With plenty of time, I'd learned how to manipulate my energies, to direct them so I could play the piano again. Music served as my only escape from reality.

The other factor contributing to my continued sanity was the other spirit doomed to be my companion. My room-mate for all eternity, Hannah Byrons, Lord Byrons' mother.

Her rosewater scent reached my nostrils before Hannah took the chair beside me. She often complained that it wasn't even her favorite perfume. She'd borrowed it from her much-hated daughter-in-law and found herself stuck with it for the afterlife. Heart attacks could be so incon-venient.

Hannah must have been torturing some student that morning, because her girlish laughter soon filled the room. It was the only thing that amused her of late.

"Hannah, why do you bother haunting them?" Hannah found the students entertaining; I found them tiresome, and badly dressed.

"I'm just messing about." Hannah's silver curls bounced as she took her preferred seat beside me. "Can't an old woman have any fun? We have precious little to keep us occupied."

"If you call torturing minors fun. They have laws about that sort of thing now, you know."

"For a ghost, you're rather boring, Griff. Playing the piano all the time . . . rarely interacting with the students. Maybe if you follow some of the young ladies around, one of them might turn out to be the one."

I knew where she was going. "Must we have this conversation?"

She frowned. "How are we supposed to end this curse if you don't even try to find someone to fall in love with?"

I pounded out a rapid succession of random notes. They served as a perfect imitation of Hannah's litany. "That's not how the curse works. True love is supposed to find me. Besides, it's a bit of a challenge when no one can see me."

"Forgive me, Griff. Can you blame me for wanting to move on, though? It's just that I'm tired of this life."

"And what about me? I'm the one she bloody cursed. I had a career. I was *famous*."

Hannah rolled her eyes. "Well, *something* is tying me to this house. The curse must have affected me too. There's no other explanation. I've certainly tried to move on enough times."

That was most definitely true. A favorite moment of mine was when Hannah had tried to "follow the light" into one of the motion-animated lights the school had installed a mere ten years back. It had kept shutting off. She'd believed the angels had simply changed their minds.

"Then maybe—" I turned toward her, but Hannah had already gone. She was forever doing that. I was alone once again.

How could I explain to Hannah that true love wasn't coming for me? I'd been a cruel, conceited man in life.

Perhaps I wasn't worthy of love—even in death?

Prelude to the Afternoon of a Faun. I changed keys, letting my fingers fall into position from memory. Debussy fit my mood very well. And besides, my arrangement for piano had much more power than the original. Flute introduction? Bah.

When I'd first been cursed, I couldn't quite figure out how to play the piano. I'd spent nearly a month alone at the Byrons house, unable to depress a single key. But the more I worked at it, the stronger I grew. Until one day, it all came back. I'd certainly had plenty of time to practice since then.

But even the piano had lost its luster for me that morning. There'd been too many similar mornings. They'd begun to blur together. Soon, I'd be unable to separate them.

I'd gotten halfway through the tenth stanza when I heard her again. That clarinetist who'd been butchering Weber's *Clarinet Concerto No.1 in F Minor* for the past three months. A more technically stilted interpretation I'd never born witness to.

The musician had a nice tone, but the player's sense of rhythm and overall technicality were off, as he or she sped through some measures and dragged the pace through others. What the player needed was someone to work with him or her.

The music stopped, and an idea came to me. It was cruel, really, but if I was to be forced to endure such a mediocre distraction, then it seemed only right I should receive some pleasure from it. I knew just how to make that happen. Without waiting for another sound from the practice room next door, I launched into the piano accompaniment for the Weber.

Either the musician wouldn't know it and would keep playing, or they'd run screaming from the building. Both outcomes held remarkable possibilities. I tore through the lively intro that led up to the clarinet's subtle entrance and, finally, I'd arrived at the moment of truth.

The unthinkable happened.

The musician began to play the piece *with* me. In all my years, I'd never experienced anything like it. He or she hadn't run away. Though I was tempted to flee myself after that first pitiful staccato run that had been written as a series of shortened eight notes, not a sloppy tangle of slurred tones. Still, the clarinetist, whomever he or she was, kept at it, fighting through every measure. Badly.

Flying through the remaining measures of the first

movement, I kept to the intended tempo, and the clarinetist struggled to follow. The keys were new to me again, intoxicating. The accompaniment I'd learned once, many years ago, an old friend. I'd forgotten what it was like, performing with another musician. The rush, the power. My curiosity built with every note, until the first movement ended.

I let my hands hover over the keys. The other musician had performed with me. *Extraordinary.* I had to see for myself who the brave soul was.

"Griffin. That was excellent! You're certainly getting into the spirit of haunting." Hannah floated into the room, choosing to hover at the end of my piano. "But I think you'd better come with me. Quickly."

It wasn't like Hannah to have a sense of urgency about anything, so I followed at once. Hannah lowered herself to the ground and thrust her head into the wall. I stood and stalked across the room where I mimicked Hanna's actions, inserting my head into the wall just enough to see through the other side, and I jolted.

Funny, a spirit suffering from shock, but there it was. A young woman crouched on the floor, rummaging through some sort of bag. She'd wedged a clarinet reed between her lips and narrowed her eyes in concentration.

Incredible. Of all the musicians *not* to run away from our encounter, I would never have picked this girl, for she seemed as though she must be faint of heart. Her clothing hung off her frame, as though she hadn't eaten properly in some time. Her face seemed pinched, strained in profile. Then she jerked her head in our direction before she jumped to her feet and ran from the room.

But I'd seen enough of her face to identify her. I would have recognized Minna anywhere.

CHAPTER 3

KATE

THE GHOSTLY PIANIST HAD ACCOMPANIED ME. *HOLY crap.*

I didn't exactly enjoy it, but I couldn't deny it had been helpful. I pretended it was my rehearsal roommate, Igor, playing along. Until I spotted the old woman's face in the air vent. Then I froze, and when she smiled? I ran like hell.

What sounded like footsteps echoed behind me as I shot out of my rehearsal space, down the hall, and up the basement stairs. It wasn't until I burst out the front door that I breathed again, inhaling as much of the frigid air as my lungs would hold, before letting it out in a single burst. I'd never bought the whole haunted house thing before. Not really. *Man did things just change.*

Charlie glanced up from his seat in the guard shack, where he toyed with the aluminum foil wrapper from the cinnamon bun I'd given him. Two windows flanked the glass sliding door of the shack. As I approached, Charlie slid the door open and the wind picked up, raising his slicked-back, salt-and-pepper hair at the part. He snatched a ball cap from a hook on the wall inside his shack before dropping it on his head. He turned up his collar.

"Kate? You okay?" He frowned.

I shook my head, trying to take as much oxygen into my lungs as possible as I crossed the courtyard. "A face . . . I . . . saw . . . a . . . face."

He heaved a big sigh. "You're gonna freeze out there. Why don't you come on in and sit by the heater?"

Muttering something to the effect of, "At least I'm not the only one," Charlie stepped aside, leaving plenty of room between us so I could climb inside the guard shack. There wasn't a ton of room inside Charlie's domain—just enough space for a chair and a small heater. I sank to the floor by the latter, shaking, unable to get the image of the face out of my mind. Charlie plunked an entire box of Kleenex onto my lap. Grabbing a handful, I blew my nose, sounding like a pissed-off elephant. He stayed just outside, wrapping his arms around himself.

"There was an old woman's face in the air vent." I totally got how crazy I sounded. I did. I also got that Charlie was the only person at Byrons School who would believe me. "Ever seen her before?"

"I've never *seen* anything. It's just a feeling. Being here alone at night, I've heard things." He visibly shuddered.

"Like what?" I asked, though I didn't really want to know.

Charlie wiped his hand over his face. "A thud, for starters. They say the Byrons boy plunged to his death when he fell through a skylight."

"Oh God." At least I hadn't heard the thud. How could

Charlie stand all that, night after night? "Why don't you quit?" I shook my head as I realized how I sounded. "I mean, not that I'm saying you should. It's just—"

"Hold on a second." Charlie tensed and held up a hand. "Who's there?" He slid the shack door partway closed and stood at attention, his hand on the gun at his side. I wasn't sure why he even wore it. I couldn't imagine Charlie ever firing a weapon.

Movement caught my eye. I slid upward along the shack wall, until I locked eyes with a stranger on the other side of the glass. He was around my age—sixteen—and NBA tall, with blond hair that ran to his chin and too-pale skin. He wore an old-school tux with an immaculately tied bow tie. The last part wasn't surprising if he was a musician, though it was a little early for a performance.

The stranger placed a slim hand on the pane. An odd scar in the shape of a slightly curved line marked the heel of his left palm. It was those eyes of his that got me, though. I couldn't make out the color, but that didn't matter. He somehow pinned me in place with his intensity. I couldn't move.

But then his right eye narrowed, and his left remained full-on open, complete with raised eyebrow. It was a look of intense dislike, maybe even hatred.

I blinked, in case I'd imagined it. I hadn't.

"Sir, can I help you?" Charlie asked.

The stranger stared at Charlie's hand in surprised displeasure. His raised eyebrows competed with his downturned mouth—it was the kind of look most people had when they'd been grabbed by a homeless person on the street.

That didn't stop Charlie. I wasn't sure if he'd noticed and didn't care or was oblivious to the boy's expression.

Either way, he didn't move his hand from the holster at his side.

The guy rearranged his features before he turned back to me, his lip curling on one side. "I'm a new student." He spoke in a clipped British accent, his eyes never leaving mine. "Piano performance."

Why was this punk staring? Then again, maybe he thought there was something wrong with me, hanging out in a guard shack with a box of tissues at my feet.

"New student, huh?" Charlie asked, lowering his hand from the holster, a little too quickly in my opinion. He cleared his throat, finally seeming to catch on to how awkward it all was. "What's your name, son?"

The guy broke eye contact. Air rushed into my lungs.

He glanced at Charlie for a fraction of a moment, as though he'd been asked a question in some foreign language, like Ancient Greek or Mesopotamian. Though I wasn't exactly sure if that last one was a language.

But then the stranger's eyes found mine again, and all thoughts of language and confusion and anything remotely having to do with reality vanished.

A weird feeling of unexplained recognition shot through me. As though I'd been waiting for him to show up, to stand outside the shack. It was as if I already knew him, and our meeting was just a reunion.

But how could I know someone I'd never met in my life?

CHAPTER 4
GRIFFIN

THE MOMENT I MOVED OUTSIDE, A WHOOSHING SOUND filled my ears. It was almost as though the reception on one of those radios that used to be all the rage had been adjusted. I could hear everything; my senses must have been dulled before.

The scents of the November courtyard invaded my nostrils. The fresh bite of impending snow. The foul scent of exhaust from the automobiles students referred to as cars. The roar as those same machines tore past us at unimaginable speeds.

The cold nipped my cheeks and I froze in place, taking in the sensation. This wasn't possible. I hadn't felt temperature changes in years. I raised my hand to my heart. The constant thud of my once-dead heartbeat slammed against my palm. How could that be happening? I was dead—I'd been *beyond* dead for many years. Yet, there was no denying the blood pulsing through my veins.

It was as if I was *alive* again. How on Earth was such a thing possible?

Even stranger, both the girl and the guard could see me.

And the girl. Somehow, Minna herself stood in the guard's station. A wave of nausea hit me. The woman who'd stolen my life away. That was it. The only explanation for any of this was Minna's presence.

She seemed even younger than when we'd first met. Her wide, eyes were absent of the blackness I remembered from our last meeting. They glared at me that morning in a mix of shock and anger.

The guard spoke to me. "Shy, huh?" He'd asked my name. Plus, he had a pistol. *Brilliant.*

"Hardly. I'm . . . Griff." Certainly, they wouldn't connect the name "Griff" to the Griffin Dunn who'd died on the property.

Besides, it was foolish of me to worry. The man was a servant. I didn't need to explain myself to him.

"I'm Charlie, night security guard. Welcome to Byrons School." He nodded in Minna's direction. "This here is Kate Covington."

Kate. He'd called her Kate. Why would Minna use a false name all these years later?

"A pleasure." But instead of bowing or slapping palms with Charlie as I'd seen them do so often in that place, I stepped closer to inspect the girl he'd called Kate.

The roundness of Minna's face was as I remembered, but though her eyes were the same shape, the color seemed lighter. Her long, brown hair had been bound so that it ran to her shoulders in a straight, lush line. The Minna I knew had been blond. I pressed my mind to recall other details about Minna from when she'd stood in the parlor cursing me, ending my life, drowning out the pieces of Griffin Dunn I'd been.

"Kate, uh, maybe you could show Griff around?" Charlie asked. He'd taken to shuffling so much he should've been assigned to guard the ballroom.

She sniffed as she climbed out of the shack, stopping before me.

"Kate. Is it Kathleen or Katherine?" I didn't care if my voice had a hard edge to it as I spoke Minna's false name.

The girl's eyes widened for an instant before they narrowed, a scowl filling her face. "Katherine, but I go by Kate," she said in a husky voice very unlike Minna's.

Leaning in, I hissed, "I know who you are, witch." Every ounce of hatred I bore for Minna boiled up and spilled over into that single sentence.

"Nice idea, Charlie, but I think Griff can find his way around on his own."

She strode off across the courtyard then, a breeze raising the long tendrils of her constrained hair, as though it promised to blow her away.

If only I could have been so fortunate.

"Do you want a map, Griff?" Charlie asked, turning toward his boxed haven, where he began shuffling papers.

"No, thank you." But as I replied, a buzzing sound filling my ears faded. The cold receded. The scents around me dulled.

Within moments, I'd become a spirit once more.

Charlie glanced back. "Griff? Griff? Where'd you go? Huh."

I hadn't moved, but I was somehow no longer visible. Something had caused Charlie and Minna to see me and then just as suddenly *not*. Dread settled in the pit of my stomach. In all my years of entrapment, nothing like that had ever happened.

The fact that it had, on the very day I'd encountered Minna, could not be a coincidence.

She'd come for something, but only one part of me remained: my soul.

RELIEF COURSED THROUGH ME AT RETURNING TO MY room. No one would ever find me there, no matter how much I played. A large mahogany door stood on the far wall, but only I could see it. Leave it to the late Lord Byrons to build a hidden room into his mansion—a choice that had made it possible for me to have uninterrupted rehearsal space, for which I was grateful. It hadn't hurt that Hannah had defaced the building blueprints during the last remodel.

Hannah cut through my reminiscences the instant I returned. "She saw you. They both did."

"I know." I gripped Hannah's hands in mine. "It was as if I was alive. That girl is a witch come to torment me. There can be no other explanation."

"What are you going to do?" For once, Hannah seemed serious.

Of course she was serious. Minna was there, in my building. Minna, who'd stolen my life away over a child's poor choices. Minna, who'd ruined me. "I'm going to confront her."

Leaving an open-mouthed Hannah behind me, I passed through the wall. When I reached the back hallway, the sound of a lone clarinet stopped me.

Minna was warming up, running through a series of major thirds. The rich timbre of the instrument chased the normality of the action away entirely. I could never recall having heard a sound so singular, aside from my own. The tones seemed otherworldly.

I moved through the wall and into the larger rehearsal space, so I could peer into the practice room window. Minna stood with her back to me, concentrating on the music before her.

Moving from her warm-up, she launched into the *Adagio* from Mozart's *Clarinet Concerto in A Major*. I knew it well, having accompanied a forgettable sod more than a century ago on the same piece. Nothing I'd learned about Minna indicated she'd been anything other than the Byrons' nanny. If it was Minna, I imagined she *could* have bewitched the clarinet to play, but I assumed the interpretation would have been perfect then.

The young woman's review of the piece was far from flawless. With her easy warm-up completed, she took a saw to a series of Mozart's delicate runs. She may have had a lovely tone, but she would need a great deal of technical improvement if she planned to perform. A *great* deal.

Her pale skin appeared flushed from playing. It didn't seem to be from excitement, but rather from concentration. She focused on every single note with the utmost intensity, but the joy was absent from her face.

"What are you doing here?"

Startled, I jumped, the irony that she had frightened *me* was not lost. I hadn't even noticed she'd stopped playing and opened the door, or that a rush of life had already filled me. My heart beat again as though a switch had been flipped. My breath settled into an even rhythm.

It had happened again. I lived.

CHAPTER 5

KATE

THE IDEA OF GOING BACK INTO THE BUILDING terrified me. What if that old lady decided to hang out in the air vent on a permanent basis? I could've asked for another practice room, but fat chance of that. They wouldn't even switch rooms for Bernie Kopel when his room partner stopped showering in protest of the school cafeteria's decision not to stock strawberry milk.

Besides, who was to say Grandma didn't visit all of the air vents equally? I didn't want another run-in with her, but there was no way I was staying in Charlie's shack with Griff hanging around.

What a jerk! The way he'd frowned at us, as though he'd just drank expired milk. Griff had raised one eyebrow, the way you'd expect a snot-nosed rich boy to do. What kind of guy wore a tuxedo to school, anyway? Did he think he was one step away from Carnegie Hall by getting accepted at Byrons?

Maybe his outfit was all the rage in Europe, but he was going to get the crap beat out of him by the percussion ensemble if he wasn't careful.

Twisting the knob, I yanked the door open. "What are you doing here?"

He jumped, as though I'd surprised him. He cleared his throat, the sound short, stern. "Someone had to point out that you completely destroyed that last series of runs."

Wait a minute. The guy was paying me a compliment? I never saw that coming. Maybe he was cool. Some people just acted weird in social situations. A curse I was intimately familiar with. "Thanks. I didn't think you had a compliment in you."

"A compliment? You believe I just paid you a compliment. Are you daft?"

Who is this freak? Did he just clamber off the moors from an Austen novel, or what? "What does that even mean?"

He leaned forward, but not enough to cross the threshold of my room. "It means you cheated the runs. *Surely* you can understand that."

Not him, too. Next, he was going to give me a lecture. To tell me what everyone else did: that a beautiful tone would only get me so far. I was not in the mood to put up with him.

"Leave me alone. I have to go to class." I slipped Benny's cover over the mouthpiece to protect my reed. Resting him on top of the piano, I began shoving my practice books into my bag.

"You can't rewrite Mozart, and frankly, no one should try."

I shoved Benny's empty case into my bag, picked up Benny, and then pushed past him, away from his height and his intense eyes.

"Are you ignoring *me*? I am never brushed aside."

"Well, today must be your lucky day." I'd almost made it to the hallway.

Then Griff cried out. "It is no such thing. Not when you've forced me to listen to careless mistakes. Or perhaps a lackadaisical attitude is simply required to attend this second-rate school?"

"You're an ass." My face burned. "Besides, the last time I checked, you were a student here, too."

"And you're a cretin who doesn't know staccato from legato. You"—he walked toward me, his eyes digging into me the way they had before—"are an *imposter*."

"Get lost, fancy pants." Sweeping past him, I made my way into the hallway, up the stairs. My hands still shook as I put distance between myself and Griff.

I'd put up with a lot from the rich kids at school. Everything from my ragged messenger bag to my scholarship seemed to set me apart. But I'd worked my butt off to be there. Griff had no business talking to me that way. Dad had promised me I'd find my way at Byrons.

My throat closed up as I moved down the hall leading to the classrooms. It was another right, followed by another, to my first class, Scales, but I paused just outside the door. I needed a pep talk and fast.

Pulling out my phone, I fired off a quick text to Rena.
I rly ms Dad.

It was the kind of text I wanted to send to Mom—the kind of thing I actually wanted to *talk* to her about. But Mom would only give me one of those sad expressions. The kind that said I should have gotten over Dad already.

Ding! A text popped up on my notifications.

He's always with you, sweetie. He's right there. xoxo

Tears stung my eyes. I didn't bother to force them away that time.

I'd fought so hard to get to Byrons, but without Dad as my teacher, as the ultimate personal defender and cheerleader, I'd never felt so alone.

Griff was right. I couldn't hack it at Byrons. *I am an imposter.*

CHAPTER 6
GRIFFIN

Tuesday, November 22nd

ONCE KATHERINE HAD GONE, THE SCENT OF THE musty basement had dulled, the sounds of the old building fading. Even my vision had diminished, the hallway before me just a little less sharp. Not blurry, but not clear. My skin, which had seemed to stretch itself before, had relaxed as I became intangible. Until I stood alone outside the practice room, a ghost once more.

It certainly seemed as though Katherine's presence had been the trigger for the change.

I should have put Katherine out of my mind. It would have made sense to do so. Yet, I couldn't get the sensation of being alive out of my head. If being near Katherine had brought me back to life twice, would it happen a third time?

The idea had haunted me the rest of the day and night. "What an infuriating woman!"

"Are you still going on about that?" Hannah leaned forward as I entered the room, a crease forming above her brow. "I'll admit, that *was* different. I may have peeked, just for a moment. You did seem alive during your discussion with the girl."

"The girl looks a great deal like Minna, but she isn't. Yet, I change whenever I'm around her. I can't explain it."

"I can." Worry crept into Hannah's voice. She had quite the penchant for acting the mother hen. "This must mean she's the one. The one who can break your curse."

If my heart had been capable of freezing it would have.

"Dear God. After all these years." All I did know for certain was that the girl held some power over me. I had to find out what.

My own salvation could depend on it.

CHAPTER 7

KATE

Even though I went to a school dedicated to music, I had to take all the regular boring classes other high school students did. Like US History and English Comp., Trigonometry and Geography. The one good thing was that Eurythmics, which taught rhythm with movement, counted as gym, which meant no traditional P.E. on my schedule. *Thank God.*

My jury was ninety percent of my performance grade for the semester. Of course, my regular classes counted toward my report card too, but as far as the music portion of the curriculum went, performance made up the bulk. Solfège (which non-musical people called sight-singing) and Music Theory and Composition (how to actually read and write music) made up the rest.

It all added up to a pretty full plate.

Then there'd been my encounter with Griff. My heart

still pounded from it as I climbed the stairs to the first floor the following morning.

I still couldn't believe Griff had shown up in my practice room and criticized me. Why was that jerk even at Byrons? If his *second-rate school* comment said anything, he clearly didn't want to be there.

Of course, I wasn't sure I did, either—at the moment. It was kind of lucky that one of the worst classes ever was the shortest. Scales class, taken three days a week, was less a class and more a forum for public humiliation. Sure, I could play my scales. The problem wasn't playing them, but they had to be performed over two octaves (twenty-nine subsequent notes) and performed solo in front of the group. To make matters worse, I had to memorize them in all twenty-four keys—major and minor—a mandate for all clarinetists.

Yep, Scales class equaled yuckfest.

Some kids glanced up as I entered the room, but turned away just as quickly. No one spoke at Byrons. Not that I was super outgoing, but at least I'd smiled the first few classes, and tried to make eye contact. It never went anywhere. The kids were too competitive to take making friends seriously.

My phone vibrated. Mom again. She'd gone to Cleveland last night and had been calling ever since. I'd declined every call.

"Kate. Phone away, please," said Ryder, a Senior Leader, and the Byrons School equivalent of a student teacher. He ran the Scales classes for both grades and had weekly check-ins with the teachers on each student's progress. He had way more power than he should. Judging by his smug expression, he knew it.

Ryder had it all—an angel's face, thick, dark hair that only dared wave on the sides, coffee-brown eyes . . . a perfectly ironed shirt that matched his perfectly ironed pants. The girls in my class thought he was h-o-t. I thought he was a-n-n-o-y-i-n-g.

I'd gone out on a date once with Ryder, when I'd first started school. All he did was go on and on about how his family *really* owned the school, or they would have if it hadn't been donated. That was all in the first fifteen minutes.

The minutes that followed had been much worse.

That was why I'd been careful to make sure there wasn't a second date. Not that Ryder hadn't asked me out since then. I wondered why. I couldn't have been his type any more than he was mine.

Reaching into my bag for my bottle of water, I spotted my number one reed from the day before. I picked it up, staring at the fine split down the middle of the bamboo, a memento of its up close and personal time with the air vent. *Damn Ghostly Grandma.* I'd been excited about playing that reed.

I wish it hadn't broken.

Shit.

It was only a fleeting thought—I hadn't meant anything by it. Yet, after I blinked twice, the split had disappeared completely. The reed was repaired.

My face flushed. Had I done that? Of course I had.

I slunk down in my seat, keeping my hand covered. Had anyone seen? What would they say? *Calm down. It's your secret.*

Just like it had been my secret in second grade, when I'd gone to a sleepover at Colleen Ross's house. She'd had this cute doll and I'd wanted it. I hadn't meant to wish she'd *give* it to me. The next thing I'd known, Colleen was sobbing and insisting I take it. She hadn't known why.

But *I* had. That was where the *no wishing* had come in.

Mom and Dad hadn't been mad that they'd had to come pick me up in the middle of the night. Colleen, on the other hand, never forgave me. I didn't even take her stupid doll.

Sitting in Scales class, it was as if a curtain had been drawn between me and the other kids, separating us. I wasn't like them and I never would be. Maybe it was time I stopped wanting to connect with anyone.

Replacing my second-choice reed with my now-whole number one, I slipped the mouthpiece in my mouth to dampen the bamboo for play. There would be no time for a warm-up.

"Good morning, everybody. Let's get started." Ryder sat at his usual spot in the circle—right by the door—exhibiting perfect clarinet player posture: back straight, knees together, bell resting just along the knees. "Jeremy. Why don't you start? Give us E major."

After a few beats, Jeremy launched into an E major scale. His sound was full and rich, the tempo spot on, and each note hit with precision-point accuracy. The whole thing was over in less than a minute, but Jeremy had thrown down the gauntlet.

"Excellent job, Jeremy." Ryder nodded as Jeremy lowered his clarinet.

Which way would Ryder go? To the left or right? Not to me—I didn't want to be next.

But Ryder threw me a confident smile, as if he could read my mind and enjoyed torturing me. "Kate, how about you next? F major?"

The heat from the other clarinetists' glares singed my skin. The simpler the scales I got, the greater the chance they wouldn't get any of the basic ones. Ryder *never* repeated scales.

I let my fingers fall into position on Benny's keys for the first note—low F. I could do this one. It was easy. But, for some reason, my mind flitted to Griff. He'd more or less told me I didn't deserve to be a student at Byrons.

Taking a deep breath, I played, but his words followed me, shouting in my ear. *Imposter!*

F, G, A . . . Don't forget the B-flat, C, D, E, F . . .

By the time I began playing the scale in descending order, I'd abandoned the tempo and moved into slow-mo. I hit all the notes, but there wasn't much else good I could say about it.

When I lowered Benny, I met Ryder's eyes and read his assessment: not good enough. It didn't matter that I'd been playing since I was ten, practicing every day for the love of it. It didn't matter what I'd done to get into Byrons—an aced audition of the *Allegretto* from Saint-Saëns' *Clarinet Sonata,* a perfect music theory test, and impeccable references. It only mattered what I'd done *that day.* The music business, even in the classical world, had a short memory.

Since Dad died, there'd been times when I'd hated music. It would have been easier to quit, but it had become my only tie to him. I wouldn't lose that. Even if I had no one on my side at home *or* at school. Even if it meant suffering through Scales.

Ryder said some words—they could have been a criticism or compliment, most likely the former. I was too relieved to be finished with that day's humiliation to pay attention.

He moved on to another student in the group. Some person named Kimberly, or maybe Brittany? She seemed to fit the part—perky in all the right places, with a butt she probably used to bounce things off in her spare time. Naturally, Kim-bany played a flawless D-flat major scale.

There were four guys and four girls (including me) playing clarinet this year. Byrons was particularly known for its woodwind program. We went around the circle, each student completing their assigned scale.

No one struggled. No one except me. *Again.* After twenty minutes of torture, the bell rang and Ryder stood. "That's it for today, guys. Nice job."

"Yeah. Nice job, charity case," one of the boys coughed under his breath, as he left the room.

Ouch. I glanced up, but wasn't quick enough to tell which one. Besides, with their solid-colored Ralph Lauren polos and pale khakis, they all blurred together. We didn't have uniforms at Byrons, but that didn't stop most of the students from looking like clones. Dad would've told me it was good to be different. Tell that to my classmates.

We all started filing toward the door for second period US History. I'd welcome a review of The Civil War after the disaster of Scales class. Shouldering my messenger bag, which contained Benny, I walked past Ryder, who was chatting with Jeremy. If I could just make it to the door.

"Got a minute?" Ryder called.

Damn. "Sure. What's up?" I turned back to face Ryder.

"I'm sorry to break the news to you." He scratched the back of his neck, exposing an inch of bare abs. Kimbany would probably have been swooning right then. "You'll need to find another pianist to accompany you for your jury."

"What? Why? Igor's been working with me since my first week at school." Igor had bought me a pink pudding in the cafeteria once. He was cool. Even if I had caught him checking out my butt occasionally.

"He's been deported back to Russia. Apparently, he had

forged papers—really bad ones." He rolled his eyes, as if to imply Igor should have known better.

Panic swirled in my stomach. *Oh no.* "How am I supposed to find another accompanist?" Everyone knew it was much harder to perform a solo piece without an accompanist. Not only did they keep tempo, but they helped the performing musician stay in tune. Beyond that, most performances just didn't sound as good.

Ryder shrugged. "I'll ask around. Why don't you put it up on the bulletin board? Someone's bound to sign up."

Oh, yeah, sure, my classmates were *totally* going to raise their hands to help. Pianists weren't allowed to accept money for accompanying fellow students. School rules. Which meant they had zero incentive to say yes.

His eyes almost held pity, but then he popped his cell phone out of his pocket and checked his reflection. I looked on as he adjusted his hair. "Which brings me to the other thing I wanted to speak to you about. I noticed you struggled again today."

Gee, thanks for that keen observation.

He slid the phone back into his pocket, and I would have sworn his teeth sparkled when he smiled. "If you ever wanted to meet after school, I could help you. I don't mind."

He'd help me all right. *The dog.* "Thanks, Ryder, but I don't like to inflict pain on others." I walked toward the exit when he touched my upper arm, gently steering me back to face him.

Ryder's sad smile didn't reach his eyes. "You know you really need to get these scales down. They're a requirement for college auditions, and college auditions are the next step on the path for you if you want to perform professionally." He stepped forward. "I could coach you. You'd be caught up in no time."

"Thanks, but I'm good," I said, taking a not-so-subtle step back.

Ryder stepped forward again. "I like you. Can't we get to know each other better? If not through scales practice, then what about dinner? I'd like to see you again."

And I don't want to see you. "I'm sorry, Ryder, but I'm not interested."

Ryder stared at me, his brown eyes searching, totally into me. It should have felt flattering, exciting. It didn't. Warning bells sounded in my head as I finally caught on.

Uh oh, he's gonna kiss me.

"I said I'm not interested." I tried to move, but the tray of the whiteboard pressed against my back.

"Come on. You know you like me, too." He moved in for the kiss, his breath hot on my lips, his body too close to mine.

"I do believe"—a voice cut into our conversation—"the *lady* said she was not interested."

My gaze flew to the doorway and Griff, who looked self-righteous or something. His hand was at his side, one eyebrow raised. I wasn't exactly thrilled to see him after the way he'd spoken to me, but I needed help—fast.

Right then, Griff was the lesser of two evils.

CHAPTER 8
GRIFFIN

RYDER, THE POMPOUS PRETTY BOY WHO'D BEEN forcing his amorous attentions on Katherine, took a step away from her. It was about time, too. I'd heard more than enough from my position outside the classroom.

"Who the hell are you?" Ryder narrowed his eyes, twisting away from Kate. The action made him look more familiar, though that thought slid away in the face of his obnoxious greeting.

"Griff." I offered my hand. "I'm Katherine's new accompanist for her jury." Good Heavens, where had that come from? Her new accompanist? The idea both terrified and thrilled me in equal measure.

Katherine's mouth dropped open.

Ryder sneered. "How did you know Kate even needs an accompanist? No one knows about Igor's deportation but myself and the faculty." His attentions returned to Katherine, which I most certainly did not like, even if I couldn't explain why. He jerked his thumb in my direction. "How do you know if he's any good?"

Enough. It only took a step for me to tower over the boy. "I think you'll find not only that my musical knowledge far exceeds your own, but that news travels faster than you think. I wouldn't bother challenging me if I were you."

Ryder's eyes narrowed. Would he try to fight me? I would relish the combat after so many years. Even if it meant striking that *pillock.*

I'd always loved boxing. A couple of times, I'd snuck off in London when Jig thought I was resting. There'd been lessons, and then a wrist sprain. Then Mother had died.

But Ryder didn't raise his fists. Instead, he picked up his bag from the floor as he brushed past me and stormed out the door. Only when he'd gone did Katherine wrap her arms around herself. Her too-pale skin seemed even paler. He'd frightened her.

"Interesting company you keep." I clenched my fists at my sides, and then just as quickly relaxed them. "Good thing I showed up to offer my assistance."

Katherine scowled. "I was handling it."

"Certainly you were. Was that why he'd backed you into a corner?"

"I fight my own battles. I don't need your help." Looping her sack over her shoulder, she strode out the door, her long hair trailing down her back.

Ridiculous. That was the second time she'd walked away from me. I followed her into the hallway. "I saved your bedraggled behind from that lowlife. Don't I at least deserve your thanks?"

Katherine spun around. "Though I'm impressed at your

ability to use *bedraggled* in a sentence, I didn't ask for your help. I had a plan."

Intrigued, I moved closer. "And precisely what would such a plan entail, pray tell?"

She blushed, the color attractive set against her pale skin. The pencil behind her ear slipped and fell to the floor with a clatter. She picked it up, and then slid it into place. "Leave me alone. I've put up with enough of your crap already and it's only Tuesday."

Turning, she walked away. I couldn't let her leave. If she put too much distance between us, I'd fade away again.

I couldn't afford to antagonize her further. Not if she truly was the one. "Please accept my apologies. You greatly resemble an acquaintance who I haven't seen in some time. It took another encounter with you to verify you were not the same girl."

Katherine's right eyebrow shot toward her hairline. "What planet did you drop in from? Seriously?"

What a vulgar interpretation of a beautiful name. Then I remembered her predicament with her deported accompanist. "Well, Katherine"—she scowled and muttered what sounded like a well-chosen expletive—"don't forget. You need me."

She paused. "*I* need *you*? You don't even know me."

Moving around Katherine, I placed myself between her and her next class. Unlike Ryder, I gave her plenty of space. I didn't need to crowd women to win them over. My own natural charm always triumphed. "I know you need an accompanist, and I am a *brilliant* accompanist."

"Don't you have classes to go to or something? It's your second day, isn't it?"

"Let me worry about my own education." It far exceeded anything they could teach me in such an inferior school anyway. "You may meet me in the practice rooms downstairs at three o'clock, Katherine."

"My name's Kate, and I don't want to work with you. I'd rather fail."

I bit back the temptation to tell her we'd already worked together. "We both know you're much too determined to fail. Eventually, you'll realize you have no control over your situation. At which point, you'll turn to the only solution available." I pointed a finger at my own chest. "You do need me."

After our duet the previous day, I'd heard enough of her performance to speak honestly. "You aren't the slightest bit ready for your examinations. They'll tear you to shreds like they did that boy who ended up joining the seminary. What was his name?"

"Wade Whitaker." Katherine tensed, the name passing through her lips as a whisper.

I knew she would know the name. The boy was a local legend in the school, maybe even more than myself. He'd arrived already high strung. What the schedule and teachers hadn't done to him, Hannah had finished off.

No wonder he'd turned to the Lord.

"You wouldn't want to become another Mr. Whitaker, would you?" God save the convent that took such a ragamuffin. "You may meet me in the practice rooms downstairs at three o'clock, *Kate*. Don't be late."

"Go to hell."

"It would seem I'm already there." I gestured to the hallway we stood in. "Three o'clock, then."

Kate opened her mouth, a retort clearly in the making, but she clamped her lips shut. Without another word, she pivoted and then entered the first door on the right, shutting it with a soft click, though she probably would have preferred to slam it.

As I slowly transitioned to spirit form, I stared after her. Lord, she was a feisty one.

Katherine, *Kate*, may have been angry with me, but she hadn't said no.

Three o'clock, then.

TAKING A DEEP BREATH, I BEGAN TO PLAY—AN ANGRY piece at first, but then I remembered Kate and how she'd looked during our encounter in the hallway. I quickly transitioned into a compellingly quiet number. The *Andante* from Shostakovich's *Piano Concerto No. 2 in F Major*. It was too sentimental for me, but my fingers seemed to choose the piece on their own. God, I missed the orchestra. For so long, there'd been only my piano and me.

Still, excitement poured into me as though a tap had been opened. As long as I was with Kate, others could see me, perhaps an entire roomful of people. If people could see me, then I might be able to perform in front of an audience again. I *was* a musician, after all. There was no point in playing for one's self alone.

"You went to see Kate." Hannah didn't make it a question. She only sat on the very edge of my piano as though she were a songbird. Too bad she was tone-deaf.

"I wanted to see if I'd become alive again, or at least appear that way." I dropped my hands from the keys.

Hannah lowered herself to her seat beside my piano. "You came to her rescue."

"Intervening when that ruffian cornered her was simply common courtesy. Anyone would have done it."

"Most people might have. Not *you*, dear Griff." Hannah straightened the collar of her dress. "As I recall, you're the chap who looks out for himself—come what may."

Her words pricked at some long-forgotten emotions I'd shoved into the back of my mind. I hadn't always been that way. "She could be the one. I'd be a fool not to investigate."

Hannah didn't respond. When I finally glanced in her direction, she'd gone. Probably to terrorize more students. Whatever the reason, I was grateful. I didn't want the company or the questions.

The end is coming.

I jolted in my seat as a voice seemed to fill the room, and yet only my ear at the same time. I sat in silence, waiting for more, but the voice didn't repeat itself. Maybe it was Hannah playing a joke, or even a wandering spirit?

The end is coming, it had said. Once, I would have given *anything* to hear those words. Why then, did they fill me with such dread?

CHAPTER 9
KATE

THE NEWS THAT IGOR HAD GOTTEN HIMSELF DEPORTED freaked me out more than I wanted to admit.

I could've gone to my student advisor and asked for help, but I knew she'd only tell me to figure it out myself. They were big on solving your own problems at Byrons. Sometimes that was cool, but mostly it sucked. Couldn't my problems be solved for me? At least until I graduated high school?

And when Griff had showed up and offered to be my accompanist, it was easier to let Ryder believe it was true. I hadn't planned on making the after-school rehearsal, but what choice did I have? At three o'clock, I made my way to the rehearsal rooms.

My feet started stepping to a rhythm before I even realized someone was rehearsing. One-two-three-four-five-six. A waltz—like a bizarre Strauss piece gone wrong.

Normally, I wouldn't have paid attention. Byrons was a music school after all. But chills skated over my skin as I recognized the pianist. It was the same musician I'd been hearing through my practice room wall. The one who had accompanied me.

Music emanated from my practice area, just as it had on the mornings when I'd heard it. But the room was dark, and the door open. Each of the other rooms sat empty—lights off, doors open. Where was the music coming from?

I reached for the light switch. My hand shook, but I forced it still. I wasn't a wimp.

Light filled the cramped area, but it was empty. No piano player. The piano sat untouched as the riveting music continued, a series of complex notes pouring through the wall, a river of emotion.

I checked the air vent. No old woman. Still, the sounds of the piano filled the space, just as they had yesterday.

I wish I knew who was playing the piano.

Damn! I did it again.

As if on cue, a section of the wall popped open, revealing a large, door-sized opening. "What the heck?"

Taking a step forward, I swung the make-shift door open wider. The piano sounded louder for a split second, until it halted. Peering around the frame of the opening, I found Griff sitting at the bench with his fingers poised over the keys. His expression seemed strained, distorted, like I'd just interrupted him in the middle of performing surgery or something.

His pale lips parted into a round O. I couldn't tear my eyes away from them.

Griff swallowed. A million questions waited in his eyes. It was like we were suspended in time.

"There you are, British Invasion."

"How did you open the door?" Griff demanded, jumping to his feet.

"I don't know. I thought you opened it." But then I remembered. I'd *wished* I could find out who was playing the piano. My face heated, but I forced my breathing to slow as I took in the dark paneling, ending at a dusty fireplace and mantel.

Keep it casual. "I never knew this secret door was here." *Casual, not awkward.*

"That's the idea behind a hidden door, you see." He rolled his eyes to the ceiling. "It was part of the original house. This school is teeming with secret passages and hidden doors. This room was a library."

"How do you know anything about this place? Didn't you just start here?"

His eyebrows shot up. "They have . . . a . . . site. I would have assumed you'd investigated things *before* you enrolled."

Of course I had. *Sort of.* "I didn't see anything about it. I'll have to look again." *Or at all.*

Griff's space easily exceeded the size of at least six practice areas combined. I took a few steps into the room, shutting the door behind me. Only the dim winter light remained. The two windows were below street level, so they didn't brighten the place up. Beyond that, there were no lights on. How did he read his music? Easy. He didn't have any.

There were two other pianos pushed against the wall, but they'd clearly seen better days. Griff's grand piano appeared to be in the best shape and dominated the room. The weird part? Although everything else was dust-covered, that instrument was immaculate. Someone had polished it until it gleamed.

Griff crossed the space and flicked a light switch. Instantly, the soft light flooded the room. He squinted and stared at the lightbulb hanging from the ceiling, like it surprised him somehow.

He sat down at the piano, and then proceeded to run his fingers over the keys in a short, agitated piece that seemed to reflect his mood. He wasn't looking at me, just taking an extended solo.

If he was going to ignore me, I had better things to do. "Now's obviously not a good time. See you around." I moved toward the exit, leaving Griff and his secret room behind.

"Kate." Griff was at my side before I cleared the threshold. "You don't have to go."

He frowned for a moment, hesitated another, and rested his hand on my arm. A burst of heat forced its way past my two layers of clothing

I backed up, easily yanking my arm from his. "Maybe you shouldn't keep people waiting." My own mother did a good enough job of ignoring me. The rest of the Byrons students weren't far behind. I didn't need to add him to the list.

He frowned. "Must you be so . . . so abrasive?"

"Must you be so annoying?" My contribution to the conversation wasn't going to stand out in the tact department, either. "Look. I'm sorry."

"We do seem to rub each other crossways at times, don't we?"

Rub each other crossways? "Oh! Rub each other *the wrong way!*" My cheeks flamed. Why was I blushing? He seemed to bring out the worst in me.

"I do not need a vocabulary lesson from an American. I am perfectly capable—" But then Griff closed his eyes, pressing the pad of his thumb against the bridge of his nose. He released a slow breath before he looked at me again.

He was blushing, too, his pale face pink. His long, blond hair glinted under the light.

Something inside of me moved, shifted. *Who are you, Griff?* I realized with a jolt that I actually wanted to know. "I'm sorry."

He forced a grim smile. "Why don't you warm up? We'll get started when you're ready."

"Okay, but just so you know, I have to catch the bus at five." I slid Benny's bag from my shoulder.

Griff glanced at the clock on the mantel, which looked like it had stopped working in 1970, given the layer of dust on it. There were enough cobwebs covering the clock that they almost completely obscured its face.

He chuckled. "Then we'd better get started."

God, he was beyond a mystery. There was only one thing I knew for sure.

Griff's eyes were hazel.

CHAPTER 10
GRIFFIN

AFTER SO MANY YEARS OF INTANGIBILITY, THE SWITCH to a more solid form made everything more vibrant, as though my surroundings had been out of focus before. My vision seemed more acute, smells stronger, the pads of my fingers more sensitive. The piano keys were even more inviting. Anticipation thrummed within me like one of the wires in the electric lights. Soon, I'd not only get the chance to play, but accompany someone else.

At least I would if that someone else would quit fussing over her reeds. Infernal waste of time, playing a wind instrument. In my time, I'd simply appeared, and a superior piano was provided for me.

She swapped reeds, and that reminded me of the news I'd have to share with Kate. I'd gotten her some new music. Knowing Kate even for such a short time, I could almost anticipate her reaction—a response I feared and awaited in equal measure.

"I got you something today." Rising, I handed her the clarinet part of my new selection. Here it was. The moment of rapture. She'd either send me the heavenly smile of an angel or the hellish glare of a demon.

"What's this?" Kate frowned, staring at the pages the way someone might interpret a foreign language.

"Your new jury piece. I found your old one in Igor's music bin. Clearly, he didn't have time to pack it before he was shipped back to the country of his birth."

"How did *you* get into Igor's music bin?" She planted both hands on her hips, eyes narrowing with the ferocity of a cornered animal. "And what business is it of yours?"

"Are you going to spend all afternoon questioning me about trivial nonsense, or are you here to accomplish something?"

"What was wrong with the Weber?" she asked, tugging a worn copy of Weber's *Clarinet Concerto No. 1 in F Minor* from her bag. "I've been practicing it ever since last summer. I wanted to get a head start on things."

At least she'd pronounced the composer's name correctly—*Vay-ber* instead of *Web-ber*. She wasn't a total wretch. "It's not the right piece for you."

It was a common mistake many new Byrons students made. They'd try something too challenging, believing it would win them points. Usually, it failed to impress.

"I don't know why you think you know anything about it. You're a piano player." She began packing up her reeds, which meant if she had to take them out again, there would be more preparation, more delays.

"*Pianist.* The Weber isn't your strength. Too many staccato runs. Your inferior performance of Mozart's *Adagio* yesterday was quite telling."

Avoiding her eyes, I opened my own copy of the Brahms, spreading it out across the piano stand. A necessity only until I'd had the chance to memorize the piece.

But Kate tipped her chin, crossing her arms over her chest and trapping her clarinet at an off-angle behind them. "And how do you know what my strengths are?"

"Should I assume that you are going to be a prima donna the entire time we're working together? I was under the impression you wanted to learn."

"I didn't ask for a teacher. I need an accompanist." She curled her lip. "What could you possibly teach me, anyway? We're equals."

That was most definitely not true. "Are you asking *me* to audition for the part?" I set my jaw, but just as quickly forced my mouth to relax. I was only working with her to break my curse—her jury didn't matter to me. Not really.

"Perhaps you should just . . . chill." I believed that was the term? "You have to leave at five. We've already wasted time."

Kate hesitated. I understood her challenges around receiving criticism. Many artists suffered from it. Though not me, of course.

No one had ever criticized me.

"What's the piece?" She turned her attention to the pages I'd given her. "Johannes Brahms—*Sonata for Clarinet and Piano in E-flat Major*."

"It's beautiful. It will show off that gorgeous tone of yours." The words slipped past my lips before I realized it.

Kate's pale cheeks colored again. "You think my tone is gorgeous?" Her eyes sought mine. What color were they? Certainly nothing commonplace.

I had to force my attention from her face. From the single freckle on the bridge of her nose. From her pale lips as she wetted her reed and attached it to the clarinet's mouthpiece in preparation for play.

"Yes. Now . . . . the time." I gestured to the damaged clock once more, out of habit. "Let's just take it from the top of the *Allegro*."

Slipping the pencil from behind her ear, she took several moments to scan the first page. She marked the paper in four places before she set the pencil down and turned to me. Kate nodded once, and then began to play.

Dear Lord. Has she been possessed? Why was she playing everything at full volume? And too fast?

She'd gotten only ten measures in when I stopped her. "This entire intro is meant to be played *piano*. That's quiet, in case you hadn't heard." Brahms had most certainly rolled over in his grave.

Kate scowled. "Jeez. I'm just reading this for the first time. It would be easier if you played, too."

"You aren't ready for me to accompany you. Stick to the basics. Please take it from the top, Katherine."

"Fine, but my name's Kate. I told you to call me Kate."

"You can stand there all afternoon arguing with me, but it won't help you in a few weeks' time."

She opened her mouth, and I awaited her rebuttal. It was there on the tip of her tongue, ready to fly in my direction. Yet, Kate held back. Perhaps she realized the truth in my words.

Instead, she positioned the clarinet against her bottom lip, took a breath, and then began.

All I could hear were technical flaws. I wished I hadn't. I remembered all too well what it was like to be reprimanded during piano lessons. Except my piano master corrected my performances by swatting my back until my playing improved.

I stopped her at the bottom of the second page.

"What did you think?" she asked, for once, her voice devoid of sarcasm.

Clearing my throat, I sat up straighter. "That was . . . mediocre at best."

Kate's smile faded.

CHAPTER 11

KATE

MEDIOCRE AT *BEST*? HAD I HEARD HIM WRONG? "WHAT are you talking about?"

Griff stood and picked up the music. He stared at it before tossing it on top of the piano. "Measures 10, 19, 39, 80, and 81 had articulation problems, your intonation was off in measure 108, and tell me, how could you ignore *all* the interpretation markings?"

The reality of his words slapped me in the face. "I usually skip them on a first run through."

He threw up a hand, turning back to the pages before him. "Not with me you don't. And the runs? I've never heard such a sloppy interpretation."

There he went about the runs again. The backs of my eyes stung.

No. No, you will not cry in front of him.

"You aren't playing jazz, Kate. This is Brahms." Griff

spat out the composer's name, frowning in my direction. I didn't know whether he'd taken offense on his own behalf or on Brahms's.

"It wasn't that bad." My cheeks burned with indignation. To put myself out there like that and then have him call me on the carpet like a sophomore was too much.

"You weren't on the receiving end of that atrocious—no." Griff shook his head, coming to stand at the end of the piano bench. "It wasn't that bad, you're right. It's just . . ."

"What?"

"When I agreed to help you, it was because I thought you were a serious musician."

I bristled. "I am."

"You're capable of so much more." His attention seemed to flicker to my mouth. "Your embouchure needs work. Firm up your lip against your bottom teeth. That will help with your articulation."

Maybe it was the way he offered that advice, the uncharacteristic softness to his voice, but it sounded like pity. I wouldn't accept that from him. "I know what an embouchure is, Griff. I didn't start playing yesterday."

"Don't you get it? I'm trying to help you."

"If insulting is helping, then you're doing a bang-up job, fancy pants."

Griff moved closer, his intensity forcing me to stare into his eyes. "Ask yourself this. Why *exactly* do you want this? Why are you fighting so hard to stay at this school if you don't want to improve?"

Biting my bottom lip, I thought back, remembering the first time Dad had taken me to the symphony. The clarinetists' keys had gleamed under the spotlights, and the music had been magical. To be on stage in the middle of it all, a part of something—that was what I wanted.

"I'll never get in with a symphony if I don't make it through this program, for starters." It was a pipe dream. The odds were beyond stacked against me, but it was *my* dream.

Griff nodded, his brow creasing. "Admirable goal. Very much so, but we both know that until you're able to work with a teacher, to accept help, you're only meeting *half* your potential." His voice softened as he spoke the words, making them harsher somehow.

Turning away from him, I twisted Benny apart, placing the pieces in my open clarinet case without wiping them down—a cardinal clarinetist sin. I'd had a teacher. The best ever. And he was gone. I'd never hear his advice again. It'd left a hole in my heart.

Zipping up my case, I shoved it into my bag and whirled around. "You know, the next time you decide to change my music, perhaps you should try consulting *me* first."

Without waiting for his reply, I rushed out of the room and up the stairs, toward the front door and the bus. I had to get away. No way in hell was I going to let Griff see me cry.

The South Hills, where we lived, was one of many communities—like Oakland, the North Side, or Mount Washington, all connected by bridges—with Pittsburgh sitting in the center of them all. They called Pittsburgh "The City of Bridges." Dad had once told me we had 446 of them. Just thinking about that made me miss him all the more.

By the time I'd crossed my share of bridges that night to get home, Mom was watching CNN in our townhouse. She worked at a large investment firm, which meant financial news was sort of her thing. She practically peed herself every time the stock ticker updated. Then again, she was generally over-excited every day of the week.

If only I could just sneak past her to my room? My day sucked bad enough without having to get into it with her, too.

"You never called me back, Kate. I called five times." She kept her voice even and cool, but it was clear she was pissed.

"I'm sorry. Bad day." I walked down the hall to my bedroom, and then set my bag inside the door. I returned to the living room and leaned against the doorframe.

"Want to talk about it?" she asked.

I opened my mouth to spill—the way I would have before, when Dad was alive—but I'd learned my lesson. She'd only tell me I should quit, and offer to get me out of Byrons and enroll me somewhere else. "No."

"Okay. You don't have to tell me, honey." She smoothed out the front of her dress pants. "But we do need to talk. Maybe you'll sleep in tomorrow? We can have breakfast." She brightened.

"I have juries coming up. You know I have to practice. I can't do that here."

"Kate—"

Here we go.

"Come and sit by me for a second."

I did as she asked, but concentrated on my worn boots.

"Things have been going really well for me at work. And my company has floated—"

God, I really hate her corporate jargon.

"—this idea to me about taking over a director role in Los Angeles. Obviously, that means you'd have to leave the Byrons School, but there's an excellent Young Leaders Prep

Program at the local private school near the office. I think it'd be good for you."

California? Young Leaders? What was she thinking? "I'd hate it. That's not what I want to do."

"Do you know how competitive the music industry is?" The words *you'll never find a job* whispered around the room like a ghost.

"Dad would never have asked me to go to some business school." I spoke the words softly, but Mom closed her eyes as though I'd shouted them. I could still remember how excited he'd been when I got my acceptance into Byrons.

"Byrons School! No way, pumpkin, that's awesome." He'd cheered and held up the letter, waving it around like a flag.

"Dad, you can't call me pumpkin anymore. I'm not a little kid."

He'd stopped dancing, and then lowered the letter, handing it back. "I guess if you aren't a kid, then we shouldn't go out for mint chocolate chip at Scoops to celebrate." He'd shrugged, but the smile had remained.

"At least listen to me."

I blinked, tearing myself from the memory. "I am listening."

"I'm not saying you can't follow your dream. I'm just saying you should have a backup plan."

"How? With what free time? You know how much work I have to put into my music. How am I supposed to fit in a second career path?"

"Katherine—"

"Kate! It's Kate, Mom, not Katherine. Why are you trying to make me into someone I'm not?"

"Not everyone has to choose a job they're crazy about. Once you're out of college, you'll have to pay your bills.

How are you going to do that with your clarinet? Why not work on a backup plan now? You can still take private lessons."

Please ring. I wish the phone would ring.

Ring! Ring!

Mom's gaze flew to the phone and then back to me. "Did you just . . . " Her need to pick up won out. "I have to take this. It's the office."

As if it would be anyone else.

"Fine. I have to study anyway." I pushed off the couch and headed to the kitchen. Opening up the freezer with care, I snuck a granola bar from the back. When Dad passed away, Mom went on this healthy kick, and everything in our refrigerator turned green overnight. I think Mom had a secret hope she'd make me into a vegetarian convert.

I'd been smuggling snacks in when she was out of town for almost a year. Thank God for the Internet.

I lived on granola bars and TV dinners that I hid in the freezer behind the ice dispenser, and a box of freeze pops that Grandma Covington sent over last year. She forgot things sometimes, like I was in high school and hadn't eaten freeze pops since I was ten.

Once I made it inside my room, I shut the door. It had been another frigid commute. A bubble bath would help me thaw. Peeling off my clothes on the way to my bathroom, I left a trail behind me, not bothering to pick it up. I turned on the water in the bathtub, twisting the faucet to the next-to-hottest setting. The only one I could get away without burning myself. As the water level rose, long, wavy fingers of steam filled the room, clouding the mirror.

I added the bubbles to the tub, the warmth teasing me the instant my toes hit the water. I sank down under the surface for a moment, reveling in the heat. I wanted to erase everything from my mind, but between my mother, Griff, and Ryder, they'd managed to press every one of my buttons.

Before I realized what I was doing, I'd navigated to the Music icon on my phone. I typed *Sonata for Clarinet and Piano in E-flat Major*. Brahms was first on the list. It was only ninety-nine cents. A bargain. With the press of a button, I'd bought it, and a little pie filled up slowly letting me know the track was downloading.

Unbidden, my mind slipped back to Griff and my performance that afternoon. My performance of The Brahms hadn't been that bad, had it? Goose bumps rose on my arms. I turned the tap back on, adding another blast of hot water.

Bumping the volume to eighteen, I popped my earbuds in and lay back against the tub. The notes soared into my ears, the clarinetist's tone and passion filled my head and heart. The piece was a brilliant mix of technicality and artistry.

But the more I listened, the more I couldn't help comparing my own practice to the version playing through my phone. Each note had its own weight, its own purpose. Whereas I'd torn through the piece. Too fast. Too loud. Too everything.

"Katherine?" Mom knocked on the bathroom door. "Kate?"

"Yeah?

"I've got a couple of overnights coming up. Then I'm going out of town on the 7th for two weeks. Why don't I call Rena and see if you can stay with her?"

I opened my mouth to say *yes, please*, but I stopped myself. I was sixteen. The school seemed to think I was adult enough to solve my own problems, maybe I was adult enough to stay on my own, too. "I'll be fine, Mom." *Just go, already. Besides, you know you want to.*

"I don't know if I like the idea of you being here alone, Kate."

I bit back a laugh. I was always alone, but I didn't bother to point that out. I just stayed under the rapidly chilling water.

There was silence on the other side of the door for a moment. "You're sure you'll be okay?" I could tell from her tone of voice that she *wanted* me to be okay—wanted to leave. I was the only thing standing in her way.

What did it matter? I'd been alone for longer than she realized. "Have a good trip."

"Thanks. I—" I waited, wanting her to worry about me, hoping she'd offer to stay. After a pause, I heard my mother's steps fading away. *So much for that.*

A loud sound jolted me. The Brahms. It was still playing through my headphones.

Until you're able to work with a teacher, to accept help, you're only meeting half your potential.

Griff's right. The Brahms is perfect for me.

The Weber was too much. Which, I suddenly recalled, was what Dad had said before I'd talked him into working on it.

Sighing, I tugged on the stopper, releasing the bath water. It looked like I'd be eating a supersized portion of crow tomorrow—in front of Griff.

CHAPTER 12

GRIFFIN

My body shifted in Kate's absence. The scents of the musty room faded. The sounds of the school brass ensemble's practice session muted. In moments, I'd gone from feeling one hundred percent alive to one hundred percent dead.

As my own adrenaline evaporated, I stared at the open door, half hoping Kate would return.

She hadn't liked what I'd said. Had I ruined my chance at breaking the curse?

"If she's the one, you're doing a fine job of it." Hannah's face lit, as she floated into the room.

"Do you really think Kate's the one for me?" The idea wasn't terrible. Kate *was* beautiful, and kind when she wasn't being so unbelievably caustic and disagreeable.

"*Duh*," Hannah said, employing the much-hated

current vernacular. "Of course. Though if I were her, I'd never come back. Especially after all that *mediocre, at best* nonsense. Really, Griffin, would it have killed you to be a little kinder?"

A strange squirming sensation twisted my spectral gut. Could it be I was experiencing guilt? "I owed her my honesty."

"Ah." Hannah nodded, her wise eyes zeroing in on me.

"She must be the one, but I'm not interested in her romantically." Kate certainly intrigued me, but it was nothing more.

"That's why you asked so many questions and spent half the time staring at her. How do you expect to kindle the flame between the pair of you if you're so unpleasant?"

Bloody hell, if Hannah didn't speak the truth. I had been watching Kate—not just her playing, but *her*. "It doesn't matter. She walked out—she's decided to go it on her own. There will be no more rehearsal sessions."

"Not necessarily." Hannah wriggled her eyebrows. "Try playing it cool, as they say. Keep your distance for a time. Then, when you see her again, maybe she'll feel differently. Maybe you will, too?"

"Playing it cool. For how long?"

"Maybe a few days. A week. Absence does make the heart grow fonder."

"Yes, I suppose." To my surprise, disappointment rose inside me. Of course, it most definitely had nothing to do with romancing Kate and everything to do with my newfound addiction to being alive.

"And then, when that window has passed, try again. Try not to see her as someone who could free you, but someone you could love. Someone with whom you *could* develop a relationship."

Hannah made sense, but God—a relationship with Kate would be like playing with fire. One had no idea how great the cost would be until one thrust a hand into the flame.

CHAPTER 13
KATE

Thursday, December 1st—Fourteen Days Left Until Juries

As it turned out, I didn't see Griff at all the next day. I went downstairs to try the secret door in my practice room, but other students were in my room rehearsing. It seemed strange to ask to interrupt their session when I'd probably run into Griff in the hall.

I never did. He didn't materialize in any of my classes or between sessions.

A week passed by in a blur of the seriously mundane. I kept my distance from Ryder whenever I could, arriving at classes late and leaving the instant the bell rang. The Monday after Thanksgiving break, I put up several requests for an accompanist on the school bulletin board, but no one came forward.

And, of course, Ms. Jennings in the front office was super unhelpful. "Don't be afraid to approach people, Kate. Be proactive. Take charge of your life."

But no one came forward, so I kept working on my own. Of course, my self-esteem did a nose dive every time I picked up the Weber, but when I worked on Griff's Brahms piece, something was missing.

Griff.

He was a pain in the ass. I'd never met anyone more self-involved. But his words stuck in my head, like a message on an extra-sticky post-it note.

You're only meeting half your potential.

None of that mattered, however, because I was without an accompanist and without options. I had no idea how to find Griff—the office had a privacy policy that kept them from releasing other students' class schedules.

Griff had disappeared—like the ghost in the air vent.

The following Thursday morning, I trudged across the snow-covered courtyard in front of the school. We'd only gotten a couple of inches. It would be mush by lunch. Someone, probably Charlie, had put up white twinkle lights on the balcony and wreaths on the windows. The place still looked like a freaky haunted mansion.

"Mornin', Kate," Charlie called as I walked past the guard booth.

"Hey, Charlie." I tossed a sandwich bag at him. Charlie caught it before gravity took its course. "Sorry, but it's only Cheerios today. The best I can do."

"Kate." He shook his head. "You really don't have to do this."

"I know." I didn't stop to chat. My brain was occupied with how to best use that morning's rehearsal time and put the face from last week out of my mind. But then I hesitated, every thought but one floating away.

Griff is in the lobby.

Where had *that* come from? It felt like a premonition or something, but I wasn't psychic. Still, there was no denying the feeling. I could just *tell*.

Stepping inside, I flicked on the lights. Griff sat on the very middle of the upward stairs. Our gazes locked, and, for a second, it was like I had just a little bit less air than I was supposed to have.

He didn't say anything, just fixed me with an unflinching stare.

"Nice of you to show up." I tried to force my voice to sound casual instead of defensive. Epic fail.

That arrogant smirk of his sent the tiniest of butterflies whirling around in my stomach. "I thought so, too. They should give me an award just for being here, don't you think?"

"But I thought you were going to accompany me. I've lost seven days of rehearsal time already."

"It was my impression, that you preferred not to work with me. I have neither the time nor the interest in such dramatics. You can always work with *Ryder* on your piece."

Oh, man. We'd reached the part where I had to apologize. He was right—about all of it. "I'm sorry."

Griff blinked, his eyes widening. "I beg your pardon?"

Anger bubbled up inside of me. It sucked having to apologize once, but twice? Still, I needed his help. I wouldn't get it by acting bitchy. "I'm sorry. You were right."

"That's something you should probably get used to." He smirked, the smile stealing a little more of my breath away. "About which part?"

I hated practically begging him for help. "I'm not ready for the Weber. And I am . . . an imposter."

His smile faded as he leveled his gaze at me. "What do you mean?"

"I don't belong here. No matter how much I practice, it's never enough, okay?" I squeezed the shoulder strap of Benny's case.

"Kate, that's not what I meant—"

"No. Let me finish, please." I had to work with Griff. There was no one else. That meant I had to make things right. "I may not belong, but I have a scholarship and I have to keep it. Otherwise, my mom won't let me stay in this school. My jury is too important to screw up. Will you work with me?"

Again, he threw that stare of his my way, kicking the butterflies up a notch. Standing, he turned and moved toward the steps leading to the rehearsal rooms. "Come on, then."

"What? Really?"

"Well, since you asked so *nicely*." He winked at me, which caused my stomach to do this weird little flip all on its own.

I thought of about twenty different levels of sarcasm I could reach with my next statement, but goading him had lost its appeal. The truth seemed the better option.

"Thanks."

BY THE TIME I REACHED HIS REHEARSAL ROOM, GRIFF was already playing the piano. His brow furrowed over his closed eyes. Long strands of hair hung down on either side of his pale face. His hair reminded me of an angel's. Bright gold, with white highlights. Intense feeling seemed to pour from every note as he played a familiar Rimsky-Korsakov piece with a fluidity that made it seem easy. As though a child could play it. That was *so* not the case.

Forcing my attention from his face, I got water to soak my reeds and set everything up on a small table at the end of Griff's grand piano.

"*Scheherazade* is one of my favorites." I tugged a tube of cork grease from my bag and began applying it to the bands that helped hold Benny's pieces in place.

"Mine, too." Still, he didn't look up.

"The story always sucked me in. A Persian king who married a different virgin each day, only to have them executed the next morning." *Stop babbling, Kate.* "Until Scheherazade was brought to him." *Put your clarinet together.*

Griff opened his eyes. They seemed even brighter than before as they locked onto mine, as though the gold flecks had been magnified somehow. "She told him a story that lasted one thousand and one nights. By the time the tale ended, the king had . . . fallen in love with her." He continued to play as he finished the story.

Heat rose in my cheeks. "It's a romantic piece. I never took you for a romantic."

Griff smiled, but it was a shuttered expression—one that hid secrets. "Yes. Well, to quote a certain clarinetist at this school, 'you don't even know me.'" His voice sounded benign enough, but his words stung.

"Excuse me for making conversation."

He cocked an eyebrow. "It was hardly conversation. It was a judgment."

God, I hate it when he's right.

"Did you have a chance to look at the Brahms again?" Griff asked.

"I did. I listened to a recording as well." That's when I noticed he was dressed in the same outfit again. The fancy vintage tux. "Don't you own any other clothes?"

He glanced down quickly and continued playing, as though it were no big deal. "It's my prerogative to repeat my attire, isn't it?" But his cheeks flushed. I'd upset him.

"Sure. Sorry." I tightened the single screw on Benny's thumb rest for something to do. Then it suddenly hit me what day of the week it was. I groaned. "Scales class is this morning."

"That's all right. We can review your scales for today." He ran his fingers up and down the keys again in a double-octave scale and then stopped. He grinned at me before switching to a soft piece that I probably should have known the name of but couldn't place.

Listening to him, my observation from last week came back to me. Griff sounded like the musician I'd been hearing in the mornings. "How long have you been a student here?"

Griff didn't seem surprised by my question. "I transferred last week from a school in England. You won't have heard of it." He didn't meet my eyes. Dad always said you could tell someone was lying if they didn't meet your eyes.

Taking a reed from my shot glass, I attached it to the mouthpiece. "I've been hearing someone play the piano in the mornings for the past three months. You sound identical to that musician."

Griff's face was unreadable. "Are you suggesting I broke into the school before I became a student to use the piano?"

When he put it like that, I sounded like an idiot. "No.

Whatever." I took the mouthpiece in my mouth and began to warm up, my fingers flexing over the keys.

"What if it's a ghost?" He was smiling. He'd decided to mess with me. *Wow.* Didn't know fancy pants had a fun side.

"I don't believe in ghosts." I suppressed a shudder at the memory of the face in the air vent.

"And you attend school here?" He switched to a softer piece of music.

His eyes bored into mine. *Griff really is hot.* I cleared my throat and tried to do the same for my head.

It was obvious Griff preferred to let the piano do the talking. He'd begun with the Rimsky-Korsakov, the single scale, and finally this familiar, angst-driven piece. Ah, I remembered. It was a piano version of *Danse Macabre* by Saint-Saëns.

After a time, he glanced up and gave me a small smile. "What do you say you and I try and get along now, eh?"

"Yeah. That'd be nice." I blew a warmup note into Benny, then ran through a quick C major scale. Of course, no one ever asked me to play C major. That was probably the easiest scale in existence.

Griff finished up and then regarded me over the piano. "Why don't you play another scale? How about A major?"

A major. Three sharps. Bringing the clarinet to my lips, I ran through the scale. I got most of the sharps, but basically it was crash and burn time for Kate.

"That was atrocious," Griff said when he'd picked his jaw up off the floor.

"Don't you know any other word? Or is that your preferred term when it comes to my playing?"

He shrugged. "So far, I've found it to be the most appropriate."

"What happened to getting along?"

"Point taken." Closing his eyes for a moment, he took a deep breath, acting like he was savoring it or something. Then he released it and opened his eyes. "Let's start at the beginning. You're trying to play these too fast. You rush into them and that's where you get into trouble. Take the notes in groups of four, then play them over and over. Give me A, B, C-sharp, D. Just keep repeating the same four notes."

"Got it." I nodded and began to play.

He stopped me after the fourth note. "Cut the tempo in half."

Yeesh, I hated dropping tempo. I'd even put it above giving blood. But I didn't want to have to deal with another nightmare Scales class or, worse, earn more attention from Ryder.

Taking a breath, I started slowly with the first four notes. Again and again, I repeated those notes. As I got more comfortable, I sped up.

I repeated the process with the next four. The next four, and the next, followed, until I'd covered all twenty-nine notes over two octaves. In less time than I would have expected, I'd moved from half to full tempo. Maybe I wouldn't make an ass out of myself in the scales round that morning? At least not if Ryder picked A major for me.

"Better. Much," Griff said.

The compliment warmed me down to my bones. His opinion shouldn't have mattered, but damned if it didn't.

We continued working together as the free minutes before the start of my classes slipped away. Even when Griff wasn't playing, he still commanded attention at the piano. I kept staring, and, each time, I'd catch him watching me.

After rehearsal ended, I packed up my books. I hadn't

expected to have a good time that morning, but I had. "You're a surprisingly good teacher."

Griff chuckled. "It amazes me how frequently you're able to make an insult seem complimentary."

Oh, man. I always managed to say the wrong things where he was concerned. "Sorry—"

"I'm only teasing," he said, stacking music into neat piles on top of the piano. "You should continue to work on these with your private instructor." It wasn't an unusual statement. Every music student had a private instructor to coach them outside of class—everyone, but me.

"I don't have one." My throat tightened. The urge to run away again rose up in me, but I forced myself to stay in place. "I was working with Brian Covington, but . . . he died right after I got accepted at Byrons." I bit my lip lightly—anything to stave off the tears that usually followed whenever I spoke about Dad.

"You've been studying here without a teacher?" Griff asked, surprise in his voice as he wiped down the keys on his piano with an ancient-looking rag.

"Yep." I cleaned Benny's exterior with a microfiber cloth, removing the invisible salt and oil left behind by my fingers. There was no point in taking the instrument apart. I'd only need it again for Scales.

"You're a very determined young woman." Griff leaned against the piano. "Wait, Brian Covington . . ." He left his incomplete statement hanging in midair.

"He was my father." I slung my bag over my shoulder, waiting for the inevitable questions, but Griff didn't press. It was obvious, to me at least, that he had a past, or maybe even a present, he didn't want to share with the world.

We were so similar.

"Thanks for this morning."

"You're welcome. See you at three?" His voice was softer, absent of condescension.

Again, his eyes met mine, but that time, I almost forgot to breathe. Those eyes, set into his almost painfully beautiful face, trapped me. As did the puzzle he presented, with his words that alternated between cruel and kind.

And he probably looks hot in jeans, too.

"See you at three," I said, turning and hurrying out of the room. I hated that I was always running away from Griff, but it had to be safer than running toward him.

CHAPTER 14

GRIFFIN

Finding Ryder was ridiculously easy. He stood behind the door to the stairwell. From what I could tell, he'd chosen that spot so he could watch Kate without her being the wiser. He was too spineless to be much of a threat to her, despite what he'd pulled the previous week.

I'd sought him out because I wanted Kate to have a chance at succeeding in Scales class. Even if it meant a little subtle intervention on my part.

Moving up behind Ryder's right ear, I whispered, "Assign Kate A major." It was awkward, making myself sound like a vulgar American.

After decades of hearing them speak, it wasn't difficult to adopt the accent when I needed to, but the way Americans routinely slaughtered the King's English made me shudder. I hated mimicking them, but sounding like a local would hopefully make Ryder assume the thought was his own.

Ryder turned, and then inspected the stairwell. "Who's there?"

Something about him seemed familiar, but I couldn't place it.

He couldn't see me, but he'd definitely *heard* me. After several moments, he passed through the doors and into the hall, sparing one more glance at the stairwell before entering the Scales classroom. The bell rang, and I waited several beats before following.

Once I neared Kate's classroom, my feet dropped to the floor as my body suddenly became solid. Kate sat just inside the next room—the only explanation for the change. The scent of someone cooking reached my nostrils, and the distinct odor of perfume clung to the hall. Music sounded clearer, louder. Everything seemed more in tune.

Hanging back, I stared through the window in the classroom door at an angle, hoping to see or hear Kate play. How would she do? Would she remember my advice? Teaching Kate had been more gratifying than I would have imagined. After we'd gotten over the initial rough patch, Kate had listened to my advice and had made adjustments.

I quite liked teaching. What a pity I'd made that discovery after my death.

Then Ryder's muffled voice reached me through the door. "Kate. A major." I held my breath as several seconds of total silence followed. Had she forgotten it? Was she nervous? But then her tone reached me in the hallway, full and rich as she ran through the scale with ease, hitting every note.

"Brilliant!" I whispered the word, resisting a shout as I punched my fist into the air. She'd played it perfectly.

"Kate. Nice job. *Really* nice job," said Ryder. "Sarah, how about E-flat major?"

And then the next musician played a scale, and the next, but I found myself too excited to listen. Kate had done an excellent job. It wasn't that she didn't have the ability; she'd lacked patience.

I began to wonder if Kate and I didn't have more in common than I'd originally thought.

The bell rang a short time later. I waited across from the classroom door as the students filed out. I heard Kate talking, but I stayed in place, waiting to see if she needed my help. Her face seemed tense. Not a good sign.

"How is everything going with your new accompanist?" Ryder asked, again blocking the door. "I would've spoken to you sooner, but you've taken off after every class."

Kate narrowed her eyes. "His name's Griff and he's amazing." She sounded defensive.

After a moment, she spotted me from across the hall. Her answering smile could have lit a thousand suns. Before I could even fathom what to say, she ducked under Ryder's arm and ran toward me, and then threw her arms around my neck.

It had been so long since anyone had held me. It stole my breath away.

Slowly, I brought my arms around her and squeezed her against me for a beat. In my time, such a gesture would have been highly inappropriate. Heat surged through me at the contact.

And then Kate let her arms drop and took a step back. "I aced it." Her pale skin glowed, her loose hair framing her round face, hugging her porcelain skin. "Thank you."

"You . . ." *Are beautiful.* Where had that come from? "You did an excellent job on your scale."

Her grin spread wider. "You were listening?"

"I was. What's the point of life if you can't risk getting caught without a hall pass now and again?"

"Cool." She gave me a thumbs up. "It felt so good. For once, I didn't embarrass myself."

"I'm very pleased for you, Kate. You have the talent. You must simply sharpen your skills."

"Thanks. And thank you for helping me," she said, her voice small as she glanced down. "I like you better when you aren't being a jerk."

"I daresay I like you better, as well. We have to get to class." No point in raising suspicion. "But why don't you try some embouchure exercises while you're in classes? Try and press your bottom lip out with your teeth and make the shape of a seven with your bottom lip and chin."

I pressed my thumb to the center of her chin and instantly realized my mistake. My skin burned where it met hers. Suddenly, I found myself remembering her body against mine, her arms around my neck. Touching Kate, in any way, was a distraction.

Kate blushed. "I'll try." Her voice had a rasp to it.

I dropped my hand. "See you at three?"

"Yep," she said as she turned and walked to class. She glanced back once, her smile slipping away from her face, as though she wasn't sure why she'd grinned in the first place.

I couldn't get the burning sensation I'd felt when I touched Kate out of my head. Had I ever felt quite that way when I'd held a woman? Stunned into inaction?

Everything about Kate was different. Even me. And it was high time I acquired some different clothes.

RETURNING TO MY PIANO, I LAUNCHED INTO THE Grieg *Piano Concerto in A Minor*. Naturally, I skipped over all the sedate horn parts at the beginning to get to the meat of it. The piano part was the only thing audiences came to hear anyway. But soon, I'd unconsciously transitioned to my own sonata, working in a new melody line. I'd composed many pieces before—hundreds. Yet the new part didn't compare to my past work. It was soft . . . gutsy and different.

Like Kate.

My curiosity at following the growing musical theme in my head refused to be ignored. My fingers roved over the keys, my mind repeating a mantra—the time of my meeting with Kate.

Three o'clock. Three o'clock. Three o'clock.

Working hard to commit the piece to memory, I ran through the section. Only when I'd finished did it register what I'd done. "I've just written music for Kate."

I'd never composed for anyone other than myself. Ever. I'd never even had the drive. That day, I realized I could easily tell her story in a million other pieces.

"What's become of me?"

"I can't answer that, but you can start by changing clothes. Here." Hannah brandished a bag at me. As usual, she'd just appeared beside me. If I hadn't already been dead, her arrival might have done me in.

"Clothing? Where did this come from?"

"From the young men's locker room. They seem to be about your size." She shrugged. "I may have been listening in a little."

"Hannah." Though I was less than thrilled by Hannah's invasion of my privacy, Kate's comments about my clothing had thrown me. I'd given her a weak explanation, but there was no telling how long it would hold up. I peered into the bag, taking in the denim and flannel ensemble. "Dreadful."

"The style is quite different now, as you've seen for yourself." Hannah waved me away. "But what isn't?"

"Do you think Kate is really *the* one?" Hannah's eyes widened.

I chastised myself inwardly for even mentioning it. "I don't know. She's coarse, abrasive, challenging . . ."

"Arguments are healthy in relationships. Maybe she's what you've always needed. Someone to disagree with."

"Perhaps." Kate was intriguing, and I'd be a fool if I ignored the growing attraction between us. Yet, could it turn to love? I couldn't answer that.

Hannah laughed, but it was short-lived. The smile slowly disappeared from her face, as though it had melted away. "Do me one favor, Griff darling."

"What is it?" I tried to tune her out, not wanting to hear the rest.

She gave me an indulgent look. "Don't get hurt."

My fingers froze on the keys. "Whatever do you mean?" When I turned, Hannah had gone.

What an odd statement for her to make. If I were to pursue Kate romantically, I'd assumed it would be *she* who got hurt. Hannah, however, made it sound as though I was the one at risk.

Preposterous.

CHAPTER 15
KATE

As Mr. Weinstock droned on and on about Trigonometry, I fought to keep myself upright. My last class of the day was dragging. Weinstock's intro lesson on Pythagorean identities wasn't helping.

If I saw one more fraction that day, I was going to scream.

I glanced at the door again, scanning the window set inside it. I'd kept catching myself looking for Griff all day. He'd been amazing earlier when he'd come to watch me ace my scale. Oddly enough, it was something a friend would do. That was it. Yeah, it was cool. *A friendship thing.*

God, why did I throw myself at him? My whole face heated at the memory. He'd probably wanted to run.

But he hadn't seemed like he wanted to bolt. He'd wrapped his arms around me. Drawn me closer to him. His body had been lean, muscular, and warm. The heat of him had seeped through my clothes and burned my skin.

When it was over, he'd seemed as shaken as I was. And when he'd held me . . . it had felt like I was right where I should've been.

My heartbeat echoed in my ears as I ran downstairs after class. The door to Griff's room lay just ahead, through the practice room. I should've slowed down and played it cool, but he'd never know if I rushed down the hallway.

I swung around the corner and opened the door. Griff was there, just as he had been the day before, but with one marked difference. His shirt was off. I got a good look at his pale skin and a lean, muscled stomach before I even understood what was going on.

Again, my face was on fire—my standard reaction around him. "God, I'm sorry."

He glanced up, horrified. "Kate. I'm—uh—I apologize. If you could just give me a moment."

"Yep." I stepped back into the adjacent rehearsal room and tried to put the image of Griff's bare chest from my mind.

Some shuffling and what sounded like confusion went down before he called out, "I'm truly sorry. You can come back in now."

Griff was handsome before—something even a total idiot wouldn't have missed. Now, in jeans and a flannel shirt that seemed fitted to every muscle in his amazing chest . . .

OMG.

Then guilt crept in. Had he changed clothes because I'd commented on what he'd been wearing? No, Griff wouldn't care what I thought. Would he? But why was he changing now, right before we were supposed to meet?

I tore my attention from his chest and forced myself to

look upward. A quick glance confirmed he was staring at some sheet music. *Thank God.*

"I'm glad it went well this morning." His brow furrowed as he spoke.

"Yes, um, thanks for your help."

He must have thought my response was strange, because he asked, "Are you all right?" His accent sounded so cool. Had it always been that way? He'd said *all right* with the tone of *right* moving from high to low, versus how we Americans said it, from low to high. It was kind of . . . hot.

"Yeah. It's just been a busy day." I unpacked and assembled Benny, then attached that afternoon's reed, lining it up, checking it for splits. Griff waited with surprising patience on the piano bench. "Why are you being so nice today?"

His brow creased as he considered my question. "You did ask me not to behave like a jerk, as I recall."

"I guess I didn't expect you to listen."

"I am, at the very least, a man of my word, Katherine."

Why the frig was he calling me Katherine again? "It's K-Kate."

He smiled a smug, knowing sort of smile. As if he'd known what I'd been thinking about him in the jeans. *Ugh.*

"How did you feel the first time you ever played your clarinet?" His mouth flattened, as though he didn't care all that much about my answer and only asked out of courtesy.

I should have told him to stuff it, but the memory was so immediate I couldn't stop myself answering.

"I'd just picked clarinet as my instrument at school. All the other kids had rented their instruments from a music store, so I thought that's what I'd do. Dad picked me up after school one day, and there was this case inside my room. I opened it up and there was the most beautiful clarinet. The keys gleamed."

Tears pricked the backs of my eyes. I missed Dad with a sharp grief I couldn't push down. I sucked in an unsteady breath.

"And when I played it, it was perfect. It was as if the instrument had been made for me. And it felt *right*, like I was supposed to choose the clarinet. I didn't get a single note wrong. Though I was only playing *Mary Had a Little Lamb*." I laughed at my own story, but stopped when I caught Griff watching me, a small smile on his face. "Should we get started?"

"Certainly. I'm going to add the accompaniment today. It starts where you come in." Griff positioned his fingers on the keys. His eyes were bright, his expression almost overeager. "Begin whenever you're all set. I'll join you."

It had been several hours since Wind Symphony rehearsal, so I dampened my reed for play. A couple of scales and a set of thirds later, I was ready. When I glanced up, Griff was watching me. Waiting.

With a quick nod, I jumped in. He followed.

And he was wonderful. He wove his part in and out of mine, the light notes urging me forward, setting the scene. It was magical—

"Stop." Griff held up a hand.

"What's wrong now?" Impatience ripped through my voice. I'd been enjoying that.

Griff chuckled, his laughter deep. *Sexy.* "You don't take criticism very well, do you?"

"I guess not."

Maybe because I was my own worst critic? If I'd been honest with him, I would have said I got so defensive because . . . well, because I didn't want him to say some of the things I'd already thought about myself. I didn't want him to tell me I didn't belong at Byrons.

And I needed to belong . . . somewhere. "Sorry. Again."

"It's all right. Taking criticism is something we all have to learn."

I searched his face for signs of sarcasm. There were none.

He ran his hand through his hair. "You're too bold. You need to savor this music. Enjoy it. These aren't notes you want to cut off. Ease them in and out."

"I don't understand." I tried to make myself sound less defensive. The very least I could do was be nice.

"Imagine what you're playing is like a secret you're sharing with the audience."

"Still not getting it." I wanted to. It was obvious from his advice so far, and from his own skills as a pianist, that he knew what he was talking about.

Griff stood and walked around the piano. For just a beat, he reminded me of a lion, with his blond mane and intense eyes. "Pretend you're humming the notes to an audience member. You sidle up to him or her . . ." He moved in, standing close enough to make my knees buckle. "Then you share your secret. Da-dum . . . da-da-da-daaaa-dum." Griff sang the first bar.

His breath caressed my ear, sending my head spinning. Griff's pleasant voice, combined with his close proximity, made my skin tingle, though he hadn't touched me.

Turning back to the notes on the page, I dove in.

Griff rushed back to the piano, filling my peripheral vision, but the notes demanded more of my attention. The more his advice rolled around in my head, the more the piece did start to sound like a little secret. The piano coaxed the message out of me, starting first as gentle accompaniment and then becoming more demanding as the piece progressed.

I stumbled on some of the more advanced sections, but kept going. It was the first time Griff let me get that far. When I finished, I glanced up.

His expression was unreadable. "Again."

Flipping the pages, I found the beginning and started once more. Griff followed.

Again and again, we worked on the piece. For the first time in over a week, I began to think I might have a chance at passing my jury.

Instead of feeling relieved, my stomach had tied itself into knots. It had nothing to do with my upcoming test, and everything to do with the way I'd felt when Griff had whispered into my ear.

CHAPTER 16
GRIFFIN

Friday, December 2nd—Thirteen Days Left Until Juries

KATE AND I FINISHED FOR THE DAY AND SAID OUR goodbyes. For Kate, she'd gone off to experience a weekend at home. For me, my own weekend stretched out, long and devoid of entertainment.

I'd believed Kate to be one thing. Yet, there were layers within her that I hadn't even begun to explore. Like harmonies buried within a piece of music, she was more fascinating than I'd first realized.

She had to have been the one destined to break my curse. There was no other explanation. Then there was her resemblance to Minna. Was it mere coincidence? Or was Kate somehow related to the witch. If so, was she one herself?

So many questions, and there was only one thing I knew for certain.

Kate's eyes were gray.

CHAPTER 17

KATE

Tuesday, December 6th—Nine Days Left Until Juries

By four thirty the following Tuesday, and after six more rehearsals with Griff, I was all like, *Weber who?*

We weren't playing the Brahms to tempo yet. Still, I was actually okay with it. After my continued success in Scales, I could deal with slowing down.

"Very good," Griff said. "Now, we're going to run through this one last time."

"Can we take a break?" My bottom teeth had imprinted themselves into my bottom lip. *Ouch.* "My mouth is killing me."

Griff's face seemed unreadable as our gazes locked. We'd been circling one another all afternoon, each baiting the other, then backing off in a dysfunctional dance. "Perhaps you should have chosen another profession?"

Plugging my fingers in my ears, I stuck out my tongue. "Seriously, the whole jerk thing? You *were* supposed to stop that."

A smile broke across his face, like the sun rising. "Sorry. You've come a long way, Kate. You've been working hard. Your runs are even and you're only missing *some* of the notes." He winked at me as I opened my mouth in protest. "Now I want to bring you back to focusing on your tone— infusing more emotion into your performance."

"I thought my technical issues were the problem."

"They *were* your problem." Griff rubbed his hands together in quick succession, his eyes lighting. "You're tackling that aspect brilliantly with coaching. *My* coaching, I might add."

I rolled my eyes. "So glad you don't have a self-esteem issue, fancy pants."

His right eyebrow shot toward the ceiling. He'd been favoring that one a lot that morning. "If I may continue—I want you to bring back the emotion in your tone. That's where you excel. We mustn't lose your interpretation of the music."

"It's not something I've ever consciously thought of. I've just played."

"Make me believe in the notes you're playing. Let go, Kate." With Griff's eyes locked onto mine, I couldn't have turned away from him for anything.

"Let go of what?"

He rested one of his hands on the back of his head. "Yourself." Griff let his hand drop. "I don't know, just . . . let go of whatever you're holding onto. You're getting the notes, but you're overthinking it."

That was definitely something I did—often.

"Try something for me. Section A needs to be graceful,

but muted. Perhaps instead of a secret, you might envision you're whispering into a lover's ear."

Because I have so much experience with lovers. "I think I've got it."

"Maybe." He glanced down before locking eyes with me once again. "You could play it as though you're whispering in *my* ear."

He stood and positioned himself on the other side of my music stand. My breath caught.

Oh jeez.

Griff.

Griff wanted me to play like I was whispering a message into his *ear*.

Help.

Tension crackled in the room—between us, around us. The pressure of the moment pushed into me as I stared at the unmoving notes on the page.

Griff reached out and cupped my cheek. A tingling sensation shot to every part of my body. "Don't think about all of the classes and rehearsals. Don't think about your scholarship. Think about your father, Kate. Remember how you felt when he first gave you Benny." Griff's voice wasn't sarcastic or impatient, but soft.

"Watch out. People will think you care." I held my breath, waiting for his answer, wondering about it more than I should.

"I *do* care." His voice was low, the moment between us morphing into a quiet sort of intensity. "Think about the good things, Kate, not the bad. Your music has a way of tying you to your father. Use that. Search for him in the notes. He's there. He's waiting for you in every measure."

"Okay. I'll try." The stark notes on the page in front of me blurred, and I squinted to focus—to zero in on anything other than Griff's closeness or the rapid pounding of my own heartbeat.

He backed away and took a seat at the piano.

I closed my eyes. All of the things that had been choking me, pressing down on me for months, waited. My scholarship. Mom. Dad. Loneliness. Being alone was the hardest out of all of them, not that Griff would understand. He couldn't know what it felt like to have no one see you.

And when had I last played the clarinet for fun? Somehow, it had become a chore; it'd turned into something I did, rather than something I loved. Dad wouldn't want that for me. He'd want to hear me play the way I always had, as though my own heart had been written on the page.

Bringing the clarinet to my lips, I drew a breath and blew into the instrument, filling up the barrel, positioning my fingers to form the first note. Griff joined in. And I imagined the day Dad gave Benny to me—how it felt when I'd played for the first time.

A warm feeling blossomed in the pit of my stomach. It started small and filled me up. One note at a time, I sank deeper and deeper into the memory. Individual notes didn't matter, the *feeling* did. The notes weren't hurdles; they were long-awaited friends.

Dad was with me. A memory of the weight of his hand on my shoulder rose up.

We used to take these walks in the woods near our house when I was little. I'd forgotten about that. The smell of damp earth and lush trees filled my nostrils. The heat from the sunlight streaming through the sycamores warmed my skin.

Through Brahms's composition, I told a story. About a man lost. The notes represented the practice sessions Dad had driven me to, the new music he'd introduced into my life. My tone embodied my pain. Pain I felt knowing I'd never hear his voice again. My fear that I'd forget the sound of his voice.

But the longer I played, the more a sense of calm washed over me. Soon, Dad could have been standing beside me. If I relaxed enough, played enough, I'd hear his voice. *Come on, Kate, you can do this. I believe in you.*

Something changed inside of me then. It shifted and moved and grew. The pain threatened to rise up, to tear me apart, but I kept playing.

How could Griff have known that Dad and my old life were waiting for me, buried inside the measures of the Brahms? Maybe letting go was the key to loving my music again? And God, I *needed* to love it. It was a part of me.

Griff's piano accompaniment wove in and out of my melody line. As the music progressed, I became less conscious of memories of my father and more aware of Griff. Of how we'd moved from two people playing our separate parts to two musicians on a journey together. The room hummed with our energy. The more we played, the more it built, spurring us on toward the ending. Though the piece had begun as a gentle creation, it was anything but. Griff and I became one person as we played, two souls united.

When I reached the final note, I held it, as it faded to nothing. There were no more notes left to play.

It was just me, Kate. Alone again.

Lowering Benny and blinking away the tears burning in my eyes, I stared at the page. Several beats passed, and Griff hadn't said a word.

He hated it. Disappointment crashed over me and I shook, focusing my gaze on my shoes. He'd probably played with some incredible musicians.

And then there was me.

I wanted to crawl under the piano and hide.

Griff cleared his throat, sitting up straight on the piano bench. "That was . . ."

Shitty? A complete travesty?

". . . breathtaking."

There was no way I'd heard him right. I gripped the side of the piano for support. "What?"

He stood, running his finger along the top of the piano's music stand. When he fixed his stare on mine, I couldn't move. Like on the first day we'd met, and every day since. "That piece—what you just played—was remarkable, *magical*."

"I'd forgotten it could be like that." Tears spilled down my cheeks. "How did you know? About my dad, I mean?"

I waited for him to say something snarky in that uptight tone of his, but Griff didn't outwardly react as he took a step toward me. "Because that's where I find my mother."

The gravity of his words squeezed my heart. "I didn't know."

He didn't meet my eyes as he reached my music stand, running a finger along the top. I shuddered, as though he trailed it along my skin. "I'm not you, Kate, but I've felt pain, too. You aren't the only one who's . . . *broken*."

"I don't want to be." That one sentence had to be the hardest I'd ever spoken, and I'd shared it with the boy who'd insulted more than complimented me—one who'd called me an *imposter*.

Griff stepped around my music stand, so that he was less than an arm's length away. I met his eyes and my breath hitched. He had the prettiest eyes I'd ever seen, and I lost myself in the mixture of brown and green and gold.

He removed the pencil from behind my ear, and the

sensation of wood sliding against my skin sent a chill rippling through my body. He placed my pencil on top of the piano. Then, with care, Griff took Benny from my stiff fingers and rested him beside the pencil.

He'd taken away my shield. It was just the two of us, standing there in the quiet hush of the late afternoon.

Griff took my hands in his. "You make me feel things I don't understand, Kate."

My heart throbbed, then seemed to halt as I processed his words. I couldn't breathe. I did my best to stand tall, trying to retain some semblance of dignity.

The quiver in my voice shot that hope down real fast. "Why are you helping me? I don't see what you're getting out of it."

"Neither do I," he whispered. And then his mouth was on mine. The lightest brush of his lips against my own. We leaned toward one another, our bodies not quite touching. Griff's kiss—that simple, bone-searing kiss—heated me from the outside in.

It lasted only a moment, before Griff drew back, his eyes locking onto mine. It seemed as though some internal war waged in his irises. I wanted to know, wanted to understand all of him.

That scared me, more than anything. I'd never wanted anyone before, not really, but Griff . . .

"Ah, Kate." Griff sighed and began to turn away.

No. Don't turn away. Don't stop.

"Griff." I barely choked out the word, but he must have heard. Maybe one word from me was all he needed.

He whipped around and crushed his mouth against mine. It wasn't the soft brush of lips from before. It was a full-on, heated kiss. Our lips moved together in unison. They met again and again. The hunger that had been building between us had to be abated. My world slipped sideways. Dizzying arrays of thoughts I'd never had and feelings I didn't understand rushed me.

He slid his arms around me, as he had in the hallway the other day. But it was different, too. This time, Griff's fingers pressed into my back, as though he couldn't risk letting me go.

Though my head only reached his shoulder, but we curved against one another perfectly. It was achingly familiar. God, it felt right. It was the way things were supposed to be.

He swept his tongue into my mouth. I struggled to get closer as my lips parted under the pressure. He dragged me against him, sparking every part of me to life. Despite his weird clothes and his conceited attitude, Griff was all guy. I could taste it in the salt of his lips, the firm muscles straining through his clothes.

No one had *ever* kissed me like that.

Then, just as suddenly, Griff broke the kiss. We separated, standing an arm's length apart, chests heaving as though we'd run a mile.

It was like my heart had forgotten to lock up all of its doors at the end of the night, and Griff had snuck inside.

Oh no. I was in trouble.

CHAPTER 18

GRIFFIN

Kate tasted of mint and a sweet undercurrent I couldn't identify. I smoothed back a shining lock of her hair, reveling in the sensation of the strands between my fingers.

Good lord, I kissed Kate.

I hadn't meant to. The Brahms had pushed me to such an action. I'd performed many a duet in my time, but somehow, we'd connected through the notes on the page with an intensity I'd never experienced.

There'd been a single tear on her face. She'd locked those eyes of hers onto mine, and that had been all the prodding I'd required.

"Katherine."

She drew a small breath, her brow creasing. My complicated vixen seemed to be fighting some internal battle. Working up a caustic response of some sort. Her shield.

How well I knew.

"I hate when my mother calls me Katherine."

"But what about me?" I couldn't read her expression until she blushed.

"It feels different when you say it." Her voice sounded unsteady. It became clear to me then. As if I hadn't realized it from her earlier response to my kiss. Kate did desire me as much as I did her.

I dipped down and claimed Kate's lips once more. Our mouths moved as one. Our tongues danced as we explored one another, savoring the moment. Kissing Kate transformed me. She'd become my oxygen. Kate was everywhere, her breath hot against mine, her close proximity awaking every part of me. Energy sizzled around us, between us.

It was the nearest thing to Heaven I'd ever get to experience. Any more and I might forget myself.

"Griff." She whispered my name on a sigh.

"My name's Griffin." I wanted her to know me as the boy I had been. Not the distorted manifestation of the person I used to be.

Kate drew back gently, but only an inch, breaking our kiss. "Griffin."

"Yes." My newly restored heart throbbed. My voice sounded breathless as I trailed my palm down her lower back, a freedom I would never have had in my day. Thank Heaven for progress.

Then something changed in Kate's expression. Whether it was remembered or something she feared in her future, I couldn't say. All I knew was that she backed away.

She grabbed her clarinet and then began to pack up. She hadn't even gone through her usual cleaning ritual—just shoved the pencil I'd removed back behind her ear as though it lived there. "No. I don't want this." Placing her hands against my chest, she pushed me back, gently, carefully, as though I might break.

Stunned, I stood stock-still. "I don't understand."

"I'm sorry, Griffin. I have to go to work." She shut her clarinet case, closing the latch, and shrugged into her coat. She took three steps backward before she turned and walked out of the room.

"Kate." I called her name, hating the pleading note in my voice. But she'd already gone, her steps on the stairs a series of fast-paced, pattering sounds, like a Mussorgsky piece. I couldn't remember which one, because her haunting, ethereal sound and the fast-fading memory of her kiss had taken over my mind.

I waited, expecting to transform to my ghostly self, but nothing changed. Kate had gone, but for once, I'd remained the same as when she'd been there. *Why? How?*

Was it possible our kiss had broken the curse?

Relief surged into me at the thought. Of course! It worked in all the fairy tales, though I was hardly Prince Charming.

I had to go after her. Even if I only got to see her for one more second, it would be worth it. I pulled open my door and ran through, slamming it shut behind me. My blood rushed through my veins with the force of a raging river.

I'd only just made it out of my room when someone cried, "Griff!"

I halted at the sound of my name. It was the guard. He could apparently see me, even though Kate had left. The curse *had* to be broken. I was alive.

A discussion with this bloke would only slow me down, but Kate liked him. If only I could remember his name. "Hello . . . uh . . . er . . ."

"Charlie," he offered, not seeming at all offended by my

memory lapse. "How was your first day? I didn't get to ask you last week. Did you do well?"

"My first day . . . of *classes*?" No one had asked how my day had been in such a long time. Not since Mother. I smiled. "Yes, thank you."

Charlie beamed, as if he'd known the answer all along, but had only been waiting for my confirmation. "Good. My shift is about to start, so I better vamoose."

He'd almost made it to the stairs when I called, "Charlie, have you seen Kate?"

"Kate? She's about to catch a bus, I think." Again, his kind smile surfaced. "She works at this place in town—a coffee shop. Coffee á Rena. Do you know it? Over by Market Square."

Of course I don't know it. I'd been dead for over a hundred years. My caffeine intake had been nonexistent in that time.

But then I remembered Kate and considered how she might answer the question. "I'll find it. Goodbye, Charlie."

"'Kay, bye, Griff," Charlie called as I raced forward.

Again, my instinct was to ignore him, but I found myself stopping anyway. "Thank you for the information, Charlie." Pivoting on the spot, I took to the stairs, elation ripping through me as I made it to the lobby.

Students cursed me as I moved past them. Cries of, *Hey, man, watch it!* and *After you, asshole!* filled the lobby.

They can see me! All of them can bloody see me!

There was no sign of Kate anywhere in the main lobby. As I passed through the front doors, however, I spotted her just past the gates.

An enormous machine of some sort pulled up with a squeal. The gigantic metal beast carried dozens of people.

"Kate!" Either she didn't hear me over the noise of the

machine or she ignored me, for she didn't respond. I had to try again. "Kate!"

That time, she heard, turning on her heel, her eyes rounding as they met mine. I ran after her across the courtyard, dodging the sea of students. What should I say? The options piled up in my mind as I crossed the courtyard.

Kate, I'm a ghost and I think being with you makes me alive again? That would certainly not end well.

I halted just before the boundary, gripping one of the iron gates as though it were a lifeline. "Kate, don't go." *Good, start with the basics.*

"Goodbye, Griffin." Kate moved toward the open door of the waiting machine.

"I thought we had *something*." *Please let that be the correct word choice.*

"You don't want this. You don't want me." She shook her head.

The memory of our kiss spiraled into my mind. "I do want you."

Kate turned and climbed into the machine. The door shut after her, and the machine began to pull away, just as my body faded away to spirit form once more.

Without thinking, I placed one foot over the boundary, and the significance of what I'd done slammed into me. Thunder rumbled in the distance. The sky darkened.

"No, no, no, no." I all but whimpered the words.

As though a switch had been flicked, night fell, rain poured once more, and all the lights in the building lit. The scene before me faded as an unseen force dragged me backward across the pavement, toward the house. And my curse pulled me back in time, to the parlor where I'd performed, to the very place where I'd watched Jonah die.

My neck turned of its own volition—forced me to watch

as Jonah fell amidst shards of broken glass. I couldn't close my eyes. No matter how I tried to block out the images before me, I had to watch.

May he be bound to this house until true love finds him . .

The curse echoed in my ears as a whirling funnel of glass rose into the air, spinning of its own volition, and sank into my chest, just as it had all those years ago. I was helpless to stop it as the blanket of darkness fell over me, reminding me that I was still a prisoner. Maybe I always would be.

CHAPTER 19

KATE

Twenty minutes later, I found myself on the sidewalk outside work, down the street from Market Square. The square was a cool little brick and cobblestone deal that covered only fifty feet or so in distance, but it was packed with cool restaurants and tiny shops, along with the iconic PPG building, covered in glittering glass.

The smell of Primanti Bros. assaulted my nose, and my stomach rumbled. A kielbasa and cheese on some good old Mancini's Italian Bread would rock right about then, but I was already late for work.

Shrugging my bag with Benny onto my shoulder, I crossed the street. Coffee á Rena sat at the entrance to Market Square.

On the outside, Rena's shop was a squat, brown building. The only bit of color came in the form of a small neon sign that read *Psychic Readings*.

Shutting off the display on my phone, I used it as a mirror to check my reflection. Resting my fingers against my lips, I closed my eyes and let myself remember Griffin's kiss. His lips had been soft, sending waves of sensation through me. No guy had ever made that happen.

I'd only been kissed twice. Once by Jaycee McGill, my old boyfriend, and the other from Ryder. Ryder *definitely* hadn't counted. His kiss had been pushy, with too much tongue and too much saliva.

But when Griff kissed me . . . his shoulders had been warm and solid beneath my hands. There'd been nothing rough about his kiss. He'd been gentle, though the way he'd groaned gave me the impression he would have preferred not to be. Our bodies had pressed together, and somehow, it was like someone had turned a light on inside of me.

And it was a really good first kiss. It was a really good *anytime* kiss.

Until I ran away from him like the freaking idiot I was— for the second time. Or maybe it was the third? Who was counting?

But he came after me.

I pushed that thought away and the front door open. Griff needed to get out of my head. Jaycee and Ryder couldn't hurt me the way he had the potential to.

Rena had put up Christmas decorations everywhere, creating an oasis from the cold and crowded city streets. Red velvet bows were attached to the back of every chair and twinkle lights had been strung along the walls and over the battered, upright piano. Colorful beanbag chairs had been positioned in very inconvenient locations between the tables, like an obstacle course for customers. It was all very festive.

Last year, Rena had put up an inflatable Santa outside. Of course, he'd been stolen and hung from the top of Fifth Avenue Place on my first day of work last New Years', so Rena had sworn there'd be no more outside stuff.

"Kate!" Rena wore large purple cat earrings. She'd gotten a few inches taken off her blond and turquoise hair again. The band The Police blared over the speakers as she danced her way over to me. Rena was always dancing. I recognized the song as one of Dad's favorites, though I couldn't name it. "How are things going? How's your mom? It feels like I haven't seen you in forever."

I shoved my bag under the counter and tugged out an apron from the shelf below the register. I quickly tied it into place. "Mom's trying to enroll me in the Young Leaders Program."

Rena grimaced. Even she would have had to struggle to put her trademark positive spin on my heinous news. True to her Rena-ness, her characteristic smile bounced back so quickly that I almost didn't notice her hesitation. *Almost.*

"People deal with grief in different ways, Kate. Give her time." She wrapped an arm around me, pulling me into a half hug.

"Too bad she wants to deal with it in California. I don't want to go. Dad's here."

"But he's not. He's *here.*" She took my hand in hers and pressed it to my heart. Rena's brow furrowed. "He'll be with you no matter where you go. Your mom's just trying to move forward."

"By spending all her time on the road and shutting out her own kid?"

"I'm not saying I agree with it, but it's her way—for now. Maybe she'll change her mind?" She squeezed my shoulder.

She was being way too optimistic. Maybe that was because Rena had known my parents *before*.

Back when I went to public school, none of the kids had seemed to get along with their parents. Mine were my rock. They came to every event—even the school bake sales. There wasn't a time I couldn't look out into an audience and spot my parents' smiling faces. That had sure changed.

The bell rang above the door. Every muscle in my body tensed. *Ryder.*

Before I could ask Rena to take my place, she'd moved into the back room.

As Ryder navigated to the counter, memories of *that* moment in the classroom and Ryder's almost-kiss sent invisible spiders crawling over my skin. "Hello, Ryder."

"Hey, Kate. I had no idea you worked here." He smiled, setting what looked like a camera bag on the counter. The letters PPT had been stitched in large, gold text on the front.

Yeah, and my grandma's a French chimpanzee. I put on my best smile and tried to ignore the jumble of anger and unease twisting my stomach into knots.

Maybe I could divert his attention. Get him out of there before he tried to start something with me again. "Are you taking pictures or something?"

He shrugged as he stared up at Rena's colorful menu. She'd written it with ten different kinds of chalk—not exactly easy on the eyes. "I'm part of this group. We do paranormal research, scope out haunted places. They meet over at Duquesne."

"Huh." Maybe he *had* just wandered in by accident? Duquesne University was just up Forbes Avenue—all of five minutes away. "I didn't know you were into that stuff."

Shit. *Don't encourage him.*

He smiled, his face lighting. "Honestly, I'd rather do investigations than play the clarinet, but when your dad's in the symphony."

Ryder's dad, Mr. Robb, was Principal Clarinetist with the Pittsburgh Symphony and president of the Byrons school board. Talk about a reputation to live up to. I'd almost feel sorry for Ryder—if he wasn't an ass.

"Yeah. I guess so. What can I get you?"

"Just a coffee."

"That'll be two-fifty." He slid over a card. I was careful not to touch his fingers as I accepted it and swiped it on the aging machine behind the register. I set his receipt and card on the counter, and then turned to fill his order. Picking up a paper cup with Rena's scripted logo on the side, I began filling it with that day's Columbian blend.

"Will you join me?" There was hope in his voice, but I'd experienced firsthand how he could go from being an admirer to a pursuer in seconds flat.

"I can't. I'm working, Ryder. Here's a to-go lid." I popped a lid on his drink and then set it on the counter in front of him. "Cream and sugar are over there." I pointed out the small station that also held stirrers, stops, and cozies.

But Ryder didn't seem interested in half-and-half. He leaned over the counter. At least there was a barrier between us that time. "Why do you keep pushing me away? You know, we could be good together."

My face heated. *This is how he wants to play it.* "Normally, I only date guys who actually *listen* when I talk. Since you're not hearing me, there's pretty much no freaking way we could be good together."

Tipping up my chin, I met his eyes. Dad used to say I

needed to make eye contact if someone tried to attack me. Even though Ryder hadn't tried that, I liked to be proactive. If the eye thing didn't work, then I'd grab the pepper spray Rena kept under the counter.

"I don't want this sludge anyway." Scowling, he smacked the paper coffee cup sideways across the counter, spilling its contents all over the floor and narrowly missing my arm.

"Hey, punk." Rena's voice cut into the conversation from somewhere behind me. I spun around. She'd grabbed her brother Mark's old baseball bat. Rena wouldn't hesitate to use it if she needed to. "This is a business. You've got about two point two seconds to leave before I call the cops. Got it?"

"Whatever." Ryder turned and walked toward the exit. He stumbled over a beanbag as he crossed the room, but he finally jumped over the last cushion and opened the door. The instant it slammed shut, my breath came out in a whoosh.

"Who the hell was that?" Rena asked, leaning against the counter. She'd tipped the bat, so it rested back against her shoulder.

"Some jackass from my school. We went out on a date once. He won't take no for an answer."

"I've had my share of those. You seemed nervous around him. Has he tried to hurt you?"

I thought about the day at the whiteboard and Griff . . . *Griff*. I touched my lips again, remembering his kiss, and a melody of calm filtered into my brain.

"No. I told him to get lost."

"That's good, at least. I don't get a good vibe from him at all. His aura is all funky."

I couldn't help grinning, despite Ryder's freak-out.

"The last thing anyone needs is a funky aura. Let's change the subject, please. I don't want to talk about that jerk anymore."

Rena tossed a cloth towel at me. I caught it before it landed on my head. "We'll forget about him, but if you're in trouble . . ." She stared me down again, probably contemplating locking me up for my own safety and calling the police.

"I'm okay, Rena. I'd tell you if I was *really* in trouble."

She reached behind my ear, plucked out the pencil I'd forgotten was there, and then extended it to me. I took it and shoved it into my bag beneath the counter, Rena said, "That's something, at least."

The dishwasher kicked into a new cycle in the room behind us, making whooshing sounds in six-eight time. She flipped the switch on the grinder, and we didn't talk until it finished running through its routine. Rena set the baseball bat in the closet and leaned against the counter.

"What's going on with you? You look like you haven't slept in weeks."

"You know how it is, Rena. I have juries coming up."

Rena replenished the reservoir of coffee beans attached to the grinder. "I think you need to take some time off. Take this week. Just focus on school. You're trying to do too much. I don't even know how you can set foot inside that creepy school, anyway."

"Rena, come on. I was going to tell you I need more hours, not less." I was about five hundred dollars short on my expenses for next term. If I lost that scholarship, though, I'd be short a lot more than that.

Rena shook her head. "It's illegal for me to give you too many hours. You're a minor."

"I'll be seventeen in a few months."

"Seventeen is still a minor. Plus, I can't afford it. Why else do you think I haven't given you hours in a couple of weeks? There's no money in coffee."

Rena was right about the money in coffee. I'd worked at Coffee á Rena long enough to know it wasn't exactly lucrative. Reading people's fortunes rarely paid the bills, either. At least she had a surprisingly steady business for Pittsburgh, which wasn't exactly known for being a mystical place.

The two of us straightened up behind the counter, dumping used coffee grounds and cleaning the empties, but the case was closed. It wasn't until we'd put the last of the mugs into the dishwasher that a slow grin spread over her face.

"Are there any nice guys you like? That guy, Ryder, was kind of a jerk, but there's got to be someone else in your life."

Rena was always scanning the shop for her "nice guy" and kind of extended that to me. She'd gotten married straight out of high school to a guy named Rufus who ran a record store in Queens. Rena had moved in with him right after they'd gotten married. Six months later, she'd moved back to Pittsburgh.

Apparently, Rufus had been growing some questionable plants in the spare bedroom.

Rena rested an elbow against the polished counter. "Come on. Dish! You gotta give me something." Her blue eyes lit, showing off the internal warmth Rena had always had, since the moment we'd met.

Griff's face popped into my head. That blond hair of his. Those eyes. I blinked the thought away.

Rena was the closest thing to a real friend I had. "I don't know. There's this guy at school. He's helping me with my jury piece." My heart started beating like crazy.

"Name please?"

"Griff. He's a pianist."

"Oooh. Is he any good?"

I blushed at her clearly unintended double entendre. "He's the best musician I've ever heard."

"He sounds *hot*." She bit her lip, clearly enjoying my embarrassment.

My whole face burned. Griff had looked incredible in jeans and flannel. "Yeah, pretty much."

"What's the problem? Why don't you want to talk about him?"

"Up until today, he spent most of his time insulting me, but then he . . ."

"He kissed you?" Slowly, Rena's face split into a grin, her eyes rounding into giant, twin circles.

"What?" My face had to have turned every shade of red there was. I'd have to Google how many were out there.

"It's obvious, Kate. You've touched your lips about fifty times since you walked in. I figured you got kissed, is all."

My fingers rested on my bottom lip. I dropped them. "My lips are just chapped."

"Kate, come *on*. This shop is my love life. Can't I live vicariously through you?"

"It was just a kiss. That doesn't constitute a love life." *Damn.*

Rena laughed. "Oooh! Girl! There *was* a kiss! And how do you feel about him? I mean, it's obvious, but I wanna hear it from you."

Oh, great. It's that *obvious?*

How could it be, when I didn't know how I felt? "I don't know, Rena. He's just a guy."

"Sure." She laughed again, but then a customer came in, and I was saved as Rena turned to take her order. Picking up three empty coffee pots from under the counter, I carried them back to the kitchen sink.

Even though we weren't talking about Griff anymore, I couldn't stop thinking about him. His kiss had made me feel tingly and hyperaware. Like I couldn't get close enough.

Whew.

Griff was too suave, too good-looking, too *everything*. He was one of *those* guys.

There was no way he didn't have a girlfriend back home. Some rich British girl with an estate and lands or something. That was the way it went in books.

No way was Griff meant for me.

But, there'd been an overwhelming theme of weirdness between us—that déjà vu, mumbo-jumbo sensation that I'd known him *before*. Rena would have called that fate. I couldn't say if I believed in that stuff one way or the other, but how could I ignore my gut instinct that I was right where I was supposed to be? I'd even known instinctively what his kiss would *feel* like, how I'd react.

I wanted him even though I didn't know exactly *what* it was I wanted.

I didn't share any of those things with Rena, because she'd pull on her psychic hat and start sensing things. I wasn't ready for that.

Every instinct screamed at me to find Griff, to go back to him. Sure, I could stay there and hide, but I wasn't a coward. If anything, I routinely ran *toward* danger.

And man, Griff was dangerous. I'd never felt anything like I had when he'd kissed me. I wouldn't go my entire life without experiencing that again.

If Rena'd asked me to break it down, I couldn't have pinpointed who Griff was to me, or our status as a couple, but I did know one thing. I'd lied to Rena.

Because Griff was anything but just a guy.

CHAPTER 20

GRIFFIN

Wednesday, December 7th—Eight Days Left Until Juries

THE NIGHT PASSED IN A TEDIOUS NUMBER OF SECONDS after I'd been forced to experience the worst moment of my life—my death—again. I'd survived it before. If I could call what I'd been doing all those years "surviving."

Despite the pain of reliving Jonah's death, it hadn't scared me off from wanting to see Kate. On the contrary, I could still remember her mouth on mine—how it had sent a tide of heat throughout my very being. I'd never expected to feel that way again. I'd given up hope.

I'd kissed her. Three, possibly four times. Had it been too soon? What if I'd scared her away? The mistake would be all mine.

I hadn't heard Hannah enter the room until she took up her position beside me. Then again, she *was* dead.

"Why do you think others can see me when I'm around her?" I asked, flattening the Brahms against the built-in music stand on my piano. "Is she the one? Or does it have something to do with her resemblance to Minna?"

"I don't know. I have an uneasy feeling about it. Did you ask her about her family? Did you try to pinpoint her tie to the witch?"

"Not yet." I'd done everything but ask questions. At least those that should have been in the forefront of my mind.

"There must be more to the curse, then. If it was just about you falling in love, it would be broken by now. I may have eavesdropped." She at least had the common courtesy to appear chagrined.

But the invasion of privacy was the least of my worries. "I don't love her." I blurted the profession too quickly.

Hannah sat down and rested her hand on my shoulder. "Are you certain, dear boy? The way you look at her tells a different story."

She'd hit too close to the truth. Time for a change of topic. "I've been hearing this voice—three times in the last two weeks. One that says the end is coming. Ever heard that?"

"No. I've never heard any such thing, and I've been all over the grounds and off the estate."

Lord, I envied Hannah her freedom. "Why do you think I'm hearing it?"

"Kate," Hannah said, without an ounce of hesitation. "The strange voice, Kate's arrival . . . it's all leading up to something."

Tapping my fingers against one another, I considered her words. "*What* is the question. And how will we know an answer when we discover one?"

"I don't know." Hannah patted me on the back. "I'll steal some more clothes for you and leave them. There aren't many to choose from, you being the height you are, but I'll try."

"Thank you."

"We're going to have to come up with a different solution if you're going to stay with Kate. The owner of the attire you wore yesterday complained to the office. He's putting up a reward for the pants." She chuckled, and then she was gone, but her words echoed in my mind.

If you're going to stay with Kate.

Even as recently as a day ago, I wouldn't have been able to imagine such a thing. Yet, Kate meant more to me than I wanted to admit. My mind flashed through a million images of her.

She belongs to me.

Where had that line of thinking arisen from? Imagining Kate as my own was dangerous territory. We could never have a future. It had been the cruelest sort of torture to kiss her.

Yet, I couldn't stay away. I wasn't sure I ever could again.

The end is coming.

BY FIVE FORTY-FIVE A.M., IT BECAME CLEAR KATE might not have the same goals as I did. The front door hadn't moved a fraction, the heavy piece refusing to even rattle against the force of the wind. Still, I waited for the door to open, pacing, or at least the best I could do for a spirit.

By the time the clock reached a quarter till eight, I'd

given up hope of seeing her. Kate wouldn't come to my room to rehearse. I couldn't explain the disappointment rushing through me.

Sinking down through the lobby floor to my piano, I took my seat and launched into a piece that hadn't even been written for my instrument. Barber's *Adagio for Strings* was the only work that would convey my emotions that day. The piece was after my time, but one of the benefits of being a ghost at a music school was exposure to new, fresh compositions.

Some of the newer works were a little too untraditional for my taste—like Philip Glass, for example, with his bizarre, contemporary creations. Still, there were so many other wonderful composers I did enjoy—Ferde Groffé, Aaron Copland . . . the century I'd barely gotten the chance to live in had much to offer musically.

If it hadn't been for my curse, I would have been included among those masters. I would have made them all look like fools. But there was little point in thinking about it. As one of the students who used the rehearsal space beside Kate's put it, *that ship had sailed.*

My ears popped, as though clearing themselves. The piano keys became firmer, the texture sliding against my skin as I played. Footsteps sounded outside my door and it swung open.

Snapping my head up, I met Kate's gray eyes as she peered around the doorframe. Gone was her ponytail. Her hair hung down around her face in loose, silky strands. Her cheeks were already flushed. Had she taken greater care with her appearance that morning?

My fingers froze on the keys. "Good morning." I churned out the greeting, my voice rusty. My heart throbbed inside my chest. Had there ever been a woman more beautiful than Kate?

"Sorry I'm late." She opened the door the rest of the way, shutting it behind her once she'd passed through. "And I'm sorry about running out on you like that yesterday."

"It's all right. Tell me why you ran. I thought you felt—" I cut off my own words. I sounded pitiful, like a broken-hearted schoolboy. I had a reputation to uphold.

She swallowed. "I don't want to get . . . hurt."

"I can't promise that won't happen, Kate. Sometimes I hurt people. I don't do it intentionally, it just happens."

"So do I." Kate's voice cracked with her confession. "That's why you and I are the way we are." She pulled a disposable handkerchief from her purse, dabbing at her eyes.

"Meaning?" I stayed rooted to my place behind the keys. The urge to rise, to hold her, tore through me. I resisted, barely.

"Meaning it's better to keep everyone away."

Her words slapped me in the face. She couldn't know my past. Couldn't know me. Yet somehow, there was a stanza of truth to her statement.

"They can't hurt us if they can't *see* us." Kate stood there, her bottom lip quivering. It had cost her to say those things, to risk breaking the rules she held so closely to her heart.

All of it weighed down on me in that moment. I'd never taken anyone seriously, never allowed them to know me. To do so . . . would have been a strategic weakness.

Now this girl with a ratty knapsack and a terrible staccato technique had burst into my life and revealed truths I'd never known about myself.

"Do you still want to work together?" Her voice shook, long tendrils of chocolate hair slipping over her shoulder as she met my eyes. I wanted to run my fingers through the strands.

Standing, I walked to her. "No. I don't want to work just now."

Disappointment colored her face. She nodded, turning to leave. "Okay. I'll practice on my own. I just thought—"

"Don't go." I spoke too quickly, touching her elbow to halt her retreat, guiding her back to face me. "What I mean to say is, I've performed in cities all around the world, studied with some of the greatest musicians imaginable, but nothing that has happened to me in all the years of my life" —I swallowed—"could compare to your kiss."

And before she could utter another word, I swept in and kissed her. Her mouth was exactly as I remembered, her full lips soft against mine. It should have been a quick, gentle kiss, but Kate *ignited* something within me.

"Griff." She pressed closer, our mouths moving with urgency against one another's.

"Call me Griffin."

"Griffin." My name on her lips was a sigh and a groan all at once. "I don't understand this. We hate each other."

Something twisted inside of me. That was what she'd believed? And why not? I'd given her enough evidence to suspect it. The honorable thing would have been to push her away. To let her fail her jury and leave the school. Far better for her if she didn't become entangled with me, but maybe I didn't want to be honorable.

"I could never hate you."

Her face softened. "I could never hate you, either."

Somewhere in the distance, a bell rang, signaling the impending start of classes. Kate broke away.

"I'm sorry, but I overslept this morning. I have to go to

class." Her whispered observation was tinged with annoyance.

"Please don't go." I claimed her lips again, sweeping my tongue into her mouth as I finished the sentence in my head. *Not ever.*

Breaking away, Kate sucked in a breath, holding the moment for much longer than I would have liked. "Okay." She released a slow burst of air. "I won't go."

Standing on tiptoe, she kissed me that time, pressing her warm, sweet body against mine. It shouldn't have worked with the difference in our heights, yet somehow, we seemed perfectly matched.

"Kate." I ground out the word. Things couldn't go on as they were. Not if I hoped to continue behaving as a gentleman. I'd already crossed several lines.

She pulled back a fraction. "Don't speak. It's better if you don't talk and ruin this by saying something obnoxious."

Laughter rolled up in my throat. It felt so good to laugh, to be alive. To be with Kate. "You're right. But I do believe you should *skip* classes." That was the proper word, wasn't it? "We'll work on the Brahms."

"I just want to know what you're hiding from me."

If it was possible for my blood to get any colder, it would have. "Whatever do you mean?"

"I've been hearing you play for the past three months. Charlie has been hearing you play for years. Then you accompanied me two weeks ago in the morning. What's going on?"

My mind snapped up to tempo, trying to fabricate a plausible explanation. But somehow, I didn't want to lie to Kate. Not after what she'd seen in me.

"Can't we just *be* today? I dreamed all night of the

moment you would walk through those doors this morning. Let's not spoil it with—"

"The truth?"

"With what I'm certain would be an awkward confessional. Tomorrow, you can ask whatever you'd like, and I shall answer." My conversation with Hannah came back. Kate could be the one to break the curse, but what would that mean? What sort of future could we have? I would sort everything out, but if I could just have one day with her . . .

She stared at me hard, but then nodded. "Tomorrow, then."

For one day, at least, I would postpone my doom.

CHAPTER 21

KATE

MY DAY WITH GRIFFIN, SPENT IN HIS WEIRD PRACTICE space, was proving to be the best one of my life. He was just so, well . . . *interesting*. He talked about everything from politics to music to science. Even though he was seriously smart, I never once felt as though I couldn't keep up or I didn't belong.

I could just be me. Just Kate.

We lay on one of the dusty divans and talked for hours, Griffin on his back, his long legs hanging over the edge. I'd curled up on my side with my head against his chest. His fingers traced lazy, tantalizing circles on my collarbone. I would seriously internally combust if he continued.

"How do you feel about the Brahms now?" Griffin asked, moving from my collarbone to the side of my neck. Oh, Holy Mother. Focus on the question. Answer his questions.

"Better. You were right, I had a lot of work to do."

"Mmm." The sound reverberated in his chest. "Words I never thought I'd hear."

"Don't let it go to your head."

"Too late." He chuckled. "Where did you grow up?"

"Here, in Pittsburgh. My parents were from here. We never left."

"And you live with your mother still? What's your mother like?" His voice sounded strange, almost strangled.

"She's a *bitch*." I spat out the words before I could stop myself. "I'm sorry. That sounds so mean. My mom really isn't that bad." We just have this huge gap between us. A missing measure in a piece of music. "We were close, once."

"Your relationship with your mother sounds complex."

"Things have just changed since Dad. I know she loves me, but it's not the same." *Shut up, Kate.* We'd only just kissed, and there I was spilling my guts to Griffin. Yet, he didn't pull away or look at me like I was a freak.

Griffin's hazel eyes locked onto mine. His fingers trailed along my upper arm to my shoulder. I shivered. He couldn't have missed my reaction. He caught everything. "Tell me about your father."

"He died in a car accident." My throat thickened.

"Not how he died. Tell me about him. What did you like most about him?"

Relief washed over me. Griffin didn't say *I'm sorry* like everyone else had.

Not only that, but Griffin wanted to talk about Dad. No one ever wanted to talk about him anymore. Especially not Mom.

"He was patient. With me. With everybody. He'd sit and listen. He never seemed to judge anyone. He had a big heart." I swallowed. "He was tall, like you, but really muscular. Sort of like a papa bear. He was my best friend."

Griffin threaded his fingers into my hair. The pads teased my scalp, easing the pressure in my chest, but building the heat in my belly.

"He had this band, The Standards. They played jazz standards, that sort of thing, on the weekends. His day job was in engineering."

"What did you like least about him?"

I cleared my throat. "He was hairy."

"I beg your pardon?"

"The man had chest hair that was like a sweater. He shed everywhere. It was disgusting." I could almost hear Mom's voice, teasing Dad about getting his chest waxed. I snorted and caught myself.

Somehow, that memory hadn't hurt.

Griffin slid a hand to his head, chuckling, the whole of his attention seeming focused on me.

"You're different. From other guys, I mean. From Ryder," I confessed.

Griffin turned me to face him, bracing his hands on my shoulders. "The way Ryder acted—it's not the way gentlemen are. You're worth so much more than . . ."

My heart must've stopped beating. I waited, my face flaming, my body screaming at me to kiss him again, but I wanted him to finish. "Yes?"

"I suppose what I'm trying to say is, you're worth waiting for." His eyes burned into mine. "You're . . . *everything*."

Did my body actually just catch on fire?

God, I was falling for Griffin so hard. I could only hope my fears wouldn't become reality. I wasn't ready to have my heart broken again.

CHAPTER 22

GRIFFIN

The darkening window caught my eye. Our day together was at an end. "Will you have to go home soon?" I asked, noting the sadness in my own voice.

"Won't you?" Her voice sounded young.

I frowned. "Not exactly. I don't have a place. Not in the sense you would expect, anyway. I'll be staying here tonight."

"What? Why? Won't they find you?"

Her last question almost made me laugh out loud. Over a hundred years and they'd yet to locate me. I doubted things would change overnight. "It's a long story, but no, they never check this room. I stay here a lot."

Kate shuddered. "I don't really like this place. It's creepy, and I think I saw . . ."

"Yes?"

"A ghost. I spotted this face in the air vent."

Guilt nagged at my soul. Hannah shouldn't have let Kate see her, but I chuckled despite myself. "I thought you didn't believe in ghosts."

"I never used to, but . . ." Kate shook her head. "Don't you *feel* it? There's a feeling about this place, like something bad is going to happen."

My smile evaporated. "Yes, I guess I do. I've never liked this house."

A funny look crossed her face. "You say that like you've been coming here for years."

Bollocks. That had been careless. "Will you stay with me tonight, Kate?" It was a bold question, but one that begged to be asked.

"Fine, but it doesn't mean I'm going to let you get into my pants or anything." She cocked a single eyebrow.

I roared with laughter, but it died in the wake of the all too serious way she regarded me. After witnessing how that cad, Ryder, had acted, I couldn't blame her.

"I feel things for you, Kate—I won't pretend otherwise—but I understand you are a young woman worthy of far more respect than a tryst in a forgotten schoolroom."

"In that case, yes." She settled back against the divan, then changed positions again, and then once more. Her restlessness was catching. "I know you said no questions today."

"Yes." I fought to keep from visibly tensing, but my jaw locked. I couldn't help it. I hadn't had a conversation like the one we'd shared in years, let alone had anyone ask me questions. I didn't want to lie to Kate, but I might be forced to.

"Would you tell me about where you grew up? I've never been to England."

Ah, so that was all. Americans seemed to have a rapt fascination with Britain. Perhaps they still regretted defecting all those years ago when they set out for the colonies.

"Very well. I was raised on a small estate—only a couple of dozen rooms." I guided her head back against my chest, so I could toy with her hair.

She bit her lip, and it twisted my stomach into knots. "Was your estate in London? Did your parents live there?"

"My parents lived separate lives. I grew up with my mother in the country, in Warwickshire. There are rolling hills, a small village, strawberry fields, a castle, lots of green." I could picture it all in my mind. I'd loved Fulton House, the name of the house where I'd grown up. No one had stared at us there. There were no prying eyes, only lush lands and horses, so there was little talk of the woman who'd gotten herself with child out of wedlock by a titled lord.

I'd have given anything to go back there again—just once—but I couldn't explain any of it, so it seemed better to direct the questions if I could. "How many rooms does your estate have, Kate?"

She smiled, scrunching up her face in that endearing way of hers. "Seven."

"It's a flat then?"

"Not exactly. I live in the suburbs, in a townhouse. The only green I get to see is our little four-by-five-foot plot of grass in front of the house. I can't imagine having the kind of land you're talking about. And fresh air? Forget it."

Right in that moment, I couldn't help feeling sorry for her. The places in the world that I'd seen—they'd been incredible, but nothing compared to Fulton House. "Back home, the air is so brisk, it burns your lungs when you breathe."

"You miss it." Kate spoke softly as she took my hand in

hers. That simple act of empathy threw me. We should've had nothing in common, and yet . . .

"Yes. I do, actually. Like most people, I don't think I truly appreciated it until I'd left it behind."

Her eyes drifted partway closed, but it seemed to have more to do with the intentional torture I inflicted on her scalp than a need for sleep. "And your father? He's back in England?"

I stiffened. There was something about my parents being combined into a pair, when they'd shared little in their separate lifetimes. Not even me. "My father is dead, too."

Kate wrapped her arms around me, forcing me to drop my hand, holding me close. "I'd tell you I'm sorry, but that's so insincere. When you've lost someone, there aren't enough words in the world to bring them back. Would you tell me about them?"

"Let's see. My mother, Miriam, was a very sweet woman, but also very ordinary. She had very few aspirations in life that I knew of, but she wanted a home of her own. A place to read and dream. She found that, I think." She was the only one who I ever showed my true self to, before Kate.

"And your father?"

"My father, Alfred, wasn't . . . kind. He failed to share with my mother that he was already married to someone else . . . a lady of high society. Of course, my mother came from a good family, as well. To avoid a scandal, my father provided her a home in the country in exchange for her silence."

"You weren't close?"

What a gross understatement. "I met my father exactly one time, when I was five years old."

She blinked. Such a thing would have been hard for her

to envision, when Kate's own father had obviously loved her. "I can't imagine what that must have been like."

"I can still remember walking down the stairs. The wood railing had been polished until it gleamed, and it felt sort of slippery." A smile tugged at the corners of my mouth. "Anyway, when I got to the bottom of the steps, my father was waiting in the study.

"Somehow, I knew who he was, and I—" Emotion rose up in me. I swallowed, a poor attempt to force the feeling away. "I ran to him with my arms outstretched, but he held up a hand and said, 'Stop, boy.' I can remember shaking, because no one had ever spoken to me that way before."

"What happened?"

"He turned to Mother and said something akin to, 'This bastard is going to be my only heir. You've done right by him, but we'll need to work hard to make sure he succeeds me.' And that was it. He just left." I didn't share the satisfaction I'd felt when I'd learned he died alone.

"What an ass." Kate shook her head, her hands fisting at her sides as she readied herself to fight battles for me. Once Kate's loyalty had been won, it was a fierce sight to behold.

"Undoubtedly." I relaxed. "Music was always my escape. When I'd just turned eight, a great piano player moved next door. She gave me lessons."

Kate rubbed her thumb over the indentation on the heel of my left hand. I began to pull away, but she was too quick. Frowning, she turned my hand over.

"Why do you have a mark branded into your hand?"

Leave it to Kate to find the one piece of evidence that could truly identify me as, well, *me*. "Childhood accident. It's nothing."

She trailed her finger over the spot where the thin line had been forever imprinted. "Want to talk about it?"

"No." Enough questions. "We're a lot alike, you and I." I guided her head to rest against my shoulder, wanting more from her, knowing I wouldn't try to take it. "I feel like I can say anything to you, and you would understand."

She snuggled deeper against me, and it was as if she was supposed to have been there all along. "I feel the same way about you."

Her poignant expression told the story—every indescribable emotion I experienced, she'd felt, too. I'd never expected to be understood again. I'd been cursed to hell, but somehow, I'd been handed a dream. I only hoped it wouldn't end.

CHAPTER 23

KATE

Thursday, December 8th—Seven Days Left Until Juries

No sooner had I left Griffin for a stop in the restroom than Chopin sounded from the back pocket of my jeans. Why was Mom calling so late? She probably wanted to talk more about her upcoming trip to California and the Young Leaders Program. God, she wanted me to be like her. Even down to the prep school resumé.

"Hey, Mom." I shoved the phone against my ear as I reached the bathroom. A gate had been placed across the entrance. The words *Closed for Maintenance* in red lettering stood out against the yellow plastic.

Unfortunately, that meant I had to go to the even creepier first floor bathroom. It had never been a favorite of mine. The green tiles seemed overly dark and chilling.

Mom's voice filtered into my ear as I reached the stairs. "Kate, hi. I thought you weren't working tonight."

What did she care? She wasn't even in town. "I'm not working. I'm with a friend."

"Are you coming home?" Her disbelief shot through the line.

Oops. "I thought you left for your big trip today?" I kept my steps light, and the phone at my ear.

"I'm leaving tomorrow morning." Mom used her stern voice. The same one she'd used when I thought I could make my own clarinet reeds out of her bamboo plant stand for my sixth-grade science project. *Fail.* "I want you home right now. Don't make me come down there and get you."

Oh. "I'm sorry, I got my days mixed up." It sort of scared me that I'd lost track. Not that I'd confess that to her. "I'm with a friend. I'll be home soon."

My face burned. A friend. Griffin wasn't just a friend. He was . . . what? A boyfriend? I wished I knew more about Griffin. Then maybe I could tell Mom about him.

For the time being, we needed to keep a low profile. Unanswered questions would only send Mom into Overprotective Mode.

I reached the upstairs bathroom, and one of the old lamps, the refurbished ones on the wood-covered wall, flickered and went out, sending the hallway into shadow.

Katya. I jolted as a cool breath passed over my ear. I whipped around, but there was no one. That place was seriously getting to me.

"Kate? Kate, are you okay?" Mom's voice sounded through the phone.

I pushed the door open and let out a breath when the lights came to life. "Yeah, it doesn't matter. I promise I'll be home soon." Crouching down, I checked the stalls. Empty.

Katya.

"What the hell?" I whipped around a second time, but there was no one there.

"Kate?"

Thunder rumbled in the distance. Where had that come from? It'd been snowing before. Maybe one of those weird December thunderstorms.

Breath whispered along my collarbone. Turning, I faced myself in the mirror and froze. My phone slipped from my fingers, dropping into the empty sink, clattering loudly against the porcelain.

A woman stood behind me. Our faces were almost identical—only our eye color differed. Her eyes were blue, not my gray. Still, the similarities were close enough. Then I began to notice the differences. Her hair, a pale blond, was far lighter and longer than mine. She'd swept it into a bun on top of her head. She was taller, too.

I opened my mouth to ask her name, to figure out where she'd come from and how she looked so much like me.

But then she scowled, her mouth scrunching up like an old woman's. "What could you possibly have been thinking? Him. Of all the creatures on this Earth, you pick the one who destroyed me to love!"

She shook, the material on her dress quivering. That was when I noticed she wasn't just wearing a dress, but a maid's uniform—and an old one, from the looks of it. One that trailed to her ankles and ran up to her neckline.

Spinning around, I met her eyes. "I'm sorry. Who are you?" I forced the words out in one long string, before she could say more.

From the sink behind me, my cell phone rang again. The ringtone sounded muffled, distant, which didn't make any sense.

"The end of everything came because of Griffin Dunn, Katya." The woman ground out the words. Her voice sounded evil and gravelly, like something straight out of a horror movie.

A slice of fear trailed the back of my neck, racing down my spine. Who the hell was she? And what had Griffin ever done to her? Sure, he could be a jerk, but I couldn't imagine him doing anything that would have ticked this lady off.

"Look, I have to go. My mom's on the phone." I spun around and grabbed the phone from the sink—just as it stopped ringing. Awesome.

"No one's there. No one is searching for you." The woman hissed the words into my ear. I jerked my head to find her already beside me.

She shoved her hand against my chest. Not hard enough to hurt or even send me backward. Before I could tell her off, a wash of warmth poured over me. Almost like I'd slipped into the bathtub and cocooned myself in a world of bubbles.

What was I going to say to her? Something. I couldn't remember. My phone fell to the tile floor. I couldn't hold onto it anymore. From somewhere in the distance, music started up. The piano. It was Griffin. No one else could capture that fiery intensity.

"That's better." The woman drew her hand away. I jerked forward, stumbling a step until she placed her hands on my forearms, righting me. "Good. Now, keep up."

She opened the bathroom door and then stepped into the hallway. I *needed* to follow her. It was as if there was a cord attached to my chest, leading me. I'd been waiting my entire life to follow it.

I couldn't go back to Griffin. Not yet.

A breeze blew over my skin as I followed the woman. She climbed the stairs. Students weren't supposed to go beyond the second floor. I opened my mouth to tell her, but before I could get the words out, I didn't care.

She seemed to know where she was going. Why shouldn't I follow? She was so pretty. So nice. What could it hurt?

The woman quickened her pace. It didn't feel like I was walking, but I moved forward anyway. One step seemed to count as ten or twenty. The thunder picked up. A flash of lightning outside. I should have been asking questions, but I didn't want to. This was okay. I was warm, safe.

Up and up we climbed, until we'd reached the top, and moved past the ropes discouraging students from entry. I'd never been to the fourth floor. Why had she brought me there? The air pushed down on my chest.

The storm sounded louder up on the top level. We turned a corner and I saw why. That section of the fourth floor contained a wide catwalk with banisters on either side. Three interior skylights dominated the center of the walkway, overlooking the first floor parlor below. A series of sconces threw low light into the hall.

Sheeting rain slammed against the windows, the sound competed with the piano for my attention. *When did it start raining?*

"This way." The woman didn't turn as she beckoned for me to move toward the skylight.

Why are we here? The question filled up my mind and my mouth, fighting to reach the surface, but the warmth took me over again. I couldn't ask. I didn't want to ask.

The rhythmic pattering of the rain on the roof hypnotized me. I followed, warm and dreamy.

We stopped a mere foot from the skylight. That was when I noticed him. A little boy lay on the ground, his small face pressed against the glass, forehead first. He was dressed in period clothes—though which period, I couldn't say, with socks that came up to just below the hem of his pant legs.

We'd only stood there a moment when a loud crack sounded and the glass shattered. With a startled cry, the boy plunged through the skylight. A loud thud, combined with a sickening crunch, followed.

My heart thudded as my head cleared. "Oh my God. We need to call an ambulance. We have to get help."

"Katya. Don't you want to see what's down there?" Again, the woman's voice made the reality around me fade, as though it didn't matter.

Warm. Everything seemed warm. Of course it did. *It will all be okay.*

But even as a small voice in the back of my mind screamed that it wouldn't be, that I didn't want to see, I peered over the opening. Staring downward, I spotted the body of the boy on the ground below.

Someone familiar also stared at the boy.

"Griffin!"

He didn't answer me. Didn't move at all. A look of horror filled his face. Before I could call him again, what looked like a hundred shards of glass rose into the air on their own and slammed directly into the center of Griffin's chest.

"Griffin!" My voice rang out loud and clear.

"He took everything from us." The woman leaned in behind me until her lips brushed against my ear. "May he be bound to this house until true love finds him. Then let him be repaid in kind."

Then she placed a hand against the middle of my back

and shoved. *Hard.*

No, no! I was going to fall through the skylight. I had to stop her.

I wish to live. In a flash, the cord that had been tying me to this woman snapped. I slammed my hands on either side of the skylight as the weight on my back faded, and then, just as quickly, dissipated.

The warm, fuzzy feeling evaporated totally. I got myself to my feet. Outside, the rain had stopped, replaced by the fat, wide snowflakes I'd remembered. Moving to the window, I scanned the sky and spotted twinkle lights on houses in the distance. The sounds of trucks barreling over the Fort Pitt Bridge on their way north dimly broke the silence. Turning back, I searched for the skylight, but it was gone, capped off by some black covering as if it had never been there.

Tremors hit me. I gripped the windowsill, trying to keep my own sense of balance from knocking me over.

"Kate." Griffin stood at the doorway, as though afraid to come any closer. Anguish morphed his face, pinching his brow, widening his eyes.

There were still impressions on my hands from the rim of the skylight. Suddenly, I understood. It hadn't been a dream. Shudders traveled through me.

"You were dead. I *saw* you die."

When Griffin spoke, his voice sounded raw. "Please give me your hand." He didn't try to touch me. It was as though he wanted me to decide if he should take his next step. "Please." His voice cracked.

I couldn't move. My feet had frozen in shock. "I can't move my legs." Tears spilled over my cheeks.

"I've got you. I've got you, love." Without another word, Griffin swept his arms beneath me and carried me away from the skylight, toward the stairs. "It's tomorrow now, Kate. I think maybe we need to have our conversation. I have to tell you who I really am."

Whatever Griffin had to say, I had a feeling it would alter things between us forever.

CHAPTER 24

GRIFFIN

KATE WAS OKAY. I'D FOUND HER. THANK GOD I'D GONE to the ladies' facilities to search for her. I'd found her communications rectangle. Then I'd heard her scream my name. When I'd run to the fourth floor landing, my breath had clouded the air—it'd been that cold.

She'd been fine when I'd reached the fourth floor, but none of that mattered.

"G-Griffin?" The temperature had dropped, and Kate shook quietly against me. She was going into shock.

The silence of the house overwhelmed me as I carried her down the hall. The thick carpeting padded my foot-steps, but I could remember when it'd been all wood. My past and present were colliding again.

"Where are we going?" Kate asked. She burrowed her head into my shoulder, her nose resting on my collarbone.

"Somewhere we can warm you up." I forced cheerfulness into my voice.

We needed a fire. I ran down the steps to the second floor and chose the first door on the right. With care, I set Kate in front of the large fireplace. But when I turned to it, I found the opening covered, a gold lock laying against the semi-transparent glass cover.

"Damnation. We shan't have a fire then." That's when I spotted the electric heater that stood by the hearth. I twisted its knob and it made a whirring sound before a blast of warmth shot from it. Kate lowered herself to the floor in line with the air flow.

An office worker had left a white sweater hanging over the back of a chair. Grasping it, I settled the material over Kate's shoulders.

"Why were you on the fourth floor?" I took her hand in mine, noting her long, slender fingers. Fingers she'd run through my hair earlier. But that had been five, no ten minutes ago. We'd past the point of no return.

"I don't know." She barely voiced the last word. That, in and of itself, was so un-Kate-like it seemed horribly wrong.

"I don't understand. What were you doing up there?" My words sounded stiff—as cold as the icy rivulets of water running along the windows moments ago.

"I don't know." Kate wrapped her arms around herself. "I was in the bathroom talking to my mom on my phone, and then this woman showed up." She drew closer to the heater, a shudder ripping through her.

"What woman?" A woman had talked to Kate, and then she'd ended up near Jonah's skylight.

"I don't know her name. She called me *Katya*." Kate bit her bottom lip. "She looked like me. Except blond. She had a German accent. She was dressed in some sort of maid's uniform. She wanted me to come with her."

It can't be.

But there could be no other explanation. Minna had returned to the Byrons house. She couldn't have been alive. It would've been unnatural, impossible. "What did she say?"

"She was angry. She yelled at me for getting involved with you." Kate moved closer to the heater. "And then I followed her. I don't know why. I just did. Then I saw you die. How is that possible?"

Sooner or later, Kate would've learned the truth. I'd known that from the beginning. Yet, why did it have to be at that moment? After the wonderful day we'd shared? "You're overtired. Maybe you should lie down."

"I'm not overtired." She shook her head. "I just watched two people die. One of them was *you*. I think you owe me an explanation."

The waiting, the keeping secrets, had come to an end. Letting out a mighty sigh, I sat down across from her. "The little boy was Jonah Byrons. The scene you witnessed . . . happened."

Kate paled. Dark smudges rested below her eyes. In the dim light, she appeared so like Minna that I almost backed away. "What do you mean, it *happened*?"

"You told me about the face in the vent—that you'd heard the building was haunted."

Kate nodded.

"You're right. The building is haunted." She'd think I'd gone mad. *Maybe I have?*

"By who?" Her expression remained frustratingly unreadable.

"By me. I'm the ghost of Byrons School. I'm Griffin Dunn."

CHAPTER 25

KATE

THE HOT AIR FROM THE HEATER BURNED MY ARM. I couldn't move. My butt had glued itself to the floor.

"I'm dead, Kate. Or, more specifically, *cursed.*" He seemed to have fixated on one part of the fireplace that had begun to crumble. Little pieces of brick and mortar had collected beneath it. The stone had fallen to pieces, just like our relationship was. Imploding before it even began.

The hard part of me, the part that rocked at putting up walls, fought to rebuild the protection I'd had in place before Griffin tore it down. But I couldn't work fast enough.

"Is this some kind of joke?" My voice cracked. Why couldn't I have been smoother, cooler? Why did I have to care?

But explanations hurt. They were always the prelude to some big letdown. I couldn't deal with that from him. I jumped to my feet. I had to get away. How could I have been so stupid as to think a normal guy could like me?

"I knew this was too good to be true. But I never thought you'd end up being certifiable." Then my eyes widened as something even worse occurred to me. "Did you make up this whole story so you could get out of being with me?"

"No. I swear I would never. Please, Kate. Let me explain."

"No, I'm done."

But Griffin reached up to rest a hand on my arm and I froze. That tingling feeling, the one that seemed to take control and turn my brain to mush, followed. Why couldn't my body dismiss him the way my mind wanted to?

"You can't go, not yet. I mean, you're free to." He released my arm. "But you know what happened doesn't make sense. And you were right. The pianist who accompanied you a few weeks ago in the early morning was me."

I dropped to my spot beside the heater. Maybe it was idiotic of me to hear him out, but so many things had happened in that house that I couldn't explain. "The woman"—I hiccuped—"looked like me."

"Yes." Griffin nodded. "Her name was Minna. She's the one who . . . cursed me. She's the reason I'm here."

"Curses aren't real. They're just things people read about in fairy tales."

He shaped his lips into a grim smile. "I thought so once, too. Until the night I died."

Sharp pain lanced my heart at the words *I died.* I tried to think up a response, but there was nothing. "Go on."

"She blamed me for the death of Jonah Byrons, the charge who was left in her care. She was . . . distraught. I couldn't reason with her."

Why was he telling me that? Why?

None of it was real—but hadn't I seen Griffin get knocked backward? His blond hair sprawled across the floor behind him? Hadn't those shards of glass driven themselves into his chest?

Still, I found myself asking: "Why would she pin something like that on you?"

He frowned, a world-weary expression filling his face. "Jonah had taken an interest in music, and he wanted to hear me perform. The boy was deformed. I thought him hideous. I told him to stay away, but he must have snuck upstairs to watch me from the skylight. It couldn't hold his weight and it shattered. The boy fell to his death." Griffin cringed. "The boy's nanny, Minna, was heartbroken. She started shouting words at me in German—some sort of spell—an incantation. She condemned me to this house. I can never leave as long as the curse is on me."

I couldn't talk. I could only sit in silence as the words rushed out of his mouth in a jumbled confession.

"I don't know all of the curse because I didn't understand most of it. The only thing I remember is: *May he be—*"

"May he be bound to this house until true love finds him. There was more, but I can't really remember. It's all blurring in my mind," I whispered, then stopped myself. I hadn't meant to talk about the words the strange woman had spoken at all. It would make it all real.

"What else did she say?"

"After that, nothing. Except . . ." My throat tightening at the memory of the weird pressure on my back. "She tried to push me through the skylight."

Griffin blanched. "But you stopped yourself from falling. How?"

Oh, no. That question forced me close to the heart of

my own secrets. *It was nothing. I just made a wish that I would live and poof! I lived.*

But there was no way I could explain what had happened. I couldn't even explain my wishes to myself. "I don't know. Who was she? Why does she look like me?"

Griffin clenched and unclenched his hands. "That first day when I met you . . . do you remember how I stared at you?"

"Yes. I thought you were obnoxious." My voice sounded scratchy. My throat ached from screaming.

"That's probably accurate." He tossed a wry smile in my direction, but it slipped away as quickly as it had appeared. "I'm dead, Kate. But both you and Charlie could see me at our first meeting. You talked to me, you looked almost exactly like Minna, *and* you found my hidden door."

"It's a coincidence. Who cares if we look alike? Oh." More puzzle pieces clicked into place. "That's why you called me an imposter. It wasn't because of my playing."

"Of course not." He waved the discovery away as though dismissing an insect and not my biggest fear. "How well do you know your family? Where they came from?" His eyes burned into mine, maybe searching for secrets I wasn't hiding.

"What do you mean, how well do I know my family? They don't have anything to do with this." But the memory of the woman's face kept popping up. We could have passed for sisters. We weren't, though. Dad would have told me about her. It's not like we had many relatives in the area. Both Mom and Dad had been only children.

He rose to his knees. Griffin towered above me, but again he didn't crowd me. He only squeezed my hands. My breath hitched. An hour ago, I would have met him halfway.

We would have kissed. In that moment, he'd become a stranger.

"I think you're related to Minna. I don't know how, but I'd wager you have powers, Kate."

In a matter of seconds, memories of all those wishes I'd made came back to me. All those years of hiding what I could do.

If only there was a way I could block out the last twenty-four hours. Maybe everything from the moment before Griffin kissed me. Then I wouldn't know what it felt like for him to hold me.

Knowing would only make it that much harder to walk away.

"Look, I don't have any powers. I'm just a music student."

His eyes raked over my body, sending my face burning again. "Can you explain, then, why I become solid, alive, and others can see me when I'm with you? Can you explain what you saw tonight? Or how I play piano just like the pianist you've heard in the mornings for months?"

"No." None of it made any sense, but I was so past the point of being able to process it. To me, everything he told me seemed like an excuse. A reason he couldn't be with me. And just then, I was tired of people not wanting to be with me.

"You're the only thing keeping me alive in this moment. What if you're a witch, too?" Griffin took both of my hands in his. It hurt. Not because his grip tightened, but because it would be the last time I let him touch me. "Don't you see, Kate?"

"What I see," I said, surprised I somehow managed to keep my voice even, "is a guy who changed his mind about me. Someone who went to some great lengths to end a relationship that hasn't even started."

He paled, his contact the only warmth in the world. "Look me up if you don't believe me. Use the cobweb. Search for Griffin Dunn."

The cobweb? The Web. The Internet. It would have been funny, if it were a different day and he hadn't shared what he had. He sure was going to great lengths to convince me he was dead.

God, I couldn't go there. I needed space to think. "I'm done listening, Griffin." I tugged my fingers from his.

He shook his head, as ruffled as I'd ever seen him. Maybe he'd always been like that on the inside. "You have to know. You could be in danger."

"No." The tears were coming. Traitors. I couldn't stay. "The only danger to me is you."

Backing up, I spun and ran. Away from all of the messed up things he'd said. I just couldn't shake the feeling that, as crazy as it all sounded, I was somehow running in the wrong direction.

Heart in my throat, I flew out of the room and down the hall. Each step seemed more difficult than the last, as though I tried to run through a swamp, or fight my way out of a dream. But it was no bad dream. I'd pinched myself too many times to believe otherwise.

I had to get away from the school—from Griffin. I burst through the front door of the building. When the blast of cold air rushed against me.

"Kate?"

I screamed. I couldn't help it. I didn't know who I expected to see, but Charlie's face in the dark courtyard seemed so out of place, so *normal* compared to the freak-fest I'd just left.

"Are you okay? What are you still doing here?" His eyes were so kind behind his serious expression. "Did someone hurt you?"

"Ch-Charlie." I started sobbing like an idiot. He patted my arm, but I couldn't answer. What would I say? I'd just spent a day with a guy who claimed he wasn't even alive?

Charlie's attention zeroed in on me. "Okay, I'm not going to ask you any tough questions, but I just need to know. Are you hurt?"

"No." Aside from being freaked out and having my heart ripped from my chest and thrown on the ground? I was great. I tried to pull away from Charlie. I had to get out of there. "I have to go home."

Then it hit me. I'd left my coat inside, and my wallet.

How would I get home? I couldn't call Mom. She'd just see it as more ammunition to get me to agree to the California thing.

Before I could have called my dad anytime day or night, and he would have come. He would have been pissed, but he would have come.

Charlie gripped my arm. "The busses stop running after midnight."

"After midnight?" How had it gotten so late? Mom would've been worried sick. I reached for my cell phone, but remembered I'd left it in the bathroom. No way was I going back in there.

"You can't walk it."

"I kn-know." My world had been turned upside down. Nothing was familiar.

Charlie's face softened. "Let me call you a cab."

"Do you know what that'll cost me? I live all the way out in Bridgeville."

"I got a friend, a guy who owes me a favor. Just go in the shack. I'll call him. You can wait in there where it's warm."

"Thanks, Charlie."

I shivered without my coat. I didn't glance back at the house as I stepped inside the booth. Charlie dropped a hoodie over my shoulders. It smelled like spearmint.

I took a seat on the chair inside the shack to wait for Charlie's friend and held my hands over the heater. I wasn't too thrilled about heading home and dealing with Mom, but she was a known entity, at least. Whereas Griffin . . .

The cab pulled up to the curb about ten minutes later. "He's here." Charlie had returned from the front gates, where he'd been waiting for his friend. Probably freezing, too.

"Thanks." I moved past him. The cold air smacked me in the face, making my legs unsteady. I began to shrug out of Charlie's hoodie.

Charlie touched my arm. "Keep it."

I wanted to smile and tell him everything would be okay. But how could I when some intrinsic part of me had broken? "Thanks." I couldn't drum up any words of comfort. There'd been nothing tranquil about my experience inside that house.

"Charlie?"

"Yeah?"

"I left my clarinet and my bag downstairs." I pushed down the bubble of panic threatening to close off my throat. The idea of leaving Benny behind was like voluntarily giving up a limb, but it had to be done.

Charlie's eyes widened. He seemed to brace himself. "I'll make sure no one takes them."

"Thanks." I climbed into the cab's warm interior. It smelled faintly of tobacco and Taco Bell—an oddly comforting combo. I rattled off my address to the cab driver before turning back to the window.

My breath hitched. Griffin stood on the balcony, his pale form semi-transparent in the rush of falling snow. My heart ached, as if I'd left half of it behind in Byrons School with Griffin. I raised a hand to touch the glass as the cab pulled away. My eyes stayed on him until the last possible moment.

Street signs blew past me as we left the North Side and headed toward the West End Bridge. The farther we traveled, the heavier my eyelids became, until I couldn't prop them open anymore.

The instant I closed them, the voice filtered into my ear as though I'd been sharing a cab.

The end is coming. Blood of my blood, the hour of my vengeance is near.

A chill swept over me, as potent as any I'd experienced on the fourth floor. It was cold, so cold. *Too cold.* Surely, if I opened my eyes, I'd see my breath.

"Hey, we're here." The driver's voice jerked me awake, and I opened my eyes to find him knocking on the ceiling of the cab's interior.

"Thank you." I reached into my pocket in vain.

"Charlie's taken care of it." He shot me this wide smile, which told me the guy probably didn't owe Charlie any favors. Charlie must've paid my fare in full, out of his own pocket.

"Thanks." I climbed out of the cab and into the night, crossing the darkened row of parking spaces until I reached my small front porch. Searching the rocks hiding in the small plot in front of the house, I found our hide-a-key and let myself in.

Locking up behind me, I leaned back against the door. "Mom?"

But there was no answer. I checked all three bedrooms, both bathrooms, and the basement, turning on every light in the house as I went. I lifted one of the slats on the blinds covering the font window and stared out into the inky darkness. Her car was gone. Where was she?

We didn't have a house phone, and without my cell, I couldn't call her. Maybe it was better she wasn't there. I didn't want to think about the question Griffin had asked me. The one about my family and how well I *really* knew them.

He'd called me a witch. Or, at least, he thought I might be one.

Maybe it's best if you don't make any wishes, pumpkin. They always seem to come true in the weirdest ways.

But that didn't mean anything. The whole thing was ridiculous. I knew who my parents were.

CHAPTER 26
GRIFFIN

Mɪɴᴜsᴄᴜʟᴇ sɴᴏᴡꜰʟᴀᴋᴇs ʀᴇsᴛᴇᴅ ꜰᴏʀ ᴀ ʙᴇᴀᴛ ᴏɴ ᴛʜᴇ backs of my neck and hands before melting. When had I last felt snow? Breathed it in? Back home, for certain. Snow had fallen across our quiet fields. Deer had raced across the frozen grass, leaving trails in the white. When I'd been smaller, Mother and I would partake of heated chocolate in her study. I'd play for her.

But that night's snow was different. It only reminded me how far I was from home. I'd never see Fulton House again. And it was likely I'd never see Kate, either. That realization was more unbearable.

Emptiness enveloped me. The cold prick of the falling snow faded. Soon, I could no longer smell it. The wind's bite couldn't touch me. Something clattered to the ground, and I realized I'd been holding Kate's electronic rectangle.

I was a spirit once more.

Standing on the balcony, I watched as the hired car took Kate away into the night.

Some dim part of me sensed Hannah. "She could have died tonight." My words were calm, controlled, but inside me, it was chaos.

I reached for the railing before me, but I didn't have the strength to make the connection. My fingers slid through it as if it were constructed of water and not iron.

"Do you know what happened?" Hannah took up a space on the balcony beside me. She toyed with a set of beads around her neck.

"Minna showed her my death. Then tried to kill Kate. Thank goodness she cried out, otherwise, I might not have found her in time." I hadn't seen Minna with Kate; however, her description of the woman was too compelling to ignore. "I should have expected something bad would happen to Kate if we allowed ourselves to become entangled."

"You could never have predicted this. Besides, it was inconceivable to you that you could ever love anyone other than yourself."

I faced Hannah, doing my best to ignore her knowing smirk. "Love? Rubbish."

"You intervened when she was endangered, you've been coaching her twice a day. This isn't the Griffin I know."

"Kate's just an amusement. It's hardly love." But even I recognized the lack of conviction in my own words.

"Is that why you just tore through the house screaming her name when she disappeared?"

I winced at the memory.

"Amusements are quickly forgotten, but love . . ."

"Hannah." I opened my mouth to argue my case, but closed it.

The memory of Kate's gray eyes flashed into my mind, bringing with it the sensation of her hand in mine, her mouth on mine.

Kate made me want to be different. Better.

How could I have fooled myself so completely? Kate wasn't just an amusement. She was everything.

I *had* fallen in love—with Kate.

But she'd almost died because of me. My hands fisted. I hated the sudden feeling of helplessness that followed.

"I don't know what I'll do if something happens to her. She claims she doesn't know anything about Minna or being a witch. She was shocked when I told her my theory. I think she's convinced she's from a normal family. "

"But you don't believe her?"

"She's definitely not familiar with Minna or the curse. No."

Hannah frowned, seeming thoughtful. She placed her hand on my shoulder. "Maybe it's better if you two have some time apart."

"Time apart? Why?" It was the last thing I wanted. I loved her. I needed to see her again. To try and explain.

"Because . . . of this." She left the balcony and returned just as quickly with a parcel. She unwrapped it, her brow furrowed in concentration. The simple act of tearing the paper probably exhausted her more than collecting the item itself had. After several moments, she drew the paper aside and revealed a book.

On the cover was a picture of me, taken on the night of my performance at the Queen's Hall in London. Beside it, written in small print, was the title: *Chasing Griffin Dunn.*

"God." I accepted the title from Hannah, staring at my

own face—the face of the other me. The one who used to be alive. We were different people.

But even that did not surprise me as much as the author's name.

"Liam Underhill?" *Dear God.* That was a name I hadn't heard mentioned in over a century. "Is he any relation to Jiggory Underhill, my old manager?"

"He is. A great-great grandson or something or other."

"Where did you find this?"

Hannah sighed, resting her index finger against the cover. "There are several bookshop window displays. There's even a concert."

One of Jig's descendants wrote a book about me. I'd barely begun to think it through when I latched onto Hannah's words. "A concert? Of what?"

"I don't know, but my point is, Kate's bound to see this. And when she does . . ."

"I told her the truth about me tonight, Hannah. That's why she's gone. She didn't believe me."

"Can you blame her?"

"No." The jumbled thoughts in my mind rearranged themselves until a new melody began to form. "But maybe this is exactly what I've been needing?" I didn't bother to fight the grin forcing its way onto my face. "Kate will have to believe me now."

"I don't think you're seeing the broader picture. Kate might believe you, but what about the people who've seen you since you've been with her? That boy, Ryder. The security guard, Charlie."

"Hadn't thought of that." I handed the book back to Hannah, who accepted it.

"We'll have to hide you . . . that will be easy enough to do."

"I'm not going to hide, Hannah." My own words surprised even me.

"Just walk away. Protect yourself. You've certainly done it before." Hannah shook her head as she picked up the wrappings.

"I think . . ." No, whatever I'd become, it wasn't indecisive. "I love her, Hannah."

Hannah sighed, clasping her hands together. "I knew it! I should have placed a wager on the outcome. A pity I've no money."

"Glad you find my romantic life so entertaining." But I couldn't be angry with her. "It doesn't matter, however. She won't be back. She didn't believe me."

"She loves you, Griffin."

My heart must have stopped. Again. "You can't know . . ."

"I may be dead, but I'm still a woman."

Kate, in love with me? Yet somehow, I believed it as surely as if Kate'd told me herself. She continued working her beads with more intensity, the clacking sound sending little echoes scattering over the bricks.

"I think we need to find someone to help you, Griffin."

"I'm listening." *Pointless though it may be.*

"They have people now—psychics they call them."

"Like a fortune-teller? They're two-bit hacks who con money from the weak."

"Perhaps you're right, in some cases. But there are those who seem to tune in to a wavelength of a different kind. One of them might be able to call on Minna and find out about Kate and your curse."

"You're suggesting I contact a clairvoyant? How? Purchase an advertisement in the *Times*?"

Hannah chuckled. "No. Kate works at a coffee shop, and her boss, Rena, is a seer—"

"Probably an untrustworthy swindler."

"On the contrary, she's quite reliable. I attended a séance there once. I was most impressed. Ask Kate to arrange it."

"You're fooling yourself, Hannah. How can I ask anything of her after what I've done, after the position I've put her in?"

"It's worth a try."

"Fine. What happens if this Rena picks up on the fact I'm dead?"

"She's a psychic. I'm sure she comes across strange things all the time."

"I'll ask Kate to have Rena come here. If she'll even speak to me again."

"I can take a message to her." Hannah raised an eyebrow, waiting.

"Do it." I didn't want the chance to talk myself out of it. "Send for her, but in a couple of hours, after she's had some sleep. And don't scare her, Hannah. If you do . . ." I let the threat hang in the air.

"Why, I wouldn't scare a soul, Griff. You know that." Before I could argue the point, Hannah faded to nothingness, leaving me alone with my thoughts.

I suppressed a smile as I stared out into the night. Kate. Kate was the one. The one who would free me. And she would be back. Especially if everything Hannah said was true.

And Hannah was always right.

CHAPTER 27

KATE

When I opened my eyes, the digital clock beside my bed read two fifteen a.m. Panic shot through me.

Griffin.

But I couldn't think about him. Not yet.

Shoving the covers aside, I jumped out of the bed and flicked on the light. I tugged on a pair of jeans and a sweater —one Dad had bought me last year for my birthday.

I padded out into the hallway and glanced into my mom's bedroom. Empty. Same as it had been when I'd arrived home. That was super strange and not like her at all. I searched every square inch of our home, but the townhouse was empty. Even the basement.

How could I ever explain what had happened with Griffin? Even then, my brain struggled to figure it out. There had to have been some logical answer.

The things I'd seen, though . . . like the woman in the bathroom . . . two people dying . . .

There was nothing rational about any of it.

How well do you know your family?

Did Mom still have that old bible? The one with her family tree? It wouldn't take long to search for it. At the very least, I could prove to Griff that he didn't know what he was talking about. I hesitated outside the doorway to her room; I didn't want her to come home and find me searching through her stuff, but it had to be done.

Turning on the lights inside my parents' room, I reached for the bible on the bottom shelf of Mom's nightstand. Sliding to the edge of the bed, I flipped open the front pages until I found the family tree section.

Each side had been filled in for at least four generations. They were names I recognized. Dad's parents. Mom's parents. I knew everyone on the list.

Moving straight to Dad's dresser, I yanked out the first drawer, sending Dad's old shaving box rattling on the wooden top. I searched the contents of the drawer. A prayer card from Dad's funeral, an address book, and a stack of random receipts.

Dad had been an expert at hiding things. There was this time we'd played hide and seek when I was a kid. I'd looked everywhere, gone around the house dozens of times.

He'd been lying on the couch with a blanket over him the entire time. The blanket had matched the couch exactly. He'd had to give himself up.

Sometimes the best hiding places are right in front of your nose—something that's hidden in plain sight.

Dad's teasing smirk filled my head. That time suddenly felt very far away, as though I'd aged a century since we'd played that game.

Something hidden in plain sight.

My eyes flew to the shaving box. When I was a kid, I'd called it the Box of Secrets.

"What's the box for, Daddy?" I'd ask him.

"It's a box of secrets."

My eyes would grow round. "What sort of secrets?" I'd try to pry it open, but I never could.

He'd shake his head. "I don't know. There's no key." Then we'd make up stories about what secrets might be inside and go on grand, pretend adventures looking for the key.

When I got older, Mom had told me he kept his shaving supplies in there. He'd locked it so I wouldn't mess with the cream and get it in my eyes or handle the razor when I was little. It had lost its magic for me then.

I lifted the box from its home. It wasn't heavy as I carried it back to my room. It also wasn't overly large, about the size of a really thick paperback book. The wood warmed my hands somehow. As though its contents had been heated. Resting the box on the bed, I tried to open it, but the lid wouldn't budge. I turned the box upside down. I even shook it. Something soft rattled inside. I turned it upside down. Nothing.

But who locks a shaving box? Especially one placed so high up I never could have reached it as a little kid.

A string of unusual symbols had been carved onto its lid. They'd always seemed familiar to me. But just like when I'd first seen them, I had no idea what any of them meant. I turned the box over in my hands, searching each side. No keyhole.

Where a keyhole would normally have been, a tiny tree shape had been cut out inside a metal circle. Its branches extended beyond the little tree-shaped hole, wrapping around the box in a series of carvings.

"Ouch!" Jerking my hand away from the box, I stared at my finger. Something had broken the skin. I didn't have to look hard, either. Protruding from the small circle was a tiny blade, as long as a pinhead and razor thin. It tugged against my finger. It was almost as if the blade itself had sucked some of my blood before it withdrew and merged back inside the box.

A moment later, the tree symbol changed color, turning bright red as what I could only assume was my blood filled it. It spread, trailing from one end of the tree to the other, until each of the markings had been stained crimson. A soft hissing sound filled the room, and then the blood, my blood, faded away, like it had been absorbed into the box.

A soft click followed. The box popped open.

What the hell kind of box was this? Did Dad know what had to be done to open it? Dad hadn't wanted me to see what was in the box. That yucky feeling I always got when I did something wrong rushed over me. Maybe I should have left it alone?

But if I wasn't supposed to see what was inside, how was I able to open it? Was the box about something bad he'd done? I lifted the lid.

Talk about anti-climactic. I didn't know what I expected, but there wasn't much inside the Box of Secrets except some papers.

The first was a birth certificate. At least I thought that's what it was. It had been written in another language. German, maybe. I could translate enough to understand the important points. It was for someone named Katya Christel.

Under what I assumed was the parents' names section,

a woman's name, Daniela Christel, had been listed, along with another, very familiar name: Brian Covington.

My dad had another child with some other woman? *Oh my God. Not Dad.*

There was an address, too, in Baden-Württemberg, Germany. And a date of birth—February fifteenth, 2000. It was my birthday.

My chest heaved as I stared at the document in my hand. What the hell? Did I have a sister? But a sister with the same birthday as me? Unless I had a twin? But why was she in Germany? And how come I'd never met her?

Warning bells sounded in my head, but I blocked them out. Setting the paper aside, I reached for the next item.

A baby picture of me. It was the same one that still sat on Dad's desk in the spare room. He'd refused to replace it, no matter how much I'd complained.

A smile tugged at my lips. I turned the picture over. On the back, in my father's handwriting, it read *Katya, my Katherine. Two days old.*

A cold fear slammed into my gut. Katya. *Minna* had called me Katya.

According to everything I'd found, *I* was Katya. And I was German. Griffin had been right.

At the bottom of the box, I found a final piece of paper —a series of lines and notes on some sort of parchment. A family tree. I glanced at the names; they were all people I'd never met and wouldn't recognize if I had. At the very bottom, I found a name: *Katya.*

My gaze swept over the other names on the tree. Goose bumps washed over me and I shook, but not from the cold.

Minna. There it was. Three steps above Katya's on the tree. Minna Christel.

God. And if Griffin had known about that, what else

had he been telling the truth about? Had he really been cursed?

Something moved in my peripheral vision, and I glanced up to find my mother standing in the doorway. A suite of emotions hit me at once. "Mom? Who's this Katya person?"

A pained look crossed her face. She let out a slow breath. "She's you. You're Katya Christel."

I swallowed; my overworked brain could only latch on to one fact: "You're not my mom?"

She wrapped her arms around her torso like she was giving herself a hug. "Oh, baby. I am your mother, just not by blood."

"What?" Whatever I'd thought I'd find in the box, it wasn't that. Never that.

"Honey, I'm sorry. We never wanted you to find out like this."

"Is Dad really my father?" I choked out the question. My room spun. I fisted my hands in my rumpled bedspread as I waited for her answer.

"Yes, he was."

The world I'd known, every belief about the *Kate* I'd been familiar with, spiraled around me in a vortex of confusion. "I don't understand. Why didn't you tell me? Who is this Daniela?" My voice sounded flat, cold.

Mom walked over and sat beside me on the end of the bed. She rested her hand on my shoulder, but I shrugged it off.

"Dad met her on a work trip before we'd gotten together. Their romance didn't last long. Daniela ended their relationship, and your Dad left Germany." She shook her head. "But when we were on our honeymoon in France,

Daniela found us. Your dad didn't know about you until Daniela contacted us."

"It wasn't an affair?" I didn't want to think about Dad cheating on Mom, even if she wasn't my real mom.

"No. Things happened so fast for us." She smiled through the tears slipping down her cheeks. "We were married in less than a year. I couldn't have any kids of my own, but you know Dad, he didn't care. He just wanted me." Mom blushed.

"You couldn't have kids?"

"No. We figured we might adopt one day. You were an unexpected answer to prayers we hadn't even said yet. Then your dad met you. I couldn't say no to him."

I could hear Dad's enthusiasm in her words, almost visualize it. When something really mattered to him, his eyes would brighten, and he practically bounced off the floor.

"We loved you immediately. You were just instantly a part of our lives—like you were supposed to be here. You have your dad in you." Unshed tears rested on the red rims of her eyes.

Someone, some invisible person, must have reached inside and squeezed my heart. That was what it felt like anyway. I focused on the worn tread on the carpet by the door instead.

"Did he have a DNA test or anything to prove I'm his daughter?" I held my breath.

"You know your dad. When Daniela told him you were his daughter, he didn't need to hear anything else. He signed the custody papers and you came home with us."

"But what if I'm not his? She could have lied. I could be anyone's kid."

"No, you couldn't." Mom smiled again. "You have his eyes. It was so obvious you were his daughter."

"Where is she? Daniela, I mean?"

My mom frowned—the look she got when she was trying to come up with the right thing to say. "Sweetie, we got word she died almost a year after we brought you home. It was the day you started taking your first steps."

Daniela, my *real* mother, was dead. How could my parents have hidden something like that from me? "How did she die?"

"I don't know. The letter wasn't signed and there was no return address. You know the song your dad used to sing to you?"

"Yeah."

"Daniela used to sing that same song to you when you were a baby. *For all who roam without a home, follow love, follow light, follow peace.* Remember?"

"I remember." I swallowed down the acid rising up my throat.

"She wanted your dad to know the song so you'd have something from her. Daniela was a musician, too." Mom chuckled. "She had to translate it from German. He wasn't very good at pronouncing the words."

How can she possibly laugh about anything when my life is falling apart?

Mom rested her head on my shoulder. "I'm sorry you had to learn the truth this way. But know this, Kate. I'll always be your mother."

God. I'd been confused about who I was before, but I'd never known myself at all.

At one time, I'd thought I could trust my parents, that they would always tell me the truth. I didn't know if I trusted myself anymore, let alone anyone else.

"Why didn't you guys tell me?"

"Daniela begged us to keep your identity a secret. She claimed it wasn't safe."

"Why?"

My mom glanced behind her shoulder for a moment, before leaning closer. "You came with two sets of papers. One with your German identity and an American one Daniela had had made for you. She didn't just ask us to take you. She asked us to *hide* you. "

"From who?" A rushing sound filled my ears as I processed her words. Memories of Minna trying to force me through the skylight rushed at me.

"I don't know. We just took you and did what she asked, but we think her family was involved in some sort of witchcraft."

"They were witches?" My voice dropped so low I wasn't sure she heard me. "That's why I wasn't supposed to wish for anything?"

My mom looked fearful. "It seemed safer to just do as Daniela asked. To get you as far away as possible and never mention the *M* word."

It took me a moment to get what she meant. The *M* word. Magic. A headache began, pounding at the base of my skull. "Did anyone ever come after me?"

"No, Kate. After the first couple of years, we grew more comfortable. Nothing ever came of it."

Why did that have to be the one time she got my name right? When I'd just found out it didn't even belong to me? "Do I have any brothers or sisters? Or is it just me?"

"Just you."

"What happens now? You go to California and I go to an orphanage or something?" *Oh, God.*

"Kate Covington. You are my daughter. It doesn't

matter whether or not my name is on your birth certificate. I'm the one who raised you. I love you."

"I love you, too, Mom. But I don't want to go to California. I can't."

"Don't worry about it. I haven't even boarded the plane yet. One thing at a time. We can talk more over Christmas break, okay?"

Novocain-like numbness kept some of my larger feelings at bay, but it wouldn't last. Sooner or later, I'd lose my shit. "Where were you last night?"

"Looking for you. You didn't answer your phone." Leaning over, she wrapped her arms around me just as she'd done when I was a child and I'd gotten sick. "Where were you?"

"I was with a friend, like I told you, and then I came home. I forgot my phone, though." Mom had deep smudges under her eyes. She'd probably driven all over the North Side and the city looking for me. "I'm sorry I couldn't pick up."

"I'm just glad you're okay." Mom touched a hand to my cheek.

I wanted to melt into it and forget anything bad had ever happened. "I think I wanna be alone for a while."

Mom stood, kissing my head. "Okay, Kate." And with that, she turned and walked out of my room, leaving me alone.

Maybe it was better that way. If I was in any kind of danger, would it extend to Mom? Maybe going out of town would keep Mom safe.

She'd been gone less than a minute when the skin on my arms prickled with gooseflesh as the temperature dropped. Where was that cold coming from? Mom hadn't opened a window. But then my stomach knotted with dread.

Oh my God, Minna. She'd followed me home.

Click, click, click.

Click, click, click.

It almost sounded like . . . typing. I glanced in the direction of my laptop. The screen had illuminated. My heart pounded as I watched a message appear on my computer screen, one letter at a time.

A message I wasn't typing.

Kate, I'll be waiting for you. I hope you'll come back to me. — Griffin

I reread the message several more times. I didn't understand everything I'd experienced with Griffin or what I'd found out about my family, but he'd been telling the truth about a lot of things. And he seemed to know more about my family than I did. I should at least hear him out.

Besides, as stupid as it sounded, I wanted to hold his hand again.

CHAPTER 28
GRIFFIN

Friday, December 9th—Six Days Left Until Juries

A MILLION MOMENTS SURELY PASSED WHILE I WAITED for Kate. Would she come? What if she didn't? Within a few weeks of knowing her, my tightly bound, caustic personality had somehow unraveled and been laid bare for all to see. I'd never realized how vulnerable love could make me. Yet, what I felt for Kate far exceeded mere love.

From where I sat at the foot of the upwards staircase. The quiet of the lobby shifted. The sound of the heating system grew louder. A slight chill brushed my skin. My body stretched, my heartbeat thudded. It could only mean one thing.

The front door squeaked open. Kate stepped inside and paused, leaning against the doorframe. Her red-rimmed eyes were puffy. She'd been crying.

"You're late."

She jerked a thumb to the door behind her. "Charlie wanted to know how I was. I gave him a scare last night."

"You gave me one. I wondered if you'd come back." I longed to hold her, to tell her it had all been a bad dream. But that would have been a lie.

"You were right," she said, her whispered words just reaching my ears.

Oh, that can only mean . . . "Tell me."

"My parents . . . well, my mother isn't my mother." Tears trailed down her face. "I have a different name. *Katya.* Just like Minna called me. I'm Katya Christel. Turns out I am related to Minna."

There was nothing I could say. No way to ease the hurt that had overtaken her. "How do you know?"

"I found a family tree and a birth certificate." She crossed the lobby and then leaned against the banister for support. "I'm not even Kate." Her voice broke at the tail end of her name.

I stood, but kept my distance. No point in sending her running again. "No matter what discoveries you make, you are, first and foremost, always Kate."

"Thank you." Her gray eyes were more serious than I'd ever seen them. "And . . . there's more. I Googled you this morning."

Pity I had no idea what she was talking about.

"You . . ." She withdrew a printed piece of paper and thrust it toward me. Damnation. That blasted book with my picture was front and center on the paper.

"I tried to tell you." I reached into my pocket and offered her the communications rectangle she'd left in the bathroom. I was pleased to be rid of it. Though it had played Chopin all night, it only featured the one song.

She trembled as she took back the square, returning it to her bag. "Everything you told me was the truth?"

"Yes. I'm sorry, Kate. I didn't know how to tell you. Then I had to." It was the worst sort of moment.

With care, I rose to my feet. I took a single step in her direction. She didn't run.

Every part of me ached to hold her again, as I'd done the day before. Would my future be void of moments like that?

"I didn't get to read it all, just the sample, but . . . the Griffin Dunn in this story . . . died in 1902."

"Yes." I tried to keep my voice even. Didn't break eye contact.

"He was a murderer. Did you kill that little boy?" Her eyes crinkled at the corners.

Why did that have to be the one piece of information she'd picked up first?

"I'm not a murderer, Kate. I was selfish—cruel to Jonah. But I've never taken a life." My throat thickened with emotion. Why? I'd become a master of concealment. Someone who kept his emotions locked away, but somehow Kate had the key.

Kate didn't argue, but seemed instead to focus on her shoes. "Last night, on the balcony, you appeared to . . . fade away. You seemed *transparent*."

"It's like I explained. When you are with me, I am living, breathing. Yet, in your absence, I return to what I was."

"A ghost." Her words sounded strangled.

I nodded. "When you left, I changed back. Perhaps having Minna's blood in you means you can always see me."

"Then show me. Disappear in front of me or something." She placed her hands at her hips. A spark of Kate's usual fire flashed in her eyes.

"I can't. You're making me appear this way. No matter what I might want, I have no control over your effect on me." I did not fail to comprehend the double meaning in my own words. "You'll have to trust me."

"Do you know how hard it is for me to trust people?" Kate covered her face with her hands, peering at me from behind slim, white fingers. "I don't think I have a choice. I still have to pass my jury."

An invisible lance pierced my heart. She only wished to associate with me for the purposes of a school test? "Benny is still downstairs. Everything is just as you left it." I held out my hand.

"Griffin." All of her emotions were laid bare in her expression—longing, fear, confusion . . . and love.

So, it wasn't *solely* about her jury.

I framed her face in my hands, tracing the shape of her lips with my own. I took my time, reacquainting myself with her mouth, memorizing the softness. It was a sweet, gentle sort of torture that sent my blood singing.

Thoughts and words and everything in between melted away as she pressed her body against mine. I cupped the back of her head, prepared to ravage her mouth, when I remembered where we were. Forcing myself to break our kiss, I stepped back, my own breath heavy. "You'll be the death of me."

Her pink tongue darted out to lick her lips. My throat ran dry.

Dear God.

"We should rehearse for your jury."

"Okay, but I'd better not regret giving you another chance, fancy pants." Despite her sarcasm, her voice wobbled. She was just as jarred by our kiss as I was.

"My trousers shall remain ever-fancy in your eyes."

But though she laughed, I couldn't shake the unsettled sensation in my stomach. Kate had revealed exactly what I'd believed from the beginning—that she had a direct connection to Minna. I'd been so concerned about hiding my past from Kate, but what if she was the one with the secrets?

WE DECIDED IT BEST TO FORGO REHEARSAL THAT morning, to discuss Kate's findings. She sat near the fireplace in my room, with a large pile of disposable handkerchiefs from the ladies' facilities on her lap. Her fingers were intertwined with mine, but that didn't help her shaking. I couldn't tell if it was from her emotions or the temperature. Kate seemed to be perpetually cold.

"God, when Dad told me the box was a box of secrets, I never thought he meant it. We used to make up games, adventures about it, you know? I never believed there could be anything important inside."

"He probably assumed there'd be safety in giving it an obvious name."

"It worked." She sniffled, bunching her arms around herself even more tightly.

"I'm sorry for bringing you into this." Taking one of the handkerchiefs, I wiped at a stray tear she'd missed. "You believe me now, about the curse? About Minna?"

"Yeah." Kate bit her bottom lip.

"I just wish I knew why she suddenly appeared out of nowhere and why she tried to kill you. I can't even pinpoint how you stopped it from happening." My own nerves jangled at the memory. That Kate had survived was a miracle. One I didn't deserve.

"Don't freak out, okay? I have a . . . secret, too."

I remembered all too well my own feelings the previous night when I'd been in her position. "Whatever it is, you can share it with confidence."

"Whenever I let myself wish for something . . . deliberately . . . I get it. I *always* get what I want."

I toyed with the hem of her shirtsleeve. "There's nothing wrong with being determined."

She shook her head. "No, it's more than that. If I wish a bus would come early, it does. If I want a good grade on a test I didn't study for, I get it . . . don't you understand? If I wish for something, it always happens."

"But everyone wishes, even subconsciously."

"Not me." Kate leaned toward me. "Listen to me. I could win the lottery if I wanted to. My parents knew the truth. That's why they asked me not to make any wishes."

"You said Minna was a witch. You thought I was one, too. What if I am? What if I've been working spells or something this entire time without knowing it?"

Then something occurred to me. "And you think that's how you ended up on the fourth floor?"

"I know it." She shifted on the hearth. "I made a wish."

I drew back, focusing on her face. "And you wished to end up on the fourth floor."

"I didn't mean to. It was just a random thought. I wished to learn the truth about you."

"Looks like you got your wish." I made no attempt to filter the acid from my tone. "And you couldn't wait a single day?"

"Griffin, I—"

"No, Katherine. I promised I would explain everything to you today, and you doubted me. You doubted my word."

"No—"

"Do you think me dishonest?"

"No, I—"

"Find me fearful?"

"No—"

"Then what could you have been thinking?"

"I was thinking I'm in love with you, dammit!"

My mouth fell open. I couldn't dream up a single response. "Love?"

"Yes, you big jerk. I love you."

Kate's words washed over me. A balm on my scarred soul. She loved me.

"I wanted to know more about you. Do you think I wanted to be on that stupid fourth floor?" Kate stood, her face flushed, her chest heaving.

"I would have told you. I just needed time." If I was going to win Kate, I would be unable to hide even one piece of myself from her. And I didn't want to.

"I've fallen in love with you, too, Kate."

She bit her bottom lip, her eyes wide. I held my breath for one . . . two . . . three . . . four quarter beats.

"No one's ever been in love with me before." Her voice sounded small—shy in a way Kate most certainly was not. Dropping to her knees, Kate slid her frigid hands into my hair.

My breath caught as she brushed her lips against mine. The room rocking back and forth like a metronome as our mouths met again and again. We kissed while all the world spun around us. Until Kate rested her forehead against my chest and drew me close.

"You see the problem we face? You're alive, and I'm . . ."

"Temporarily indisposed." Kate's smirk returned. It was good to have her back.

"Yes," I said. "I don't have the answer as to how to break this curse, but I know you're the key. Your connection to

Minna and your ability to transform me into a living, breathing human being can't be for nothing. There has to be a reason you're involved."

"That's it." Kate jumped up, her face pure sunshine.

"I don't understand. What is it?"

"Don't you see? All I have to do is wish your curse away." She closed her eyes, bunching up her face. "I wish to free Griffin Dunn. I wish to end the curse against him."

Kate opened her eyes, and I kissed her, softly, just a faint brush of my lips against hers. She tasted like salty tears and sweet dreams about to be broken.

"That means the world to me, my dearest. Yet, I have a feeling much more will be required before this curse changes one way or the other."

But she shook her head, denial reigning supreme. "You'll see. I'll fix this, and we'll be able to stay together."

"If your wish comes true, then I promise to give you the world." If only I could find a way to explain to her my wishes had stopped coming true the moment my life had ended.

"WHAT HAPPENED AFTER YOU DIED?" KATE SAT NEXT to me on the divan, where I'd just spent the past fifteen minutes or so plundering her mouth.

"I don't remember anything that happened when I died. There was just this point a few weeks later when I confronted Minna. That's when I figured out what happened to me for certain. Then the Byrons closed the house and I was on my own."

"And you've never left the grounds in all this time?"

I shook my head, suppressing a shudder at the thought

of what happened every time I tried. "I can't leave. You heard the curse."

"Then how were you in my room this morning?" She seemed less afraid then—more curious.

Grimacing, I took her hand in mine. When Hannah had suggested visiting Kate, it had sounded like a good idea. "That wasn't exactly me, though the message was mine."

She tensed. "It wasn't you?"

"It was Hannah. She's the other spirit here. She's much more . . . let's say *diverse* in her pursuits."

"Wait." She sat up, her eyes narrowing. "Is Hannah an old woman?"

Oops.

"Young lady!" Hannah's outraged cry filled the room. "You have no business calling me old."

To Kate's credit, she didn't flinch, but stood, sliding her hands to her hips. "You."

Part of me had assumed, rather naively, I would never have to introduce Kate and Hannah. "Kate, may I introduce Hannah Byrons."

"You're the one from the practice room." Kate let out a long, slow breath.

Hannah took her preferred spot beside my piano. "Yes."

"You had no business showing up in an air vent, scaring me, and ruining my number one reed. Who do you think you are?" Kate trembled.

Hannah raised a hand to her throat with all the haughtiness of an Italian opera singer I'd seen perform once. I doubted Hannah'd ever been spoken to like that in her entire life—or *death*. "Griffin told you. I am Hannah Byrons. The lady of this house."

"Well, you're a terrible host, lady," Kate spat.

I bit back a laugh.

Hannah fanned herself with her hand before sparing me a glance. "I like her, you know. She has gumption."

"Oh, she does." The pride I felt for Kate slipping into my voice.

"So help me understand. *She* can leave the building," Kate jerked a thumb at Hannah, "but you can't? Why?"

"Whenever I try to leave, something pulls me back to the parlor."

"And the parlor's where you . . ." Kate's eyes held nothing but intense understanding.

"Where I died, yes. Then I'm forced to witness Jonah die all over again . . . I suffer my own death again, as well. As you've surmised, it wasn't a pleasant one."

"That's how it has been in the past. But if you'll recall my suggestion, you might have a way around that," Hannah said.

"What suggestion?" Kate asked, seeming much more comfortable in Hannah's presence all of a sudden.

Hannah let out a breath. "What I'm thinking is, perhaps, with your connection to Minna, you'd be able to ask her about the curse, Kate."

"I don't exactly have oodles of conversations with dead people." Kate shredded one of the disposable handkerchiefs.

"No, but your friend Rena can." Hannah lowered herself to the edge of the brick fireplace beside Kate.

"Rena? What does Rena have to do with any of this? How do you know her?" Kate ceased her destruction of the paper products.

"She's a clairvoyant," Hannah offered. "I attended a séance there last October. Simply *delightful*. All the best spirits were in attendance. Oh, and I may have followed *you* there, just once or twice."

Kate gaped. "How am I supposed to ask her? *Hey*

Rena, contacted any freaky ghosts lately? It's not exactly typical employer-employee conversation." She must have caught something in my expression, because she added, "Sorry. I wasn't trying to say *all* ghosts are freaky, just *some*."

"Noted." I winked.

"Regardless of whether or not you've discussed it, Rena can contact spirits, and, more importantly, she *has*." Hannah patted the top of Kate's hand, but only managed to sink right through her. "If you can, I would ask her to help. She wouldn't be as shocked as someone, er, normal, might be."

"I don't see why not." But Kate bit her lip.

"Hannah, could you leave us, please?" I kept my eyes focused on Kate.

After a pause, Hannah answered, "Of course." In the space of a breath she'd left us.

The instant she'd gone, I took Kate in my arms. "If this Rena woman can't help us, that's all right. All I know is . . . I want to be with you."

"And I want to be with you." She pulled me close, her short, compact body a compliment to my own taller, gangly one. "I'll call Rena today, and maybe we can . . . go and see her."

"Wait. Hold on." I released her, turning to meet her eyes. "You remember what I told you about leaving. I simply can't." My newly restored heart pounded in my chest.

"I know you haven't been able to in the past, but you say you're alive when we're together. What if that means you can just walk out the front door when you're with me?" Kate balled up the handkerchiefs around her and then tossed them in a dust bin that probably hadn't been emptied in years. "Besides, Rena won't set foot in this building. She's terrified of it."

"You must be joking." A psychic being afraid of a haunted house? Who'd ever heard of such a thing? It was almost an insult to the spirit community.

Kate waited. How different I'd become from the jaded man I'd been even a few weeks ago. Kate and I had been together only two days, and already I didn't want to deny her anything. "Of course I'll try to go." I nodded, though my nerves remained taut.

"It'll be all right. This time, there will be something different about it—leaving I mean. You'll have something you didn't before." Her infectious smile returned, taking over her face.

"What?" I swallowed.

"Me. I'll be beside you." As if for emphasis, she interlaced her fingers with mine and squeezed.

"That, in and of itself, is a dream."

I only prayed it would be enough to save me.

CHAPTER 29
KATE

Freezing rain hit the windowpanes like sticks on a snare drum. I tapped along with the rhythm on the side of my bag as I walked. It should've been a totally different kind of day. I'd fallen in love, found out I had a different name, and discovered I had a different mother.

Somehow, despite everything I'd found out, I couldn't stop smiling. Griffin loved me.

Thinking of Griffin reminded me of my promise to contact Rena. Grabbing my phone, I texted her.

cn u do a séance 4 me?

Need ur hlp w/smth

I pressed Send and was about to stash my phone when it vibrated in my hand.

Mom.

Her picture took up the small screen. I could've ignored

her. Just put the phone in my bag and gone to class. It would've been easier to deal with her later.

But she had answers.

"Kate, are you coming to class?" Ryder's voice snapped me out of my trance.

When I glanced up, he had that nasty look on his face again. The one he'd worn when he'd dumped his coffee on Rena's counter.

"Who are you, Ryder, Suzy Hall Monitor?" A scowl pasted itself on my face.

Ryder's eyebrows jerked upward, like two twin caterpillars. "We're starting now. If you're coming, take your seat."

I glanced back at my phone, but I'd missed the call. *Thanks a lot, Ryder.*

My fingers felt stiff and tired as I trudged into the classroom. This was bound to be fun. I pulled Benny's case out and put his pieces together.

"Who was that hot guy you were with the other day?" The whispered question came from my right. Kimbany sat at the edge of her seat, a grin on her face. Clearly, she seemed to think we were besties, but whatever. She wanted an answer, I'd give her an answer.

"My boyfriend." Of course, as soon as I said the words, I wondered if I shouldn't have kept my big mouth shut. Griffin hadn't exactly said he was my boyfriend, but after all, he'd said he loved me.

"Your boyfriend? OMG. For reals? He's yummy-looking." Kimbany winked at me.

I didn't bother to suppress a smile as I thought about Griffin with his shirt off. "Yes, he is. I wouldn't tell him, though. He sort of has a pretty high opinion of himself."

"He has a right to, looking like that. It's amazing, really —his resemblance to the guy who died here," she said.

My blood chilled. "What do you mean?"

"Well, there's a plaque over by the piano studio. You know the wall that features all the different musicians who appeared in the school over the years? The one I'm talking about honors this guy who died here, like a hundred years ago or something. Griffin Dunn."

"Really?" I tried to keep my voice even, but curiosity took my heart rate up to *presto*. I'd seen the wall, but I'd never spent much time reading the historical markers. I doubted most people even knew they were there.

"Totally. I just happened to notice the Dunn one before I had a theory lesson. The picture on the plaque is a little grainy, but the guy looks so much like your boyfriend."

Clapping broke us apart. "Okay, let's get started," Ryder said.

Vaguely, I heard him leading the class, but mentally, I wasn't in the room anymore. I'd had no idea about the plaque. Would I have been onto Griffin sooner if I'd known?

What a shame no one even seemed to know it was there. Griffin deserved so much more.

SCALES CLASS WENT QUICKLY. SOMEHOW, POSSIBLY through divine intervention, I nailed my E-flat major scale. Yet, I couldn't concentrate on my success. My heart wouldn't stop racing. I had to see the memorial.

After class ended, I bolted out of my seat and down the hall. I looped around the floor so Kimbany wouldn't think I had any particular interest in what she'd said. Cutting back by the brass classrooms, I headed over to the piano section. I almost didn't see the plaque because it wasn't large—maybe the size of two regular sheets of paper, side by side.

I stopped when I found it, and so did time. A picture of Griffin, pompous-looking as he stood next to a grand piano, dominated the top section. He appeared cold, without a hint of a smile. My eyes locked onto Griffin's in the photo. It was like meeting the eyes of a stranger. Swallowing, I read the text.

Griffin Dunn of Warwickshire, England, born August 29th, 1886, was believed, despite his tragic demise at the age of sixteen, to be one of the most notable pianists of his time. Mr. Dunn began appearing internationally by age ten after he was discovered by Jiggory Underhill, his London manager. Noted interpretations included Beethoven's Moonlight Sonata, *which Dunn performed to a full house in London only weeks before his death. Mr. Dunn gave a concert at the Byrons estate on December 17th, 1902, at the request of Lord Helmrick Byrons, the ironworks magnate, who wished to sponsor Mr. Dunn. Tragically, the virtuoso died under mysterious circumstances following his performance. He was later implicated in the death of ten-year-old Jonah Byrons. But though a dark history shades his life, Griffin Dunn remains a musical icon and will leave a legacy of performances so powerful, they are beyond imagination.*

Below, the text, in small print, I read a single line aloud, "Sponsored jointly by the Underhill Family and the Byrons School of Music."

"Ah, so you found their quaint commemoration, did you?" Griffin asked from somewhere behind me.

I didn't realize I was crying until he spoke. He turned me around to face him.

"Love," he said, frowning. "You're crying. What's

wrong?" He reached up and wiped away some of my tears with the pad of his thumb.

My voice shook. "People really believe you murdered that little boy."

"Maybe they should believe it. He was only a child. Perhaps it's my rightful penance to be trapped here." He shrugged. The action made him seem so young. He could have been any teenager in any school in America. But he wasn't. He was a 130-year-old specter from England.

"No. You had no idea what he was planning to do." I stepped into his space and held him, wrapping my arms around him. "Your life . . . everything that's happened to you. You never even got a chance to live."

"Shh. I learned to deal with it all a long time ago." Griffin gave me a stiff pat on the back, drawing away. He didn't meet my eyes. The conversation was over.

Swallowing, I glanced at the plaque again. "You were born in 1886?"

He grimaced. "Does that bother you?"

I wiped at my tears and forced a straight face. "Yeah. Who knew I'd fall for an old man? Kinda creepy."

Griffin burst into laughter.

"You'd better get out of here. What if someone sees you beside this plaque?" As if on cue, I glanced up just as Ryder passed us on the other side of a support beam with a camcorder—probably the same camera he'd come into Rena's shop with.

Ryder didn't seem to see us, but then he glanced back. I quickly looked away, bringing my gaze back to Griffin's.

Griffin must have caught the expression on my face, though, because he glanced up just as Ryder walked down the hall. "That bloke hasn't been bothering you further, has he?"

"Mostly I try to avoid him. Though he came into Rena's shop the other day."

He raised an eyebrow. "And you felt this information was of so little import that you failed to mention it?"

"I handled it."

"Kate—"

My phone beeped. I pulled it out of my bag and scanned the screen.

What's going on? Can you come here at 3:30?

My face heated as the sensation of Griffin watching me took me over. "I got a text from Rena."

Griffin cocked an eyebrow in that equally endearing and frustrating way of his. "You're beautiful, dearest. A pity I've no idea what you just said."

Snorting, I offered him the phone. "Read it. It's called a text message."

"What a redundant title." But Griffin took the phone anyway.

I pretended not to notice his hand shaking as he read. He really was nervous about leaving the school. He'd see soon enough that the curse was broken. That was just how my wishes worked.

"A far cry from Western Union, but it will do." He held out my phone.

"Good." Taking the phone back, I keyed in my reply.

Yeah. See ya.

I pressed the Send button. When I glanced up, I caught Griffin's questioning gaze on me. "Can you meet me in the lobby at three?"

Griffin tensed. I didn't blame him. I'd have been freaked out, too. "Of course."

"It's going to be all right. I know you don't want to do this, but we need to try." I reached up to kiss him one more time. For just a second, I felt wobbly and out of tune, like those times when I couldn't hear the notes right and had trouble matching pitch.

Griffin's hot breath hit my neck. "Go to your classes before I decide to keep you."

I wanted to do anything but go to class, but I had to keep my grades up. Byrons didn't make exceptions for curses. "See you soon." Turning, I sprinted toward my next class, just as the bell rang.

CHAPTER 30

GRIFFIN

A STRANGE TASTE HAD WORMED ITS WAY INTO MY mouth, as though I'd been forced to digest substandard music. If this didn't work, I could be hurled into my own nightmare once more. God, I wanted nothing better than to leave with Kate and never return.

"Griffin!" Kate rushed up to me in the lobby, her face flushed. "I missed you."

Wrapping my arms around her, I tugged her close. "And I, you." When we parted, I blurted my news. "I haven't changed back."

Her eyes widened, and she rocked back onto her heels. "You haven't changed back since after Scales?"

She ran a finger along my collarbone, just above the neckline of my shirt. Lord, she had no idea what she was doing to me with that feather-light touch of hers. Things a gentleman could certainly not repeat aloud.

"No. Never. It probably signifies something ominous."

"Are you sure you want to do this, Griffin? Because we don't have to. I can tell her no. We can stay here."

"Are you saying you changed your mind?" Hadn't she been the one to talk me into such a foolhardy adventure in the first place?

"Even if we don't leave and can't talk to Rena, I'll understand. I'll still sneak into the building to see you." She smirked. Clearly, Kate saw nothing wrong with that image.

I, on the other hand, could visualize the scene Kate described all too clearly. Kate, stealing into the building, running into my arms. Kate aging while I remained paused in the middle of a concerto—for all eternity.

Then Kate dying, leaving me. Never living. Never moving on.

"No. I don't want that for you." The words tumbled from my mouth.

Kate's expression grew serious, her mouth straightening into a thin line. She'd read the finality in my voice.

"I love you. That was part of the curse, remember? I had to fall in love? Now I have—with you." Of course, I was terrified, but if I could leave with Kate, it would all be worth it. "Let's try it."

She drew in a slow breath and tightened her grip on my arms. "I'll be right beside you."

"Then I would go anywhere with you, Katherine." Even straight to the gates of hell.

Kate squeezed my hand, guiding me outside into the December chill. She slowed as she reached the veranda, and we stepped down into the courtyard. Christmas lights flashed in my peripheral vision, brightening the bleak afternoon. The smell of snow burned my nostrils.

"No matter what happens, just keep walking," Kate urged.

As though I could do anything else. I kept that thought to myself, however. The last thing I wanted was for Kate to think I didn't want to accompany her. Kate slowed as we approached the front gates.

Berlioz's *Symphonie Fantastique* filled my head. I couldn't help but hum the main theme from *March to the Scaffold.* "Daa-daa-dadada."

"Stop it," she hissed. "Berlioz is hardly going to put us in the right frame of mind. He was a depressed whiner."

Kate's musical knowledge pleased me, as did her take on the composer. I chuckled. "I don't know. I quite like his idea of getting back at an ex-lover through composition."

"It was totally pathetic. He should have gotten over it. Eaten a pint of ice cream or something."

"*Not* Berlioz then . . . We need something to take our minds off things. Mm." A game Mother and I used to play came to mind. "What's your favorite rainy-day music?" I glanced up at the cloud-covered sky. The white puffs were thick and heavy with snow that had yet to fall.

"Felix Mendelssohn, *Song Without Words.*"

"Not a clarinet piece?" We had twenty, maybe fifteen more beats until the boundary. My heart lodged itself in my throat.

"No. Clarinet pieces just remind me of how much work I have left to do." She sounded unconcerned, though she gripped my hand tighter within her own smaller one.

We were almost there—maybe ten beats away—our combined footsteps hitting the brick in near-unison.

"We all have work left to do, my dearest."

She snorted. "Except, apparently, you."

"We can't all be *me,* I suppose." But I realized, with

surprise, that I wasn't serious. "Actually, there are so many pieces I'd still like to learn. Even more that I want to—" I stopped myself. I was going to say *perform*.

Kate's eyes caught mine, understanding evident in their gray depths. Still, she didn't press, didn't ask for an explanation of the dreams I'd allowed to play *pianissimo* in my mind for so long.

"No." I stopped just inside the gates. "I can't, Kate. I just can't." My hand shook in hers, and I hated myself for that small weakness. I couldn't watch Jonah die again.

Kate took both of my hands in hers. "If you don't want to, I understand."

I let out a breath of air. Blessed relief. "Thank you, but we both know I'd be a coward if I didn't try this."

"Let's try together, okay?" Slowly, she began walking backward, leading me along. "I'm here. I'm right here with you." A few students milled about the courtyard, but they didn't seem to have noticed us. A good thing, since I might've vanished at any moment.

I counted off each beat, closing my eyes and letting Kate lead me.

One.

Two.

Three.

Four.

Five.

Six.

DEAR GOD. WE'D MADE IT THROUGH. NOT ONLY HAD I crossed the boundary of the gates the way a free man might, but we'd moved a block down the city street, beyond the property altogether. We walked along the thoroughfare, Kate's hand clasped tightly in mine.

Suddenly, she stopped in the very center of the sidewalk and her face lit. "We did it. Oh my God, you're—"

"Don't." I pressed my lips against Kate's, silencing her.

Her mouth came alive as she parted her lips against the onslaught. She whimpered, pressing her body against me, sweeping her tongue along mine. Every part of me awakened then, drawn in by her kiss, and our closeness. I broke the kiss, losing myself in the depths of her gray eyes, wanting to get lost in the rest of her.

"You'll be the death of me, Katherine," I whispered, drawing her closer, her warmth making me feel every degree of cold that filled the air around us. It wasn't enough. I wanted Kate wrapped around me, her skin against mine.

No. That couldn't happen. It was one thing to love her as I did, to kiss her, to *want* her. Making love to Kate would cross every boundary of propriety. I couldn't allow that, even if she seemed wholly unconcerned about her virtue.

A smile took over her face, making her seem, for an instant, like a glorious angel beneath the rays of the winter sun. She took my breath away.

"Griffin, aren't you happy? We made it outside."

I couldn't risk any excitement at passing through the gates. *Not yet.* Otherwise, I'd never be able to stand it if I found myself forced to return.

"I am happy. Perhaps . . . overwhelmed is a better word choice." I'd say no more, lest I undid my good fortune. "Mozart, *Piano Sonata, No. 5, in G major, Allegro.*"

"What's that?"

Taking her hand, I led her down the street. Ridge Avenue, I believed it was called. "My favorite rainy-day music. It sounds like raindrops to me."

"I don't know that one. Will you play it for me?" She turned away and the sun might as well have set.

"Of course. It will be the best performance you've ever experienced."

She chuckled, but remained silent, allowing me to take in my surroundings.

"Do you want to catch a bus? We can walk, but it's kind of cold." Kate wrapped her arms around her torso and mimicked shivering.

"Let's walk. If you don't mind." After being confined to the estate for so many years, I didn't want to take my eyes from my surroundings. I had no interest in stepping onto one of the great machines when I could stretch my legs.

It had been many years since my coming to Pittsburgh. I could say with certainty that the avenue hadn't looked like that when I'd first arrived. Mammoth buildings rose from the ground in all shapes and sizes. Some of the original homes still remained on the opposite side of the street, but boasted signs declaring them as businesses. People walked every which way, most with packs slung over their shoulders.

Even the streets had changed. Gone were the uneven cobblestones, gone were the horses and carriages. The world had developed around me. True, I'd witnessed much progress from behind the windows of the Byrons house, but I'd found it easier not to look. It only reminded me how many years I'd lost. That sort of thing could drive a man mad if he let it.

The concrete sidewalk spread before us in one long, level path. A large machine blew past. A horn blared.

"There are so many automobiles." There were dozens of them, maybe more. Everywhere. Hannah had told me they filled the streets. They flashed by us, their colors reminding me of a flock of brightly-colored birds.

An odd sensation blossomed in the pit of my stomach. We were entering Kate's world. Mine had ended, my era as dead as I was.

"Have you ever ridden in a car?" Kate asked.

"Once. It didn't have a roof. I remember it as being quite cold. We had to stop four times to get it started up again." I tread carefully on a sidewalk mangled by tree roots, its surface crested periodically as it changed from uneven brick to broken gray stone and back again.

"Things are probably a little different." Kate wrapped one arm across her chest. The other hung at her side, her hand intertwined with mine, helping me to keep the frigid cold at bay.

"A little." We continued moving through the park—past buildings I'd never seen, never dreamed would be there.

"I've heard you play Beethoven before—in the mornings. *Moonlight Sonata.*"

"Yes. Guilty."

"You play another song in the mornings. I don't know who the composer is." She closed her eyes. "The one that goes . . . da . . . da-da . . . da . . . da-da-da-da-da-da-da-da . . . daaaa."

Numbness crept over me. She'd not only heard one of my pieces, but could sing it back to me? "Yes, it's one of mine. The one you just sang is called *Redemption.*"

"It's amazing."

Kate's opinion shook me to the core. I couldn't muster my usual arrogant response. "Thank you. My turn. Music for when you feel . . . happy?"

She frowned, the edge of her thin nose wrinkling as she

considered my question. "Handel, *Water Music, Suite No. 1, Hornpipe.*"

"Handel. I never would have chosen you for a Handel girl."

Her smirk returned. "I'm full of surprises. Dad used to play Handel on Sunday mornings. We'd make bacon and eggs and . . ." Her smile faded. I didn't push her. I squeezed her hand the way she had mine.

We passed through a park in silence, and then beneath a bridge of some kind. Things had changed. In truth, there weren't too many more surprises until we reached the beginning of another bridge.

At the foot of the yellow-steeled structure, the reality of the ever-changing world slapped me in the face with the strength of a mother whose daughter had been compromised.

The icy wind whipped against my face as I stared upward, gawking. The structures touched the sky. More cars sped across thoroughfares there.

"Do you see those buildings? The height?" They'd been much shorter when I'd first arrived. The air was so clean, no smog or dust. The black cloud that had hung in the air over the city, gone. Everything seemed . . . different and loud. Extremely loud.

"What's your favorite happy piece?" Kate asked, guiding me across the bridge. Our breath formed tiny clouds as we walked. Men and women alike stared at me as I crossed the bridge, probably amazed I could be outside without a coat. Goodness, but I regretted that choice. My fingers had turned numb.

"*Night on Bald Mountain*, Mussorgsky."

"Why?" Her voice shot up. "It's not a happy piece at all. It's scary and evil-sounding."

I shrugged. "I am a spirit after all, am I not?"

"But not evil," she said. "You could never be evil."

That time, I had no problem identifying guilt when it surged up. I'd been cruel to Jonah Byrons, and he'd died because of it. If I'd only been able to look past my own prejudices.

But I couldn't argue with Kate. The Griffin she saw in me was the one Mother had seen. My mother wouldn't have blamed me for Jonah's death, either. Maybe it was time I stopped blaming myself, as well.

THE FIRST THING I NOTICED WAS COFFEE Á RENA HAD been loaded with so many different pieces of furniture it resembled some sort of bizarre upholstery shop. A variety of colors I'd never known existed, along with the wonderful smell of coffee, assaulted my senses.

"Kate!" A petite woman with hair in shades of blond and an ungodly turquoise hue danced behind the counter to the most bizarre music I'd ever heard. An odd band with a flower on it adorned her head. She resembled the top of a bakeshop cake.

"Hey, Rena." Kate embraced the woman briefly before releasing her. "This is Griffin."

"Oh, *this* is Griffin?" She winked at Kate. "Nice job, girl!"

I turned to search behind me for the job Kate had completed. Once again, I had the distinct feeling something had been lost on me. "I'm delighted to meet you, Rena." I bowed.

Rena's eyebrows shot up, her eyes widening as she

patted Kate's arm. She offered me her delicate hand. "Aren't you just the little player."

"I play piano, if that's what you mean?" I took her hand in mine and placed a chaste kiss on her knuckles before releasing her. Yet, Rena wouldn't allow me to pull away. She clasped my hand tighter and closed her eyes.

I turned to Kate, but she seemed focused on her friend. If she found such behavior unusual, she didn't question it.

When Rena opened her eyes, her entire demeanor had changed. She no longer seemed the lighthearted, flowery sort I'd first perceived. A look of awe, bordering on fear, crossed her face.

"I'm getting such an unusual vibe from you, Griffin." Rena leaned closer, a distinct crease forming in her brow.

"I would imagine so. Is there somewhere we might talk in private?"

"Absolutely." Rena grabbed a piece of paper with the words *Out to lunch* on it and stuck it to the door. Locking up, she gestured for us to follow.

Our trio made its way through a doorway behind the counter. I'd only just passed the threshold when the door shut behind us with a click, submerging the room in near-total darkness. The only light came from a high window near the ceiling, its glass distorted, making it impossible to see out.

But Rena touched something on the wall and more light filtered in. My eyes adjusted. I'd expected a dark space with mystical stars and candles. Instead, the room had been painted in a rich yellow shade, with tones in red and brown. Framed photos of Rena with various children covered the walls. A small kitchen took up a corner of the room. Rena flipped the switch on a metal device in the corner. Soon, the sound of water boiling began to fill the room.

"How about we get comfortable?" Rena gestured to a grouping of pillows on the floor. "Why don't you take your shoes off and have a seat? I'll make us some tea."

Heat rose in my face as both Rena and Kate removed their shoes. It seemed an oddly intimate gesture, but Kate tugged on my hand, guiding me to the cushions.

"I'll, er, leave my shoes on for now, thanks." I tried to sit up straight, but the seat Kate had chosen for me kept sinking beneath me, hissing as a snake might.

Rena busied herself pouring tea into wide, blue mugs. The vessels were very different from my mother's china, but they had their own charm.

"Here you go, Griffin." Rena offered a steaming mug to me, and I fought the temptation to decline. No one should ever consider preparing tea outside of Britain. Our need for Rena's assistance, however, far outweighed my need for the perfect brew. I raised the cup to my lips.

The first scalding sip reached my tongue, bringing with it a collection of flavors—a floral and citrus amalgamation most potent. "I'm pleasantly surprised, Rena. This is excellent."

"What? You don't think I know how to brew tea?" Rena smiled. "It's an imported Darjeeling. I had a sense you might prefer it. I've learned to follow my instincts."

"They're good instincts." I could remember sitting in a London restaurant drinking an almost identical brew. But that had been ages ago. Another life. Another Griffin.

Rena laughed. "You are trouble, aren't you? But then again, I've always been a sucker for a man with a British accent." She offered a mug to Kate and took a seat on the pillows opposite us. "What's going on? Why the need for a séance?"

"Do we need a reason? Perhaps we were merely curious." I wasn't quite ready for my second confessional in less than twenty-four hours, but the moment had arrived.

She regarded us with a certain degree of suspicion in her eyes. Since I'd yet to be on the receiving end of Rena's scrutiny, I shifted in my seat which sunk beneath me, yet again.

Heaven help me. "I've been cursed, Rena." I blurted out the words.

Rena's eyes darkened a fraction. "Cursed how? By whom?" She set her tea on a low table beside her.

"By a German witch named Minna Christel." I sounded oddly conversational, as though I'd just said, *Try the salmon, it's divine.*

Rena jumped to her feet. "Are you out of your mind? A witch?"

Kate squeezed my hand. "I know this is super hard to believe."

Rena shook her head, crossing her arms in front of her chest. "Oh, no, I'm not having a problem believing it. Witches are real. They're *too* real. And you don't want to go messing with one. When did this happen?"

"1902." Kate spared me from having to answer. "Griffin's been stuck in Byrons School. He's the ghost. And . . . since this all happened over a hundred years ago, I'm pretty sure the witch who did it is six feet under."

"A hundred . . ." Rena dropped to the cushions and brought her knees to her chin. She let out a long breath, after which she seemed calmer. Her arms and shoulders lowered. "If you're cursed, that explains your aura."

"Aura?" Griffin asked.

"Yeah. We all have them. Yours is yellow-green, which shows me your creativity. There's something more, though.

A black strand threaded through it, around it. I've never seen it before. It's like"—Rena paused—"a cage."

What an accurate description. "Any idea what it means?"

"It usually indicates the person is depressed or has a dark soul. It could mean there's some sort of badass entity attached to you." She stared at me, her gaze hitting mine with all the intensity of the first measure of Beethoven's *Symphony No. 5.* "Why hasn't anyone seen you if you've been living in the Byrons building all this time?"

"I'm dead. I only appear alive when I'm with Kate."

"Uh-huh." Rena stared in my direction with her unflinching gaze.

"You know the legends. Everyone's heard him play piano. All the guards talk about it. They won't even go in there at night." Kate narrowed her eyes on Charlie's behalf. "You should apologize for that, by the way."

My stomach knotted. Why should my own gut twist and turn in such a way? Was I feeling guilt for scaring Charlie? Should I even care? But, I did. I cared because Kate did.

"No way." Rena brought her hand to her mouth, her entire expression shifting as she bounced in her seat. "But you can't be, you just can't. But who else could you be?"

"Er, Rena?" I asked.

"You're Griffin Dunn, aren't you?" Rena launched herself to her knees. "Griffin Dunn, the pianist."

At that moment, there seemed little point in hiding anything from her. "You know of me?"

"Now I know why you look so familiar." Rena smiled, excitement lighting her eyes. "I've been reading about you. Your story, I mean. There's a man who wrote a book about you."

Damnation.

"You know about that book?" Kate caught her bottom lip between her teeth, but released it.

"Yes. You know I love biographies." Rena reached into a bag behind her and extracted the Underhill book. "The author is some guy named Liam Underhill."

"I'm familiar. Underhill is connected to Jiggory Underhill, my old manager."

"He's a relative. Maybe a great-great-grandson." Rena waved the book in front of me, but then set it down when I didn't take it. "This Liam also manages Griffin's, uh, *your* estate now. That's why he has access to so much information. Underhill's hosting a concert tonight at the Byham Theater and *I* have tickets. I snapped them up the moment they went on sale."

"Cool," Kate said. "But how strange is it that you just happen to have that book."

"It's not strange at all." Rena shook her head. "Everything happens for a reason, Kate."

As Kate and Rena continued chatting about the details of that night's concert, I stared at the copy of Liam Underhill's book. The very idea that someone had written a book about me . . . I could imagine all too well what one chapter would have been about.

"I suppose this book carries a line of nonsense about how I murdered Jonah Byrons." It would make sense that it would be chock full of lies. I finally picked up the book, but didn't skim the pages.

"Mr. Underhill believes you're innocent, Griffin. So do I." Rena patted the back of my hand. The action reminded me so much of something Mother would have done that I pulled away.

"Thank you." I truly meant it. I'd been blamed for so long for something I didn't do, I'd grown numb. *Almost.*

"Wow. This is . . ." Rena said. "Back to why you're here."

"We want you to contact the witch who cursed Griffin," Kate said. "There's also more."

"More? I mean, how much more could there be? You're already dating a hot British guy who's been dead for over a hundred years. Not to mention you want me to contact some witch's spirit, so you can find out about the curse she used on your boyfriend. Is that right?"

"I think you've covered it so far, yes." Impatience grew within me. I wanted Rena's help, but I also wanted to get started. For once, I wasn't in the school. I wanted to soak up as much as I could before I was forced to return, as I absolutely expected to be.

"How could there be more?" Rena sank to her cushion again.

"I'm . . . I'm related to the witch who cursed Griffin." Kate's voice sounded strained, but she launched into a shortened explanation of what she'd learned from her mother, her encounter with Minna, and even what had happened when Minna had attempted to push her through the broken skylight. Her jaw tightened when she shared she had a different mother.

"I'll do what I can today," Rena said. "This isn't exactly an easy job. It's not like we can place an order for the precise spirit you want to speak with."

"But you'll try?" I asked.

Rena nodded. "Yes. I'll try."

My mind ran through some possible consequences of what we were about to do. What if Minna appeared and tried to harm Kate again? What if we called another spirit? What if nothing happened?

Despite my hesitation at leaving the Byrons estate, I would try anything for Kate. She made me believe I had a chance. She'd given me a reason to live again.

CHAPTER 31
KATE

Rena used a small piece of white chalk to draw a line around us, closing our little group in so we sat together inside the circle. She sprinkled salt along the line.

"What's up with the salt?" I looked on, impressed. Rena had a knack for pouring salt exactly along the line. I would have been wearing it.

Rena didn't look up as she worked. "The salt is to purify the circle. It keeps the bad mojo out. It sounds like you two have got some bad mojo going on."

"Er, excuse me? Bad mojo?" Griffin's brow furrowed. "I'm not familiar with the term."

"Don't ask." But I smiled to soften my words and pushed down the impulse to get to my knees and press my lips to his. A few days ago, he wasn't a part of my life. *Not really.* But then there was our kiss, and he'd told me he loved me. *Everything* had changed.

Rena clasped our hands and we formed a circle of three. "Now close your eyes. I want you to clear your minds—both of you. Try to release the noise from your daily lives. Open yourselves up and be ready to receive a message".

Ready to receive. Got it.

"Right," Griffin said. "Ready to receive. Got it."

His long, slim fingers intertwined with my own felt right. I was where I was supposed to be.

"I want you to relax. Take slow breaths in and out. Focus on this moment," Rena said.

I focused on the steady in and out of my breath.

The warmth of the room wrapped around me, cocooning me. The spicy scent of chai tea with a twinge of cinnamon tickled my nose. Outside, a truck rumbled by. But soon, there was only the in and out of my breathing and Griffin's hand in mine.

"That's it. Calm, cool, ready to receive. We humbly call forth the spirit of Minna Christel." Rena's voice sounded a million miles away. Dreamlike. The room grew hotter. The air harder to breathe. The tea smell choked me, thickening my throat. I could no longer feel the place where my hands joined with Griffin's and Rena's.

Cool air rushed me, as though someone had opened the back door to the shop. The tea smells were erased, replaced by the scent of wet dirt—the same ozone-rich fragrance that kicked up whenever it rained. The sound of bird calls filled my ears. The earthy scent grew, overpowering all other sensations. Fresh air filled up my lungs. They burned from the clarity.

"Please open your eyes," Rena said. But no, that wasn't Rena's voice. It belonged to someone else.

Popping open one eyelid, I peered out. "What the frig?" I jumped to my feet. I was in the woods. No, in an actual *forest*. Tall conifer trees surrounded me, allowing in light in small patches. A weird sort of pressure boxed me in, making me light-headed. My breath clouded around me.

I searched for the source of the voice. Then, just as suddenly, *she* was there, taking my hands in her surprisingly warm ones.

"Katya." She smiled as she spoke my birth name in a thick German accent. The woman had long, dark hair that curled at the ends and framed her welcoming smile. She was beautiful. I would have known her as my mother even if we didn't share the same eyes or an identical tumble of dark hair.

"Daniela?"

"Yes, my dear." She reached a hand out to touch my cheek, but I backed up, yanking my hands free from hers.

I wrapped my arms around myself. "Don't touch me, okay? You can't just interrupt our séance and expect me to run into your arms. This isn't fair."

"I know it isn't, Katya—"

Who does she think she is? "My name's Kate. You don't get to name me." There I was, fighting with another mother about my name.

"I'm sorry, Kate. You're going to think I'm a terrible person, but I don't have much time. I'll be quick about this. I had to protect you."

As much as I didn't want to listen, my curiosity got the better of me. "Protect me from what?"

"From Minna. I trust you know who she is by now, since you know me."

"Oh, yeah. I know her. She's the psycho nanny who cursed Griffin—my boyfriend and tried to kill me."

Daniela blanched. "Goddess, yes, I know. I put a

protection charm on you, but obviously its power has waned. I'd thought I had every inevitability accounted for."

The questions I'd wanted to ask Minna herself rushed to forefront of my mind. "What happened to Minna? What made her turn into the woman I met last night?"

"Minna changed everything. Her emigration to America to follow Helmrick Byrons was only the start. She became obsessed with caring for Byrons' son, but it was after his death that she destroyed our family."

"When she cursed Griffin?" I asked.

Daniela nodded. "Yes. The curse on Griffin Dunn was an act of revenge. Regardless of what Minna wanted, it was Jonah Byrons' time. It was not, however, Mr. Dunn's. She played with fate and took an innocent life."

"What happened, you know, afterward?"

"Dark magic always exacts a price. In this case, it was our family's power." Daniela's expression remained cryptic. "Yes. Minna is the one who placed the curse on Griffin Dunn. She was a witch, but more importantly, *you* are one, too."

My skin cooled at her words. "I kind of figured that out for myself already." Still, hearing it stated so plainly brought everything home. Images of fairy-tale books where cruel witches with green skin were vanquished ran through my mind. "Why did you give me up?"

Confusion raged inside my head. On the one hand I was annoyed that Daniela had interfered with my plans to talk to Minna, to get information from her. On the other, this was my birth mother. I hadn't even known she'd existed before this week. There were too many questions percolating in my mind, clouding my thoughts.

"Minna corrupted our power and it began skipping generations, though we all have the power of divination."

Daniela began to pace, throwing a glance over her shoulder every few steps. "I knew the power would be handed down to any children I had. I went into hiding, kept to myself. If I never had any children, then the line of power couldn't be corrupted."

"But then you met Dad."

"Yes, your father just appeared on my doorstep one day. He'd been on a hiking trip and wanted to use the toilet. He stayed for a week afterwards."

I remembered Rena's promise that coincidences didn't exist. A musician just happened to land on her doorstep with a tie to the Byrons estate. That was a set up if I'd ever heard one. "What happened? How did he end up with my mo—with Jennifer?"

"I had a vision about you, before you were born. One in which Minna found me and took you. I ended things with Brian even though I loved him. Always remember that, Kate. I loved your father. I love you. I would never have given you up if there'd been any other choice."

I pushed her comments about loving Dad and me out of my mind. That still felt *wrong*. Maybe it always would. "Wasn't Minna dead? Wouldn't she have been over a hundred by then?"

"She died when you were a child, though her life was still unnaturally long. I've always believed it was her commune with the dark that prolonged it. Also, her hatred for Mr. Dunn spurred her on and her spirit clings to this world, waiting for revenge."

"She obviously had children of her own. Why didn't she just deal?"

"Katya," Daniela said, that time succeeding at touching my cheek. "Kate. To love a child is both a great and horrific thing. You would do anything to protect them.

"She believed so much in her vengeance that she wove the curse to pass through our family line—a blood curse. That's why she cared so much about continuing the Christel line. It was the only way to ensure this particular type of curse lived. It lives in your blood now."

"That sounds . . . evil," I said.

"Very. Minna would have manipulated you, rooted you in darkness. I did the only thing I could. I gave you up, hid you, and had a powerful protection enchantment placed on you. Now that you're the only one of us left, you are the owner of the Christel magic."

My mind swam with the information Daniela had given me, but finally latched onto one concept. "Does that mean *I* own Griffin's curse?"

"Yes, and it will all come to an end, soon. Griffin Dunn has fallen in love. You'll have one chance to break the curse. On the anniversary of Griffin's death. You are the last child of the Christel witches. You may be our only chance to end this."

"Can't I just undo the curse? Decide to cancel it?"

"You must purge the curse from the bloodline or all will be lost." But as I stared into Daniela's eyes, her face a mirror of my own, she slowly faded. "Be careful in the Byrons house. Some of Minna's magic still remains, even if she does not."

I blinked. In an instant, I'd returned to the room where Rena sat with her eyes closed. Griffin and Rena still held my hands. The smell of damp earth receded.

"I'm not getting anything from her," Rena said, opening her eyes.

"Kate?" Griffin tightened his hold on me.

I'd just seen my mother. My birth mother. My *real* mother. And she'd gone just as quickly as she'd appeared.

"Kate, you're freaking us out here, girl." Rena had taken to patting my face. It was just annoying enough to snap me out of it. "What's wrong?"

Though my eyes had slipped into focus and found Griffin's, I couldn't stop shaking. "I saw my real mother, like through a vision or something. She told me I have powers."

"Dear God." Griffin ran a hand through his hair.

"She also said I'm the new owner of a curse. *Yours.*" The room began to spin around me, my vision growing fuzzy. I was a witch. And the one person I wanted to save most in the world was the one person I'd somehow been holding prisoner.

CHAPTER 32

GRIFFIN

KATE PALED, HER EYES SLIDING BACK INTO HER HEAD before she could utter another word. She slumped back against the cushion. I patted Kate's cheek, yet she didn't stir.

"How did she see something, but you didn't?" I asked.

Rena got to her feet and went to the sink. She opened a couple of drawers before she extracted a small towel from one. She twisted the faucet and began running it under the water. After a moment, she shut off the tap and rung out the towel. "The universe shows us what it wants to, although that may not always be what we want to see."

"The cryptic interpretation of a true seer."

Rena gave me a grim smile. "I apologize for being a cliché." She handed me the damp cloth, which I placed on Kate's forehead.

"Come back to me, my darling."

Kate opened her eyes. "Oh." She forced herself to a

sitting position, which left her in my lap. No hardship for me. "It wasn't a dream?"

"Girl, I don't think so." Rena brushed a tendril from Kate's forehead, the way an older sister might. It seemed as though Rena had done a fine job of filling in for Kate's mother. A pity her own wasn't up to the challenge.

"Daniela called Griffin's curse a blood curse. It's passed through every generation of Minna's family since her—which means I own it now. I'm the last remaining descendant of the Christel witches." She locked her fingers together, bringing them up under her chin. "I didn't know."

Before I could answer, bizarre music began to play. Rena reached into her pocket and pulled out a pink, communications rectangle. Didn't Kate call it a seller phone? "Excuse me, guys. I'm so sorry but I have to take this." She held the thing to her ear. "Hey, Mark! How's it going?" Her voice trailed off as she left the room.

"Are you afraid of me now?" Kate's voice shook.

"No." It would have made sense for me to fear her, knowing what I did, but I couldn't bring myself to.

"*I'm* afraid of me."

Her fingers were cold as I pressed them to my lips. "You have my absolute trust and devotion."

"Sorry about that, guys." Rena returned, replacing the seller phone in her bag, grinning from ear to ear. "My sister-in-law is expecting, and she just went into labor two weeks early! I have to drive up to Grove City to stay with the kids."

That explained the pictures of Rena with children. They must've been nieces and nephews.

"Congratulations, Rena. That's excellent news." I plastered a smile I didn't feel upon my face. Despite my regret over how I'd treated Jonah, I was still not fond of children.

"Thanks. Anything else you found out during your

vision, Kate?" Rena sat down across from us, but it was clear she was simply too excited to focus on my curse in that moment.

"Daniela said I'll have one chance to break the curse—on the anniversary of Griffin's death."

"December seventeenth," I offered. Memories of the Byrons house on that night resurfaced inside me—the carefully chosen decorations, the society surrounding me, Lord Byrons and his pungent cigars . . .

It would have been my first Christmas without Mother.

Rena stopped fidgeting and her eyes flashed to meet mine. "A little more than a week from today is not much time."

"Thinking back, it probably explains the voice." There was little point in keeping that anomaly to myself—especially from a clairvoyant. "I've been hearing a voice that keeps saying *the end is coming*."

"It's a friendly sounding voice, then?" Rena asked.

"No." I straightened, taken aback. "In truth, it sounds quite evil."

"Griffin has a little trouble with sarcasm." Kate patted my arm. "But it's not happy at all, and I've heard it too. On the way home the other night. The voice said *The end is coming. Blood of my blood, the hour of my vengeance is near*."

Rena frowned, casting a glance at the clock and her seller phone before focusing on us again. "I don't like it, Kate. Maybe I should stay here. See if Mark can get a sitter."

"No. Your family needs you. We'll be fine for now." Kate squeezed Rena's hands.

"She's right, you know. There's nothing you can do right

now, anyway." Though I tried to sound reassuring, I couldn't ignore the depression seeping into my veins.

Sighing, Rena reached for a turquoise flowered bag that matched the stripe in her hair and withdrew two strips of paper. "Why don't you two take my Liam Underhill tickets?" She waved the papers in the air. "I think it's important for Griffin to go. Besides, I'll never make it now."

She handed the tickets to me, and I glanced down at them.

The Byham Theater Presents
The Life and Music of Jiggory Underhill
Friday, December 9th at 7:00 p.m.

Shock coursed through me as I absorbed the words. "Jig didn't even know how to read music, let alone write it." I handed Kate the tickets.

Kate offered the tickets back to Rena. "I'd like to, but I don't have a car. That'd be pretty late getting home by myself. I mean, early mornings are one thing—no one's awake—but this late . . ."

Rena slid her hands into her pockets "Stay here tonight." She frowned, as though warring internally with herself.

Her gaze lingered in my direction, narrowing slightly before easing up. What did she truly see when she looked at me? "My apartment's just upstairs. Take a break from the curse for the evening. We'll tackle it when I get back. Just be *responsible.*"

For some reason, Kate's face pinked. "Rena, I—"

"I am always, at the very least, responsible. Thank you, Rena." I said, not bothering to hide the relief from my voice.

An evening alone with Kate outside of that wretched house . . . I couldn't imagine it.

"Sure, and Griffin? Try and keep a low profile at this thing. They could have pictures of you." Rena smiled as she moved toward the steps leading to her lodgings. "And feel free to borrow any of Mark's things. He stays here sometimes when he has to go into the city. He's got a few suits in the closet. Kate knows where they are."

"Thanks, Rena. Don't worry, I'll lock up and everything when we leave." Kate got to her feet.

"I'm gonna get my things together." Rena turned to leave the room, then stopped and glanced back. "Don't get frustrated about today, Griffin. Spirits aren't on direct dial, okay? We'll try again."

"Thank you, Rena," I said, but as Kate squeezed my hand, I understood that the same thought had crossed both of our minds.

We could try again, but what if we didn't find answers?

CHAPTER 33
KATE

Hours later, we walked out into the swirling snowflakes, the bite of the dropping temperature nipping at my cheeks. It wasn't far to the Byham on Sixth Street, but I took us in the opposite direction and into Market Square. The place had been decorated for the holidays with a fake Bavarian village and a Santa Claus cottage. Crossing the cobblestone street and the old bricked square, we moved through the crowd.

My heart pounded so hard it blocked out all other sound. I felt about five years older in Rena's black sheath dress. I'd brushed my hair until it shone and curled at the ends, just around the middle of my back. Griffin had borrowed a dress shirt, flat cap, and coat Mark had left at Rena's. Mark was tall and wiry, like Griffin, though just a bit shorter, so that Griffin had stayed in the pants he'd been wearing.

Since there was a chance there could be photos of Griffin at the event, we figured we were better off being late.

"I'm curious as to what we're going to find tonight. Jig didn't have anything to do with music. I was the one who'd come here to perform, though I wouldn't have if he hadn't pushed things."

"Why did he?" I asked.

Griffin met my eyes. "I was about to become a pauper. At least according to Jiggory, though I thought my accounts were healthier than what he'd described. That's what I was doing in Pittsburgh in the first place—trying to find a benefactor. Lord Byrons had been about to offer to become my patron."

"You didn't have any family or anyone back home to take care of your estate? Take care of you?"

"No." He frowned. "Mother had died while I was traveling. My father, two years before that. I had no siblings. I mean, there was Clarissa, but it wasn't serious."

"Who was Clarissa? Your girlfriend?"

"She was . . ." He looked uncomfortable.

I blushed. It was obvious who she was from the look on his face.

"She was my lover, Kate." Griffin averted his gaze.

Damn. Jealousy busted into my chest then, a ferocious break-in that held my heart in a stronghold. I could imagine his eyes taking in another girl, the same way they had me. I couldn't stand it.

That Clarissa person had probably been worm food for more than fifty years. Still, tears burned the backs of my eyes.

"Come on, you." Griffin placed his hand on my waist and ushered me around the corner, gently guiding me so my back pressed up against one side of the building's brick exterior. Though we stood feet from the crowded square, the alleyway had no lighting. The blackness surrounded us on all sides.

"I've loved no one before you, you foolish girl. Do you understand? You are the only one who has my heart."

"It's not like I should have expected you to be celibate."

"Good. Then what's the problem?"

"It's just . . ."

"Kate?" His voice held concern, but also exasperation.

"I didn't know *her* name before. You know, Clarissa? I figured there had to be someone. It was easier to write it off when I didn't know her name."

"Right." His lips grazed mine, and my anger melted away. "It's immaterial. You're the only one I want."

Griffin swept his tongue into my mouth, and the rough brick of the building rubbed against the back of my scalp from the pressure. My body softened against his. Under normal circumstances, I would have been freezing my butt off, but I'd grown overheated. After a moment he stilled, letting his warm hands fall away.

"You make me forget things, Katherine."

A chill passed through me. "Such as?" My voice came out in a breathless whisper as he drew back.

"We're in a public square, with many other people, and here I am practically devouring you. We could have destroyed your reputation."

I smirked. "I'm sure my reputation will survive just fine." A clock chimed. "Come on. I think we can sneak in now. It's not far to the theater."

Griffin interlaced his fingers with mine. "As you wish." He fell into step beside me.

The short walk gave me the opportunity to think about later, when we'd be alone. Memories of his searing kiss in the alley rushed me. What if Griffin wanted to sleep with me? We had a downtown apartment all to ourselves with no supervising adults and a whole night ahead of us. Plus, the anniversary of his death was approaching and we didn't know what that meant. What if he disappeared in a week and I lost him forever?

Mom had put me on the pill last year—"just as a precaution." Other than fighting to remember to take it, I'd never thought much of it. Benny had made up the whole of my love life.

Things had changed, though. I loved Griffin. He did say I was worth waiting for.

But what if *I* didn't want to wait?

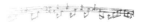

THE BYHAM THEATER SAT ONE TO TWO BLOCKS OVER from Market Square, depending on who you asked. I was used to walking. Downtown Pittsburgh was small enough that you could walk from one end of town to the other in less than twenty minutes. There was no point in paying for a taxi.

We dashed through the theater's side entrance just as an attendant moved to close the door. We rushed inside, and I glanced up to thank the usher who'd let us in. It turned out to be the last person I wanted to come face-to-face with.

"Ryder. What are you doing here?" *Oh, no! I forgot he worked here.*

His entire face lit up. Great. He'd probably think I was into him. Did the guy have an off button?

"Kate. Nice to see you," said Ryder, who straightened,

the golden tassels on his usher's uniform glinting in the glare from the recessed lighting.

"What, no special greeting for me, Ryder?" Griffin moved his hand to my back, simultaneously supporting me and setting me on fire.

Ryder narrowed his eyes. "You're the piano player, right? What's your name again? Gaston? Gus?"

"Griffin. He's my boyfriend." *Ha! Take that!*

"Boyfriend?" Ryder's face fell, but he recovered quickly. "Wait a minute. You look familiar."

Griffin cocked an eyebrow. "Since we've had the misfortune to meet before, I'm hardly surprised."

Ryder took a step forward. I placed a hand on his chest, promising myself I'd wash it later. "The show is about to start. Don't you have to give us programs or something?"

"Yeah." He pressed two programs into my hands and snatched the tickets from my fingers before eyeing them. "You're in the third row, middle section, far right. Just go through these doors." He gestured to the set of double doors just ahead.

"Thanks." With a final glare in Ryder's direction, I let Griffin guide me to the appropriate row. We took our seats. My breath caught when I glanced down at the program.

A picture of Griffin standing next to an older, dark haired man dominated the cover. *Jiggory Underhill with student, Griffin Dunn* read the caption. I ran a hand over Griffin's face in print.

"Student." Griffin's voice shaded with disbelief.

The house lights dimmed then. Applause filled the room as a man entered from stage left and removed the microphone from the stand. He seemed relatively young, maybe thirty or forty, with neatly trimmed, dark brown hair and wire-rimmed glasses. We were seated close enough that I could see his face. He had kind eyes.

"Good evening. I am Liam Underhill. Thank you for coming. Jiggory Underhill, was a unique talent. I wish I could say I inherited his gifts, but sadly . . ." He shrugged and the audience laughed. "Jiggory's work breaks all the rules when it comes to classical music. His compositions are passionate and powerful. It's obvious why he taught so many wonderful musicians everything they know, including Griffin Dunn, whom you'll find a photograph of on your program cover. He's the subject of my new book, which my publishers will thank me to tell you is called *Chasing Griffin Dunn*. Jiggory taught him to play the piano."

Griffin tensed. That last comment had not gone down well.

"But let's let the music speak for itself, shall we? Here is *Desperation* by Jiggory Underhill." Liam backed away and jogged down the steps to take a seat in the front row. He glanced in our direction as he sat, freezing for several beats before finally taking his seat.

Shit. He saw us.

A lone pianist walked onto the stage. He took a seat, raised his hands to the keys, and then began to play. No symphony backed him. He simply launched into a torrent of notes with no introduction, no warm-up. I couldn't have moved from my seat for anything in the world.

Desperation was one of those pieces that made the hair on the back of my neck stand on end. It was all-consuming. It drudged up every thought, every emotion I'd ever experienced and squashed them. It was the sort of music that made me recall things like the last birthday party I'd had with my dad, the first time I knew I really wanted to get serious about the clarinet, the day Dad had died . . .

The music dove into my chest, tearing out my heart, gutting me, forcing me to relive the good and the bad. Tears spilled over onto my cheeks. I didn't bother to wipe them away. The piece mesmerized everyone in the room, as though a magical creature had written it, like the fairies I used to read about in books.

Or just maybe . . . *a ghost.*

CHAPTER 34
GRIFFIN

THE BASTARD. THE THIEVING, SCHEMING BASTARD. Jiggory had stolen my music and taken credit for it.

And if that wasn't insulting enough, they'd hired a pitiful musician to attempt my compositions. My jaw set as I stared down the pianist on stage. As though any practiced pianist would have missed my markings on interpretation for that last measure.

Rage pounded *forte* through my veins. My hands shook.

Kate tensed beside me. *She knows.* Her fear and concern for me were almost a third person sitting between us.

I couldn't meet her eyes. Instead, I fought to keep my fingers from moving against my thighs—from hitting the notes on an invisible piano as if I were the one performing.

After the applause died, Underhill returned to the stage. "Wonderful, wasn't it?" A chorus of murmured approvals echoed from the audience. "I was fortunate enough to find this journal containing all of Jiggory's music." He held up a thick, brown volume—one all too familiar to me.

My journal. How had Underhill gotten it? But of course. I'd taken a copy with me to America, so I could work on my songs during the boat ride over. I'd never told Jig. Clearly, he'd found the journal after I'd died and had claimed it as his own.

That stung more than I wanted to admit. I'd once thought of Jiggory as a friend. He was the closest person to my own age I'd known when I'd lived, though ten years had separated us.

"It was heavily damaged when I discovered it and had to be restored, but I've been able to bring it back to what it once was. You'll find a complete listing of Jiggory's works on the back cover of your program." The young Underhill held my journal aloft. My fingers twitched as I forced myself to stay in my seat. To identify myself would surely cause an uproar and wouldn't bring us any closer to breaking my curse.

Opening the program on my lap, I flipped through dozens of advertisements before I found the performance order listing the songs to be played that evening. As I'd expected—every one of them was mine. The two longest would be first. The titles reached out to me from the page, old friends, but then I realized what would be played next.

"This next piece, *Redemption*," Liam Underhill said, "was one Jiggory wrote while he was mentoring the brilliant concert pianist, Griffin Dunn."

No. Not Redemption—anything but my favorite piece.

Kate gripped my arm. "*Redemption* is your piece. He stole your music!"

I couldn't speak. I'd only managed a nod by the time the first note filled the hall. The audience was clearly entranced by the music, and they would never know it as mine. I shoved my fist in my mouth.

I'd composed *Redemption* after I'd learned of Mother's sickness, when there'd been too many miles between us for me to return to her side before her death. I could recall exactly how I'd felt when I'd first penned the melody. Grateful to my mother for all she'd given me, but also devastated. After she'd died, I'd never gotten the chance to go home again.

The music soared over the audience, tormenting my heart. There were too many memories attached to every note. Each stanza made me recall the pain of my mother's loss, of enduring the curse itself. All too soon, it was over, leaving the room silent.

Then, in a wave of motion, the audience jumped to their feet in a standing ovation. Their applause rocked the theater, making the soles of my feet vibrate. That's what it would have been like. That's what I would have had the chance to experience if Jonah hadn't fallen and I'd lived.

Not only had Jig taken credit for my work, but he'd cheated me out of that experience. He'd taken my life from me using a far different method than Minna.

After the applause ended, Underhill rose to his feet and spoke from beneath the stage. "We have much more for you, but now it's time for a brief intermission. Thank you."

Applause rang out, and then the house lights went up. Underhill lowered the speaking mechanism to his side. He instantly directed his gaze at Kate and me.

We rocketed to our feet in unspoken agreement. Kate gripped my hand, and I let her lead me up the aisle, toward the exit. Thank goodness she'd taken the initiative. Could I have navigated back to Rena's through the rage clouding my vision? Doubtful.

"Excuse me. Sir. Miss."

Underhill.

He was almost directly behind us. I glanced back, and his gaze locked onto mine.

Damnation. A side door opened, and dozens of audience members filed into the aisle in front of us.

"Keep walking." Kate spat the words into my ear.

"Please, excuse me." Underhill's voice sounded more urgent. "Please. Young man."

Kate led me down one of the side aisles and through another door. Soon, the exit was in sight, but the crowd blocked our escape. So close, and we'd been boxed in.

"There's nowhere to go." Kate spoke so softly I almost didn't hear her.

The door in front of us opened and shut, and soon Underhill positioned himself in front of us. I could only stare at the man who could have passed for Jig himself. He had Jig's long nose and pale blue eyes. He had also inherited Jig's ears, which curved out to the sides just slightly. Which one of us was the ghost?

"Hello." Underhill cleared his throat, roughly. "I'm sorry for stopping you. It's just . . . do you realize you are the spitting image of Griffin Dunn?"

"They say everyone has a twin," Kate offered.

Lord, she's a terrible liar.

"This is more than a small resemblance." Underhill smiled, his face growing more animated by the second. "You could *pass* for Dunn—the likeness is simply remarkable. Are you a relative of his?"

"No," I said, making my voice sound intentionally cutting.

"I've been searching for such a long time for information on Mr. Dunn." Underhill sounded desperate, but it was clear that, to him, Griffin Dunn was merely a problem to be worked out. In his mind, I'd died long ago. I was no longer a person, but a myth. "He interests me a great deal."

"It would help if you got your facts straight." I kept my hand on Kate's arm as though she was the only thing grounding me.

"I beg your pardon?" Underhill asked, clearly confused.

Kate tugged on my arm. "I think we'd better go."

She was absolutely right, but I couldn't stop myself. The truth burned in my heart and had to be spoken. "Jiggory Underhill was a liar and a thief."

To his credit, Underhill's affable smile dropped only a fraction. "A thief? No. Jiggory was a very talented musician. He worked alone most of the time, so we know little about his process. However, his body of work is extraordinary. He was quite prolific."

I'd been quite prolific.

I was *still*.

"Jiggory worked alone because he stole someone else's ideas—Griffin Dunn's. Jiggory had not one ounce of musical talent within his body. He obviously didn't care for Mr. Dunn and certainly acted as no mentor."

"That's not true. He *did* care. He tended to Mr. Dunn's estate; he invested his money, as well. There's an endowment in his name dedicated to the arts every year since Dunn's death," Underhill argued. "I took over management of Fulton House several years ago."

"Fulton House?" My childhood home. *Dear God, it still stands.*

"Yes. It's Mr. Dunn's ancestral home. Can we talk about

this after the performance? You have some very curious things to say," Underhill commented.

The smarter course of action would have been to walk away without a word. Yet, how could I let that man believe Jig had written any music, let alone the hundreds of pieces in my journal?

My music.

"We have to go. *Now.*" Kate pulled on my arm with more force than before.

I brought myself up to my full height. "If you desire the truth, Mr. Underhill, all you need to know is in the back corner bedroom on the second floor of Fulton House. The mantel moves."

Allowing the exchange had been foolish of me. It became clear once I allowed Kate to lead me away. I'd said far too much.

I had to get out of the theater before Underhill realized who I truly was. Otherwise, we'd have a hell of a lot more to concern us than stolen music.

THE SNOW HAD PICKED UP, SENDING THICK, FLUFFY flakes plummeting from the sky. I swiped them from my face as I allowed Kate to lead me away from the theater and back to Rena's shop. As if she sensed my mood, Kate said nothing, the only indication of her presence her slight footsteps on the pavement and her firm grip on my hand.

Hearing my music performed, knowing what Jig had done . . . it made me long to go back to who I was before Kate. When I couldn't be hurt, when no one made it past my personally erected barriers. But Kate had changed everything. Only then, as we strode along in silence, buffeted by the wind, did I recognize I'd been stripped of my carefully designed facade, unable to comprehend the next measure.

My music had been an extension of my being, and Jiggory had taken it and claimed it for his own.

There isn't a damn thing I can do about it.

Silent blocks passed, and, before I realized it, we'd reached Coffee á Rena. Warmth enveloped us as Kate let us in, locking the door in our wake. I trailed her to the top of the stairs, where she dropped her coat on a chair inside the foyer before moving to the kitchen.

Rena's kitchen was tiny—much tinier than my kitchen at Fulton House, though I'd spent little time in it since my childhood accident. There was a U-shaped counter that took up one section of the room. A small, round table had been set up in front of the window. Lights from the buildings outside illuminated the night sky. Snow still fell, resting on the outside sill and framing the windowpanes in white.

Kate lifted a blackened orange teakettle onto the stove. There was a soft click as she turned a knob. Flame sparked to life under the kettle. "Tea?" She didn't wait for my response, but reached into a cabinet above her head. She set two cups onto the counter.

"That is exactly how my mother approached any problem I had while growing up. She'd make tea." Seeing Kate perform the same familiar motions calmed me. "'Have a cup of tea, Griffin, love,' she'd say. As though the answer to all of my problems lay in the dregs." I rubbed my face, trying to force the memory back from where it came. It was so much easier when I didn't remember.

Kate smiled. "She sounds like a smart woman."

"She was. I wish I'd appreciated her more."

"I know what you mean." Yet, Kate didn't elaborate as

she arranged about five or six biscuits on a plate and placed it on the table. "Have a cookie and talk to me."

Her direct approach jarred me, though it shouldn't have. That was the very essence of Kate. Her innate ability to speak her mind was what had attracted me to her in the first place. "There's nothing to talk about."

Kate added tea leaves to a strainer overtop a black and white, polka-dotted teapot. "Cut the crap, Griffin. What's going on in your head?"

"Leave it, Kate."

"Why?"

"Because I can't change any of it. Because I asked you to."

Kate stopped fussing with the tea and leaned back against the counter. Her long dress moved with her. She glanced down at the program and opened it to the page with Jig's biography. "It says here that Jig and a Clarissa Benton were married. Is that your Clarissa? The lover?" She picked up a mug from the counter and put it back down as though she'd changed her mind.

"Yes. The very same." Perhaps I'd known all along what I'd felt for Clarissa wasn't love. That I'd thought of her so little since my time in purgatory served as proof of that. Still, she'd said she'd cared for me, as had Jig. Had they been using me? Hoping to get to my music and my fortunes all along?

When I had died, Jig had taken over my life in my absence—a most unsettling revelation.

"I don't understand. Jiggory stole your music and your lover. I also don't think it would be a stretch to assume he skimmed money from you, too."

Her words drudged up old memories from my distant past. "I trusted Jig to take care of me. Too much, apparently.

I knew there was a reason I'd never told him I was composing. He told me I couldn't even afford our boat trip back to England."

"Exactly. And don't you think that deserves some sort of discussion, or a reaction from you at least?"

Numbness seeped into me. "What sort of reaction were you expecting?"

"Something, Griffin! Get pissed, get mad, like you were back in the theater. Yell, throw something. Show some emotion, because you've been seriously ripped off. By Jig, by Clarissa, and by Minna. I think you've earned the chance to show it."

"It happened over a hundred years ago. I can't change it. You have remarkable perspective when you're dead, Kate."

She flinched. "Don't. Say whatever you need to, but don't say that."

"Why? Regardless of what we've learned today, I *am* dead."

We stood like that for a collection of silent moments. A tear slipped down Kate's cheek. "It sounds so final."

"For most people, it is." I tried to radiate nonchalance, but so many thoughts were spinning around inside my head, colliding with one another.

I'd never trusted anyone, not really. At what could possibly be either the end or the beginning of my existence, I'd been faced with needing to trust someone. What was I holding on to?

"Tell me."

Her simple words unlocked something inside me. Jig's betrayal burst through me, as though a dam had been broken—a tide of emotion I couldn't swallow back. I wanted to hit something, but as I looked around Rena's tiny kitchen, there was nothing, save for a few ugly cow figurines sitting on a shelf. They seemed to stare back at me, goading me on, willing me to destroy them.

Kate must've read my mind, because she went to a closet, then opened the door. Reaching in, she slid out a punching bag. "Looking for something to hit?" Kate stepped back, giving me free access to the bag.

The first hit on the target, its leather as smooth and rich as butter, brought sweet relief. I envisioned Jig's face on the front of the cool exterior. "I knew there was a reason I never told him I was composing." One, two, three, four, five, six . . . My punches had transformed into the underlying tempo of my own morose waltz.

"The bastard! And *she* claimed she loved me."

Wham!

"Those were my compositions, Kate."

Wham!

"Griffin—" Kate called out, a lone, soothing voice in an empty concert hall.

"My creations are in the folio Underhill held up. And no one will ever know!"

Wham! Wham! Wham!

"Griffin, please—"

"No one will ever know I wrote it." But as I spoke those words, I heard in them the egotistical creative of the past. Someone I'd ceased to be. It all had to do with the beauty in the room with me.

"Griffin." Kate's voice drew me back a fraction of an inch to the present. "Griffin, please. Your hands!"

I moved to throw another punch, but then caught sight of my hands. The source of my livelihood and connection to my greatest love after Kate: *my music.*

A piercing wail filled the room as the kettle came to a boil. Kate moved to switch off the flame, but though she'd left my side, my gaze never strayed from the horrific sight before me.

Blood dripped from my bruised knuckles. They'd puffed up, vague reminders of their former selves. Each finger ached, but I hadn't broken any of them.

Tears spilled silently from my eyes. They turned to choking, gasping sobs that threatened to bring me to my knees. All the years, all the days and nights I'd been alone, and I'd never cried—not once. It had taken this betrayal, this moment of ultimate pain, to let open the floodgates.

"It's okay." Then Kate was there, not caring that I might get blood on her dress, unafraid of the raging emotions she'd encouraged me to unleash. She wrapped her arms around me and held on, as though we stood amongst the waves, the only stable beings in the world.

My anger and sorrow seeped out of me then, and I sagged against a nearby stool, weary. Kate withdrew, crossing the room to search the cabinets.

She rifled through two before finally locating the object of her search in the third—a white box with a red cross on it. She opened it, pulling out bandages and gauze, along with tubes full of who knew what. She filled a bowl with water and ice, and then retrieved a towel from one of the drawers. Running a cloth under water, she returned to me with her findings and rested them on the nearest counter. She took my hand in hers and began to dab at the knuckles on my left hand, while at the same time guiding me closer.

"You know, when I was a kid, I entered a songwriting contest. My entry was really good, too." She lifted my left hand into a bowl of ice water, and I sighed as some of the sting abated.

"Did you win?" I asked, my voice a raw modulation of its usual tone.

She shook her head. "No. This girl named Suzie Summerhouse won."

I swallowed, wiping away my tears with the back of my sleeve. "She sounds abhorrent."

Kate smiled. "She was a smug little bitch, if that's what you mean." She cleaned the cloth under running water and returned to me to work on my right hand.

My skin stung. I held still.

"She won because she stole my song. She knew one of the judges and they swapped out the pieces."

"What happened?"

Kate sprayed something vile on my hands and started wrapping them. "Nothing. She won. The school orchestra performed the piece in front of the entire town. My dad and I went to the judges, but it was fixed. She won."

"And that was it?"

"Yeah. She's an unwed teen mother now, I think." Mischief filled her eyes as she worked quickly, taping my hands.

Though my bruised skin stung, and my knuckles ached, her touch made my body thrum in anticipation, innocent though her ministrations were. "Your point?"

"My point is sometimes the good guys don't win. They lose. And it doesn't mean the people who lost are losers. It just means the people who won are assholes."

"I like your logic, crass though it may be."

Taping complete, she leaned back. "Jiggory and Clarissa won the first round, but they don't have to win the second."

"A boxing metaphor?"

She shrugged. "It seemed appropriate."

Kate raised my hand to her lips, placing a gentle kiss on my now-bandaged knuckles. Turning away from me, she crossed the space and dropped the cloth into the sink. Only then did she turn back to face me as she slid onto the counter. "I know it's your music. I see you, Griffin. I *see* you."

There had once been steps separating us. One or two, perhaps ten . . . I bridged those in the space of a heartbeat. My hands came to rest on the counter on either side of Kate. Two more beats passed, and my mouth was on hers, rough, determined. I traced her bottom lip with my tongue, biting it, teasing it. She sucked a breath in as I lifted her onto the counter. I found her lips with my own and the pace of our kisses increased as our mouths met with urgency. I needed her. Craved her. I couldn't get close enough.

Her hands fisted in my hair, making my body harden and gooseflesh raise on my skin. She opened her mouth against my persistent tongue, her body growing pliant as I moved my knee between her knees. An unspoken understanding grew between us.

It could all end at any moment, and we could lose one another. I couldn't imagine dying again and never having known Kate the way I was meant to.

Our mouths moved over one another's as we pushed toward something undefined. I should have run away and let the curse pull me back to the house, both for her safety and my own sanity. But then, in the brightness of Rena's tiny kitchen, with my hands stinging and the December wind howling against the window, I understood it had been a lost cause from the start.

Kate has always been meant for me.

"Let me love you." I kept myself very still, waiting for her approval.

"Okay." She gasped as I pressed a soft kiss against her skin, the smooth rise of her collarbone tempting me.

"If you don't want to be with me, Kate, you've only got to say so. I don't want you to do anything you don't want to."

Kate regarded me for at least a hundred moments or more, before she slid off the counter and pressed a kiss to my jaw. "I *never* do anything I don't want to do."

My breath halted entirely. *Dear God.*

CHAPTER 35
KATE

Griffin carried me into the darkened guest bedroom as though I would break. Most people usually assumed I didn't want to be cared for that way, but I did. I wanted someone to look out for me. He made me feel loved. Neither of us bothered with the light—probably a good thing, since that would've meant he'd catch me blushing like the freak I was.

The sensation of the cool comforter against my bare arms shocked me as Griffin pressed my overheated body back onto the bed. Every one of my nerve endings pulsed, responding to his explorations.

What was I doing? I'd just said I wanted to make love. I'd never been with a guy. Yet, this was Griffin. If we never broke his curse, I'd want the memory of his arms around me. I'd want him to love me forever.

Then my thoughts vanished, and my mouth was on Griffin's, my body molded to his. His lips drove me crazy, my head an out of control Ferris wheel of thoughts and emotions. "But I've never—"

He kissed me again, and I stopped voicing my objection. Griffin pulled back nonetheless. "Don't worry. Neither have I."

That certainly was not true, the dog. "But you said—"

"Shh." He kissed the center of my forehead, and then placed a finger to my lips. "It's true I've lain with a woman before, but I've never made love to anyone. I've never loved. With you, everything is my first time."

His words were sledgehammers, knocking down my walls. Griffin would be mine. Even if that one night was the only chance I'd have to pretend we'd be allowed to stay together.

"You can have everything—every part of me is yours for the taking." He kissed me again, his heart pounding where my hand rested against his chest. I ached for him, for the words he'd shared with me in the hush of the kitchen. Words, I understood, that had been hard-won. Griffin would never have been a boy who loved easily. Yet, he loved me.

He found a sweet spot on my neck and grazed the sensitive skin with his lips. I shuddered and arched my back, pushing myself into him involuntarily.

"Kate." He made my name sound like a song.

He probably would have made the next move, but the urge to feel his skin against mine took me over. The first button on his shirt came undone with no effort, as though I'd had help. The same with the second, third, and fourth . . .

Oh my.

I tugged off his shirt and touched his chest, feeling muscle and the rampant beating of his heart.

He sucked in a breath when I ran my hands lower on his stomach. His skin was warm, burning under my touch, like he had a fever or something.

He reached up and placed a hand on my breast, and my face flamed. I'd never considered myself to be well-endowed in the chest department. Would he care?

We shed our clothes, parting only for the seconds it took to slip the fabric from our skin. Once the barriers had gone, his mouth slipped to the soft skin he'd only previously explored through my clothes. I arched my back, dizzy with the feel of his lips.

Griffin's long fingers splayed over my stomach, and I ached for something I didn't know existed. His mouth moved on mine again as his fingers played me like the keys on his piano—expertly, tenderly. Waves of pleasure coursed through me as he brought me closer and closer to something. I moved on the bed, antsy, unsure, yet totally certain of what I wanted—for him to release me from this torture, to feel his skin against my own.

I tried to say his name, to call out, but I was incapable of speech. Griffin pulled closer. "I want you more than air, more than anything." His words were barely audible in the cocoon we'd created for ourselves.

"Then make me yours. Please make me yours." A tear ran down my cheek, and I touched it, realizing it wasn't mine.

"I love you. No matter what happens . . . I will love you, forever." His whispered words brushed against my ear.

And then he was everywhere as he altered his position,

our bodies joining. As our connection deepened, we moved together in a composition of entwined limbs and furious tempo, accented by hopes we'd both been afraid to do more than whisper, and everything changed between us.

CHAPTER 36
GRIFFIN

Saturday, December 10th—Five Days Left Until Juries

Hours later, at midnight, I found myself being pulled from the arms of a sleeping Kate and into a blackness that brought me to Byrons School. Again, I'd been dragged to the parlor and forced to relive it all again. Jonah's death. My own. It had been my biggest fear, when I'd left the grounds yesterday, and it had come to fruition.

Pain had shot through every one of my limbs, but it quickly faded as I rose to my feet, a spirit once more, back in the clothing I'd been wearing at the time of my death. It was so much harder to be in that place since I'd known what it felt like to make love to Kate.

Memories of her body intertwined with mine filled my mind. They helped me pass the time as I waited for her arrival.

When the first rays of light hit the courtyard, anticipation began to build within me. Kate would be there soon. But the longer I waited, the more I began to believe she wasn't coming. As the sun rose, I realized not a single student had passed through the gates. Come to think of it, there was no Charlie. Was something wrong at the school?

But no. It was Saturday.

Kate wouldn't be coming to school.

A crushing depression followed. We had a few days together at best. I would lose her for two of them. Just a sign of what to expect in the future—a world with no Kate.

A chill danced over my skin. The air grew colder, my hearing sharpened, and the change came on. Soon, my heart beat again.

"I missed you this morning." The sound of Kate's voice jerked me away from my self-pity.

I could sense my face lighting up at the sight of her. "Kate."

"Why did you leave?" Kate stood at a distance, her arms wrapped around herself, Mark's coat over one arm. She must've thought the worst of me, even believed I'd walked out on her on purpose.

"I don't know. I was in bed with you"—I took one step closer, then two—"when I found myself torn from your arms. I ended up here."

"You got pulled back? Like you did when you tried to leave before?" When I nodded, she relaxed visibly, her shoulders losing some of their tension.

"Yeah." Who cared if my voice broke on the word as I stepped into her arms, her vanilla scent assaulting me. And had I just said *yeah* instead of *yes*? What was the world coming to? "It seemed worse this time, though that may have been because I was forced to leave you."

"I don't understand," she said, resting her head against my chest. "If I own your curse, why did you get pulled back? I didn't send you away."

"I thought perhaps it had something to do with my prowess in the boudoir?" Accepting the coat from her, I slid my arms into the warm material and then buttoned it up, relieved for its comfort.

"No, um, your *prowess* seemed just fine to me." She looked at the ground.

I tipped her chin. "And you were exquisite."

She blushed. *Ah, exactly the reaction I was hoping for.*

I brought my lips to hers. It was a brief, searing kiss that sent my heartbeat thudding all the more.

"Your hands." She gestured to my unbruised knuckles.

"When I changed back, the bruises healed—the one bright side, I suppose. Though I would have preferred to wake beside you." We observed one another. Former strangers caught up in the unfamiliar game of love.

"We have to find an answer, Griffin." The wind whipped longer strands of her hair into her face. She brushed them aside, as her brow creased. "Do you think we could get into Minna's bedroom?"

Real fear seeped into my soul. Minna hadn't been at the Byrons House in over a century, but that didn't mean she hadn't left an impression. The idea of going to her room left me feeling as uneasy as when we'd first left the grounds. "You don't want to go in there."

"Why not? What's there now? Have they remodeled the room?" Kate asked.

"They tried, but they were unsuccessful at finding someone who would work in it."

Kate laced and unlaced her hands as she stared up at the house. "Minna's not haunting it is she?"

"No. It's just a feeling. Hannah says it's dark. The room reeks of something that isn't right. No one has stayed there *since* Minna."

"Then that will give us a better chance of finding something. I say, up we go." She gestured forward.

"Aren't you frightened?" I asked, sorry she'd stepped away to walk to the front door. "This could be highly dangerous, especially for you. She tried to kill you only two nights ago."

Kate bit her lip, then released it. "I'm terrified. But I'm sort of masochistic. I always choose the scariest path."

"Why?"

"Because the scarier it is, the more of a chance it's the right one."

I pulled on the door handle. "Ah, hell and damnation. It's locked."

"Let me see if I can open it," Kate said.

My eyes flickered to her profile as she placed her hands on the door. After a collection of moments, I heard it.

Click.

Kate tugged on the handle and the door swung open.

"Impressive," I said, forcing my voice to sound even. It wasn't the fact she could do magic that unnerved me—it was the ease with which she'd just applied it.

Soundlessly, I gripped Kate's cold hand in mine and we took to the stairs. As we reached the fourth floor landing, we climbed over the ropes blocking off the floor from students. Not that they were needed. Even I noted how the entire atmosphere changed, as though the level had been cloaked in a heavy shroud.

We turned the corner on the top floor, coming to a stop at a dead end. A single door stood there. A tremor of uneasiness vibrated through me at the sight of it. "Here we are."

Kate expelled a breath. Releasing her hand from mine, she reached for the door handle.

"We don't have to do this. There could be some other solution." Even as I spoke the words, I knew there wasn't. That was our best chance at discovering the truth, outside of another séance with Rena.

"If you think I'm giving up on you so easily after last night . . ."

"If the very least I can contribute is to open the door for you, then so be it." I eased myself in front of Kate.

The instant I gripped the doorknob, the metal scorched my skin and I tore my hand away. A raised *B* stood out for only a moment before the letter faded away entirely.

"Maybe I should try?" Kate stepped forward.

"No."

"She's my relative, Griffin. Maybe I'll be able to do it."

"And what happens if it burns you?"

"Then you'll bandage me up this time." Before I could argue further, Kate grabbed the knob and turned it without incident. When she pushed on it, the door swung open, only to smack the wall behind it.

I blinked. We may as well have traveled in time.

CHAPTER 37
KATE

MINNA'S ROOM EASILY PASSED FOR THE LARGEST TIME capsule I'd ever seen. I'd expected musty, emptied quarters. The space gave the impression she'd just stepped out for coffee or something. I suppressed a shudder.

Honestly? Her digs kind of surprised me. No creepy altars or weird voodoo dolls anywhere. Instead, she'd pinned up quotes from Shakespeare and Yeats. I remembered both from my public school English class. Several bible verses had been written in pencil on the pale yellow walls. Not exactly the type of thing I'd anticipate from a witch.

Do not say, I will do to him as he has done to me.—Proverbs 24:29

Vengeance is mine, I will repay, says the Lord.—Romans 12:19

I pointed to the verses. "Five bucks says those are about you."

Griffin's mouth turned downward in displeasure. "I daresay you're right."

"But why Bible verses? She was a witch."

"Easy. These quotes eliminate suspicion." He paused in front of a picture hanging above the desk. A little boy with somber eyes stared back from the frozen image. He would have been cute, except for the ridges of scars that covered one side of his face. The photo seemed so lifelike. As though he were about to launch himself out of the frame.

"That's Jonah?"

Griffin moved as if to touch the picture, but then seemed to think better of it, letting his fingers fall to his side instead. "Yes."

Way to go, Kate. He probably didn't want to talk about it. "I'm sorry. It was stupid of me to bring it up. I mean, who else would it be?"

"It's all right," Griffin said, sadness stealing into his voice. "I'd assumed there would be some remembrance of him here."

Did he want me to talk to him about it, or change the subject? I couldn't be sure. Yet, I wanted to understand Griffin. I *needed* to. "You didn't know him?"

A faraway look filled his eyes. Griffin was probably experiencing it all again—Jonah's simple request and Griffin's own not-so-straightforward death. "No. He wanted to know me, and I thought myself above him. My reasoning seems faulty now."

Griffin faced me. He'd had 115 years to remember it. He might have been haunting Byrons Hall, but I thought it was more the other way around.

"I certainly never wished to see him die. I was spoiled,

indifferent. I was cruel, not kind. I only wanted to be left alone. I don't want to be remembered as a murderer."

"I know the truth," I whispered. Griffin had been cruel —pretty much the biggest ass imaginable—but he wasn't to blame for Jonah Byrons' death. Then Daniela's words from my vision came back to me. "Daniela told me that it was Jonah's time to die, but it wasn't yours. She said that Minna would have known that."

"That doesn't make what I did it any better, does it?" Griffin moved away, and the moment broke apart.

Any questions I had faded away. If I pushed him right then, he'd close himself off. It would have to wait.

Returning to my own search, I pulled on the closet door and jumped. A row of gray uniforms hung in the closet. I shoved my fist against my chest. "Talk about freaking me out."

"I feel like we're missing something that's right under our noses." Griffin stood by the window, staring out at the freedom he no longer had.

"Yeah, I know what you mean." It was as though the room held some sort of unmet expectation. But what was it? I placed my hand on the wall, leaning against it. "What are you hiding, room? I wish I knew your secrets."

A cloud must've passed overhead or something, because the room got dark too quickly. As the space dimmed, writing came into view on the walls. It was as though someone had written on them with chalk or a white crayon, and I was the black light. I turned around in a circle, reading the phrase that had been repeated over and over, at least a hundred times. My heart pounded to the cadence of the words with each repetition.

Jonah is dead.

Griffin let out a low whistle. "Now we're getting to it."

"No kidding." Letting my gaze trail the writing, I read on.

"Kate, would you have a look at this?"

I turned and caught Griffin staring up at a skylight. "What is it?"

He touched my forearm. "Look closer. There's something written in the dust. I almost missed it, but it's there."

Squinting, I leaned forward, just able to make out the jumble of words. "It's another language. German maybe?"

"Makes sense."

I blinked. In the instant I closed my eyes, I went from *guessing* the words were German to *knowing* they were. I could also translate them. I hadn't even wished for that one.

"God, Griffin."

His eyes were full of concern. "What's wrong?"

"I can read those words. I know what the writing says."

Griffin's eyes widened as he took my hand. "And?"

"It says *bitte verzeihen Sie mir*." I ran my hands through my hair. "How can I read German, Griffin? What's happening to me?"

He sounded calm, but his eyes were wild. "I don't know."

Wrapping my arms around myself, I did my best to squeeze out some of my discomfort. It wasn't happening. "It says *please forgive me*."

"Somehow, I doubt that's meant for me." Griffin chuckled. I didn't know how he could find humor in our situation.

"Maybe it was meant for Jonah?"

We stared at one another, the silence stretching between us. As I moved closer to the bed, I spotted a spiral of writing above the headboard—a written tornado of random words.

Griffin Dunn.
Murderer.
Wastrel.
Killer of dreams.
The blood of my blood will destroy him.
Destroy.
Hate.
Cold.
He will walk amongst the living with his heart ripped out.
Pain.
Die!
Die!
Die!
Die!

A sickening sensation twisted my stomach. The hatred that seemed to cling to the walls like a thick paint closed in on me.

Some smaller words had been written closer to the headboard. I leaned forward to read the rest of the writing. As though a door opened, the bed shifted, and I fell, down, down into the darkness. Away from Griffin and the tight little room, my mind and body frozen with fear.

AS MY EYES AND MIND CLEARED, I REALIZED I STOOD alone. In the distance, the sea churned, sending a frigid breeze in my direction and making me shudder. The rustling of the grasses that dotted the dunes acted as the only other sound. The salt air tickled my nose.

Then I saw her, Minna. *Where am I?* I swallowed down acid that rose in my throat.

I'd ended up behind one of those dunes and I crouched down, even though Minna hadn't reacted to my arrival. I was pretty sure she didn't even know I was there.

Minna paced, waving her arms wildly in the air with every step. "The little brat bested me. How, I cannot say, but I should have been able to take her life. Dunn loves her. It would have destroyed him."

Minna. Her voice wasn't loud, or abrasive, or even scary. It sounded as though it belonged to some mousy, church-going school girl, whose only private battle was with acute shyness.

Her skin color had altered from chalky white to pale charcoal. Her blue eyes had shifted to red. Her hair had begun to fall off in clumps, leaving patches of gray and white behind. She laughed, the sound maniacal, before bursting into tears and sobbing.

"No!" She held out her hand, palms out, and closed her eyes. "Be patient, Minna. 'The end is coming. Blood of my blood . . . the hour of my vengeance is near.'"

Before I could process it all, I found myself back in her room at the Byrons School.

Griffin knelt over me, a panicked expression on his face. "Kate, what happened?"

"Minna." Her name tasted bitter on my tongue.

Griffin blanched. "Did she try to hurt you again?"

"All I know is one moment I was here, and then the next I was somewhere else. I'm not even sure Minna knew I was there."

"You never left, so it must have been another visualization of some sort." He rubbed my shoulder. "Tell me."

Though the room'd had a benign feel to it when we'd first walked in, the atmosphere had grown darker. I had to get out. "Not here. I think we've found everything we were going to anyway."

Griffin bent down and swept me up. My breath shot out of my lungs, his actions reminding me of the night before. Even though he didn't shut the door, a glance confirmed the door had shut itself, closing the rest of the school off from Minna's nasty magic once again.

Daniela's words came back to me. *Some of Minna's magic still remains, even if she does not.*

The pressure of Minna's presence had eased once we'd reached the hall. Griffin and I moved through the school, the silence of Saturday making my experience with Minna seem freakier since it had ended.

It wasn't until Griffin brought me to a garden behind the school that he set me on my feet. I tried to calm myself, sucking in deep breaths, hoping to erase the memory of Minna. Griffin settled me onto a stone bench. "I thought a little fresh air would do." Snow fell in thick flakes, dotting his golden hair in a mass of tiny, frigid polka dots.

"Thanks." Sounds filtered in from the street—horns honking, dogs barking. The snow-covered haven where Griffin had taken us seemed like a different world. The weird little garden had a stagnant look about it. There it was easy to imagine that Minna, herself, had sucked all of the life out of the Byrons estate.

"What did she say?" Griffin asked, brushing back my hair.

"She was angry. She said I'd bested her the other night, that something stopped her from killing me. I don't think she knows about my wishes."

Griffin turned away, staring out toward the house and the snow clinging to its roof. I didn't like the faraway look he

STEPHANIE KEYES

had in his eyes. It took him away from me and the little time we had left.

Catching his hand in mine, I led him back to me. "Can we get out of here? I mean, based on what happened last night, I think we have until midnight before you get pulled back, right?"

Griffin's eyes flicked to the house and then back to me. "I *think* so."

"Then let's go, Cinderella." Tugging on his hand, I led him out of the side gate and into the street, a much faster exit than last time. I didn't want to waste another minute.

Somehow, the curse had to be broken, and making wishes just wasn't going to cut it.

CHAPTER 38
GRIFFIN

"You really know how to show a man some entertainment." I entwined my fingers with Kate's as we walked under the archway signifying the entrance of St. Michael's cemetery. The sun had peeked out, sliding through the trees in the still-early morning. "Why are we here, exactly?"

A small smile tugged at her lips. "After that freak show in Minna's room, I needed some fresh air. And I wanted to show you something."

Kate didn't seem particularly eager to elaborate. There was no point in pushing. Together, we walked through pine trees that stood amongst the graves like ancient guardians. Eventually, she led me to a single headstone, bordered in evergreen, standing beside a small pond. When I read the engraving, all became clear.

Brian Covington

Beloved husband and father.

Follow love, follow light, follow peace.

"Griffin, this is my dad. Dad, this is Griffin. I love him." Her voice cracked on the declaration.

I wrapped my arms around her, pulling her against my side. "I'm delighted to meet you, sir. Apart from that unfortunate hair situation, I've heard only the best things."

Kate giggled. "He would have liked you." But despite her laughter, her eyes had filled with tears when she met mine. She forced a swallow. "Why didn't he tell me?"

"I don't know." I shook my head. "All we have to go on is what you've read, but I don't imagine he'd have lied unless it was to protect you."

"Like you did?" She pulled back, her eyes filled with understanding, not accusation.

"I'll do anything to protect you."

"I know." She touched my arm before turning back to her father's headstone. Something about her position and the way the sunlight glinted on her long, chocolate-colored hair caught my attention. A melody began to build in my mind.

"Kate, do you have anything to write with, and maybe a piece of paper?" I clenched and unclenched my hand, itching to get at least the major theme on the page before I lost it.

She frowned but searched her coat pockets. "Here." She handed me a pencil and a small slip of paper with printing on one side. "Will these work?"

"Yes. That will do. I just want to get this down." Brushing snow from a nearby rock, I sat and positioned the small strip of paper on my knee. With practiced precision, I drew a single staff and a treble clef. Next, I added in the notes of the melody. After I'd captured the basic theme, I stuffed the paper into my pocket and offered her the pencil.

"Did you get it all?" she asked, taking the pencil and slipping it behind her ear.

"It's a start. Enough that I'll remember it later." There was more I wanted to say, but a strange tugging sensation in my gut drove the words from my mouth. "Goodness, that's—"

"What?" Kate asked, alarm coloring her voice.

"There's a—" But the sensation of being pulled continued. Rather than fight it, I decided to follow it. I turned in the direction it led me, allowing it to draw me through the cemetery, across an open green, and toward a hill, upon which a single grave stood. No formal headstone had been placed there, only a lone cross. It was a simple iron creation with an even more basic epitaph inscribed into the metal.

1886-1902

Here lies G. Dunn

Murderer

My breath evaporated at the sight. Could it be? Was that why I'd been drawn to the grave? "I think this is my body."

"Good morning! I can't believe I've run into you both." Liam Underhill's voice had my head snapping in his direction.

Dear God. Had he heard me?

"Good morning, Mr. Underhill," Kate said.

I didn't see any point in formalities. "Have you taken to following us now?" How much had Underhill heard? Kate's gaze locked onto mine, and I knew she wondered the same.

"I'm sorry we weren't properly introduced last evening.

I'm Liam." Underhill offered his hand to Kate. She accepted it.

"Kate Covington."

"Nice to meet you, Kate."

How odd Underhill hadn't asked my name after all his questioning the previous night, and then that morning's interruption.

"You know, I slept terribly last night," Underhill said.

"I'm so sorry to hear . . . perhaps you should partake of some sleeping pills." I could feel Kate's gaze on me, but I didn't meet her eyes.

"You should be sorry, Mr. Dunn."

My heart thudded as he spoke my last name. "You must be mistaken. My name isn't Dunn." A bold lie, standing beside my own grave. I kept my attention riveted to Underhill.

"Isn't it? Why not be honest with me?"

"I'm honest with my mother. Few others deserve my truths." My hands had balled into fists. I forced myself to relax, my fingers to unclench.

"I'm sorry, but what is it you wanted, Mr. Underhill?" Kate asked.

"Liam, please." Underhill grinned, obviously thrilled she'd asked. "I was awake all night because I Skyped my assistant early this morning."

What in hell is he talking about?

"And the funny thing is, we've recovered the journal you so casually mentioned." Liam stared out at the city's skyline, partially visible from where we stood. "What I want to know is how did you know it was there?" He'd seemed so easy-going before, yet suddenly he affixed me with an unflinching gaze.

I'd never expected to see Underhill again when I'd

shared that information. What was I supposed to tell him, the truth? What good would it do? Whatever Liam Underhill was, he wasn't a fool. I had to tell him something.

"Mr. Underhill, I understand you fancy yourself a bit of a historian. Some of us are just better at our research. Kate, we really must be going."

"You're right." Kate moved into position beside me.

"Just a moment. Before you go, I have something to show you." He reached into his back pocket and pulled out a small case, before popping it open. With some effort, he withdrew an aged photo of me.

It pained me to see myself as I had been, so full of promise.

"Wow," Kate said, her eyes flashing to mine. "You do look a lot like that guy. That's not you or anything, though. That picture's really old."

Bless her quick thinking. I could almost overlook the bad acting that accompanied it.

"This is a picture of Griffin Dunn that was taken in 1901. To Kate's point, you do look a lot like him. If we're being honest, you look exactly like him," Underhill said.

"People look like one another all the time. It's a rather common occurrence you're bothering yourself over, isn't it?" Stuffing my hands into the pockets of my trousers, I did my best to pretend I couldn't feel the biting December cold.

"The similarities you share with Griffin Dunn are clearly identical. You even hold your body the same way he did." Underhill regarded me with his usual placid smile, but his eyes were working the puzzle, trying to sort me into my proper place.

"And how is that?" I kept my expression blank.

"As though you were preparing to run to the piano and begin a performance." Underhill bent down and dusted off some traces of dirt from the cross that marked my grave. It should have been overrun with weeds, practically illegible. It wasn't.

"What exactly are you getting at, Mr. Underhill?" Kate asked.

"Liam, please. It's just you look like Griffin Dunn and you knew the exact location of the music. There are times when you even speak the way he would have. Are you a great-grandson?"

Relief passed through me. Whoever he believed I was, it wasn't myself.

"He's the last of the line." Kate bit her lip and then released it. "There's been so much bad press about his great-grandfather that he didn't want to share who he was."

Quickly, I performed the maths in my head. "Actually, he was my great-great-great-grandfather."

Heavens, I've grown ancient.

Underhill's brow furrowed. "I had no idea he even had a child. There's been no record of it, and I swear I've seen all of the records."

"Would you tell anyone you're related to someone who was accused of murder?" When Underhill didn't respond, she said, "Yeah. Didn't think so."

"The journal you told me about didn't just hold the compositions that I'd discovered, but nearly twenty more. All handwritten, I might add. I have to have it all authenticated of course, but many of the pieces, well . . . they're pieces my relative supposedly wrote."

My jaw clenched. Jig didn't know a sharp from a flat, a whole note from a sixteenth. He'd taken my music, my ideas, my lover, and, with all probability, my money. "Perhaps your relative wasn't as honest as you first believed."

"I can't answer that, since I didn't know him. If there's

been a mistake, however—if Jiggory did take credit for Dunn's work . . . you could be responsible for letting the world know the truth.

"And also, you may be in line to inherit Fulton House. Of course, I'll need to prove you're you. We'll need a DNA test, and I'll need to see your papers, but those are small matters."

The very idea of me inheriting my own house was preposterous. What did it matter, anyway? It wouldn't last, this being alive. I was only human if I was with Kate. Even that might not be for much longer.

Underhill turned to me. The relief I'd felt when he questioned me about being Griffin Dunn's heir vanished when he glanced at my hands, limp at my sides. Instinctively, I drew them behind me.

"Mr. Underhill. I told you about the journal because I wanted you to know what a lying, scheming mongrel Jiggory Underhill was. Now that word has gotten out, my job is complete. You may keep your tests."

Turning my back to him, I stalked from my grave. I needed to keep moving, keep thinking. Especially since Underhill had become an unanticipated complication.

I was almost out of time to break the curse.

Almost out of time with Kate.

CHAPTER 39
GRIFFIN

AFTER WE RAN INTO UNDERHILL IN THE CEMETERY, Kate had taken me to her place. Since Kate's mother had left for California, we'd spent long hours talking in the silence of her townhouse. It couldn't last, however. We both agreed it was better to bring me back to the estate than risk being pulled back.

Kate had also made the unilateral decision to drive her mother's car. She'd been nervous about the process, but it had been quite a bit faster and warmer than the public transport we'd taken to get to her home in the first place.

The cold formed a vice around me as I watched Kate drive away into the night. If there had been any way I could have stayed with her, I would have. Instead, I was back at the Byrons estate, staring after taillights on a car that had long since left me behind.

I glanced down at my hands.

Solid.

Cold.

I hadn't changed back. Thank goodness I still had Mark's coat.

"You there."

I snapped my gaze in the direction of a security guard. Not Charlie, but the weekend guard I hadn't met. "Yes?" Where was Hannah when I needed her?

"Move along, please. This is private property."

"Yes. Yes, of course." I wasn't going anywhere. There was no way I was experiencing everything with Jonah again for that tosser.

"Now, please, sir." The guard gestured to the gates.

"What's that?" I asked, pointing to the window behind him. "There's someone up there. It's the ghost of Byrons School!"

The guard turned, and I used the opportunity to sprint toward the side lawn.

"Wait!"

Uh oh. Clearly, I hadn't distracted him as much as I'd hoped.

"Hannah!" I hissed through my teeth.

"Sir! You're trespassing!" The guard shouted behind me. A crash sounded, but I didn't bother to stop. Maybe I could scale the building on the side?

Run through the front door. The whispered words in my ear jarred me.

I'd no sooner processed them than the front door creaked open, the sound so loud that it had to have tipped off the guard. I ran through it, heard it slam shut behind me. On the top step of the downward staircase, I slipped, nearly plummeting to the landing below. My knee plowed into the rung of the banister.

"Dammit!"

More footsteps sounded collectively behind me, an incessant drumming I was moments away from being thrown out of the building. I had to escape, to get back to what I knew. Refusing to waste another second of time, I continued down the rest of the stairs and around the corner into Kate's practice room.

My secret door stood open, and I ran through the instant before it slammed shut behind me. Leaning back, I tried to catch my breath, but my chest heaved violently.

Footsteps sounded as the guard passed by my hiding spot. I held my breath. After a moment, they started up again, fading as he continued his search. No doubt chasing me would provide even more fodder to keep the security guards' collective panic in full swing.

Even if they heard me playing, they'd never find me. They wouldn't be able to see the door. Only Kate seemed to have that ability.

Sinking to the floor, I forced my breathing to slow. I sensed I wasn't alone. "Thank you, Hannah."

"You're welcome." Hannah floated onto her usual perch beside my piano. "I've hardly seen you. You must tell me everything." Her round form all but shook in anticipation.

"Whatever do you mean?" I moved to the piano bench, still out of breath from my sprint down the stairs.

My hair hung over my eyes, a chaotic curtain. I brushed it aside as I spun around to face the keys. I began picking absentmindedly at the Brahms piece, thinking of Kate's smooth skin.

"You've lost all focus. Aren't you supposed to be ending

the curse, so we can move on? Instead, you're running around the city, skirt chasing."

"Kate doesn't wear skirts." I didn't bother to keep the wry note from my voice.

"I'm serious. I know you love her. What are you going to do about the curse?"

I didn't deny it that time. "Rena has offered to help us. Kate had a vision of her mother. We learned something's going to happen on the anniversary of my curse. We'll have one chance to end it then."

"Goodness. That's only the start of your problems, I'm afraid."

I stiffened as I heard his name, but I didn't stop playing. "What do you mean?"

"That boy, Ryder showed up here late Friday night with the equipment the *Prats* use."

Prats was the term we used to refer to investigators of the supernatural. Ryder wouldn't be the first to explore the house. The Byrons estate had teamed with all manner of ghost-hunting amateurs after Jonah had died. Whenever a new team had showed up, Hannah'd had entirely too much fun with them, pushing the toy cars they'd brought and driving their equipment into a series of high-pitched frenzies. Although I didn't encourage her, the results amused me.

I'm a ghost, Griffin. I'm supposed to haunt people. It's what we do, she'd informed me.

"Ryder's a spirit hunter? Wonderful. If he's searching for me, I've gone and given him a good head start."

"Whatever do you mean?"

"Kate and I went to a concert on Friday night, and my picture was on the program. It was hosted by the man who wrote the book about me."

Hannah pursed her lips, proceeding to pace and float simultaneously, as we'd both been prone to do.

"Apparently Jig stole my music and passed it off as his own work. Ryder was there, Hannah. He worked at the theater. He must have come here after the concert ended. And here I've been bandying about like no one could possibly recognize me."

I transitioned from the Brahms and began picking out the melody from the cemetery. I'd checked my pockets earlier for the paper I'd written on, but it must have fallen out. No matter; it was still fresh in my memory.

"I wouldn't chastise yourself, Griffin. It'd be quite a leap for him to assume you're actually *you*. And he was asking questions about you even before the concert." She toyed with the lace collar of her dress. "He checked in at the office to try and get a glimpse of your records, visited the registrar's, and followed Kate the day she found the plaque about you."

A smile tugged at the corner of my mouth. "Hannah. Were you spying on him?"

"What?" She brought both hands to her chest. "He's been too pushy with *our girl*."

Our girl. It warmed me somehow to hear Hannah refer to Kate that way.

A scowl settled on my face. "I hadn't realized how much of a pain in the arse Ryder was going to be."

"Maybe he needs to be frightened a little." Hannah sounded thoughtful. She was already planning something.

"Maybe." I returned to my music, my fingers finding the notes to another section from Berlioz's *Symphonie Fantastique: Dream of a Witch's Sabbath*. It seemed the most appropriate piece of music for the moment. After a time, I sensed Hannah drift away.

How ironic that part of me found it a relief to be back in my building, where I belonged.

But even that was an illusion. I didn't belong anywhere. Not anymore.

CHAPTER 40

KATE

Sunday, December 11th—Four Days Left Until Juries

After I dropped Griffin at the school, I drove back home, worrying the entire time I'd be busted for driving without a full license *and* after curfew. Fortunately, there weren't many people on the roads after I got out of the city. And before I realized it, I'd pulled into the parking space outside of our townhouse.

I ran to the house, unlocking the door and letting myself in before quickly dead bolting it behind me. It was well after midnight. Not a soul around to interfere with my plans. Good. There was something I needed to do.

Alone.

The e-reader my dad gave me a couple of Christmases ago sat on my dresser. Pressing the power button, I started it up before navigating to the Store icon. I typed one word into the search field: *Witchcraft*.

I hit enter.

Skimming the titles, I found lots of manuals for things like spell casting or working with herbs. There was even a primer on the Wiccan Wheel, whatever that was, which went through the Wheel of the Year. Probably important, but not what I was looking for. I scrolled more until I found *Unlocking Your Inner Witch: A Beginner's Guide to Connecting with Your Power*. It was only $4.99 for an e-book.

A minute later, I'd downloaded it and began reading.

There are many who will claim evil does not exist in the world—that the practice of Wicca does not allow the entrance of evil into it. I guarantee evil is everywhere, however, whether or not you choose to look for it. The study of Wicca and what the masses refer to as witchcraft are quite different. Wicca is a religion of light and nature, but it is when witchcraft merges with that belief that things can grow dark. Therefore, the most important skill a young witch can learn is protection.

Okay, not what I wanted to hear. I already knew about the bad stuff. After all, wasn't I related to Minna? I skipped ahead. I didn't think I was ready for anything too complex, but the chapter on meditation seemed like a good idea. Maybe I'd learn something, *anything*.

"Casting your first circle. Mm. Burn sage to purify the space and dispel negative energy. Sage, great. Well, this is gonna have to do." I grabbed a bottle of air freshener and sprayed my room, trying not to inhale.

"With chalk, draw a circle on the floor as wide as you

are tall." I discovered a packet of large, colored chalk—the thick kind they made for little kids' fingers—in a drawer in the hall.

Perfect. One hot pink circle coming up. Since I had carpeting in my room and I didn't want a mess to clean up, I improvised. I laid a bed sheet on the floor and drew my circle on the sheet instead. I followed that up by pouring salt around the outside.

Once the circle was in place, I scooped up four tea lights and an aim-a-flame, then set the candles at the four points around the circle. Following the instructions in the book, I closed the circle in behind me. Walking around the circle three times, I chanted, "Cast the circle thrice about, to keep the evil spirits out."

After my third lap, I sat cross-legged on the floor and clicked on the flame, then lit each of the candles.

Nothing remarkable happened, so I returned my attention to the book. The next instructions were to meditate, something I'd never done. I closed my eyes and tried to calm myself.

Breathe in, breathe out.

Breathe in, breathe out.

Breathe in, breathe out.

Keeping my eyes firmly shut, I whispered my request. "I wish for the truth. Show me what I need to know."

The light behind my eyelids brightened for an instant, and then images began to flicker before me.

Griffin.

The curse.

Jonah.

All things I'd seen before.

"I wish for more. Show me how to save him. Tell me about Griffin's curse."

The Soul Separation spell . . .

The words took over my mind for a moment, sending chills to my core. I swallowed.

"What is the spell? How do I break it?"

But more images came then, of me falling . . . dying . . . bleeding.

The sacrifice is great. The words echoed in my mind, and my throat closed. I couldn't speak, couldn't move, and the pictures vanished as quickly as they'd come.

Did that mean if I kept on trying to save Griffin, I'd die?

Shaking, I opened my eyes and then jumped to my feet. I rushed to my bedside table and turned on another light, and then the bathroom light. I turned on the TV, but even that did nothing to blot out what I'd seen. I switched off the e-reader and tossed it across the bed. I proceeded to eye it like it was a snake, ready to strike.

It was just after one thirty in the morning. Moving like someone about a hundred years older, I followed the book's instructions for closing out the circle.

Every time I blinked, I saw my death. I couldn't get the images out of my mind. No matter what I did, they filled my head and heart to the brim. Muscles I didn't know I had throbbed. A thick blanket of exhaustion wrapped itself around me. Still, I'd gotten some information . . . the Soul Separation spell.

If only I knew how to break it.

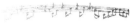

IT WAS JUST AROUND SIX THIRTY IN THE MORNING when I parallel parked Mom's car at a meter a block over from Coffee á Rena, so Rena wouldn't see it. She'd know right away I'd been driving without a license—after all, she'd been the one who'd taken me out to practice after Dad had died.

I'd tried to get some sleep after the ritual, but there was no chance of that. Witnessing my own death didn't help. I jogged to the entrance of Rena's apartment. On weekdays, she always opened at five, but Sundays weren't exactly hopping in the 'Burgh, so she unlocked the doors at ten. I punched in the security code and waited for the system to disarm, rocking back and forth on my heels in the dark to keep warm.

When the alarm was off, I let myself inside and armed it again. If Rena had gotten back from Mark's, she'd be up. If she hadn't, her apartment still felt cozier than my place.

If she *had* made it back, it was the perfect time—maybe the *only* time—I'd get to really talk to her. I spun around and found Rena at the top of the stairs, waiting.

"Kate." She gave me one of her warm Rena smiles before frowning. "What are you doing here, girl? You do not do mornings. Want some coffee?"

"God, yes." Coffee would be a lifeline. "Are you an auntie again?"

"I am." Rena grinned and tugged her phone from her pocket. In an instant, a picture of a red faced, screaming baby girl filled the small screen. "This is Stella Marie. She's already a little ball buster."

"Congrats, Auntie. She's cute." Kicking off my boots, I wiggled my toes inside my fuzzy socks before following her up the stairs and into the kitchen. I spared the guest room a glance as we passed by. Memories of my night there with Griffin warmed me.

Rena poured coffee into a mug. "Here." She offered me the steaming brew. "This is a nice French Roast. Should perk ya up just fine."

I took the cup and sipped. The caffeine greeted my body like a long-lost friend.

"Did you and Griffin have a nice time on Friday?" Rena's face lit as she added sugar to her coffee. The longer I went without speaking, however, the faster her face fell. She wasn't a mother, but she *was* psychic.

"Can we talk about something else for a minute?" I wasn't ready to share details about the exchange with Liam Underhill, let alone reveal that I'd had sex for the first time. Not yet, anyway. "I got an e-book about witchcraft and I tried some meditation."

She sipped her coffee, regarding me over the rim of the cup. "Let me guess. You saw something you didn't want to?"

"How'd you know?"

"That's what happens with visions. They don't show us what *we* want, usually only what we need to see."

The warmth from the mug heated my hands. The cozy room made the events of last night seem far away. "Do you think they're accurate?"

"Sometimes. Sometimes not." Rena seemed thoughtful. "Do you want to talk about it? What did you see?"

"See and *hear*, you mean."

She halted her coffee cup's progression halfway to her lips. "You heard something, too?"

"A voice. It said something about a Soul Separation spell and a sacrifice that would have to be made. Does that mean anything to you?" I drained my coffee cup.

"No. I don't know anything about spells and sacrifices. I don't like the sound of it, though. Maybe it's Daniela trying to tell you something?"

Annoyance ripped through me. What good was Daniela anyway? She'd deserted me, and then shown up once to give me some cryptic information.

"On second thought, this doesn't sound like her style." Rena added cream to her coffee. "What made you try meditation?"

"It seemed like the least complex thing in the book. I thought it would be good for me to try to do *something* to help Griffin. I didn't bargain on creepy voices and death visions." Crap. I hadn't meant to share that little nugget.

"Death visions? Who died?" Rena gripped her cup, leaning closer, searching my face.

"Griffin." The lie weighed on my tongue as it slipped out.

"Death visions don't always mean *death*. Besides, Griffin's already dead."

Instant relief. "So it could mean something else, and there's no point in freaking out?"

"None at all. Maybe *I* can work on this with you, Kate. I mean, that is why you're here, right?"

"Yeah."

"Okay, then let's try something . . . a meditation to calm you."

I shook my head. "No, I don't ever want to do that again."

Rena took my cup and set it on the table. She guided me over to the cushions in the living room and I sat down, cross-legged. Rena took a pillow across from me. "Meditation isn't inherently evil, Kate."

"What if I see something freaky again?" My stomach clenched.

"Take my hands and close your eyes. Breathe in and out, slowly. Let the tension go. Relax."

"I'm scared." I felt like the world's biggest idiot for blurting my fears out loud.

"I'll be right here. Now, keep breathing in and out. Focus on the sound of your breath."

The memories of what I'd seen were too fresh in my mind. I didn't want to relive those. Still, maybe I'd been meditating the wrong way? That sounded like something I'd do. Maybe working with Rena would help me figure things out.

"If any thoughts turn up, gently push them away. Focus only on the sound of your breath. Nothing else matters. Clear your mind." My hand grew heavy in hers. Second by second, my panic began to abate. Everything was warm and cozy. The terror slowly subsided.

"Imagine your body is filled with a white light. That light is pouring into your body, filling you with positivity. The white light pushes your fears out. Let out a long, sharp breath."

I followed her lead and exhaled deeply, releasing the negative energy. Drawing in a slow breath, I envisioned it as nothing but white light, filling me up, cleaning me from the inside out.

Follow love, follow light, follow peace . . .

The same voice filled my head and my ears, all at the same time. I jolted, my eyes flying open.

Rena was right there, her calm blue eyes meeting mine. "I'm with you. It's okay. Close your eyes and let it come. You're safe here. You know that."

Safe. I was safe. Still, it was hard to go back to medi-tating after a strange voice had recited the song Dad used to sing to me when I was a kid. Though I did my best, there were no more voices. The show was over for the day.

For the next half hour, Rena led me through a medita-tion ritual on how to open myself up to and close myself off from energy. It was a simple series of steps I could practice at home, where I envisioned white light cleansing my body and removing negative energy.

When we'd finished, I no longer felt jittery or out of control. Unfortunately, I hadn't learned anything more about the Soul Separation spell or the sacrifice. All those experiences and I was no closer to finding a way to break Griffin's curse than when I'd started.

CHAPTER 41

GRIFFIN

Monday, December 12th—Three Days Left Until Juries

KATE AND I SPENT MOST OF SUNDAY TOGETHER, WITH Kate arranging another late-night drop off at the school for me, just before midnight. The hours between when I last held Kate and her return wore me down like a lagging horn section I'd once performed with. Though I remained in solid form, I found the idea of sleep foreign. The very notion that I might need rest left me too jumpy to consider the prospect.

I'd played for several hours, but soon I'd tired of even my own music. I'd climbed the stairs to the lobby to await Kate's arrival. I reclined on one of the chairs in the foyer, in total darkness. Though the idea might have terrified some, I was one of the ones haunting Byrons School. I had nothing to fear from the place.

A light flicked on, and I rose to a sitting position, my eyes taking a moment to adjust.

"Waiting for anyone special?"

Ryder had on some sort of black uniform, a headband with a light attached to it, and a pack on his back. In his hand, a small device emanated a whirring sound.

"Good morning, Ryder. On your way to a costume party, I presume?"

He stepped farther into the room. "No. I'm on an official investigation."

"For the circus?"

Ryder scowled. "No, the Pittsburgh Paranormal Teen Club."

"I can certainly see why they accepted you for membership with your attire." I needed to get away. Although I'd remained in human form overnight, how could I ensure I would stay alive even for the length of the conversation? "I wish I could say it's been a pleasure, but that would be a lie. I see little point in those." I brushed past him on my way to the stairs.

"Do you?"

I stopped.

"Why are you lying to Kate, Griffin?"

I hated the sound of her name on his lips. "I've never lied to Kate about anything. I've never needed to."

"Does she know you're Griffin Dunn?"

"Griffin Dunn? You're insane." I burst into laughter, though inside I reeled. "Don't you think I'd look like, I dunno, a rotted corpse if I were Griffin Dunn? He died ages ago."

The equipment in Ryder's hands sounded off the closer he came. Once again, I was struck by this sensation of the familiar, as though I'd met him before. It vanished when he spoke.

"I thought so at first, but when I heard Kate and Kimberly talking in class about how Kate's hot boyfriend looked just like the dead guy on the plaque, I had to check it out."

"Ridiculous." I wasn't hot. I felt comfortable in the room —not overheated in the slightest.

"Is it? The thing is, though, I've always been very good at puzzles."

"Your point?"

"Fine. You're supposed to be enrolled here, but the school has no record of you. None of the teachers even know who you are. There are no students named Griff at this school."

My heartbeat quickened. "Poor record keeping, obviously."

"The first time I met you, you had on that fancy old suit. It was like something they would have worn a hundred years ago."

He *did* remember meeting me. That simpleton. "What's wrong with going a little"—I latched onto a word Kate had used and hoped it was the right one—"*retro*? Clearly, I'm wearing current clothing today." I gestured to the shirt I wore, another of Hannah's finds.

It was Ryder's turn to laugh. "Those aren't even your own clothes you're wearing. Students have been reporting missing clothes for a week. Plus, there's your shirt."

"What about it?"

"It's got Garry Murphy's last name on the back."

Ah, Hannah. She wouldn't have understood she'd need to search for something like that.

"Besides, he's the only one here whose clothes will fit

you." He narrowed his eyes, as though inspecting an insect under a microscope. "How are you even able to appear this way? And what would a ghost need with clothes?"

I had no choice but to deny his accusations. "You're mad. I'm not a ghost, Ryder. I'm just a little down on my luck." I hated even admitting that much to him.

"The suit you wore when we first met is exactly like the one Griffin Dunn wore in this picture." He held up the program from Friday, an evil grin on his face. "Details, Griffin. It's the little details that matter." He tapped his head three times with the program. "And then, of course, there's the video footage."

What in Heaven's name is he talking about? I gave him a tight smile. "Is this about Kate? You want her for yourself, don't you?"

Ryder's face reddened. I shouldn't have baited him, but I had to keep the upper hand.

"Well, it's me she wants. It's me she *loves*." I allowed a triumphant grin to form on my face.

"For now. Once I show this to Kate, she'll change her mind."

Ryder opened a black rectangle, one larger than Kate's seller phone, and held it up in front of me. At first, it appeared as though I was staring at my own reflection, but then, I appeared on the screen from a distance. Horror washed over me as I witnessed myself being dragged across the brick courtyard by some unseen force, before fading from view. A moving picture, much like the demonstration I'd seen by the Lumière brothers before my death, but on a much smaller scale.

"I've been watching this place for weeks, adding the cameras slowly when I knew I could. This is a film, a *video*," Ryder said, like he was speaking to a child.

"I'm familiar."

"Are you? Because someone who died in 1902 might not have gotten a chance to see a film."

I would have sworn sweat broke out on my brow. I hadn't perspired in a century. "Ryder, you're a fool and your accusations are preposterous. And this is clearly fabricated evidence."

He thrust a finger in my direction. "After all the surveillance I placed in here on Friday, I'll get even more proof. I will bring you down—at *any* cost. Then I'll make Kate *mine*."

I hadn't meant to hit him, but it was surprisingly easy. My fist made a solid connection with his jaw. Ryder flew backward, landing on his arse on the hard floor. He glowered up at me, his fists at the ready as he got to his feet.

The front door creaked. "What's going on here, Griffin?" Charlie rushed into the lobby from his station outside. "Did you just punch Ryder?"

"Apologies, Charlie. I'm meeting Kate for rehearsal early, and I heard noises. I thought I heard someone snooping around but didn't realize it was him."

"I wasn't snooping around," spouted Ryder, his eye already appearing to blacken.

Charlie's eyebrows shot heavenward. "Your gear isn't exactly helping your case, Ryder. You weren't trying to do a ghost hunt again, were you? They've turned you down before."

"He's a ghost, Charlie. He's not even alive," Ryder announced, his hands on his hips, as though he'd made the pronouncement of the century.

"Preposterous." I drew myself up, turning away from Ryder.

Charlie's gaze locked onto mine for a moment. "Now Ryder, he looks pretty alive to me."

"It's a trick," Ryder said.

"I say a full mental evaluation might be in order, Charlie. Clearly, the boy is disturbed." I almost felt sorry for Ryder. He'd discovered the truth, and I had no choice but to try to discredit him.

"I have video," Ryder said, holding up the device.

My heart stopped. If he showed the video to Charlie, what would happen? Would Charlie believe him?

Charlie shook his head. "Ryder, I'm sure you have many things on those gadgets of yours, but you've broken my trust. I'm not much inclined to believe anything you have to say."

Ryder scoffed, getting to his feet. "The headmaster loves me. I'm like a second son to him. I'll tell him who Griff really is."

"Who is he?" Charlie asked, his face expectant.

Uh oh.

"Someone we all know, though we've never formally met." Ryder grinned.

I drew my fist again. "Give me a reason, you prat."

Charlie scratched his head. "Ryder, who is he?"

Ryder smirked. "A murderer by the name of Griff—"

"That's a reason." Drawing back my fist, I punched Ryder in the cheek. My honor was at stake. Only a couple of hundred years ago, those words would have resulted in a dawn appointment in my home country, with drawn weapons and a second in case I lost.

"Griffin. Come on now." Charlie's hand rested on my shoulder, making me pause. "He's not . . . um . . . don't do this to yourself, okay?"

I could see the words written on Charlie's face. *He's not worth it.* Charlie was taking my side. Glancing down at

Ryder, I noted I'd knocked him out. Good. Maybe I'd get a moment to destroy the device with Ryder's evidence.

"What the hell is this?" Kate stood in the doorway, glowering at the lot of us.

"Kate, dearest. This, er . . . this isn't what it looks like." *Oh my.*

CHAPTER 42

KATE

AFTER HOLDING THE CIRCLE AND MEDITATING THAT past weekend, it seemed as though I was a little closer to solving the problem of Griffin's curse. I knew the name —*Soul Separation spell*. I just had no clue what to do about it.

As to the death visions, I'd just omitted those from the story when I'd shared it with Griffin the day before. There was no point in making him freak out any more than he already was.

Staying up late so many nights had taken its toll, so I'd decided to sleep in that Monday. I woke up to find an email from the school with my official jury time. Thursday, at noon. Griffin and I needed to rehearse.

I'd never expected to walk into the school and find Griffin and Charlie talking over Ryder's unconscious body.

They looked like two kids who got busted raiding a candy store.

"Is someone going to tell me what's going on?" I demanded.

"Kate, darling, I just . . ." Griffin frowned.

Charlie hemmed and hawed. "Um, well now, Kate."

Griffin stepped toward me. "I must speak with you."

"Griff, you're going to have to answer some questions about this whole thing." Charlie patted Ryder on the cheek.

"Of course, Charlie. You have my word," Griffin said.

"I know it." Crouching down, Charlie turned back to Ryder and proceeded to pat him on the cheek some more.

"Come on. Before he wakes up." Griffin pulled me toward the stairs.

I wasn't going to get any answers in front of Charlie, so I let him lead me away from the lobby. But the moment we reached Griffin's room, I whirled around. "What's going on?"

He thrust his hands into his golden locks. "Listen. Ryder knows who I am, or thinks he does, anyway."

A slice of fear drove down my spine. "What?"

"He had a video of me on that black square of his—he caught me being pulled back on Friday night. He's going to turn me in." Griffin seemed panicked. "It looked pretty compelling, Kate."

"There's no way he got permission for something like that. He must have snuck in over the weekend."

"Ryder said he placed cameras around the school. Is there some way we can destroy it all? Should we throw the technology out the window?"

"No. It wouldn't be worth it. That equipment's expensive and I'd get in real trouble. He's probably already uploaded it to the cloud anyway. Ryder's anal."

Griffin frowned. "Once again, I have absolutely no idea what you just said, though it's intriguing."

Kate rolled her eyes, grinning at me. "My point is, we can't destroy it, so the only thing we can do is try and discredit it."

"How?"

"I don't know yet."

"Brilliant."

"Look, my jury's Thursday at noon."

"We still have a lot of work to do. We're not ready for Thursday."

I spared Griffin a glance. "At least I have you to help me. I don't know what I'd do if I had to figure this out on my own."

He smirked. Obviously, he'd been expecting me to say something like that. "Of course you have me. I want to help you be as prepared for this as possible."

"Thank you." I squeezed his hand. Everything would be all right. Griffin was my angel.

AN HOUR LATER, I KNEW THE TRUTH. HE WAS THE devil.

"Dammit, Griffin. Why are you never happy with anything I play?" My fingers had permanently molded themselves to the clarinet keys. The callus on my right thumb, which fitted under the thumb rest, had cracked from the cold and had started bleeding. I pressed my tongue against the indentation my teeth left on my bottom lip, trying to force the impression out.

"That's not true," he said, remaining at the piano and rubbing the bridge of his nose.

"Then back off. You're my accompanist, not my teacher."

He glanced up at me. "I thought I was performing both roles more than adequately. Or would you prefer to go it alone?"

I could hear the threat in his voice. "No, I just—"

"You don't need me to tell you that was a poor effort, because you already know. You can do this, but you need to believe in yourself. I can't do it for you." Worry creased his brow.

A glance at the clock told me it was almost eight. "Let's go again."

"Fair enough." Griffin poised his fingers over the keys.

I wouldn't be afraid of the music. I would not hold back. I would give it my all. If I screwed up, so be it. If they told me to leave, I'd go. But it was time I quit acting like a wimp and got the job done.

Taking a breath, I dove in, attacking the piece with a ferocity I hadn't before.

With my new mindset, the runs were no longer barriers I dreaded, but simple hurdles I could and did conquer. I could do it. Griffin believed in me; I needed to do the same. I would prove it to myself and to Griffin.

"Yes!" Griffin cried, his enthusiasm spurring me on. "That's it!"

I poured everything into the music. In it, I shared my deepest fear: that I wouldn't be able to save the boy I loved. And when I hit the last note, I could have hit the floor.

I knew I'd put everything into my performance.

Griffin smiled at me. "I knew you had it in you."

"*I* didn't," I said, my voice hoarse.

"You were brilliant." He caught my hand in his,

bringing my knuckles to his lips. A longing to be closer to him filled me up.

He frowned slightly, glancing at the keys. "I wanted to play something for you." Funny, but it almost seemed as if he was asking my opinion about a piece. That couldn't be right.

"Sure. Go ahead." I leaned against the piano and waited.

What a study in opposites Griffin was. One moment he was cold and callous, the next, considerate and sweet. Though he'd seemed more of the latter since we'd gotten together.

"Mm." Griffin's fingers danced across the keys. The piece sounded familiar, though I couldn't place it. My gaze darted to his face, and I paused.

His eyes were closed, his fingers flying as though on fast-forward. He'd totally lost himself in the music and in each note. I stepped closer. I didn't want him to stop. It was a new brand of magic, though—the kind Griffin made entirely on his own.

He'd been brilliant before, passionate. In that moment, Griffin changed, almost as though opening before my eyes. His expression reflected his pain, his fears, and his loss.

The bench creaked as he moved, almost physically coaxing the music from the piano. I rested my elbow on the end of the instrument and listened. As arresting as his appearance was, the music drew me in even more.

He'd made me a part of that moment, enveloped me in the piece. That was his gift. I could *feel* his love for me, his need for me, in every note.

And then he stopped on a bold chord, his eyes closed, head hung, breath heavy. He glanced up, and a myriad of emotions rested in his gaze.

"Did you tell Kimberly I'm hot?" he whispered.

A blush crept up my cheeks. "Maybe."

He smirked, returning his attention to the piano.

"But don't let it go to your head, fancy pants."

"Can't. I dunno what it means." He was still laughing as he started the accompaniment for my Brahms piece.

I had to find a way to save him—no matter what the price. The world deserved to hear what I had.

CHAPTER 43
GRIFFIN

Tʜᴇ ᴅᴀʏ ᴡɪᴛʜᴏᴜᴛ Kᴀᴛᴇ ѕᴛʀᴇᴛᴄʜᴇᴅ ʙᴇꜰᴏʀᴇ ᴍᴇ, ᴀɴ endless void. My heart willed it to reach three o'clock, the mantra of her dismissal time replaying itself in my head.

Three o'clock. Three o'clock. Three o'clock.

"Hey."

At the sound of her voice, I jerked my head in the direction of the door. A wave of happiness hit me. "Hello, you. It's not three o'clock yet, is it? Are you skipping class again?"

"I missed you, too." The dark smudges under her eyes stood out against her pale skin. "More like time off for good behavior. I did well on my theory homework, for a change. It's probably your fault." She put a knee on the piano bench, leaning into me.

"I don't mind taking the blame for *that*. Now, what shall we do this afternoon?" We would probably rehearse; however, we hadn't discussed our plans for *after* rehearsal.

It amazed me how reliant I'd become on her to stave off my loneliness.

"I have to work. I'd like you to come with me."

"I cannot imagine I would excel at either making or serving coffee."

She laughed. "I agree, but I'd like to try and get Rena to do another séance."

"I don't like it, Kate. You've already had too many unusual things happen, and that was before you started hearing voices in your bedroom."

Kate frowned. "We need to find out how to end our curse."

Our curse. It moved me that she was prepared to own the dreaded thing with me. I did the only thing I could: I changed the subject. "No one's come searching for me from the headmaster's office."

"It's only a matter of time. Charlie told them you were coming to classes here." At the sound of Hannah's voice, I turned. "They are going to *remove you*. At least that was the term I think they used."

"But they can't. He'll get pulled back." Kate's eyes narrowed. "Ryder's a pain in the ass."

"Definitely. I've also heard his plans. He's organized an investigation here at midnight on the 17th," Hannah said.

A chill passed through me and I suddenly understood how Charlie felt whenever Hannah paid him a visit.

"But I thought Headmaster Withers refused to grant him access?" Kate asked.

"Nevertheless." Hannah let the word hang there, the unspoken implications of her thoughts sifting among the dust motes waltzing through the room.

"Damn." Leave it to Ryder to hound me until my very end.

"You'll need to take the greatest care. The group's planning to interact with the spirit of Griffin Dunn." Hannah shook her head. "In the meantime, take the back door when you leave, okay?"

She'd gone before I could say anything else.

"For now, Hannah's right. Let's stick to the less-travelled pathways, shall we?" Tugging on Kate's hand, I picked up her bag and led her down the hallway and out the side door.

ONCE WE'D MADE IT OUT INTO THE CHILLY, EARLY afternoon. I grabbed a small stone and wedged it into the lock on the side door. To passersby, it would give the impression the door had been closed and locked. "Let's use this as our entrance and exit. Seems less conspicuous."

"Gotcha," Kate said, leading me through the gate. Neither one of us spoke. When we'd been at Rena's over the weekend, it had seemed like quite a long stretch of time until December seventeenth. The harsh reality of my impending doom hung above us, an ominous note.

We drove to Rena's in relative silence, except for Kate's grumbling as we hit a small amount of traffic. Much like the first time we'd arrived, we found Rena dancing in the main area of the shop. No patrons were inside. How did she manage to keep Coffee á Rena open?

"Kate!" Rena cried once she'd spotted us. "And hunky Griffin! What a nice surprise this is." She set a steaming mug of something on the counter.

"Surprise. What do you mean? I'm supposed to work," Kate said. "I'm a little early, but I thought maybe we could do another séance before my shift."

"I didn't think you'd want to work today." Rena moved closer. "I thought you might want a few days off. I'll give you extra hours next week if you want, but . . ." Her gaze flickered to me and back to Kate.

But I could be permanently dead in less than a week, or worse. I tried to act as though I hadn't heard and moved from Kate's side. Another young woman worked the front counter—a slight blonde with large blue eyes. She threw me an appraising look from her position behind the counter. Once, she would have been exactly my type. That day, I simply turned away without expression.

"Let's talk in the back. Sierra, watch the front for me, honey," Rena said.

The girl must have nodded, for we were soon following Rena into the same back room where we'd held the séance before. That time, she closed the door to the room with a soft click.

"Did you enjoy the concert, Griffin?" Rena asked. "Kate didn't tell me anything. We got caught up in some other things."

Kate's cheeks turned pink. No doubt, she was considering the latter part of Friday night. The one during which I'd explored her body. But Kate soon snapped out of whatever reverie she'd fallen into. "Apparently, Jiggory Underhill stole Griffin's music and his friend and lover."

"Former-lover," I added. "I wouldn't call her a friend." Kate glanced in my direction with a raised eyebrow. "Why mince words?" I shrugged, as seemed to be the fashion.

"Anyway," Kate said, rolling her eyes, "we met Liam Underhill, and Griffin told him his relative was a liar. And where to find the originals of all of his work."

Rena shook her head. "Great job keeping a low profile, Griffin."

"What was I supposed to do?" I didn't bother to keep the caustic tone from my voice.

"Keep your mouth shut, enjoy hearing your own work performed, and move on?" Rena asked.

"He took credit for my work. He *stole* from me. Kate thinks he might have been pilfering money from my accounts. Don't tell me you would have ignored that?"

Rena seemed to consider that. "No, I don't suppose I would."

Music by Offenbach began to play, the sound scattering my thoughts. "Hello?" Kate held her cell phone up to her ear. "Yes?" She sat down and ran her hand to the back of her neck. "How do I know I can trust you?"

I stared at Kate during the pause that followed. She toyed with her shirtsleeve, tapping her foot while she awaited a response. "Meet me at Coffee á Rena, Market Square. A half hour." Kate pressed part of the phone and glanced up.

"What is it?" Rena frowned as though she already knew the answer, which she probably did, being psychic.

A worried crease puckered Kate's brow. "That was Liam Underhill. We ran into him again over the weekend," she said.

My breath lodged itself in my throat. "What did he want?"

"He has something to show you. He said something about finding the truth about Griffin Dunn." Her frown almost matched the one she'd given me when I'd first handed her the Brahms piece, yet it was underscored with a new note. Fear. "He'll be here in half an hour."

Damnation.

CHAPTER 44

KATE

RENA AND I WENT INTO THE KITCHEN TO MAKE TEA, Griffin's Band-Aid for any stressful situation.

Griffin had gone out to the upright piano in the shop to play. I'd expected him to choose the classics again, but instead, he expertly covered a piece by one of my favorite bands. He must've been paying attention to it when we were in the car.

Cool.

I heard Sierra talking and his soft-toned replies. I understood why she'd gravitated to him. Who wouldn't? Still, it did nothing to stop the little fingers of jealousy worming their way into my heart.

"Ouch!" I'd picked up the teakettle by its scalding hot sides and not by the handle. I dropped the kettle back on the burner.

"Kate! Are you okay?" Rena rushed over.

"It was stupid. I don't know why I picked up the kettle that way." I held my palms out in front of me, the skin was red and stinging. How would I ever be able to perform my jury piece after this?

But before I could answer her, the pain receded, and the redness vanished until there was no trace. The skin should have been puckered and on its way to forming some good scars, but it was unblemished. I hadn't even wished for my skin to heal.

It just *happened.* I glanced up and caught Rena watching me. "I guess I dropped it quickly enough."

Rena met my eye as she straightened up the tea leaves and cleaned the strainer. The brew was a tart raspberry. "Or your powers are growing."

"What good does that do me if I don't know how to handle them?" There, I'd said it out loud. "What if I have this power, all of this control over Griffin's curse, and I *still* don't know how to save him?"

Before all of that had begun, I'd been an outcast, a loner, but I'd *known* the world I lived in. I'd understood how things operated. But learning I wasn't who I'd thought, that my mom wasn't even my mom . . . it called everything into question.

Suddenly, I had this magical legacy and a crazy ghost witch after me. The worst part of it all was learning that I alone could save Griffin.

"I don't even know who I am anymore. I'm not even Kate. I'm just . . . lost."

Rena reached over and squeezed my hand. "You'll figure out these powers of yours. You've already learned so much."

A pair of strong, male arms wrapped around me. I leaned back into Griffin. "You'll save me, because you are *the* most stubborn person I've ever met, Katherine Covington. You won't let Minna destroy me." Griffin gently coaxed my hair out of my face and behind my ear.

The bell tinkled out front, alerting us to another customer. I straightened my shoulders. "I'd better go and see if that's him."

"I suppose you should." Griffin slid onto one of Rena's stools.

Rena shook her head. "You can't tell him who you really are, Griffin. You're dead. How do you think that would go down? Are you really ready for daytime television, boy?"

Griffin's eyes widened. "I haven't the slightest idea what that means."

"Never mind. I'll handle it." I patted his arm, leaving him with Rena. Taking a deep breath, I stepped out front. Liam Underhill was there with his kind eyes, paying Sierra for a regular coffee.

"It's on me, Sierra." I nodded in her direction, but never took my eyes from Underhill.

"Cool." She pushed a napkin and a coffee cup toward Underhill.

"Thanks for the coffee." He took a sip. "This is excellent. I'm glad you suggested we meet here."

My body had somehow become wooden, unwilling to do my bidding.

"Is Mr. Du—is Griffin here?" His eyes darted around the room.

He knows. "Come around, okay?" I gestured to the back.

He hesitated before following me through to Rena's private space. I noticed the worry on Griffin's face as I returned, only to be replaced by annoyance as Underhill walked through the door.

"Tell me, Mr. Underhill . . . you've interrupted my gravesite visits and my private meetings. Shall I expect you in my bed chamber next?"

Liam laughed, seeming completely unaffected by Griffin's acidity. "You have to understand . . . uh, may I call you Griffin?"

"No."

"You have to understand, Griffin," Liam said with a smile, "the information you've given me . . . well, it's a bit like giving a bone to a dog."

"Should we inspect you for fleas, as well?" Griffin loomed over Underhill, the six inches of height difference between them making the good doctor look like a hobbit.

Liam chuckled. "Seriously, your little piece of history is so intriguing, I've been able to think of little else." He paused then, a smile lighting his face as he extended his hand toward Rena. "My apologies, Madam. I don't believe we've been introduced."

"Rena Lane, Mr. Underhill," she said, her voice guarded. It was hard for Rena to be too reserved with people, though. Even ones she didn't trust. A goofy smile transformed her face. "I've read your book."

"Really? Well, you're one of two people. My mother will be thrilled to hear she has company." He took Rena's hand in his. "The pleasure is all mine, Mrs. Lane."

"Miss," Rena offered immediately.

Underhill smiled, turning three different shades of red at once. "Of course, *Miss* Lane."

Rena blushed.

Underhill's pale face seemed to grow even redder as he released Rena's hand.

"Uh-hm. You wanted something, Underhill?" Griffin

sneered. Man, he had that whole uppity British guy act down pat.

Liam handed Griffin a picture of a man holding up an old journal and grinning. It was the academic equivalent of a big fish photo. "Look. I had the journal at Fulton House authenticated. It's real."

"I know it is." Griffin's voice sounded hard, clipped. He reminded me of a lion, ready to strike—to tear Underhill apart.

"And, please accept my apologies, but I found this." He extracted the piece of paper Griffin had written on at Dad's grave and offered it to him.

Griffin snatched it from Underhill's grasp. "Petty theft, Underhill? I would have thought better of you."

"It had fallen on the ground. As you can see, I've returned it." Liam loosened his collar and leaned closer to us. "Curious, though. Your writing on that piece of paper matches the journal."

Shit.

Griffin went rigid beside me.

"When I found the second journal and got a sample of your handwriting, I realized you composed all those pieces. I'd never had a proper handwriting sample of yours before. I assumed the journal was Jiggory's, since it was found with his things.

"And then your resemblance to Griffin Dunn—it's extraordinary. You even have a mark on the heel of your left hand." Underhill smiled. "Griffin Dunn suffered a severe burn from touching a fireplace hearth as a child. The metal grate which held the logs was hot. When Griffin touched it, it partially branded him with part of the Warwickshire crest. Just a small part—a single line that made up the coat of arms."

Griffin rolled his eyes skyward. "Your point?"

"Do I need to state the obvious?" Underhill toyed with his collar as he regarded Griffin. "All of the evidence suggests you *are* Griffin Dunn. Beyond that, I still would have been able to identify you if I didn't have any of that evidence to support my claims."

"And why exactly is that?" Griffin's tone turned haughty.

Underhill shifted. "Because I've been standing outside this shop for the last ten minutes listening, and I've never heard anyone play the piano the way you do. You're very talented, son."

Griffin's eyes lit for a beat. In the space of a quarter note, however, his expression hardened. I could almost see his brain working overtime, trying to come up with a solution.

Finally, Griffin spoke. "It seems you have me at a disadvantage, Mr. Underhill. You know far more about me than I do about you. For example, I have no clue as to what you're after. Is it money? Are you a fame seeker? Do you want to steal my work, as well?"

Liam smiled. "If I wanted to sell your story, Kate knows as well as I do that I would have done it by now. No, it's a bit worse than all that, I'm afraid."

"Really. How so?" Griffin sat and then crossed his arms.

"I'd like to make sure the world knows you really composed all of those pieces. Beyond that, I've never believed you were a murderer. I could help you clear your name." Underhill scratched his head, as though trying to think of more.

"How do we know we can trust you?" I'd always been a pretty good judge of character, but I couldn't risk getting it wrong.

"A fair question." Liam reached into his pocket and extracted a very familiar leather-bound journal. Griffin's notebook that Liam had at the concert. He offered it to Griffin. "This journal is worth thousands of dollars. It's an academic's dream. But it really belongs to you."

Griffin's lips parted in surprise. He couldn't have seen that one coming, either. Slowly, as though moving through a dream, he accepted the book.

"Of course, you don't have to tell me anything. I can leave tonight and never contact you again." Liam dropped his hands at his sides, as though not sure what to do with them once the journal had been turned over. "But if you do agree to let me help you, your secret would be safe with me. I want to change your opinion of my family."

Griffin ran a hand over the book, a wondrous expression on his face. He'd probably never expected to see it again, let alone have it handed to him. He glanced back at Rena for a beat, and I caught her wink. What better assurance than to be vouched for by a psychic?

"I'd just like to know one thing. If it's all right." Liam removed his glasses, staring at Griffin as though his secrets lay in his eyes. "How are you still alive?"

Griffin hadn't moved in my peripheral. Liam's gift had overwhelmed him, that much was obvious. I needed to buy him time. "That's a little complicated." *Yeah, Kate. Like that's not the understatement of the century.*

Liam replaced his glasses, nodding, and grinned. "Don't you know? Complicated's my specialty."

I'D NEVER EXPECTED GRIFFIN TO TALK TO LIAM. I'D figured he'd knock him out, like he'd done with Ryder, or we'd find some way to sneak out of the building. Instead, the opposite had happened.

He'd spilled the beans—about the curse and falling in love with me. Nothing seemed out of bounds. Once Liam had processed what he could, he began asking Griffin questions about Jiggory. Then Rena and I might as well have left the room, so we did.

Rena had suggested we try another séance, but though I'd slowed my breath and focused on the candle flame in front of me, I couldn't concentrate. My thoughts were in the other room with Griffin.

"I've bookmarked a couple things you might try." Rena was skimming the book on witchcraft that I'd found online, her finger moving right to left as she slipped through the virtual pages.

"Thanks. I'll take a look." Not that it would do much good. It was amazing that I hadn't managed to burn the house down with my ritual. I couldn't imagine a second.

"I've been thinking about what you said before, about how you have no one to ask about the curse." Rena kept her eyes trained on the book as she spoke. "Maybe you can ask *Liam* for help?"

My stomach rolled. "With breaking the curse? That's the last thing we need. Liam has so much information on Griffin." Instinct told me I could trust him, but to ask him for help with the curse . . .

Then Rena's words hit me. "Why would we want to *involve* him?"

She blushed. "I don't know. It was an idea."

"Rena, do you *like* Liam?" I smiled, despite myself.

Rena laughed, but it sounded girlish, like a giggle. Rena was not a giggler. Finally, she patted my hand. "He has kind eyes and his accent . . ."

"He does. I thought so, too. It's just so risky, trusting him. I'm surprised Griffin decided to talk to him."

"I'm not. I'm telling you, he's good. What you see is what you get with Underhill."

Griffin's laughter wafted in from the other room, making me smile. A sudden urge to see Griffin almost swallowed me up. I rushed past Rena to get to him, moving into the main shop.

Sierra was drooling on the cash register, twirling a strand of her blond-highlighted brown hair around one finger.

"Marvelous. Tell me, why did you end it that way?" Liam sat beside Griffin on the bench, staring at the piano keys as though he'd never seen them before.

Griffin's face lit up. "Ah, but that's where things get interesting—the ending. The masters tend to end things in four-four with a turn-da-da-di-da-daaa and then a traditional symphonic ending. I usually choose to simply resolve the chord or sometimes not. Sometimes I change the time signature entirely. They're left expecting more, hoping for it, but they don't get it. You see?"

"Brilliant," Liam said.

I walked up behind Griffin then, wrapping my arms around his neck. It wouldn't hurt to show Sierra that Griffin was taken.

Touching my cheek to his for a moment, I asked, "What have you two been talking about?"

Rena tapped Sierra on the shoulder. "You can go for the day. It's slower than I expected."

"Thanks, Rena," Sierra tossed a lingering look over her shoulder at Griffin before stripping off her apron and heading to the back door. It slammed shut several moments later.

Liam smiled, his eyes almost twinkling. "I might have a way for Griffin to make a comeback."

"Yes. Once the tiny problem of my curse is sorted," Griffin joked, but there was a strain of sadness in his voice.

"How?" I tried to keep my voice even, though it felt like it wobbled.

"I hope you all aren't opposed to doing something, um, slightly illegal," Liam said.

"Illegal? No, not at all." After holding my first circle, having visions, hearing voices, and driving without a license, breaking the law just didn't seem important. Been there, done that. "What did you have in mind?"

I sank to one of the many cushy pillows on the floor. Griffin lifted his long legs over the bench and turned around. "Apparently, no one ever came forward to claim my estate after my death. Obviously, I never had any children, so that ruled out my having an heir."

"And in Britain, we have a habit of leaving an estate under the management of the same family. In this case, mine," Liam said. "Under Jiggory's care, the Dunn estate fell into disrepair. I'd always assumed it was bad management." Liam fussed with his glasses, raising the wire frames a fraction and lowering them back onto the bridge of his nose.

Griffin's face clouded over. "He swore up and down that I'd depleted my funds. I've never been financially minded, but that came as a surprise, even to me."

"He certainly plagiarized Griffin's music." I couldn't help fuming when I thought about Jiggery taking credit for *Redemption*. That song had obviously been important to Griffin, and the jerk had claimed it as his own.

"I'll never forgive myself for perpetuating that misinformation." Liam seemed to mean it. That warmed my heart.

"You're making up for it now, eh, mate?" Griffin asked. "Besides, you weren't responsible for any of those things. It was your scalawag of a relative."

"Let's get back to the stuff you mentioned earlier. The illegal part." I wasn't exactly anxious about it, but I wanted to know what we were dealing with.

"It's simple, really. We just have to prove Griffin is someone he's not." Liam kept his voice even, but his eyes shone with excitement.

It must've been a dream come true for him. How often had I wanted to meet someone who'd died years before I was born, like Mozart or Bach.

"Just let me know what I have to do," Griffin said.

"Well, you'll have to smile for your passport photo, but that's about it," Liam said.

"Passport?" I asked.

"For when Griffin returns to England. I think it would be for the best if we get him back to his home country as soon as possible," Liam said.

I swallowed hard as I attempted to analyze Griffin's expression from the corner of my eye. He wouldn't be interested in something like that would he? Just picking up and leaving for England?

But a grin had transformed his beautiful face, as though he couldn't imagine better. "Thank you, thank you." He clasped Liam's hand in his. "It would be more than I could have ever dreamed of. Especially if Kate can go with me."

A mix of emotions rose up inside of me. He wanted me with him. I'd been expecting him to leave with the same calculated planning my mom was famous for. But he'd *remembered* me.

That made me love him just a little bit more. "I'd love

to. If I can work it out with my mom." *God, that sounded lame.*

Griffin's face lit. "It's beyond a dream then. Thank you."

"Liam." Rena took a seat across from him. A slight blush crept up her cheeks. "How long, exactly, are you planning to stay in town?"

Liam smiled that little smile of his again, and I would have sworn he blushed, too. "I'll be heading back on the nineteenth. I have some business here for some charities I oversee. Why do you ask?"

Rena bit her lip, her trademark coolness gone. "Griffin's curse is one heck of a puzzle. If you're around anyway, what would you think about helping us solve it?"

"I'd be grateful if you would." Griffin ran a hand through his long, blond locks. "Kate's found out a lot on her own, but we need help. If I'm to have a life with Kate, then there's more that needs to be done."

If I'm to have a life with Kate. My heart pounded at his words.

"I'd be delighted. Truly, I would." Liam grinned, rubbing his hands together. "And I think I know just where we need to start."

"Where's that?" Rena asked, taking my hand in hers and squeezing.

"Minna's room." Liam's excitement would have been super contagious if he'd said anything else, but Minna's room had been a freak-out session I did not want to repeat. Griffin met my eye, and it was clear he wasn't thrilled about the idea, either. Still, Liam was right. We needed answers and we weren't going to get them by playing it safe.

It was just after five at night, so the school would probably be locked. I didn't want to put any pressure on Charlie by asking him to let us in after hours. It was better if Liam just walked into the school.

"Can you meet us at the Byrons School tomorrow? Three o'clock." Maybe it wouldn't be so creepy if we tackled everything in daylight.

"I'll be there." Liam grinned, taking a moment to plug the time into his smartphone. No sooner had he entered the info than my own phone rang.

The display read *Byrons School of Music*. Frowning, I accepted the call. "Hello?"

"Ms. Covington? Headmaster Withers. Can you come into my office tomorrow at eight o'clock a.m.? It's about your accompanist." The headmaster did not sound happy.

"Of course. I'll be there, sir."

The headmaster said goodbye and ended the call, but I'd barely noticed. Withers knew about Griffin—Ryder had video footage of Griffin on school grounds, after hours—and wanted to meet with me.

Crap.

I'D DROPPED GRIFFIN AT THE SCHOOL HOURS AGO. Driving Mom's car illegally was nerve-wracking, but also convenient. Besides, no one should have to deal with public transportation in a time of crisis.

Griffin, being Griffin, had asked me to do some facial exercises to strengthen my embouchure. When I'd told him what he could do with his facial exercises, he'd actually blushed.

Since I was just staring at the ceiling thinking of him, I figured it might be time to try the Power Unlocking exercise

Rena had told me about. An easy out wasn't going to present itself. I needed to arm myself as best I could.

Turning on my e-reader, I flipped to the page Rena'd bookmarked. Fortunately, the tools I needed to hold my circle were still in my room. I was sitting inside the circle lined with salt within minutes, my candles lit to represent each of the four elements, surrounding me. Taking a deep breath, I read the words of the Power Unlocking spell out loud.

> *"Ancient power, which lives inside of me,*
> *I call your power here to me,*
> *Help me release my fear of thee,*
> *Unlock the powers inside me,*
> *So mote it be."*

Nothing. I was still too tense. I needed to concentrate.

"Ancient power, which lives inside of me . . ."

Nothing. Third time's the charm? Taking a deep breath, I focused everything I had on finding out the truth and freeing my own inner power. I remembered how my parents had told me never to wish for anything. Suddenly, wishing was fine. And I wished to discover who I was.

"Ancient power, which lives inside of me . . ."

Light burst into blinding rays against the backs of my eyelids. The skin on my arms grew hot. The room spun. So did my stomach. I fought the jarring wave of nausea. I tried to raise a hand to my mouth, to stop myself from vomiting, but I couldn't lift my arms. Heat immobilized me, pressing in from every angle.

Fire pushed itself inside me, traveling to my core. It began to eat at me, scorching my organs, melting them, clawing at my insides. I gripped my chest as waves of pain tore into my heart, making me double over. The flames that had threatened to consume me sank deep, charring me, destroying me. Then, as quickly as it had begun, the heat damped down to nothing.

The ground rose up, and my hot skin met cool sheet as I face-planted, pressing my forehead to the floor. The inside of my mouth tasted like blood. I'd bitten my tongue. The metallic flavor coated my throat.

I lay there until my breathing slowed. I'd read that was called *Grounding*—an act of returning all of the energy from a circle to the elements. *The elements can have it.*

After several minutes, I sat up. All of the sick feelings had washed away. I could *feel* the strength in my veins, the power there. I took a deep breath, a stronger, better version of myself. I still didn't have the answers, but I wasn't afraid to find them anymore.

In my head, I asked the question I wanted the answer to more than anything. *Show me how to save Griffin Dunn.*

A flood of images of Griffin followed . . .

In England, being pushed aside by his father.

With a man who looked a lot like Liam.

Shards of glass being driven into his chest.

Dying, the last traces of light dwindling from his eyes.

Playing the piano alone in Byrons School.

Holding my hand.

Walking into a white light.

By the light of the waning moon, you will make your choice.

The same voice from before filtered into my ear.

After several beats, the images flickered out, and I let go of my breath in one slow, single stream.

Griffin walking toward a white light wasn't good.

Yet, I *had* managed to unlock my power. I just had to learn how to use it.

CHAPTER 45
KATE

Tuesday, December 13th—Two Days Left Until Juries

FIDGETING WITH MY SKIRT, I TRIED TO SIT UP straighter in my chair, but it was one of those deals that was designed to make you slide down into a more relaxed position. Not good if you were in a meeting with the headmaster of your school because your ghost-boyfriend got called out for punching some jackass in the face.

"We take security very seriously at this school, Ms. Covington," the headmaster said, pacing back and forth in front of his desk.

Sure you do. That's why you put a school on the North Side, four blocks from a crack house.

"We can't have strangers coming and going in the building."

"With all due respect, sir, he's not a stranger. He's my accompanist. He's also very talented."

"Talent means very little when compared with dishonesty. Charlie told us he's a student. That must mean he's been attending classes."

"Charlie must have misunderstood, sir. Griffin's only been coming here to work with me on my Brahms piece."

"That's not what I've heard." The headmaster sat back in his chair. "Do you realize Ryder Robb has video footage of this Griffin on the property in the middle of the night? You can't expect me to believe you were here rehearsing with him, because you weren't on that film."

"No, I wasn't here. I don't know what's on that video, but there must have been some sort of mistake."

The headmaster shook his head. "There is no mistake. When I find this young man, I'm going to press charges."

Fire kicked into my veins. Hadn't Griffin been through enough? "I guess you also believe he's the ghost of the guy who died here? Ryder also claimed that."

"That accusation is simply too outlandish. It's the time-stamp on the video and Charlie's story that have me the most concerned. That's why I'm afraid he cannot participate in your jury."

My heart shot up into my throat. "What? We've been working so hard. Igor got deported and Griffin's the only one who would help me."

"That may be the case, but this Griffin won't be accompanying you."

"Please. My jury is in two days. Two days. You can't do this."

The headmaster's expression softened. "Ms. Covington—Kate . . . all of the teachers and myself . . . we know how hard you've been working to keep up your scholarship. We'll take that into consideration for your jury."

"But Headmaster Withers—"

"I'm sorry, but that's my final word."

Numbly, I rose to my feet, tears stinging my eyes. Turning, I moved toward the door.

"One last thing . . ."

I stopped, but I didn't glance back. "Yes?"

"What *is* Griffin's last name?"

Oh, no. They could kick me out of the school, but I wasn't telling. "I don't know. I've only ever known his first name."

And before he could question me further, I walked out of the office. I needed to find Griffin before Withers did.

WITHIN THE SPACE OF A DAY, GRIFFIN HAD BECOME A wanted man. It wouldn't have been such a huge deal, except he hadn't reverted to spirit form. We weren't sure if that meant Griffin was permanently alive, but he'd been in his sort-of living form ever since the weekend.

In other words, he wasn't as easy to hide. Fortunately, both Griffin and Hannah were more than familiar with the layout of the house, which included a bunch of back staircases and hidden passageways.

At a little after three o'clock, we snuck upstairs to meet Liam. Classes had just ended for the day, but already the building had an empty feel to it. I squeezed Griffin's hand tighter as we walked. Neither of us spoke. It wasn't as if I'd run out of words, but more like I didn't have it in me to talk.

"Kate. Griffin." I whipped my head around at the sound of my name.

"Liam." It surprised me how happy I was to see him. My thoughts flipped to the conversation I'd had with Rena about her interest in him. I hoped it worked out between them somehow.

"Thanks for coming, Liam. Let's go." Griffin waved him over to our corner of the lobby. The three of us entered the back stairwell.

Liam panned the dark stairs. "It's very much my pleasure. Just one question, though. Why are we using the servants' stairs?"

Griffin grinned. "Haven't you heard? I'm a fugitive now, mate."

"What?" Liam's mouth fell open.

"One of the other students is a paranormal investigator. He caught Griffin on camera at like one in the morning. Now they think he's a squatter or something." I began climbing the steps that led to the next level. Griffin kept his hand in mine.

"Interesting." Liam trailed behind us. "Now, about Minna's room . . ."

"Are you sure you want to go in there? It's pretty messed up." I shuddered.

"If I'm being honest, no, but I have a particular knack, shall we say, for finding tiny details." He placed his hand on Griffin's shoulder. "It makes sense we should start there."

"It's evil." The sensation of losing myself in a vision of Minna seemed too fresh. No way did I want to repeat that messed up experience.

Liam patted my shoulder and I met his eyes—calm and older than his years. "Evil preys on the weak-minded, Kate, not the strong."

"Okay, but don't say I didn't warn you." I tugged on Griffin's hand. By the time we reached the top, the atmosphere had changed drastically, just as it had when I'd gone up there with Griffin over the weekend. Pressure rested on my chest, the air turning thick and soupy, like a summer fog.

"There's definitely a feel to the place. I don't think I'd want to come here on holiday." Liam's voice sounded hoarse.

When we reached Minna's door, I twisted the knob. It opened for me just as easily as it had the other day, though I half expected Minna to be there for some reason. Maybe she was, and we just couldn't see her.

"I don't understand," Liam turned to Griffin and me. "In the hallway, the air was unbearable. I don't know what I expected to find, but this room is charming."

"Don't let it deceive you." Griffin nodded in my direction.

That time, I only needed to touch one part of the wall, and the shade and texture of it changed instantly. The spiteful words Minna had written appeared out of nowhere, as though a curtain had been drawn.

Liam chuckled. "Oh my. You were right, Griffin, this does alter the mood of the place."

Some fresh air would've brightened the space up, but when I tried to move the window latch, it wouldn't budge. It was as if Minna herself refused to let any fresh air into the room. Finally, I gave up and turned back to my search. The three of us worked side by side, combing every corner, every inch of wall space in silence.

After about half an hour of searching, Liam crouched down on his hands and knees. "Griffin, help me move this desk away from the wall."

Griffin stepped forward and stationed himself. Together, he and Liam lifted the desk to the center of the room. Once they set it down, Liam returned to his inspection.

"There's some sort of contraption built into the baseboard here." He bent down to examine a small gold piece, jutting out from the wall. "I wonder . . ." He stood and stepped on what looked like a wide, flat door stop, pressing it to the floor. The creaking sound of an old spring followed, and a cloud of dust rose as a section of the wall pulled away from itself, revealing an opening.

"A lever and a secret passage . . . mmm. It would seem that your Minna had something to hide." Liam peered into the darkness without any trace of fear.

No. Not another creepy room. Whatever it was, it was going to be some sort of freak-fest if Minna was involved.

CHAPTER 46

GRIFFIN

From what I could tell, Minna's hidden space took up the entire back corner of the house. Her bedroom had been small, with enough room for a bed, a desk, and a closet. This room was at least twice its size, the chalk outlines of dozens of circles still visible on the aged hardwood.

A high table in the corner held a collection of jars—some half empty, some not—containing different unidentifiable substances. A few dried herbs hung from the rafters of the room.

"I'll turn on the lights." Kate moved along the wall, searching for the electric light switch.

"It doesn't seem as if this room is wired for any kind of electricity. That's odd." Liam moved a few candles from a sideboard and placed them on the long, large table in the center of the room. Selecting a matchbook from the same area, he struck a match and set the flame to each of the three candle wicks on the fat pillars of wax. "This will have to do, then. Here's one for each of us."

Kate tugged the shutters closed on each of the windows. "This should keep anyone from seeing the light when it starts to get dark."

"Good idea." Liam nodded his encouragement as he picked up a candle.

Kate surveyed the space. "This is her workroom. She made magic here. I can *feel* it." A new awareness had lit her eyes since she'd been experimenting with her own powers.

The place did carry the lingering sensation of energy—a sort of vibration. Goosebumps pricked my skin. "Maybe you should touch the walls again, Kate? See if anything happens."

She placed her palm on the wall. "Okay, creepy room. Show me what you've got." As it had in Minna's bedroom, writing on the walls revealed itself, slowly, as though we were watching it being written there in real time.

The writing began with groupings of neat notes. Halfway around the room, it shifted into untidy scrawls.

"Man, this woman really needed some sticky notes. *Seriously*," Kate grumbled.

"What's so odd is that, from any reading I've done on witches, they usually have a strong focus on home and hearth, order . . . they write everything in their Books of Shadows. This seems strange. She must have had problems." Liam brushed several inches worth of dust off the empty mantel.

"It reminds me of something a teacher would do." Kate and Liam both turned to me. "You know, writing instructions down on a chalkboard."

"You think she was teaching someone?" Kate asked.

"Maybe at first . . . see how the topics change here?" Kneeling, I examined Minna's writing. Notes on herbs and plants filled a portion of the space, but the writing gradually grew darker, interspersed with words like *Hate* and *Dunn*.

We were reading the history of Kate's ancestor's descent into madness.

"She clearly has no love for you, Griffin." Liam's eyes had widened.

"So it would seem." I did my best to keep my voice devoid of panic. "But no bother. All of the greats were misunderstood—Galileo . . . DaVinci . . . Richard the Lion-heart . . . *Me*."

Liam chuckled. "Good to see this curse hasn't damaged your ego."

I continued examining the walls. The more I read, the more uncomfortable the room became. Perhaps Minna's evil was shrinking the workroom, directing it to close us in.

"Interesting." Liam examined a stack of paper on the largest table in the space.

"Looks like scratch paper to me," Kate said.

"At first glance, yes, that's exactly what it is. If you look at an angle, however, you can see an impression from the writing on the previous pages." Liam grinned, the same enthusiasm he'd displayed when he'd first found my second journal taking over. It would seem Dr. Underhill loved a good mystery.

He dug through his bag and pulled out some thin paper and what looked like a black crayon. Liam made a rubbing of the page and then lifted it up to the light.

"What is it?" I stood on Liam's other side.

"Nothing that seems significant. Mostly, this looks like it was used for notes on spells, shopping lists, that sort of thing. And someone's address and a dollar amount."

"Whose?" I squinted at the notes.

"I can't make out too much, but it looks like somebody named Bywell in Dover. I'll look into it, of course." Liam opened his bag and then slipped the sheet inside.

Kate moved away. "I expected to find spell books here. Something we could search for the curse in."

"Minna took them with her, I would imagine," Liam said. "Did you notice how there are no books, but there are still some clothes in the closet? Sort of gives you insight into her priorities."

We continued the search for another hour, Liam taking photographs with his seller phone, of all things. After we'd found all we were going to, we decided to call it an evening.

"I have to do some reading I can't access on my smartphone. I'll head back to Rena's and check out that address. I promise I'll work as quickly as I can." Liam patted my shoulder.

Again, his kindness and caring jarred me. "What if there's nothing to learn?"

Liam smiled a melancholy sort of smile, but his expression said everything. He didn't know the answer.

Neither did I.

CHAPTER 47
KATE

Wednesday, December 14th—One Day Left Until Juries

My final exams for the term had been scheduled for that day, so I didn't get to see Griffin all morning or most of the afternoon. Once school ended, we'd squeezed in another rehearsal before Griffin and I drove over to Rena's for Chinese and a research party.

No sooner had I stepped inside her apartment when Rena took my hand. "Any new progress on the meditation front?"

"Hello, Rena." Griffin released my hand as he moved into the living room area. "I'll just say hello to Liam. Liam, mate!"

It wasn't until I heard Liam's answering greeting that I turned back to Rena. "You mean any more *death visions*?"

She shrugged. "I didn't want to ask in front of Griffin. I'm guessing you still haven't told him."

"He's got enough to worry about, without bringing up that." Plus, there'd been the small matter of it having been my own death I'd envisioned and not Griffin's. "How's the research coming?"

Rena leaned back against the counter and blew her bangs to the side with a frustrated puff of air. "Slower than I'd like, though it's been interesting. Apparently, the address Liam found is for a *Gayle* Bywell."

"Who's Gayle Bywell?" I fiddled with the zipper on my jacket and unzipped it, before shrugging out of my coat and then laying it over the back of a kitchen chair.

"*Well.* It turns out Gayle Bywell was a witch and an author. And check this—she wrote a seven-part series on revenge spells."

"You're kidding? Maybe a Soul Separation spell?" I crossed my fingers behind my back.

"It's possible. Liam went over to Carnegie Library to check out a few books he couldn't get to online, and to some mystical shop in Dormont today." Dark circles stood out beneath Rena's eyes. "In between serving coffee and cleaning up, I've been reaching out to my dead peeps for answers. I haven't found much, but at least Liam's been here to keep me company."

Oh really? "What's going on between you and Liam?" I tried to tease her, even if only halfheartedly.

Rena turned away from me and flipped the switch on the electric kettle. She arranged both mugs and tea bags without meeting my eyes. "He's a nice man, Kate. I've just been lending him the back room, so he can use my WiFi. That's all. It's faster than the hotel's."

I wanted to press her for more, but the doorbell rang. The delivery man had arrived. My questions would have to wait.

After Griffin and I helped Rena lay out the spread of General Tso's, Sesame Chicken, egg rolls, and fortune cookies, we all dug in. There wasn't a moment to waste in the search, so we read as we ate. The quiet stretched between us.

Suddenly, Rena sat up straighter, holding a book up front of her. "Here's some more information on Gayle Bywell, if you guys want to hear it."

"Absolutely." Liam moved forward in his seat, books stacked across his lap and on each arm of the chair where he sat. An ancient MacBook rested on the coffee table across from him.

"Okay, so this Bywell chick was associated with the Pendle witches in England," Rena said, as she grabbed a fortune cookie from the pile in the center of the ottoman.

"Who were the Pendle witches?" I separated my own cookie, but when I pulled the paper from it, it was blank. *That's freaky.* Quickly, I bundled it up and tossed it in our communal trash bag.

Liam bookmarked the page he'd been staring at. "The Pendle witch trials happened in England in 1612, I believe. There were twelve of them in the coven, and they were accused of the murders of ten innocents."

"I've never heard of it," Griffin said.

"We're probably talking about the most notorious witch-craft trials in British history, Griffin." Liam sounded shocked; apparently, that information should've been common knowledge to members of the British population. Even dead ones.

"After all that hubbub, the coven continued. Gayle Bywell was supposedly the high priestess in the early 1900s," Rena said. "I'm sorry. I thought there'd be more."

Liam patted her hand and Rena's face flushed. "It's all right. Every piece of information counts now." We went back to our individual searches until Liam spoke up a moment later. "Mm."

"Find something?" Griffin leaned over his shoulder.

Liam held up a thin volume. "I think this is what we've been searching for. *The Spell to Separate One from One's Soul*—it's part of the *Blood Curses* section." This weird, intense allegro played inside my heart, the rapid beats making me jumpy. "A spell to forcefully separate a soul from its body." He handed me the book. "Why don't you have a look at this next part?"

I took the book and laid it open on the coffee table before sliding to the floor. "This isn't a spell. Even I know enough to understand that."

"What is it, then?" Griffin's impatience crept into his voice.

"It's more like the *framework*. Bywell's telling us how to write the spell, not what the actual spell is." Damn. I'd wanted this to be the solution. Preferably, an easy fix. "Real spells have details, limitations, locations, that sort of thing."

"Is there a counter curse?" Rena had that uneasy look about her again. The same expression she'd worn when she told us about Griffin's bad mojo.

Griffin leaned in closer, our cheeks almost touching. "It's here, farther down. *The Counter-Curse for the Spell to Separate One from One's Soul*," Griffin read. "Breaking a curse is, of course, simplest when the caster is alive, but a counter-curse can be performed, provided the text of the original curse is available." Griffin stood, turning away from the book. "Damn."

"Great. There's no counter-curse, and we don't know the original curse." Why couldn't we get a break for once? Some easy information that didn't lead down a million different rabbit holes. Too bad my wishing hadn't been enough to break Griffin's curse.

"But wait, maybe there's more . . ." Liam grabbed the book and turned the page. "Oh no."

"What did you find?" Griffin leaned in, scanning the words on the page. Liam was faster.

Liam cleared his throat. "Reciting a counter-curse would be highly undesirable, for the caster must voluntarily choose to strip the curse from her blood. Blood curses, dark in their nature, require a sacrifice of a single, willing soul." Liam set the book down and turned to me. "The witch who recites the counter curse will lose her life."

"That's it?" Of course, it was. Why else would I have seen those visions of my own death? I'd known this was coming. "There isn't an alternative version?"

"To kill the owner of the curse, using a method as dark as the one they employed in the spell. He or she can't just die from natural causes." Liam cringed.

Rena came from behind me to take my hand. "Honey, this is what you saw, isn't it? That morning when you came here after having the vision. You saw your own death, not Griffin's."

Crap.

"What does Rena mean, Kate?" Griffin's voice sounded strangled.

It was exactly what I'd been hoping to avoid. If Griffin had any idea I'd been having visions of my own death, he'd freak. Yet, there was no hiding it anymore.

"I did see my own death." It took every ounce of strength I had to make myself look at him.

Disbelief colored his face. "And you didn't tell me?"

All the hurt was right there. I'd blown it. I should have told him.

I sought Rena's eyes, visually pleading with her for backup, but she reached for her tea, sitting back and propping another book against her chest like a shield. "Uh-uh, girl. This one's on you."

The ice in Griffin's eyes sent a chill whipping through me. "I believe I'm still waiting on that explanation, Katherine."

Uh-oh, we're back to Katherine again.

"I didn't want you to worry." It was the truth, but that didn't stop my own guilt from eating me up from the inside out. "And Rena said death visions could mean different things. I was crossing my fingers it wouldn't come true."

His expression didn't change, and a massive silence fell between us. We stood there, locked in a visual stalemate. We were fast-moving into the *beyond awkward* stage.

Time for a subject change. "What happens to Griffin if I recite the counter-curse, Liam?"

But Liam wasn't making eye contact with me. He just shook his head.

"Tell me. The answer's on that page, I know it is." My voice shook. "Come on."

"If you recite the counter-curse under the correct conditions, Griffin will live again." Liam continued to scan the page, running a thin finger over the text. "He'll instantly get his life back. His soul will reunite with his body and he'll go on. If you don't recite it, he'll stay as he is—for eternity. It's a bit of a one-shot deal, I'm afraid."

No wonder the visions showed my death. There was no way I wasn't helping Griffin.

"What are the correct conditions?" Rena leaned over Liam's shoulder to read the page, and blanched.

Liam continued reading. "It has to be performed on the anniversary of the curse's original casting, but only when there's a waning moon."

"A waning moon . . . that's what I heard during my meditation." *By the light of the waning moon, you will make your choice.* "What's a waning moon?"

"There are many phases of the moon, but based on the drawings here, they mean when there's just this little sliver of moon in the sky," Rena explained, shoving a fresh cup of coffee into my hand. "Friday night's a waning moon."

Shocker.

"Oh, Mother of All Coincidences." Griffin finally spoke. "But it doesn't matter. I'm staying as I am."

"No, you can't. How can we live a life with me sneaking into the building to see you all the time?" I clasped his hands, meeting the rich, hazel color of his tormented eyes.

Those same eyes grew colder, if that were possible. "That's just it. There will be no more *us*. You were an indulgence I should have ignored."

Ouch. "That's ridiculous. The point is I'm going to die—either tomorrow or later. Why would I want to live my life knowing it came at the expense of yours?"

His face softened again, changing Griffin from the stranger before me to the boy I loved. "Why would *I*?" He projected his pain in every syllable. "I've just found you, Kate. I'm not going to let you give away your life over me."

"We'll keep searching for an actual counter-curse, and if I can't find it . . . I'll write my own." Our gazes locked in an unspoken stalemate. I crossed my arms over my chest, hoping I came across as more confident than I felt.

Griffin's expression darkened before he turned away. "Liam . . . Rena . . . thank you. I'm afraid I must bid you good night." Without another word, Griffin stood and stalked outside, leaving me behind.

CHAPTER 48
GRIFFIN

THE ONLY WAY OUT OF MY CURSE INVOLVED KATE sacrificing her life for mine. Worse, she'd had visions of her own death and withheld them. She'd known all along her life would be at stake.

Part of me wanted to grab her and shake her—make her see reason. The counter-curse couldn't be the solution to our problem. I simply found the price of ending the curse *entirely* too high to pay.

Since I was unfamiliar with the city's layout, I was forced to accept a ride from Kate. We drove in silence for several minutes until Kate parked the car outside the school.

"Griffin."

"I can't." My voice broke on the word *can't*.

"But we have to talk—"

"No." I locked my eyes onto hers. "Talking happens

when there's an exchange, an actual discussion. You've refused to bring me into the conversation."

"Griff—"

"Good night, Katherine." I exited the car, sprinting out of sight past a sleeping Charlie, and then into the building through the still-unlocked side door. After reaching my room, I slammed the door behind me, the sound ringing with the finality of a dungeon door closing. And why not? Hadn't this house, this life, been my prison?

My anger wouldn't abate. Fury raged inside of me, threatening to consume me. Slamming myself onto the piano bench, I flipped up the cover protecting the keys. Raising my hands, I prepared to play the angriest, loudest piece I knew.

Then . . . nothing. My thoughts were as scattered as random notes yet to be inked on a page.

"No!" I pounded on the keys at random, the way a child does when faced with a piano and free rein. My fingers slammed out stray notes and chords as tears burned my eyes, blinding me.

What did it matter if I couldn't play? Kate wouldn't be with me. She'd be sacrificing her own life, and for what? For a grudge that had nothing to do with her.

Shoving my fingers roughly against the keys, I ignored the little stabs of pain shooting up my arms. They were reminders of what I would lose, the greater hurt to come. Exhaustion seeped into my limbs, but I kept up my assault on the piano.

The instant Kate entered the room, I knew. A physical awareness overwhelmed me. I could feel the pull of her, leading me back, guiding me to her, but I wouldn't stop. I pummeled the keys, the relentless pressure of my assault damaging my long fingers.

"Griffin," Kate said, her hand on my shoulder.

I stiffened at her touch, stilling my attack on the keys. Sweat trickled down my forehead. These were my final moments of lucidity. "How could you even consider it?" I spoke the question with a grating voice.

"You'll be alive. That's how." She guided me away from the piano.

"But what could that possibly matter if you'll be dead?"

She shook her head. "Griffin. I'm going through with it."

The end is coming.

The voice filtered into my ear again, an all-too timely reminder.

Forcing the words out of my head, I focused on Kate. *"You'll die."*

"But don't you see? The curse will be over, and you'll be able to go on. There will be nothing holding you to this awful house." Her voice came across strong and even, yet I read the closely checked terror in her eyes. "You can go on living."

"Living means nothing to me if it's an existence you're absent from."

"Griffin." She placed both hands on top of her head. "Whatever it is, however *awful* it is, this is still my decision. If it means I have to die to break the chain and save you, then that's what I'm going to do."

I took a step toward her, framing her face in my hands. "None of the notes will sound the same. I can't even play the bloody piano."

"You'll play again. You'll get over me," Kate whispered. "That's what they say."

"Never. There'll never be anyone for me but you. There hasn't been in over a hundred years."

Her warmth seeped into my skin as I held her, though

her fingers on my neck were perpetually icy. "Make love to me," she whispered.

I drew her to me, bringing my mouth down on hers, tasting the salt of our tears on her lips. Hunger burned inside me. I wanted to forget. I only wanted to know Kate, to be close to her.

We shed our clothes, and I scooped her up, carrying her to the divan. Her dark hair fanned on the cushions as I lowered her to the dusty material and our skin came in contact. In the heat and longing, in the pure innocence of that moment, I foresaw my cold future without Kate.

It didn't matter if I *could* live if it meant I'd be dead inside.

All the duets we could have played, the music we could have written, Kate's promise and my own, would be nothing more than a lost, forgotten symphony.

CHAPTER 49
KATE

Thursday, December 15th—Jury Day

At a quarter till twelve, I went upstairs to the lobby, just outside the room where the juries were being held. Griffin waited inside a shadowy alcove where he hoped he'd be able to hear me. They couldn't arrest him if they didn't know he was there.

A text from Rena popped up on my phone just as I went to set it to mute.

Good luck!!!!!

I tapped out a message back.

Thanks. Gonna need it.

The chorus from *The Funeral March* began to play as Mom's picture popped up on my phone. Mom. The information we'd learned the previous night weighed on my shoulders all at once. I could die very soon. I'd never see Mom again.

Accepting the call, I jammed my phone against my ear. "Hey, Mom."

I hadn't expected the awkwardness, but it was there. I hadn't spoken to her since I'd found out she wasn't my birth mother. Not that she hadn't tried to call me. I just didn't know what to say.

"Hi, Kate. I just wanted to wish you luck."

Huh. I didn't even think she'd remember.

"Thanks, Mom. How's L.A.?"

"Insane. The drivers are crazy." Even so, Mom sounded more relaxed than she'd been in weeks.

"I miss you, Mom."

More silence. "I miss you, too. I was afraid you wouldn't take my call."

"I'm sorry about that. It was just a lot to process." I stared at my clarinet, watching the glare from the overhead light play off Benny's nickel-plated keys. "How's the job? Do you think you'd like it?"

"I think I'm going to take it, Kate. I got to meet some of the other team members and they're great. Plus, the money is so much better. You won't need to worry about loans for college. I even found you a clarinet instructor, if you're interested."

Part of me wanted to tell her yes, that I would get on a plane right away. I would see her again, and she wouldn't have to lose me, too. Yet, I couldn't walk away from Griffin or the life I had in Pittsburgh.

"I know what you're going to say, Kate." Mom shuffled what sounded like papers on the other end of the line. "And I think you're right. Your dad really wanted you to go to

Byrons, so I'll leave it up to you. You can study wherever you want after this term."

I sat down roughly on one of the chairs in the lobby. "Really?"

"Don't blame me for hoping otherwise, though. I miss you, and we didn't get a chance to talk about everything. I had to leave at such a bad time. I'm sorry."

"I know. I'm sorry, too."

Mom sighed. "Don't you be sorry. I handled it badly. We'll talk all about it when I get back next week. But you have my word—you'll get to choose where you go to school."

"What would you think about letting me study in England?" If I could get past the whole imminent death obstacle. After all, Griffin had said he wanted me with him.

"England? That's new. When did all this come about?"

I let out a breath. "I don't know. I've been thinking about it off and on."

"Katherine." Griffin had snuck up behind me, his breath soft against my ear. "They're finished in there."

"Who's that?" Mom asked.

"That's, uh, my boyfriend, Griffin."

Griffin smirked, clearly enjoying the boyfriend reference.

"*He's* allowed to call you Katherine, huh?" Mom whispered.

My face heated. "Yeah. He is."

"Does *he* have anything to do with this whole England thing?"

"Mom?"

"Yeah, honey?"

"I love you."

"I love you, too. And when school is over, I'd like to talk about Mr. England, okay?"

"Okay, Mom." I ended the call with promises to text her after my jury, then shoved my phone in my bag.

"Let's go, lovely. You'll be brilliant." Griffin took my hand and my calm returned until I got a good look at him. He stood before me, in dress pants, a crisp white shirt, black tie, and a cap.

"What do you mean *let's go*? You're not coming with me. The headmaster said he'd have you arrested."

"Let the police come. Let them question me. You've changed *everything* for me Kate." His tight grip on my arms contrasted with the softness in his gaze. "Let me do this for you."

Excitement burned in his eyes. He couldn't wait to perform. Whatever happened, my jury would be a gift to him. A chance to play in front of an audience.

If he wanted to take the chance, who was I to stop him? Not trusting myself to speak, I nodded.

Pressing a quick kiss to his lips, I slipped past him into the main parlor. It was time to show them all what I could do.

As I moved into the room, I glanced up at the jury panel. Five teachers sat at a table on a riser: Headmaster Withers; my Solfeggio instructor, Mrs. Drecker; one of the Brass instructors, though I couldn't remember his name; Ryder's dad, Mr. Robb; and one other visiting instructor for strings I'd never met before.

I nodded to the panel and placed my music on the stand. "Hello, I'm Kate Covington. I'll be performing the Allegro from Brahms' *Sonata for Clarinet and Piano in E-flat Major*."

Griffin slipped in and took a seat at the piano.

Headmaster Withers shot to his feet. "Ms. Covington, what is the meaning of this? I informed you that this *free-*

loader would not be permitted to accompany you. Call security!"

A few moments later, Charlie ran in from the direction of the lobby, eyes wild, his unloaded gun drawn. He normally didn't work the day shift, so he must have been covering for another guard.

"Where is the perpetrator, sir?" Charlie asked.

"Right there." Headmaster Withers pointed to Griffin.

Maybe Charlie would stick up for Griffin. I certainly wasn't going to let him get detained that easily. "You don't understand. He didn't do anything. He just agreed to help me."

"Then what was he doing here in the middle of the night? Why were you here, young man?" Headmaster Withers stared us down.

Griffin shrugged. "I dunno, working out a plan to corrupt little children, I suppose."

The panel gasped. I glanced at Charlie and caught a ghost of a smile on his face.

"What?" The headmaster had turned a purplish color. "Charlie, use your cuffs."

"I beg your pardon?" said Griffin. "You plan to put me in shackles like a common prisoner?"

Headmaster Withers stood up and then stepped down from the platform, directly in front of Griffin. "You'll go with Charlie, right now."

"Good morning. Sorry to interrupt." Liam walked into the room then, his should-be-trademarked smile at the ready.

Yes! I remembered the name on Griffin's plaque—*Sponsored jointly by the Underhill Family and the Byrons School of Music.* He'd stick up for us. Maybe he even had enough clout at Byrons School to help.

Headmaster Withers stood straighter and adjusted his tie. "Mr. Underhill. I thought you'd gone after our meeting. I'm afraid I didn't expect you to attend juries. I can get you a chair."

"That's very considerate of you." How was it that soft-spoken, kind-eyed Liam could command an entire group of people with only a few words? "But I won't impose. I've just come to inform you that if you arrest Griffin, you'll be making an enormous mistake. You've no idea who he is."

Headmaster Withers frowned. "Who is he?"

Liam leaned in and whispered into the other man's ear. Though I couldn't hear, Liam must have shared something special, because everything about the headmaster changed. He visibly relaxed, his skin returning to a normal color. When Liam drew back, the headmaster glanced at Griffin. "My goodness. In that case, he is certainly welcome."

"Excuse me, Headmaster Withers?" Charlie still held the handcuffs. "Should I, uh . . ."

The headmaster shook his head. "Those won't be necessary, Charlie. It turns out that Griffin here is actually a *friend* of the school's. I had no idea."

"Neither did I," Griffin muttered under his breath.

"He can accompany me then?" *Please!* I didn't want to beg, but I would do it if I had to.

The headmaster turned to me, a smile lighting his face. "Most definitely."

Oh, my goodness. Relief, so intense that it almost brought me to my knees, shot through my veins. Griffin would get to be my accompanist! I wouldn't have to do it alone. *Hallelujah!*

But my super happy feeling didn't last long, because my new reality hit me all at once. It was time to perform my jury piece.

Help!

AFTER A DEEP BREATH, I PLAYED A SINGLE WARM-UP note for myself. Griff played a middle C so I could tune, and I matched my pitch to his. The sound filled the room, clear and confident.

I had the perfect reed, an actual accompanist, and the most important thing: me.

My focus returned, and nodding at Griffin, I began to play.

I stopped thinking about key signatures and eighth notes. All fears about tests and exams and juries and curses vanished. Everything slipped away as I mentally moved into a white space where only Griffin, our music, and I existed. The notes were so wholly tied to Griffin; he was foremost in my mind.

The moment had been made for us and us alone. The music called to me.

And I answered.

Griffin's playing matched mine, the strength of his interpretation blending with my tone. The music was a dance, and we skirted around one another repeatedly, only to come together once more.

My fingers tackled the runs fluidly, Griffin's instruction coming back to me.

Softly here now, Kate.
Make that F natural come to life.
That's it, a bit more power there.
Legato on those eighth notes, please.
Make me weep at section G.

After I hit the last note, my gaze shot to Griffin's, and he beamed, giving me a thumbs up.

"That was a true pleasure, Ms. Covington." Headmaster Withers grinned from ear to ear as Griffin moved in by my side. "And I see from your records you didn't have a private instructor. Impressive."

"I did, sir. It was my father, Brian Covington. He passed away last year. He graduated from Byrons."

The headmaster's smile faded. "Brian was a good man. We subbed together in an orchestra pit once. I remember reading about him, but I didn't make the connection. I'm sorry for your loss. "

"Thank you, sir." I glanced to the panel at the front of the room, but I couldn't get a read on any of them. The only exception being Liam, who was openly grinning. "Griffin helped me a lot." *Understatement of the century.*

Headmaster Withers rested a couple of fingers against his chin as he scrutinized Griffin. After a moment, however, the puzzled look faded and he dropped his hand. "It's a good thing he did, otherwise we'd never have known about him.

"Griffin, this is highly unusual, but I'd like to offer you a full scholarship to my school. There would be a probationary period—you did punch another student, after all. But, judging from your accompaniment of Ms. Covington's piece, it's clear we need to have you on board."

I hid my smirk. Griffin could probably teach everyone in the school—including the teachers.

Griffin cocked an eyebrow. "Thank you, sir. I'll consider it."

"See that you do. Oh, and my apologies for the mix-up." Headmaster Withers winked at Griffin. "Have a good

holiday break, both of you. Nice work, Ms. Covington."
Nodding in our direction, he returned to the panel.

"Thank you, sir." Suppressing the bubble of joy that
threatened to make me turn to mush, I tugged on Griffin's
hand, guiding him out into the side hallway and into the lobby.

Liam followed us as we passed the next student in line.
"Kate, Griffin, that was wonderful. I have to go, but we'll
speak later. I may have something. It's to do with the curse."

"Do what you need to do, by all means." Griffin shooed
him off, and, within moments, Liam had sprinted out the
front door and down the steps.

Griffin watched me with what I thought was consider-
ably less enthusiasm. Had I screwed up? What if I hadn't
done as well as I thought I had? Maybe he'd only given me
the thumbs up for show? "Tell me the truth."

He laughed. "What a change from our first rehearsal."

"Come on, Dunn. Just lay it out for me."

Running one of his fingers down the back of my arm, he
smiled. "You were absolutely magnificent, Kate. I am over-
joyed with your performance."

"Thank you. I couldn't have done it without you. You
know that, right?" When I'd first met Griffin, I would never
have guessed he'd help me save my jury and my scholarship.

He scoffed. "Of course I do. As if anyone else could've
saved your bedraggled behind."

Laughter bubbled from my lips when he used the same
words he'd spoken shortly after we'd met. He'd promised to
see me in hell, but that memory only reminded me my own
death was closing in. The laughter died on my lips.

"Please, Kate. Don't go through with it," he whispered,
his voice shaky, his words urgent. "I'm not worth it."

"You are." Leaning in, I breathed his scent and brushed

my lips against his. He sucked in a breath. "And freeing you is the right thing to do. I *feel* it."

"If it's the right thing, then why is it breaking my heart?" Griffin pressed his forehead to mine.

I cupped his cheeks. Closing my eyes, I tried to commit the feel of his face to memory. But I didn't answer, because it was breaking mine, too.

CHAPTER 50
GRIFFIN

WE'D GONE FOR A DRIVE FOR SOMETHING TO DO. KATE had seemed nervous about driving at first. After several days of carting me about, however, she'd grown more at ease. That irony was not lost on me. She'd finally learned how to drive, only to have to give it up if—

"Tell me again what would happen if we were free to leave, Griffin. If we could go anywhere, right now."

She'd only asked me to reveal the dreams closest to my own heart. "Kate, please don't ask me to."

"I'm sorry." She tapped her fingers on the wheel of the car. "It's just that I need something to hold on to."

"Fine. I'd take you away—tonight. We'd go to England. I'd marry you the moment I could." I slipped my fingers through hers. I would have given anything to take her away, to free us both.

"Marriage, huh?" Her skepticism wasn't lost on me.

"I wouldn't want you to develop a reputation. If you're going to live at my estate, then people would talk." I stopped myself. That was getting into dangerous territory, and I knew it. Each of us observed the other, the words *if only* hanging between us.

She smiled, but didn't seem put off. "I've never worried about what people think."

No, she probably hadn't. At one time, it would have kept me from courting her in public. I might even have taken steps to avoid her socially, but in this era, I found Kate's rebellion intensely attractive.

"My mom called today before my jury." Kate blurted the words out in a rush. "She found a teacher for me so I can continue my studies in California."

I swallowed away the sadness her words drudged up. "If you don't perform the counter-curse, you could walk away from this place, start again. California is supposedly quite warm." I wrapped my arms around myself and pretended to shiver.

"Don't be such a loser. I told her I wanted to study in England. If I live—" Kate glanced away. "If I live, I'm not going to spend a single day apart from you."

Relief almost overpowered me for a moment. It would have been my dream, but I'd learned a long time ago that what I wanted and what others desired didn't always match.

Silence wrapped around us as Kate parked at a distance from Coffee á Rena. We let ourselves into Rena's back door. Heavy bass pounded against my eardrums the moment we stepped inside. It didn't surprise me; Rena was a bit of a dancer at heart.

When we turned the corner, Rena and Liam were dancing together. It was a slow piece, though I didn't know it. The singer's gravelly voice made it hard to decipher the lyrics. Meanwhile, Liam looked at Rena as if she were the only woman in the world. Rena appeared to be returning the sentiment.

What an interesting development.

Kate coughed, employing a pitiful attempt at nonchalance. Liam and Rena jumped apart, both their faces reddening.

"Hi, you two." Rena's eyes were over bright. Despite our interruption, her tone held an ocean of warmth.

"Hey." Kate stepped into the waiting circle of Rena's arms. Rena returned the embrace, hugging Kate back, smoothing her long, dark hair. "Congrats on the jury, sweetie. Liam said it was awesome."

"She was amazing. Not that I'm surprised. Hi, Rena." A wave of shock hit me as Rena hugged me, as well. My former self would have been appalled. My former self could go stuff itself.

Rena released me. Patting my arm, she walked to the counter and picked up a tray with a bright orange teapot and several mismatched mugs on it.

Kate threw her arms around Liam. "Thank you, again. You saved the day this morning."

Liam grinned, his face still slightly pink from our interruption. "It was my pleasure, Kate." He patted Kate's back before releasing her.

"I just have one question. What did you say to the headmaster that made him allow Griffin to play?" She took a seat on one of the nearby cushions.

A mischievous expression took over Liam's face. "I told him that if he wanted to receive a future donation from me, he'd let you play."

"Thank you, Liam. Truly." I took a seat beside Kate and tugged her into my arms.

Liam straightened his sweater, casting a sideways glance at Rena before picking up a stack of papers from the table in front of us. "I apologize for leaving directly after your jury, Kate, but I got a phone call. It's part of the news I wanted to share with you."

"What did you find out?" I asked, as Liam and Rena sat down on the settee across from us.

"I've had my local assistant searching for descendants of Gayle Bywell." Liam pointed at Rena. She blushed, and I would have sworn on Mother's grave that Liam did, as well.

"I actually found one." Rena sipped from her mug. "Helen Bywell is the current High Priestess of a coven near Dover. She was super cool when Liam talked to her."

To Liam and Rena, that revelation was simply a fact to be shared. To me, it brought us one step closer to the counter-curse that would end Kate's life. Yet Liam, Rena, and Kate all sat around grinning, as though it was some sort of brilliant breakthrough.

"You're kidding?" Kate asked.

"What did she have to say?" I loosened my grip on Kate's hand. "What is the Soul Separation spell?"

"It's old, dark magic. The creators of many of these spells were heavily associated with necromancy," Liam said.

"Bringing the dead back to life?" Kate squeaked out the question.

"Yes," Rena said, her expression grim. "Except Griffin isn't truly dead. Not *really*."

My heart pounded, but one question begged to be asked. "What *am* I then?"

Liam tossed the papers on the table and then spun them around so I could read them. There was a bunch of gibberish at the top of the page, but the drawings told the story.

"You've been frozen, in a sort of suspended animation or something. The spell rips your soul from your body somehow. It probably doesn't hurt that Kate's the last Christel witch, either." Liam ran his hands along the front of his trousers. His eyes seemed trained on me.

Kate snuggled against me, too calm. "This keeps getting weirder and weirder. Does Helen have any ideas about a counter-curse?"

"I gave her all of the information. Helen did say it would be a *challenge* to come up with the counter-curse without the original, but she has Gayle's book. She's going to research the Soul Separation spell further. We'll be speaking again tomorrow morning." Liam didn't meet my gaze as he finished. Something about the way he said the word *challenge* made me think he would have preferred to use the term *impossibility.*

Every part of me felt etched in stone. I wasn't dead, not really, but we were no closer to saving Kate. Kate who was determined to sacrifice herself for me.

"There's something else, as well." Liam slid a large envelope toward me. Lifting the flap, I poured the contents onto the low table in front of me. I found a British passport and a paper deed to Fulton House. My throat closed up as I opened the latter, taking in the faded ink on the page.

"Your papers took some doing and almost every connection I had." Liam glanced around, as though we might be heard at any moment. "Some of them were not exactly legal. They'll get you out of the country, though."

"This address . . ." I glanced at the passport.

"It's for your flat in London."

I glanced up in surprise. "It's still been maintained?"

"I've been using it as my residence in the city," said

Liam. "I thought you might want to return there when . . . once it's all . . ."

"Thank you, though I hardly mean for you to be evicted from your home." He was risking so much by helping me.

"You deserve this, Griffin." Liam patted my hand where it gripped the papers. "I can't undo what Jiggery did to you, but I hope I've made a start. This is your life. Take it back."

My throat tightened. If only a man like Liam had been my father. Though I was old enough that our roles should have been reversed, he'd shown me the caring and respect my own father should have given me.

"What's next?" Kate squeezed my other hand, bringing me back. I'd forgotten she was holding it.

"I'll be appearing on *Good Morning, World!* tomorrow. By the afternoon, everyone will know you as the long lost, relative of Griffin Dunn."

"But doesn't that also mean they'll know the truth about Jig?" Liam looked so much like Jig. Sometimes it was hard to remember I no longer lived in the past. "It will negate everything in your book."

"Not everything, but . . . It's a small price to pay for honesty, Griffin, and I'll release an updated version." Liam patted my arm.

Rena and Liam continued discussing the counter-curse, but I'd tuned out. Even if Liam pulled off what he promised, what kind of life would I have without Kate? I would lose her, and the bleak reality was, I could do absolutely nothing to stop it.

CHAPTER 51
GRIFFIN

Friday, December 16th—Sixteen Hours Until the Counter-Curse

I squeezed Kate's arm as we walked up the steps from my room. "I'll meet you as soon as your classes free up, love."

"I don't want to go, Griffin. Even a couple of hours away from you is too many. Besides, finals are over. They're just killing time." She touched the hair framing the side of my face. I remembered when I'd first met Kate—how impassive and abrasive she'd seemed. I saw her for what she was: a vibrant, yet broken-hearted soul in a mask. She needed to heal even more than myself, and that was saying something.

I pulled her to my chest, stroking her hair. We stood just outside the classroom where the first class of her last day of the term was to take place. Students filed past us as we tried to hold onto one more moment in our private world.

"Isn't this sweet?" Ryder's voice sliced into our bubble, ugly and unbidden.

Reluctantly, I drew away from Kate and faced my adversary. "Was there something you wanted, Ryder?"

Ryder stepped in front of us. I gritted my teeth to keep my temper checked.

"I know who you are." He glared at me. "I'll prove everything tonight."

"You listen to me. If you have some quarrel with me, then we can settle this outside." *Where I will trounce his pasty, American derriere.*

Ryder laughed hysterically. "Nice try. Headmaster Withers may have let you off the hook for trespassing, but tonight's going to be the night I prove your identity. You'll have nowhere to hide."

"What's this about?" Headmaster Withers stepped up to our group.

"Headmaster." Ryder turned then, a smile lighting his face.

"Ryder was just sharing with me his plans to expose my *true* identity." I did my best to suppress my glee at the exchange, but admittedly, that wasn't much.

The headmaster shook his head. "Griffin's been vouched for. Leave it."

Ryder's face reddened. "Yes, sir."

"Attention students." A voice said through the amplification squares in the wall. "Please report to the ballroom immediately for an important school message."

"You folks should go and find your seats." Headmaster Withers smiled. "I understand it's going to be quite a show.

And your great-great-great-grandfather, Griffin . . . Let's just say I'm glad his name's finally been cleared."

My name? Cleared? I swallowed. "Thank you, sir. But how did you—"

"Mr. Underhill. He was on *Good Morning, World!* today. If everything works out, we should be able to replay this morning's interview for the students. If you'll excuse me." And with that, Headmaster Withers turned and left us.

"I'm watching you." Ryder glared at me before taking off down the hall after the headmaster, leaving Kate and I alone.

"Let's go," Kate led me toward the ballroom, but the idea of being seen by so many unnerved me.

"No, come with me. I've got the perfect place to watch."

We pushed through the throng of students, rushing to avoid the chaos. It was a bit like swimming upstream. Kate didn't say anything as we slipped into the parlor adjoining the ballroom. Faint winter sunlight trickled in through the sheer draperies, leaving random rays on the worn carpeting. We closed the door behind us, the din of the crowd fading.

Crossing the room, I stopped by the chair rail on the right side of the fireplace. "Let's hope it's still there."

"What?" Kate asked. "There's not another secret passage, is there?"

My fingertip found the button, and I pressed it, the secret door popping open with a click. "As a matter of fact, lovely, there is." Swinging the small door aside, I held out my hand and helped her in before shutting the door behind us.

"I think this wraps around part of the ballroom to the door. Usually, these sorts of things have a hidden screen, so you can listen in."

"This is seriously cool."

"Any other woman I've known would have been horrified to climb into a musty passageway. Not you." Hunting in the dark, I located the small handle. I slid a panel to the right and we had a clear view of the headmaster, as well as a large black electronic device, through a thin screen.

Headmaster Withers's voice reached us. "I'm sorry to pull you all out of class on the last day of term. Although I'm sure none of you are disappointed." Collective laughter filled the room. "You all know about the dark history our school building has. You've heard of the murder that supposedly took place here. You've also heard our resident ghost giving frequent performances and kicking most of our students' behinds."

"All. All of your students' behinds," I muttered as the students laughed.

"Shh." Kate nudged me in the ribs.

"Anyway," the headmaster continued, "there's something I want to play for all of you, so make yourselves comfortable."

A small commotion followed as the students sat down on the ballroom floor. The large square came to life, and I glimpsed Liam on the screen, a woman seated to his right. After a moment, she began to talk.

"This morning, we are very excited to have Liam Underhill with us. Mr. Underhill is the author of the book *Chasing Griffin Dunn*, which chronicles the life of a young concert pianist who died in 1902, but not before being blamed for the death of a ten-year-old boy. Mr. Underhill is in Pittsburgh, Pennsylvania this morning, at the Byrons School of Music—the location where Griffin Dunn's life ended. Good morning and welcome, Liam."

Liam smiled, seeming surprisingly at ease in front of the

camera. From what I could tell, it looked like he was in Headmaster Withers's office. "Thank you, Jane."

"You seem to have quite an interest in Griffin Dunn. Tell us about him."

Liam smiled. "Griffin Dunn is sort of an enigma. Everyone blamed him for Jonah Byrons' death, but it never added up for me. There were eyewitness accounts that claimed Mr. Dunn pushed the boy from the skylight. There were also reports that Mr. Dunn was performing at the time the boy died. I don't believe Mr. Dunn was responsible for the boy's death."

"Then who was?" The interviewer shifted to the edge of her seat.

"My research has revealed two things. Firstly, the skylight the boy fell through was crafted by Hander & Sons. There were three reported instances of other skylights by Hander & Sons cracking and leaking that year.

"Second, I managed to locate the descendants of one of the servants on staff that night. A gentleman who served water to Mr. Dunn right before he died. He wrote about that evening in a diary. If I may, I'll read a few lines." Liam held the book aloft, as though he wouldn't take no for an answer.

"Please do," the woman urged.

"December seventeenth, 1902. A dreadful thing happened this night. The poor Byrons brat fell from the skylight. The darn thing looked like it shattered. It was right in the middle of a performance by the visiting musician, Griffin Dunn.

"Then Minna Christel, the boy's nanny, came in and started sobbing over the child. She told us all that Dunn murdered him. The next thing I knew, he was stabbed in the chest with these shards of glass and then he dropped dead. No one knows quite who did it or how it happened. I don't want to tell anyone my thoughts at the house, but I think Minna murdered Dunn. He was a snobby sort of fellow, but he was no murderer. The police are investigating the wrong death, if you ask me."

I expelled a breath. I couldn't believe what I was hearing. Dim memories of a man with wide eyes and a water glass filled my head. If Liam hadn't brought him up, I might never have remembered him. Yet it was *that* man who'd truly cleared my name.

If I survive this curse, I will see everyone. I'll never ignore another person again. I'll never treat them as less than equals.

"So . . . Griffin Dunn, after all of these years, has been proclaimed innocent?" The interviewer shook her head. "Now, you're related to Jiggory Underhill, who made major contributions to classical music himself. Do you believe Mr. Dunn inspired his work?"

"No. I believe it was more a case of Jiggory stealing Griffin Dunn's musical creations." Several moments passed while Liam explained about finding my journal.

"Incredible. What led you to this remarkable find?"

"Despite Griffin Dunn's youth, he managed to have an heir. His great-great-great-grandson has come forward, with evidence society has wronged this talented musician." Pictures of Griffin as he'd been flashed on the screen, before a more recent photo—the one Liam had taken for Griffin's passport—displayed.

"Is he a musician, as well?"

"Yes. He's beyond brilliant. Definitely inherited the Dunn talent. I have no doubt he will take the world by storm one day very soon, just as his relative did over a hundred years ago."

"We'll have to have him on our show."

Liam chuckled. "I wish you luck with that. He can be quite a contrary fellow."

"Nonsense," I whispered.

"Give me a break." Kate muttered the words under her breath.

The interviewer continued. "In the meantime, a fantastic story, Liam. Thank you for joining us. The world has new music, and an innocent man's name has been cleared. What a wonderful Christmas present for the family of Griffin Dunn."

The square faded to black. "Well, what do you think?" Headmaster Withers asked the room.

Thundering applause shook the floor. My heart pounded so hard it competed for attention. The world knew of my innocence.

"Mr. Underhill has been given full access to the building, for research purposes. We'll be asking him to speak to all of you when you come back from break. In the meantime, we will be having a new plaque made for Mr. Dunn. On a final note, we're celebrating the exoneration of our resident ghost with an early dismissal for today. Have a wonderful holiday season, all of you. We'll see you back next year!" Applause shook the walls again, but that time, I didn't notice.

I slid the listening panel shut, then gently pushed Kate up against the opposite wall. "I'm cleared—everyone knows of my innocence. And it's all because of you." Desire washed over me as she brushed her lips against my own.

Kate sighed. "Griffin."

"You make me forget myself."

She chuckled. "Maybe we can leave now, and you can forget yourself in some other place that isn't covered in a hundred years' worth of dust." As if to prove her point, she sneezed.

"I desire nothing better, my darling." Pulling on Kate's hand, I led her out of the darkness and into the light.

Twelve Hours Until the Curse Expires

Kate and I spent the rest of the morning in my room. She worked on her own version of the counter-curse, whereas I paced and played intermittently. Yet, I couldn't commit to anything. The afternoon set in, and we decided to get something to eat at Lindo's, a little Greek diner Kate knew that was just around the corner.

We'd only just reached the lobby when Liam walked through the front doors, his dark hair covered in snow. "Did you see it?" A wide grin spread across his face.

"It was brilliant," I said. "Thank you for everything, mate."

"You're welcome," Liam said. His gaze panned the room. "Is there a place we can talk?"

"Is everything all right?" Kate slid her arm through mine.

"In private, please. After all, Ryder's on the prowl," I said. Turning back, we led Liam downstairs to my room. I ushered both of them inside and shut the door. "What did you find, then?"

Liam pulled out the device he'd used to search for information on Minna. "I decided to use a black light filter on some of the images from Minna's room and see if anything else came up. It did," Liam said.

"More technology?" Goodness, it truly was everywhere.

"Apparently, Minna did keep very detailed notes about your curse. They were just written on the inside of the closet wall. Normally, I'd be impressed, but under the circumstances . . . I had to have it translated." Liam held up a small, black square, somewhat smaller than the one Ryder had shown me, and began to read.

> *"Curse Griffin Dunn who has taken all,*
> *To roam the darkened rooms of the Byrons house.*
> *Through the blood of my children this edict will pass.*
> *May he be bound to this house until true love finds him,*
> *Then let him be repaid in kind."*

"My curse." Numbness crept over me. Finally, I'd heard it in its entirety.

"It would have been nice to know about the *repaid in kind* part earlier, though, don't you think?" Kate asked. "Now I guess I really get why she tried to off me."

"Minna believed you took the one she loved the most. What better revenge than to take someone *you* love away?" Liam's eyes showed his sadness. "I shared the copy of the curse with Helen Bywell. She emailed me what she believes is the correct counter-curse."

"What she *believes* is the counter-curse?" I did not like the sound of that.

"Not too many people want to go to the trouble of reversing this curse once the spell's been cast. As far as Helen knows, this is a first." Liam paced as he spoke.

"Brilliant," I said, not meaning it.

"Why would she help us? I thought the Bywells were evil." Kate leaned against me, her warmth grounding me.

"It seems we're not the only people trying to atone for the sins of their dead relatives. Helen has done a lot of research on this particular spell, but she's never known it to be performed on anyone."

"How does it work?" Kate asked.

"At midnight, cast a protection spell over yourselves—Helen's written one out here—then recite the counter-curse. Then we see what we see." Liam shrugged.

"Thanks, Liam. For everything. Griffin will have my phone. Please call him *after*. Help him, okay?" Kate's voice shook as she slipped the phone into my shirt pocket and accepted the paper with the counter-curse on it from Liam.

"I will." Liam gripped Kate's shoulders, meeting her eye. "You'll need to memorize the counter-curse. I know you can do it. You're quite a remarkable young woman."

"I will. Thank you, Liam." She kissed him on the cheek.

When Liam released Kate, he turned to me. "Griffin, may I have a moment?" He gestured to the door to my room.

"Go on. I'll be right here when you get back." Kate waved me on as she rested the paper on the piano, propping herself up on her elbows as she investigated the text. My heart hurt just looking at her, but if Liam had something to say, I owed him that much. More than, actually.

Once we'd stepped into the adjacent practice room, Liam pulled the door shut.

"Thank you, Liam." I extended my hand.

Liam clasped it, but pulled me into an embrace instead. When we separated, he drew back, cupping my face in his hands. "My dear boy, I know you don't believe you're worth saving, but you *are*."

My throat constricted, tightening so that I couldn't swallow.

"I know only a little of your childhood from my studies. Your father wasn't much of a father, from what I gather."

"No." It was quite the understatement, but nothing was to be gained from reliving it.

"Your arrogance was only ever a well-placed mask. But remember this: life only happens when we strip the masks away. You're such a remarkable talent. You don't need to hide who you are from us. Always remember that."

His words reminded me so much of something Mother would have said, that I'd almost forgotten how to inhale.

"Thank you again, for everything you've done. You've cleared my name and been a true friend."

If Liam felt rebuffed at my changing the topic, he didn't show it. "That sounds like a goodbye."

"Maybe. For now, at least," I admitted. "I think you should go. I don't want you here when . . ."

"I'm not a very religious man," Liam said, his voice rough. "But I will pray for you—for both of you—for your souls."

The end is near.

Fear choked me as the voice returned.

The end was coming.

That very night.

KATE SAT ON THE HEARTH, STARING AT THE PAPER WITH the counter-curse on it. I didn't want to interrupt her, humming softly to herself. Yet, I wasn't ready to give up hearing her voice.

"That melody . . . it's pretty. What is it?"

"A lullaby my dad used to sing to me when I was little. Daniela taught it to him, I guess." Kate didn't look up as she answered. "Do you think I'll get to see my dad again? Did you see anyone you loved?"

The suddenness of her question jolted me. "Stop it." How could I answer that? How could I ever tell her that I saw nothing but the miserable house in which we sat? "That's enough, Kate. If you think like that, it's all over." I couldn't bear that.

Hannah came into view, bringing an icy draft with her. "Ryder and his team are inside the building. They've decided to ignore the headmaster's warning."

"Bloody hell. I'd forgotten about *him*." Ryder would make things very difficult for us.

"I just wanted to alert you." Hannah sounded very faint, like a faraway memory or impression.

Seeing her then made it difficult to recall the days before Kate, when I'd found Hannah a nuisance. Instead, I remembered Hannah's company, the pep talks, and the clothes.

"Thank you for everything you've done for me. You'll be able to move on after Kate performs the counter-curse, so in case I don't see you . . ." Automatically, I attempted to take her hand like I used to, but my fingers passed through hers.

Kate glanced up then, as if finally catching on to our conversation. "What are you talking about? The counter-curse won't do anything for Hannah."

Hannah didn't respond.

"Hannah, what in blazes is Kate talking about?"

"I've been reading up on witchcraft." Kate reached up, her hand passing through Hannah's. "The Soul Separation spell only affects one person. Hannah wasn't even here when the spell was cast. She's never been cursed."

"Hannah, is this true?" Hannah had implied for so many years that she'd been cursed, as well, that I'd stopped questioning her ages ago.

But her eyes filled with tears. I could see them clearly despite the indistinct nature of her frame. "I was coming here to live the night I died. I wanted to be with my grandson, Jonah. He was very likely the only grandson I would have, since my idiot son married his harlot of a wife. I arrived the day after Jonah's accident.

"I had a heart attack. When the light appeared, I just didn't follow it. What if Jonah had been stuck here, searching for his mother or me? I stayed behind. Then Jonah wasn't here. You were."

I cringed. "You never told me."

"When I met you, well, you were so wounded. You needed me. It was nice to be needed again and I . . ." Hannah glanced at Kate. "I was afraid."

"I thought your only motivation in pushing me to end the curse was so you would be freed. But it was never about that, was it?" A cloak of guilt fastened itself 'round my neck. I'd been waiting for love to find me, yet it had a long time ago.

Hannah shook her head. "Griff. I just wanted you to be happy."

"Hannah." For the second time that evening, I found myself quite choked up. "We've had some good times, haven't we?"

"The very best, dear." She attempted to pat my hand, but hers passed through mine, sending a chill up my arm. "I'll take care of Ryder and the Prats. You take care of the two of you."

"We'll find you afterward, Hannah," I said. "If I can do something to help you, I will."

Hannah gave me a small, sad sort of smile. "Maybe it's time I helped myself. Just maybe . . ." Before I could respond, Hannah faded away.

Kate glanced at her phone. "It's eleven thirty."

"We wait." I searched her face as I took her icy hands in mine. "Should we play something?"

One last time. The words lay unspoken between us, but I knew she recognized their presence absolutely.

"I'll get Benny." She turned away to assemble her clarinet. "I didn't bring any music." She tucked her pencil behind her ear regardless.

That was when I remembered. My sonata. I jumped up and went to the piano. "I almost forgot. I have something new." She raised an eyebrow. Pausing, I held her gaze. "If we make it through, Kate, we shall perform this piece together. I promise you."

She nodded. "Bring it on."

Smiling, I walked over and set the clarinet part on the stand. "This is my gift . . . to you."

"You wrote this for me?"

"Only the clarinet part, I must confess. I wrote everything else years ago, but it was always missing something." I walked to the piano and sat down. "It was missing you, Kate."

A tear trailed down her cheek as we regarded one another. Kate finally picked up the music and looked it over. "Holy freak-out, Griffin. This is really hard!"

I smiled. "Love, you don't realize how far you've come under my tutelage."

"You think I can play this?" she asked, surprise coloring her tone.

"*Now.* Of course, you couldn't have done it without me." I winked at her.

"Fine, fancy pants. Let's get this show on the road." But her voice wasn't as harsh as it would have been once. Strains of tenderness and longing wove through it.

"Here goes." I launched into the introduction. When Kate made her entrance, it was everything I'd ever dreamed of. Her tone lent itself beautifully to the piece. For a first reading, there were few mistakes or stumbles. Maybe I'd learned to be less critical? But no, Kate had improved that much.

We stayed in the first section, avoiding the jazzy movement toward the end of the second page. Time slipped away as we performed, the notes twisting and turning, overwhelming me with their texture and complexity.

Kate and I had become one in that moment. Each note I played filled the backdrop to her rich tone. I could almost imagine us in Paris, playing in a grand hall somewhere.

Something rose up inside my throat, blocking it, stopping it from working. My hands slipped from the keys. I couldn't breathe properly. Kate set down her clarinet and came to kneel on the floor beside me.

She wrapped her arms around me, and I wrenched her closer, as though I could keep her with me if I only found a way to hold on. "Please don't do this. Please, Kate. I can't bear to watch you die for me. I can't—"

She raised a finger to my lips. "If I don't make it, get to Liam. And take Benny, okay? Tell my Mom . . . *something*."

Kate reached up and kissed me tenderly. It was a kiss steeped in loss and the greatest kind of grief. A hot and violent clash of lips and tongues. It was an eleventh-hour plea that the moment we lived in would never end. But I knew better.

Just as she finished the words, the clock, the one that had never worked before, began to strike. One . . . two . . . three . . . four . . . A death march.

The end has arrived.

CHAPTER 52

KATE

A LOUD ROARING FILLED THE ROOM, REMINDING ME OF a train. Griffin pulled me to him, like it would matter. The room began to spin, the wind whipping around us in an intense funnel cloud. Around and around the air went, with us standing in the eye of the storm. The speed of it increased, its suction pulling at us.

The vortex sucked us into a wave of black and dragged us up the stairs and straight to the parlor. When the air cleared, we were sprawled across the floor, directly in front of the piano.

My worst nightmare was coming true.

"Griffin." I reached for him with unsteady hands. His eyes widened as he scrambled to sit in front of me, edging me back toward the piano.

"Here we are again."

Snapping my head up, I came face-to-face with Minna.

When I'd first met her, she had made an attempt at looking like a normal person.

Yeah, not so much now.

Minna's gray, cracked skin flaked off as she walked, resting like dandruff on the gray fabric of her uniform. She grinned, a toothless, black-mouthed expression that sent my stomach rolling.

Focusing on her eyes, I inhaled through my mouth. "How can you be here? It doesn't make any sense. You're dead."

"It does seem a bit odd, doesn't it? But see, as the curse comes to fruition, the stronger I become." Minna paused. "It's unfortunate, Griffin, that the woman you've chosen to love is of my blood. I'd have preferred not to have to kill her just because of who she is."

Minna extended her hand forward in one swift action, as though she held a whip. Something hard and sharp and unseen lashed at my skin, as Minna magically sliced my arm open.

"Ah!" I fell to my knees.

Griffin positioned himself in front of me. "Don't hurt her. Let her walk away and I'll stay as I am."

The bastard.

Minna let loose a wicked, maniacal laugh.

The burning in my arm was unbearable, as intense as fire. Griffin looped his arms around me from behind, pulling me against him.

"It's time Dunn was repaid in kind." Extending her hand again, Minna sliced open my other arm.

I gritted my teeth. I would not cry and I would not pass out.

"He took him. My little one has gone. Oh, how he's

gone. My little one. The pain." Minna seemed lost in her ramblings.

"Run. Do it now. Wish yourself home," Griffin hissed. "It's the only way to keep you safe."

"I'm keeping us both safe." Closing my eyes, I visualized a circle of protection around Griffin and myself and whispered the spell.

> *"I am protected by your might,*
> *O gracious Goddess, let my fear take flight,*
> *Thrice around the circle's round,*
> *Evil's banished, not to be found."*

"What did you do?" Minna shrieked.

A burst of warmth shot through me, like I'd just drunk a scalding hot chocolate. A thin band of light encircled us. It had worked, but it wouldn't last.

I had only a moment to recite the counter-curse. *Oh, no!* I'd left the counter-curse in the rehearsal room.

"Kate?" Ryder stood by the door in the far corner of the room.

"Bloody hell," Griffin muttered.

"Ryder, you need to go. Take all those people with the equipment and go now." I didn't like Ryder, but he didn't deserve to die at Minna's hand any more than the rest of us.

Ryder's eyes widened as he pointed to Minna. "Who's that?"

Griffin muttered something about a fool's errand.

"Didn't your mother ever teach you it's rude to point?" Waving a hand in front of her, Minna once more used her magic and knocked the camera from Ryder's hand.

"Whoa." Ryder scrambled back, toward the piano, sweat broke out across his brow. "How'd you do that?"

Minna flew across the room in the blink of an eye and grabbed Ryder by the collar. With the wave of her hand, Minna forced him backward. He slammed against the door, where his head slumped to one side.

She faced us. "Ah, look at the pair of you. Your bond is strong. It will be delightful tearing it apart."

Bond. That was it. There was something about bonds in the counter-curse . . . What had I read? Bonds. Bind . . . *That was it!* I held my hands out in front of me.

> *"By light of moon and dark of night,*
> *I release thee from the bonds which hold you.*
> *I strip this magic from my veins.*
> *And restore life to thee.*
> *So mote it be."*

"No!" Minna screamed, her howl much like it had been the night Jonah died.

"Kate!" Griffin cried, his eyelids drooping shut as a glow built within his body, lighting him from the inside. Color flushed his cheeks. I hadn't realized how pale, almost waxy, his skin had looked before. He instantly appeared healthier. Muscles strained against his shirt. As though puppet strings pulled him from the back, he levitated a few feet off the ground.

It didn't last more than a few seconds, however. As quickly as he'd been lifted up, he was lowered to the floor once more. His breath came in heavy, uneven spurts. I rushed to his side and then cupped his head in my hand.

Griffin opened his eyes and looked at me. I searched his face, but there was only uncertainty, as if . . . as if he didn't know who I was. He stared at my hands as though my fingers were foreign and he hadn't been holding them in his own.

He didn't remember me. Tears burned the backs of my eyes, but I didn't have time to dwell on them.

Blackness closed over me as a burning sensation poured into my veins, as though I'd swallowed red-hot lava. The path of the fever traveled to every extremity. I couldn't breathe. Something was rending me in two, ripping me apart.

I was dying. But at least Griffin would go on, and the world would hear his music.

S*tay here. Stay safe.*

"I love you." I'd barely uttered the last syllable before I blacked out, and the scene before me vanished.

WHEN I CAME TO, MY EYELIDS HAD CRUSTED OVER. I forced them open and stared at the blue sky. Heavy white clouds drifted above—the kind we got before it snowed. I'd ended up on a surface harder than frozen ground. Dizziness washed over me as I sat up.

The garden flickered into focus, and I realized I sat on the same bench Griffin had carried me to the day we'd found Minna's room. My fingers trailed the cold concrete as my brain clicked into gear.

"Griffin!" I jumped up, but he didn't answer. Where was he?

"He's fine, Kate. The spell worked. You saved him."

The voice made me spin around. In the distance, a man waited on the garden path. "Daddy?" It was him. After all that time, all those moments I'd spent trying to get over him, he was there again. "Daddy!"

I ran down the path and launched myself at him. He was shorter than I remembered. He threw his arms around me, holding me tight.

"I'm here, Kate. I'm here." He stroked my hair the way he used to when I was little and I'd had a bad dream. Maybe that was what it all was. A bad dream.

"I thought I'd never see you again." Tears spilled over my cheeks and I swiped them away. I didn't want them to blur my vision. Not for one moment.

"I knew I'd see you." His eyes brimmed with tears. "I just hoped it wouldn't be this soon."

And then the memory of everything I'd learned about myself came back to me. "Dad, why did you and Mom lie to me about everything? I didn't even know my name. You just told me not to make wishes." Anger bubbled up inside me and I released him, backing away.

He ran a hand over his face. "I didn't want to. But Daniela . . . she begged me to. She told me it was the only way to protect you."

"But you lied."

"You're my daughter, Kate. I'd do anything to keep you safe. Even now." His voice echoed in the garden somehow, the slight reverberation bouncing back.

I squeezed my eyes shut, wanting things to be different. "Mom isn't—"

"She is your mother, Kate. She was with you from the moment you came home. She may not have given birth to you, but Jennifer is the mother Daniela wanted to be to you."

Mom's voice came back to me from the phone. *When school is over, I'd like to talk about Mr. England, okay?*

I'd never see her again. She'd never know why I'd gone

or what had happened to me. All of my thoughts had been on Griffin.

She wouldn't even have me anymore. She'd only have her job.

"I was so selfish." My throat parched, making my voice scratchy.

Dad stepped forward and gripped my arms. "That's impossible. You made many selfless choices tonight, Katya. You risked your own life for Griffin's. And even in your last moment with him, when he didn't seem to know you, you only wished he'd be safe.

"They sent me to help you move on." Dad squeezed my hand.

"Move on. I'm . . . I really am . . ." Knowing I would die didn't make the truth any easier.

"You died. Stripping yourself of the curse ended your life, but you knew it would." Dad patted my arm.

"I had to . . . Griffin . . ." My voice came out like a whimper, weak, strangled.

"I know, Kate, but the curse requires the sacrifice of a willing soul in order for it to be appeased. You, my darling girl, gave up yours."

"What if you took mine instead?"

The soft, familiar voice had me pivoting in place. Hannah stood in the far corner of the garden, her silver dress glittering in the moonlight. I'd never noticed it before. Or maybe I'd never seen her clearly—after all, we'd always been on two separate planes. Things must have changed since I was about to join her.

"No. I cast the spell. It has to be my soul, Hannah."

"I read up on witchcraft a little, too. The spell requires a *willing* soul. It never specified whose." Hannah walked to Dad and took his hand in hers.

The older woman patted my arm. For once, she didn't go through me. She seemed as solid as Griffin always had. "Kate, you were willing to sacrifice everything for Griffin and asked for nothing in return. I care about that boy. I always have. Now that I know he will be loved, I *can* move on. Let me do this for him."

"Thank you, Hannah." I wrapped my arms around myself.

"Well, then." Dad raised a hand to his heart. "It seems we'll have to wait a little longer to be together again, but I'm always with you."

Relief cascaded over me, a powerful decrescendo. "I love you, Dad. I'll always love you."

He grinned. "And I will *always* love you, my beautiful girl. Now, go back there and take care of Minna."

Alarm shot through me. "Take care of her? But Dad, I don't know how."

"You do, Kate. It's the words of the song. Do you remember? The one I sang to you when you were a child."

My mind flashed to Dad humming, rocking me in the chair. The memories broke over my mind like a voice hitting a particularly high note.

The song.

Dad.

The song Daniela had taught him, because she had the gift of premonition, like all the Christel witches.

The song had been a spell all along.

And before I could react, I found myself back in the parlor. Griffin held me, my body pressed up against his. Tears ran down his face in streams.

"Kate!" He held me even more tightly, his eyes widening. "God, I thought I'd lost you."

"What?" Minna screeched. "How did you survive the counter-curse?"

"Griffin. Get behind me. Don't argue, just do it," I whispered as I squared off against our enemy. "It's over, Minna!"

She laughed, a brittle sound that resembled shattering glass. "You are but a child with no understanding of your power. You cannot hope to challenge me."

Closing my eyes, I concentrated on one thing and one thing only: the song Dad had sung all those years ago. I imagined Dad and Daniela standing beside me as I chanted.

"For all who roam without a home,
Follow love, follow light, follow peace.
Just let go.
Go home."

Behind Minna, the light in the room began to change. It grew brighter and brighter until all the light in the world seemed to pour from its core, forming a spinning circle of gold. My thoughts jumbled as we sat there, staring into the netherworld or whatever it was I was seeing. Each of my knuckles burned, like they'd been bruised. I swallowed, but my throat felt as though a layer of skin had been ripped off inside.

Minna's eyes widened. "What have you done?"

But in the next instant, the little boy from the photo in Minna's room stepped from the tunnel. "Mama?"

"Jonah Byrons." Griffin's voice was a whisper behind me.

"Jonah?" Minna transformed back to the innocent nanny from Germany—the one Jonah loved. "Jonah."

"Why are you doing these things?" Jonah's voice was almost a whisper, but I could hear him clearly. "Griffin didn't kill me. He didn't make me do anything." He sounded less like a ten-year-old boy and more like a forty-year-old man. "It was an accident and it was my time. You knew this."

She stepped closer, her hand outstretched. "I can bring you back. I can bring us both back. This girl"—she gestured to me—"she has power. We can live again together, and I can take care of you as I used to. I love you, Jonah."

Jonah smiled. "I love you, too, Mama, but this isn't the way."

Her eyes softened. "My son. You've no idea how hard it was, pretending you weren't my own child. Working here was the only way I could stay in your life."

I hadn't seen it before, but that conclusion stared back at me, as though it were the most obvious thing in the world.

"I should have known." Slowly, Griffin got to his feet. "Jonah."

Jonah turned to face him. Instead of the anger or hurt I expected, his features remained neutral, calm.

Griffin cried, his voice cracking. "I'm sorry. For everything. I never meant for you to die."

"I forgive you." Young Jonah held up his hand, a small smile on his face. "You've learned to love now, don't you see? It was the only thing you ever really needed to be truly great. Let my death burden you no longer."

Jonah extended his palm. A small ball of white light shot from it, sailing through the air and landing squarely on Griffin's chest. Griffin gasped for an instant, but then he exhaled, a small, black cloud escaping from his lips before evaporating. I leaned against him. It was all I could do to comfort him.

"Come with me, Mother. Follow me." Jonah turned and slowly, incrementally, he walked into the light.

With Jonah no longer acting as a buffer, however,

Minna flew in my face. She jabbed her finger in my direction. "You will die tonight, Katya Christel. You—"

"Minna." At the sound of the new voice, Minna and I jerked our heads in unison. Ryder stood and walked toward her. What was he up to? "I forgive you."

"Who are you to forgive me, but a child?" Minna deepened her scowl. But, despite everything she'd said, it was obvious the change in Ryder threw her.

Ryder seemed peaceful. "In this moment, this *second* of time, I am not a child. We have come full circle. Ryder is one of mine, a descendent of the Byrons clan on my brother's side. I have taken his body only for a moment, to pass on a message."

Minna moved toward Ryder, but when Ryder touched her arm, she froze. "Helmrick."

"Yes." Ryder nodded. "It is I. I forgive you, my love. I should never have asked you to hide who you were."

"Whoa." *I so did not see that coming.*

"That's what she wanted. Remember the words on her skylight?" Griffin asked. "*Please forgive me.* She wasn't asking the Byrons family. She was asking Helmrick all along."

But Minna shifted to face me then. "We are not so different, you and I. We would do anything for love. We would fight for it, kill for it if we had to."

Once, her words might have rung true with me, but I wasn't the lost girl I'd been the day I'd first met Griffin. I wasn't alone anymore. I'd found my own direction and I'd guided myself.

"You're wrong, Minna. Maybe we'd both fight for love, but when it was lost, you chose revenge. Now I know: love's never really lost. It's always with us. That's the one thing you never understood."

Focusing all of my strength, all of my energy on Minna, I thought, *I wish Minna could move on.*

The white light grew bright, brighter, until it was too intense to look at directly. From between my fingers, I looked on as Minna was plucked from the room and pulled toward the light. Her screams echoed off the bare floors, making my ears sting.

Gradually, the light began to dim, until it faded to nothing, as if it had never been there. Ryder/Helmrick met my gaze for an instant and nodded before he faded away, leaving Ryder's body to sag to the ground.

With care, I turned around to face Griffin. For a moment, only our breathing broke the silence. *We're both alive. We lived.*

"Holy crap," Griffin said.

"*This* is the moment you picked to start using American slang?" I snorted, laying my head against his chest, happiness bubbling up inside of me.

"I dunno. Seemed appropriate." He wrapped his arms around me as we clung to each other. "I've been given the greatest gift, and I promise I will never let you go."

"I'm counting on it, fancy pants."

As we held one another in the now-quiet house, faint church bells began to chime in the distance. There was peace at last at Byrons School.

EPILOGUE
GRIFFIN

Monday, August 28th—Eight Months Later—FlatChap Studios, London

THE HEELS OF MY HANDS BLOCKED OUT ALL LIGHT. I wanted to sleep, to sink into a cave of darkness, but I still had so much to do. Only a bit more and I could return to my feather bed—if my two all-nighters in the studio didn't get to me first. I straightened my headphones and rubbed at my bleary eyes. "Todd?"

"Yes, Griffin." The recording engineer's voice fed through my headphones.

"Would you murder me in my sleep if I asked to record the last stanza again?"

"I kind of expect it by now, mate. After all, you're *you*." Todd shrugged from his spot in the recording booth.

A wry smile turned up my lips. "You're not going to ask me out, are you?"

Eight months on, and I'd learned to make the subtle changes to my speech that allowed me to matriculate into the London culture flawlessly. Picking up my lukewarm coffee, I gulped down the remainder.

"Nah. You're too blond for me," Todd said. "Now give me a brunette any day."

I choked back laughter. "That's me as well, Todd." I took a deep breath. "'Kay. I'm ready." My eyes flickered to the countdown clock on the wall. When Todd signaled, I began to play.

It wasn't one of my old pieces, though I'd recorded both *Desperation* and *Redemption*—my favorites—earlier. No, it was something new. A composition that had poured out of me my first week back at Fulton House.

My fingers soared over the keyboard. The coffee gave me new life. I completed the final stanza to my satisfaction. When the recording light switched off, I stood up, stretching. "Brilliant."

"Kate's here, Griffin," Todd said. "Do you want me to give everyone a break, so you two can have a good snog?"

I'd been about to deny it, but then Kate walked in and my full attention was drawn to her, as though she were a magnet. "Take five, Todd."

She'd pulled her hair into an elegant upsweep that morning. She'd dressed in boots and form-fitting trousers. A sleek blue sweater completed her outfit. Kate had blossomed under the influence of my fashion sense.

Kate's face lit when her eyes met mine. "Good morning."

"Hey, you." I kissed her, my body instantly responding to her after two nights apart.

"Sorry I'm late. I had trouble finding a hundred and thirty-one candles for your birthday cake."

My thoughts slipped away as Kate's words took hold. "Of course, my blasted birthday dinner. What age am I supposed to be again?"

Kate busied herself with assembling Benny. "Nineteen."

"Bother." I didn't want the dinner, even though it really was my birthday.

Liam had made me eighteen on all my paperwork, to make things easier for us. We'd moved from Fulton House and into my flat in Kensington in July, so Kate could start taking lessons from Sandra Ruskin, the principal clarinetist with the London Symphony. Liam had also gotten Kate into the pre-enrollment program at the Royal College of Music.

Still, no one could ever know the truth about my past, so we would always need to play our parts. That meant celebrating birthdays and aging. What a fresh concept, as Todd would say.

"And we got Liam and Rena's wedding invitation in the mail. Not that we didn't already have the date down. Mom's already booked her ticket from California. You'll have to find someplace to stay while she's in town."

"Why me?" I asked. "I have a beautiful flat."

"That's exactly why." She smirked as she busied herself with her preparations.

The door to the recording booth opened, and Todd stuck his head in. "Kate? You about ready?"

"Yeah. How's this gonna work? I've never been in the studio before." Kate placed a reed between her lips. My mind grew fuzzy staring at those lips.

"Right. Put on the headphones. I'll walk you through everything, okay?"

"Better give yourself some time, Todd. She'll need to find the perfect reed first." I smirked as Todd returned to the sound booth.

"Stop it! Leave my reeds alone. It's a process," she said as she scrutinized each one.

"How's this best man thing going to work? I've never had *friends* before." It had been a nagging worry, right along with how to get used to confining modern underwear and which mobile phone to buy.

Kate slid a reed on Benny's mouthpiece and blew a couple of notes to test it. "You'll do fine. Just care about Liam. Be there for him. You'll do great."

"Thanks." I pressed a kiss to her forehead. "So will you. Knock 'em dead."

"You know, it still freaks me out when you talk like a normal person? I don't think I'll ever get used to it." Kate put on a pair of headphones. "All set, Todd."

"Good luck." I kissed her cheek.

"Thanks. Would you hand me my music?"

"This beauty you've defamed with that pencil of yours?" I pulled the sheet music out of her bag. "Do you want me to stay here and turn pages for you?"

"I think I've got it, fancy pants."

Kissing my Kate on the forehead, I set the music down on the stand. Pride and love nearly overwhelmed me as I read the title of the piece she was about to record.

The Spellbinder's Sonata for Clarinet and Piano by Griffin Dunn.

THE END

YOUR NEXT FREE READ!

The most wonderful thing about writing is connecting with readers! I occasionally send out newsletters with details on new releases, as well as special offers and other news related to my books.

And if you sign up for my mailing list I'll send you another book for FREE.

Steph

DOWNLOAD YOUR FREE BOOK >
https://bit.ly/spell-free-book

LEGENDS, LORE, AND MORE

This was a very interesting story to write from the beginning. First, because The Byrons School was inspired by a real life location, the Byers-Lyons House at 901 Ridge Street, Pittsburgh, PA. It was the building where I attended music classes and rehearsed in a tiny, spooky, rehearsal room. I swear the temperature did drop when you walked inside. It's also the place where I met my husband and my own love story began.

The Byers-Lyons house was supposedly haunted by the ghost of a little girl, one of the Byers's children, who fell through a skylight. Distraught, her nanny was reported to have hung herself after writing *Please forgive me* in the dust of the skylight. Maids in the building reported that the message returned every time the glass collected dust. In *The Spellbinder's Sonata*, the child is a boy, simply because that was the first incarnation of the legend that I'd ever heard and it stuck with me.

I also took great pains to recreate the layout of the Byers-Lyons house. The actual building is as I described it, with a few exceptions. There is no great ballroom, the catwalk does not exist, and there is no large rehearsal space in the basement. Sadly, Minna's bedroom and workroom are also fictional. The building is now part of The Community College of Allegheny County and has been since the Sixties.

Coffee á Rena is also a fictional place. The location that I had in mind is actually a McDonald's at Forbes and Liberty in downtown Pittsburgh. Though a coffeehouse would have been way cooler. I stayed true to the rest of my locations. Lindo's, for example, is where Mr. Keyes and I had our first date. Primanti Brothers is fast-becoming a nationwide phenomenon. Market Square is still a tourist attraction in the city.

Also note that I reference a "waning moon" in the story. My editor will thank me to tell you that there are many moon phases, none of which are just "waning."

Benny was the name of *my* B-flat clarinet. I studied classical clarinet for thirteen years before I finally left music school to go into IT. Yes, I had Scales class and it was just as horrible as I depicted!

Though there was a kind Igor who bought me a pink pudding, he was never, to my knowledge, deported. He also helped me pass my first college jury without an instructor—here's to you, Igor.

A NOTE ON GRIEF AND LOSS

Kate Covington's journey to move on after her father's death was a very personal one for me. My own father went through a seven-year battle with cancer that eventually traveled from his lungs to his brain. It was ugly and difficult and cruel. Writing this book played a big role in my ability to move on.

Some of us deal by shutting ourselves away and erecting our own walls, like Griffin. Others just keep moving, running, and reinventing themselves. Then, there are those of us who lock it away, and live in denial, like Kate.

Grief is personal, but grief is also variable—some days you may forget and have energy, at other times, it will overwhelm you. Everyone experiences grief differently, yet, we all eventually take the same journey.

Remember, your grief is not for any one thing or person to define for you. Recognize that you aren't alone. There are others out there that are going through the same thing. I've been there and I hear you.

You will get through this.

If you find yourself never experiencing happiness in the

present, seeing no light in the future, finding yourself persistently unable to manage necessary daily tasks from eating and sleeping to coping at work or school, or frequent thoughts of suicide, there are folks standing by to help you. Make the call.

24/7/365 Crisis Hotline
Call: (775) 784-8090
Text: "ANSWER" to 839863

ABOUT THE AUTHOR

Stephanie Keyes is the author of over a dozen other titles for teens and adults. The Spellbinder's Sonata, her Beauty and the Beast meets Phantom mash-up, was an Amazon #1 new release. Spellbinder's was awarded the RONE Award for Best Young Adult Book of 2019 and took 2nd place in the Athena Awards for Excellence in YA and NA Books (Paranormal Category). She also writes contemporary romance.

Keyes has spoken at events throughout the US and the UK, and was a featured artist at Pittsburgh's First Night 2019. She is a member of The Society of Children's Book Writers and Illustrators (SCBWI) and Pennwriters.

Keyes is a technical writer and content strategist, teacher, and speaker. She lives in Pittsburgh, Pennsylvania with her husband and her boys, Hip-Hop and Bam-Bam, and dog, Duncan MacLeod.

BB bookbub.com/authors/stephanie-keyes

f facebook.com/StephanieKeyesAuthor

instagram.com/stephkeyes38

ALSO BY STEPHANIE KEYES

Young Adult Fantasy

The Star Child

Seventeen-year-old Kellen St. James has been haunted by the same girl for half of his life. When they finally meet outside of his dreams, he's thrust into the world of faeries, gods and goddesses—and all at his college graduation.

The Spellbinder's Sonata

A brilliant concert pianist, a clarinetist with a history of magic, and a haunted house. Beauty and the Beast meets The Phantom of the Opera in a tale of magic, music, and one dark curse.

The Boy in the Trees

Part of the Blood In the Shadows anthology, Jemma's sketched the same boy hundreds of times. The only problem? They've never met.

New Adult Romance

The Internship of Pippa Darling

Pippa's one Irish internship away from graduation, unfortunately it's with Finn Burke, the one author whose work she hates.

The Education of Uma Gallagher

Uma Gallagher's thrilled to land a teaching position in Dublin, but the last thing she expects is to find rock star Caden Hannigan in the back of her class.

ACKNOWLEDGMENTS

This book remains one of the most difficult I've ever written. It was also one of the most terrifying for me to release, because it is highly personal. I, myself, was once a classical clarinet student, hoping for a music career. I am a fatherless daughter, after losing my Dad to cancer in 2011.

The other personal side to this story, is that, while writing it, I listened to everyone's ideas about this book—except my own.

Anytime anyone gave me feedback on *The Spellbinder's Sonata*, I'd put it in. Soon, a very curious thing happened: the book was no longer my own.

So, I shelved it, assuming it would never see the light of day. The problem with books like this one, however, is that they get under your skin.

With the help of editor, Laura Whitaker, I was able to find my story and bring back the narrative *I* wanted to share. Thank you, Laura!

I wouldn't change one moment of that journey, however, because it's taught me that the first person I need to listen to is myself. In my office, there is a decal on the wall that says *Let Steph Happen*. It's a reminder that I can't let others to tell me what to write, or how to feel and think. I need to me my own voice.

Thanks to the usual cast of characters, Najla Qamber, Ashley Turcotte, the Rt. 19 Writers group, Melissa Struzzi, Ellen Roteman, and Dave Amaditz—you are an amazing team and you helped make this book possible.

Also, I have to thank my husband and soul mate, Aaron. Marriage isn't all unicorns and rainbows. It's hard work. But *this guy* . . . he has stood by me in everything I do. He's never wavered—not once.

Aaron is also the one person who insisted I see this book through because he knew it was my best. Honey, I wouldn't have made it here without you. You're still the cutest trumpet player on campus.

Finally, thanks to you, my readers. You guys are the best and I heart you 100%.

Love,

Printed in Great Britain
by Amazon